WHERE
TRAITORS
FALL

WHERE TRAITORS FALL

KATE CALLAGHAN

WHERE TRAITORS FALL

Copyright © 2021 by Kate Callaghan

First edition September 2021

Copyedited by Emma O'Connell
Formatted by Enchanted Ink Publishing
Map by Eve Siddall Butchers
Cover Design by Sara Oliver
Proofread by Sisters Get Lit.erary Author Services

ISBN: 979-8-5465-6218-2 (paperback)
ISBN: 978-1-5272-9010-5 (paperback)
ISBN: 978-1-5272-9212-3 (hardback)

Please do not consume any herbal ingredients or replicate any potions described in this book. They are highly toxic and will result in bodily harm.

The mystical language used in this series is a combination of multiple languages found in Ireland's history.

For my **mum**, who is also my best friend. The woman who **taught** me **strength**, **kindness** and **hope**, and who **listens** to all my mad plot lines with **endless patience**.

One year after Klara's coronation

Night had fallen over Malum, and any light coming in through the arched window of Klara's chambers was no longer sufficient. Klara lit another candle on the dresser while the torches on the walls lit by themselves. The presence of the full moon told her to finish getting ready before her guests arrived.

"Can I wear this?" Lottie asked, picking up a small pot of crimson lip balm that Klara had stolen from Abadan's abandoned quarters.

Klara sat at her dressing table, using a decorative pin with dark emeralds in the shape of a dragon to hold back her wavy black lengths of hair. She had to put her best foot forward when entertaining the highest of Malum's society, even if she would rather be dressed in her usual belted trousers and light shirt.

"When you're older there will be plenty of time

to use it," she said, taking the balm from Lottie's outstretched hand and applying it to her own lips.

The young lycaon had come to her room after getting ready in a flash. It helped that she had someone to bathe and dress her, while Klara refused to be manhandled—and the thought of having to touch her terrified the doomed in the castle. No servant wants their master to know what they are truly thinking; not that Klara thought of herself as a master. All she expected from those who had joined her service was loyalty, and if they remained true, they had nothing to fear from her.

Lottie pouted, sitting on the edge of Klara's bed. "But just for tonight—for the gathering."

"How about I show you how to make the balm instead? Then you can make whatever you like." Klara didn't want to argue before the creatures arrived.

"When?" Lottie demanded eagerly. "Can we make it tomorrow? Henny is meant to show me potions anyway, but you can help us."

Klara knew better than to give her an exact time, though she was pleased that Lottie enjoyed her potions and poisons lessons. When Eve had taught Klara, she couldn't wait to run from the conservatory; then again, Henrietta probably didn't throw books at Lottie when she got something wrong.

Henrietta ran the castle and oversaw the rest of the doomed. She had spent many decades in Hell, and Klara had needed all the help she could get once the queens were gone and those loyal to Abadan had been dismissed. The first time they'd met in Hell, Klara had tried to bribe Henrietta with a coin. Henrietta could have taken it and bribed her way out of Hell—and yet she had given the coin to her commander, following the rules even at her own cost. It was the type of loyalty and devotion Klara needed at her side as a new ruler.

"Soon."

"Soon. You always say soon and then you're busy—you're always busy." Lottie leaned back on the bed of dark silk sheets.

Malum and its responsibilities took Klara away at all hours, and she had learnt early not to make a promise she couldn't keep. She rose from the dresser and brushed the long blonde fringe from Lottie's eyes, forcing her ward to look at her and revealing her startling blue eyes. The eyes of a future alpha.

"I wish I could spend every day—every hour—showing you how to make every concoction under the two moons of Malum, but there is a Forest to run. So that you can run freely without being skinned for furs." Lottie went a little green and Klara cringed internally at her own harsh tone; she had yet to master the art of mothering. Without a role model, all she had was the example of the now-fallen three queens and her father, the King of Hell, to go on. "I'll try and make more time for us to spend together, okay? But for tonight, can you smile? I'll even let you stay up past the dinner."

Bribery was a last resort, but Klara had a masquerade to pull off, and she couldn't have her ward going rogue in front of the elders. Furthermore, she guessed that Lottie would be asleep long before the night ended. If she spent all night worrying about Lottie's behaviour her hair would threaten to turn blue, which would certainly clash with the silk dress from Eve's wardrobe she had dyed black and the emerald jewels that had been left in Abadan's vault for far too long. She didn't lust for jewels as Abadan once had, but when society called for it, she figured she might as well indulge in the finer things.

"Promise I can stay for the dancing?" Lottie asked, trying to hide a smile, smoothing her hands over her black trousers.

"Would I go back on my word?" Klara asked, and hated that Lottie looked doubtful. "I'll do my best," she reassured her ward.

Lottie had grown in the past year; she had only reached Klara's hip when they had first met, and now she was passing her waist. Having insisted on a black suit with a white shirt tonight, she looked like a small commander of Hell—which made sense considering how she admired Frendall like a brother, even if they weren't related by blood. Not a day went by when she didn't ask for him. Since Frendall's promotion to general upon Lilith's death, he had been busy training his own legion of demons. Klara understood his duties in Hell, just as he understood that her priorities in Malum made their visits short… and yet oh so sweet.

Klara looked at the purple amethyst crystal around her neck, her secret weapon, and unclipped it. *Once it protected me from the ghouls; now it can protect her.*

"Come here. I think it's about time I give you this," she said.

Lottie shuffled over. Klara held the chain up in front of Lottie, whose eyes went wide in surprise.

"Promise you will look after it?" she asked her ward, who nodded eagerly.

"This is a very special crystal, okay? It will glow when you are in danger, so you know to run or make yourself scarce," Klara explained, brushing the blonde hair aside and fastening it around Lottie's small neck.

"Your Majesty?" The slight knock on the door caused Klara to drop the dark green lace mask she had just picked up.

4

"Come in," she said, and Henrietta walked in wearing a simple cream dress, her hair secured by a patterned headscarf. It had been a gift from Klara when she had brought the doomed from her father's manor to the castle. Klara had told her then that she didn't have to wear the plain scarf that was a symbol of servitude and devotion, but Henrietta had insisted; it was her way of showing penance and loyalty—so Klara had swapped out the plain scarf for one with various colours as a sign of her respect and a reward for Henrietta's sense of duty.

"The envoys and elders have started to arrive, and are waiting in the foyer to be greeted," Henrietta said. "And there has been a raven from lycaon territory."

Klara had been expecting such a message; the new alpha liked to leave it to the last minute before finding some excuse not to come to the castle. That way, there was no way to convince him and his newly formed pack to attend.

"Bring it here," she said, feeling suddenly tired as Henrietta placed the parchment in her hand. She read the note, already knowing what it would say. "Matthias and his beta send their regards," she said to Lottie.

The pack's failure to attend, or at least to send an envoy, only put greater strain on Lottie's relationship with her fellow lycaons. Then again, Klara couldn't blame Matthias for the distance he wanted to put between his people and Lottie; it was her blood-right to become the next alpha. Matthias had won his position by popular vote, not by birthright, once the lycaons who had been burnt out of their homes came out of hiding when High Queen Abadan had fallen. No leaders, especially inferior ones like Matthias, liked to be seen as less than worthy. However, Klara felt him to be necessary until Lottie came of age. The packs were united under him for now, and peace between them only had to hold for a few more years. Klara wasn't sure she could handle an all-out war between the various remaining packs of Malum; there was already so much to do on a daily basis without adding that into the mix.

Still, Matthias's insecurity was no reason to snub a gathering, and it set a bad precedent. Told the other elders of Malum that Klara's invitation could be denied without a valid reason.

"I didn't want them here anyway," Lottie replied with a huff. "Matthias looks at me like he can't decide if he wants to kill me or adopt me. It's creepy. And the other lycaons who visit… I can sense they're afraid of him, but why don't they challenge him?"

"He is the strongest of the packs for now, and fear can be a powerful motivator," Klara told her, and Lottie scrunched her nose in annoyance.

"How would you like me to address it?" Henrietta asked.

"We won't draw attention to their absence. Please remove their place settings from the tables; hopefully enough venom will be flowing that they won't be missed," Klara said, knowing that no matter how much venom was guzzled by her guests, their lack of presence would be noted. Gossip was one of Malum's favourite pastimes.

"I'll order it done before you escort in your guests." Henrietta nodded in agreement and Klara tossed the parchment into the fireplace beside her dresser, watching it burn up into ash.

"Thank you, Henny, we will be down shortly."

"Can I go with Henny? I want to see them arrive," Lottie said, hopping off the bed and taking the doomed's hand.

"Have you got your mask?" Klara reminded her, and Lottie went back to the bed to grab her black lace mask. Klara tied the dark green ribbons at the back of her head over her blonde, lightly waved curls. Lottie had wanted to match Klara, so the masks were identical but the colours of the lace and the ribbons had been reversed by the seamstress.

Henrietta offered Lottie her scarred hand, and the two left Klara for a moment to gather herself. "Let the games begin," she said to the mirror.

The beauty of the masquerade, an idea she had stolen from her father, was that it put the creatures and herself on equal footing. They needed to get to know her as much as she needed to get to know them, and who didn't love to drink and dance until their feet hurt? Her first Gathering upon taking the crown had resulted in two deaths. A pixie had taken the seat of the Elder vampire Langda, whose envoy, angered by the slight, had decided to feed on said pixie. Klara had taken the vampire's life to show she would not stand for any type of violence at the Gathering. Ever since that night, petty quarrels had been kept to a minimum.

Her high heels—with a small blade hidden in one of them—clicked on the stone floor, and the skirt of her dress flowed behind her.

Chin up, back straight, no fear. She repeated the mantra to herself as she moved down the staircase. The torches shone brightly on hundreds of gathered creatures, dressed in every kind of fashion, from the giants to elves from the coast. The air was chilled and filled with the hum of voices as the factions of creatures talked amongst themselves while they waited. Only the warlocks stood out, thanks to their signature painted white masks outlined with red around the eyes. They all bowed their heads as Klara stood on the staircase. She dimmed the lights, creating the favoured shadowed atmosphere, and the doors to the ballroom—hidden beneath the two staircases—opened.

Redesigning the castle to her taste had been one of Klara's favourite tasks since becoming queen, one year ago to the day, or at least a year for Malum. Cobwebs no longer hung from the walls and chandeliers, or the statues that littered the halls. The once ruined ceilings had been rebuilt, but Klara had left areas exposed so that she could see the stars of the night sky.

Lottie joined her guardian and took Klara's hand. She winked at her ward as the creatures watched them, and she could feel the pride and jealousy emanating from the creatures below. They waited for her to lead them in, parting as she walked through, each careful to keep their distance. She smiled at this.

Klara had used the gold tapestries from Abadan's quarters to cover the arched wooden beams in the ballroom; the doomed orchestra began to play as the guests entered. Waiters carried trays—Klara had hired a few creatures from the Forest to serve as a way for them to earn coin. She could see the strain on their faces as they served creatures from other factions, but there was no room for pride when their family was starving.

Malum, under her reign, was healing—slowly. The reduction of market taxes so that everyone could afford food had been her first order, which had angered many, but Klara made it up by removing the ban on selling human goods, which increased their revenue. However, even if food and clothing were more affordable, many still paid more than they could give. The potion factories were no longer run by the warlocks and the witches so that no side could get greedy, and the creatures who worked within were fed and housed fairly. Potions were now sold to other realms, including the human world, which created more jobs and meant more pay. There was still tension between the factions, but Klara believed that in time, once everyone was on equal ground and no one was benefiting from the flawed and cruel system designed by Abadan, balance would be restored. Malum was by no means perfect; rivalry and hatred ran deep, and only time and understanding could mend it.

The envoys and a few elders filed into the room, taking their drink of choice from the trays.

"May your cup never empty and the music never stop," Klara called, standing at the centre of the dance floor in the ballroom. There was a loud cheer from the guests before they raised their glasses and drank. The creatures paired off; the dancing began.

Klara walked the room, still hoping they would be too entranced to notice the lycaons were a no-show once again. *Not even an envoy. A pathetic snub, but it sends a message.* The storm raged outside, and Klara revelled in the sound of rain hitting the protections. She loved to watch the storms that often visited the Forest, but she had been wise enough to protect the castle with a weather spell to rid it of the insidious damp Abadan had allowed to set in. The moss had stopped growing on the arched entries to the various rooms.

"Another atrocious evening. Why you insist on holding such events is a mystery to me," Elder Langda, head of the vampires, said at her back.

"Wouldn't have it any other way," Klara said, turning. She knew better than to keep her back to a vampire. "You never fail to show," she added, and Langda's red irises beamed. When Klara had taken the throne, Elder Langda had been the first to bend the knee. There had been no love lost between the vampires and Abadan, especially once the fallen high queen had taxed the human blood brought through the port. Klara had been quick to amend that. She'd needed to make allies fast.

"Any excuse to be above ground. The underground settlement can get awfully dull after so many generations. Furthermore, the smell of your youth is enchanting. So much hope and longing—it's enough to make me want to take a bite." Langda smirked.

The smell of my youth? Klara suppressed the urge to shiver.

"Your envoys seem to be enjoying themselves," she said, gesturing to where they danced hand in hand with two pixies. The previous scuffle was apparently long-forgotten, thanks to the venom and time.

Langda offered her a crystal glass of the drink, and she knew better than to reject it. She took a sip, while Langda drank the blood that Klara had had chilled especially for the occasion.

"When you live as long as we do, we don't hold grudges." Langda shrugged.

Before Klara could reply, to her astonishment, Frendall walked through the doors. His black suit was tailored to his body; a black mask concealed the left side of his face, revealing his new status as general—a scar that ran through his right eye vertically.

"If you will excuse me," Klara said.

"Who am I to interrupt young love?" Langda winked, and Klara rolled her eyes.

Frendall caught her in the crowd, and he bowed without a word and offered her his hand. Klara laughed, placing her glass on the tray. She took his hand, and an enjoyable warmth crept up her arm; they hadn't seen each other in a few moons. Their new duties and responsibilities kept them apart more often than she liked.

The next dance began and two rows of creatures formed, facing each other. Frendall and Klara circled each other, stepping back and forth, their eyes never leaving each other.

"What brings you to my neck of the woods?" Klara asked, playfully.

"I heard of a great beauty trapped all alone in the castle," Frendall said, and she shook her head. His arm circled her waist, and hers found his.

"And you thought I needed saving?" she said, raising her eyebrow.

"I wouldn't dream of it."

They separated, and Klara missed the contact. He stepped to her back this time, his breath against her neck, and the rest of the guests disappeared. All she felt was his hands on her lace bodice.

"I didn't think it would feel like this," he muttered, almost to himself, and Klara moved away in time with the music as they circled each other again. The wonder in his voice surprised her.

"It hasn't been that long," she pointed out, and he smirked.

His hand grazed hers, and she automatically tried to slip into his mind but then hesitated, sudden uncertainty creeping through her. There was something strange in him—an anger she didn't recognise, a tremor in the calm he was trying so hard to maintain.

The applause of the many creatures broke the trance. They danced closely, and Klara felt warmth radiating from Frendall as their palms hovered an inch from each other. She broke their gaze, and her eye caught the mirror. In the reflected ballroom, the light of the candles caught a glow on Frendall's cheek.

A glamour.

Taking a moment to figure out her next move, she smiled and moved around another creature. The dance came to an end; while they bowed to each other, she leant down and pulled the blade from her heel. They straightened once again as the next dance began. Laying one hand on his shoulder as his returned to her waist, Klara brought the blade to Frendall's neck.

The room froze, and the music stopped. Frendall was grinning wickedly, as though this was exactly the reaction he had wanted.

"Is this any way to treat a guest?" he said, and Klara pressed the blade against his throat.

"Whoever you are, I didn't invite you, and I have every right to use this blade because of it."

He didn't remove his hand from her waist, her body pressed so tightly against his that she could feel his heartbeat. The sensation made her uncomfortable, so she pushed herself away. "Reveal yourself—or I'll slit your throat, and your death will tell me."

They broke apart, and Frendall bowed, his shape altering and clothes changing. The slightly pointed ears gave him away as fae, his dark blue eyes fixed on hers.

"Your Highness," he said, turning his narrow shoulders to face her. He didn't have to address her as 'majesty' because she wasn't his queen.

"Who are you to take a general's form and trespass?" Klara demanded, dropping her blade to her side.

"I'm here on behalf of the fae queen. Does the Gathering invitation not extend to all allies?"

"You did not come here as an ally, but as a spy disguised." Klara had to consider what to do quickly; the whole of Malum's court was watching. She couldn't kill him. The fae queen might have intended for him to come as himself and it had been his choice to disguise himself; there was no way for her to know unless she touched him, and she had no intention of getting close to him again.

"A spy? No, my disguise was merely a jest. The queen thought you would appreciate my sense of humour."

"Since you clearly have nothing to conceal, then tell me your name," Klara ordered, stalking towards him.

He held his hands up, stepping back. "Jasper, high fae of your mother's court. So I would think twice before you raise that blade again." His smug tone made her regret lowering it in the first place.

She didn't stop, and he continued to back up to the doors. They opened, sensing Klara's presence, and she walked him out into the foyer.

"I might not be able to harm you, but I can remove you from my lands," Klara snapped.

"You didn't seem to mind my hands on you. With all your famed strength, you couldn't even tell who I was! Does your commander really mean so little to you that you couldn't tell the difference between my touch and his?" The fae stepped closer to her, and she feared the creatures in the ballroom would hear him. Rage coiled within her.

"Or maybe you did sense something? And you just didn't want to believe it."

She thought of the longing she had felt as he'd held her waist, and the sensation of emptiness when he had moved away. *It was a trick, it wasn't real; you thought he was someone else,* Klara reassured herself.

And you believe that? Jasper projected mockingly into her mind. Without realising, she had connected with him when they had touched, the same way her mother, the fae queen, had when she had dragged Klara before her in Kalos.

Don't flatter yourself. You hid yourself in the skin of another—you are nothing but a coward, she projected, breaking away from his mind.

He frowned, no longer able to reply silently. The doors to the castle opened ever so slowly behind him as she controlled them and she stepped into his space, watching his pupils dilate. She might have reacted to him as Frendall, but he was certainly reacting to her. She lifted her hand to the back of his neck, reaching up so that her lips almost touched his ear.

"Come here again without permission, and I will mount your pretty fae head on a spike," she whispered.

She felt him jerk away as the sound of the rain and a clap of thunder rattled in through the open doors. A frown darkened his handsome features, and while he was seemingly debating how to respond, she gave him a great shove in the chest. Jasper flew back through the doors and into the mud and gravel that marked the entrance to the castle.

Klara walked to the open doors and looked down at where he lay, covered in filth. She smiled, seeing Jasper's fine fae clothes ruined. He was on his feet in an instant, clearly embarrassed as he wiped himself off. She slipped the blade back into her shoe and walked out into the rain, the heavy droplets cascading down the deep *v* in the back of her dress.

Wanting him to see just how serious she was, she gripped his lapels and brought him close, trying to shake his pride from him. "Send the queen my regards," she growled.

"She told me about you, but you are so much more,"

he breathed, his face inches from hers. Her lips trembled in the cold as he gazed at them. She shoved him away before he could say any more.

Striding back inside, Klara refused to look back at her unwanted guest. She felt awash with relief as the castle doors sealed, separating them.

Elder Langda was waiting by the door. She raised her glass of blood as Klara returned to the ballroom, dripping.

"Let's get back to it, shall we?" Klara asked, though her tone stated that it was an order. The music started, and the dancing recommenced.

"The fae queen grows bold," Elder Langda said.

"An ill-timed joke. My mother does love to test my abilities." Klara tried to laugh.

"I would be wary, young queen; the fae queen is not one to be dismissed," was all Langda said before rejoining her envoys.

Klara spent the rest of the evening neck-deep in meaningless conversation and venom until the storm passed, bringing an end to the evening. She had silently hoped that Frendall would appear to wash away the lingering feeling of Jasper's hands. *It's the first contact I've had with a fae; of course I'm thinking about it,* she thought as she spotted Lottie asleep in the window seat, the end of a gold tapestry wrapped around her. The fact that she could sleep in a room full of the realm's worst meant she was indeed amongst her own kind.

Once the rest of the creatures and elders had departed in their chariots, coaches or portals, Klara sealed the doors and rested her head on the cool stone wall. She had drank more than she had intended, but it was all in the name of making and sustaining allies. She wasn't sure whether she had lost or gained points for throwing out the fae.

Who was he to come here without an invitation? I don't care if he was my mother's envoy; to disguise himself was an attempt to humiliate me in front of my guests. She knew Aemella hated the Gatherings once every new moon, but that was no excuse. *Hardly even a spy. Disguising himself as Frendall was only going to draw my attention. Maybe Mother wanted to see how far I would go?* Klara remembered the look of surprise on Jasper's pretty face when he had landed in the dirt, and a warm glow of satisfaction ran through her—only for it to be replaced with the sensation of his hand hovering over hers and a memory of the comfort that had run through her. *Is that because he was fae? Because I'm part of their kind?*

Instantly sober, she tugged at her cuffed sleeves and pulled off her heels. She made her way to bed, only to wake anxiously after a few hours to find herself in the same dress. Unable to return to sleep, she pulled herself from the soft bed and made her way to the throne room, while Lottie and the rest of the castle slept peacefully.

Klara studied her empty throne room, taking a small candle from the candelabra in the hall. The stones, cool under her feet, woke her tired body; she tiptoed, making sure the other portraits weren't disturbed. The soft snores of some were disturbed by the low growls of others. She had decided to keep the portraits, though they still chilled her—they held secrets, and many concealed rooms and passages. *Without them, the castle wouldn't be the same.*

"Forneus? Open up," Klara ordered, and the Marquis of Hell flinched at the mention of his name.

"Yes, Your Majesty? Shouldn't you be sleeping?" The oiled portrait yawned, and Klara moved the small candle's flame closer to the enchanted paint. "No need to threaten," Forneus groaned, and the gold-framed portrait opened up. Klara lifted her palm and opened the frame wider to step inside the hidden passage.

"Ignis," she whispered as she travelled down the stone steps. The candle's flame shone brighter, guiding her down the steep passage. Torches lit once she reached the secret room at its end, and she discarded the candle in the basket of others on the small bureau by the entrance. It had taken two full moons of constant searching to find all of the queens' hiding places, and she still wasn't sure if she had discovered them all.

How long can I conceal this? Father will want to visit soon, and he might be able to sense her. I could move her, but to where? Lokey might hide her, but he has his wife and a newborn to consider. The concealed chamber might be deep in the castle, but that won't stop her father from prying. *If anything, the hidden chambers will be the first place he'll look.*

"How is she today?" Klara asked, putting away the thoughts of discovery. A crystal pod shone in the centre of the small stone room.

"Improving; her wounds and scars have healed. I was worried her leg wouldn't reattach, but with the clear quartz you got from the warlocks, it seems to have taken well." Henrietta replaced the worn out crystals on the stone slab with newly charged ones.

Klara watched the rise and fall of Lilith's chest. The First Woman, General of Lucifer, and one of the three previous queens of Malum lay utterly defenceless. Lilith continued to slumber and heal. Henrietta had once asked if they should let her go, but Klara refused to give up on her mentor. She had already mourned her death before finding her, bloodied and torn, in the tunnels of the castle.

She removed one of the protective crystals from the circle surrounding her. Lilith's mind and memories were still fogged by the trauma of her soul being partially torn apart by hounds. Had Abadan not been premature in her departure from witnessing the destruction of Lilith's soul, she would have been killed instead of severely maimed.

Lilith, I know you can hear me! I need you to wake up.

She projected these words to Lilith daily, and yet the queen refused to open her eyes. When Klara touched her, she was sure there was nothing physical stopping her from waking her up. Klara wondered if Lilith just didn't *want* to wake. *Maybe she has found peace...* but Klara couldn't let her go, not again.

I need an advisor. I've put it off for as long as possible, but unless you want Elder Langda roaming the castle, then I suggest you give me some sort of sign. Every ruler needed an advisor: it was tradition. One her father had pointed out on her last visit to Hell.

"Maybe she needs more time?" Henrietta said, and Klara removed her hand from her mentor.

"Or maybe I was wrong to bring her back from the brink." Unable to express her frustration, Klara turned and punched the wall, causing small pebbles to fall to the floor. Every day new crystals were placed and healing spells chanted, only to end up with the same result. The frustration was eating away at her patience. *Perhaps Lilith wants to join her wife in the afterlife, or wherever we go when we die. If we go anywhere at all.* Thinking of Arthur, she hoped it was somewhere peaceful.

"Tomorrow might be better," she told herself. She replaced the crystal in the circle, and the bubble of protection covered the queen. Klara dug out the spare clothes she kept in the hidden room and changed into a simple shirt and dungarees. Henrietta handed Klara her boots before she had to ask.

"We can only hope she finds her way back," she said, giving Klara a knowing look. Many who came back from Purgatory weren't what they once were, and if Lilith wasn't dead, that was where she was right now.

Many thought of Purgatory as a state of nothingness and not a physical realm, but they were wrong. It was the physical realm of the in-between where a soul could relive memories. Eve had taught Klara that it took a different shape for all who visited. Once there, it was up to the soul to pass on—but many got stuck, unable to move to the underworld, where Kharon would sort the souls for Hell, Heaven or, if they did not bear a coin for passage, the River Styx, doomed to circle eternally or be plucked for servitude. However, while a soul was in Purgatory, there was a small window where they could be brought back to their physical body—but only if the soul was strong enough.

The revival came at a price; memories held no shape in time, and the soul could have been plagued with horrors for decades when only a day on Malum had passed. There was no way of telling what state the soul would return in, or which kind of memories it had been exposed to.

"Let's leave her in peace." Klara moved away from Lilith and dimmed the torches, shrouding the room in darkness, only the glow of crystals remaining. She knocked on the portrait, and this time there was only a second's hesitation before Forneus opened up.

"Will that be all this evening?" he asked, yellow eyes shining as his slumber was interrupted for the second time.

"You may rest," Klara said, and the painting settled.

She looked to Henrietta, relieved that the doomed didn't need sleep. The sun didn't grace Malum as it did

Kalos, except through a thick layer of grey clouds, but daybreak was close. Klara sometimes wondered if the sun was punishing Malum for its sin, or protecting itself from being tainted. Thievery, murder, sacrifice, dark magic... the list was endless, but that was the nature of the Forest and its creatures. Klara could improve some elements, but she couldn't change the nature of the creatures who dwelled within or beneath the trees. Nor would she want to.

"I have to step out this morning. I need you to make sure Lottie is prepared for tonight's meeting with the lycaons," she said to Henrietta, who stayed two steps behind her.

"I will see that it is done. Are you not going to sleep?"

"A luxury I can't afford at this current moment. The covens must have thought their absence from the Gathering would go unnoticed." Klara's axe appeared in her hand as they made it to the foyer. She intended to find out why the covens hadn't attended, though with the current rumour of sacrifices swirling, she suspected she knew the reason.

The demons standing to attention opened the great doors, and Klara was delighted to see her lycaon and demon guard ready and waiting to carry out tonight's mission.

"I know the venom from last night hasn't been kind to some of you, so let's get this done as quickly as possible." There was a rumble of agreement, and they set out.

Klara waited on the outskirts of the red trees that marked the edge of coven territory; she sensed the thickly woven protection spells and glamours. The lycaons and demons waited as she peeled them back. It was taking longer than she'd expected.

I wasn't expecting them to be this strong after losing Eve, she thought as she peeled back the last layer of protection. She wiped her nose with the back of her hand as blood dripped to her lip. Revelation magic was powerful, but it still came at a toll. *Much stronger than I was expecting.* She wiped her hand on her suit trousers—she had thought she should dress up for the occasion, so she had opted for one of Lilith's deep purple suits that she had had tailored, with no shirt underneath and her axe fastened to her back.

Klara motioned for her guard to move forward with her. One step onto the covens' territory, and fires lit up the red trees, marking their way to the sacrificial ring. Klara had heard reports of the covens sacrificing young creatures to restore the power they had lost at Eve's death. They couldn't command the elements as they once had nor hold their improved glamours of themselves—dark magic left a stain on the flesh—for long, and they no longer had the energy to dance under the moon until daybreak, worshipping her father so they could retain their unnaturally long lives.

"No blood is to be spilt," Klara warned the demons and lycaons at her back. "I only wish to talk with them, and when we reach the sacrificial ring, you will not draw your weapons." The protections set by the witches would only cause the drawer to end up using the weapon on themselves.

"Yes, Your Majesty," the guard replied as one, and they followed the fires to an opening surrounded by a ring of trees. The ring seemed empty, but Klara knew better.

"Your Majesty." An old crone appeared before her on the path to the ring, cloaked and corseted and blocking their way.

"I believe you missed the Gathering because you are holding a ritual sacrifice this dawn?" Klara asked, and the crone coughed into her wrinkled hand.

"Why, yes. We are sorry we could not attend. Our young ones were sad not to dance." The crone was stalling; Klara sensed her mischief.

"There will always be another. Since I am here, I would be delighted to be granted the honour of witnessing your practices; the other elders often invite me to their traditional rituals."

"There is nothing much to witness, so we did not think an invitation was necessary, but as you wish," the crone said, guiding Klara up the path at a dangerously slow pace. "Surely you have more important matters to attend to than visiting our rituals?"

"I feel that my late guardian would want me to keep a close eye on the covens."

The crone smiled, revealing a set of blackened teeth as they reached the edge of the trees. "How *kind*." Klara hadn't thought those words could ever sound so menacing.

The crone removed her hood, and an impressive black cauldron set on a pyre appeared in the centre of the ring. Witches were chanting and dancing around it under the light of the descending moon. One of them stopped dancing as Klara passed through the circle.

"Sorry to interrupt," she said sweetly, noticing the bound child with black eyes kneeling beside the cauldron. *Sacrificing a demon? How bold of them.*

"We were not aware of your presence, Your Majesty."

"Think nothing of it. I merely wish to pay a visit. I heard you are sacrificing at dawn."

"Yes—have we broken a rule?" the witch panted, sweat from her dancing trickling down her face. *That's twice a witch has mentioned wrongdoing, could be paranoia or the rumours are true.*

"It's well within your right to sacrifice a soul: one a fortnight, as the law dictates," Klara reminded her, knowing full well that they had sacrificed dozens more over the last few weeks. She wanted them to sweat.

The witches' eyes went to the guards as one, and some stopped dancing and stepped closer to one another. A part of Klara enjoyed the fear her mere presence invoked. She didn't even have to do anything. Sometimes not knowing what she was going to do frightened the creatures more than actually punishing them.

"Do continue." She sat on a fallen tree at the circle's edge as her guards took their stance behind her.

Klara watched the witches dance and chant and toss herbs and potions into the bubbling cauldron. They moved slowly and warily under her gaze until the crone ordered them to move it along, or dawn would break before the sacrifice was complete. At that the witches' painted bodies moved at a much faster pace, clearly wanting to end Klara's time with them.

As two of them grabbed the demon child under the arms, Klara noted that some of the witches wore crimson robes. It was bold to wear Abadan's colours; many had burnt their supportive clothing, but she admired their courage to remain loyal to their fallen high queen. She had been informed by the warlocks that the witches blamed her for Eve's death, and she suspected the wearing of Abadan's colours was meant to insult her.

"One moment," Klara said, just as the two witches were about to toss the demon into the boiling cauldron.

"We must complete the ritual when the moon meets the sun," one of them protested.

"I hate to break the momentum. However, I must ask—how many sacrifices have taken place this month?"

One of the witches paled, and the other shook his head. Witches weren't entirely female or male, just as the warlocks weren't all non-binary. The difference between the two opposing forces was how they gained their magic. Warlocks harnessed nature, nurtured it, used the elements for both good and self-gain so that there was a semblance of balance; but the witches stripped it, twisted it, took everything they could from it and left nothing but ash.

"Before you lie, remember that you are allowed under treaty law to make one sacrifice a fortnight, as it has always been—"

"We wouldn't..." the crone began, and one of the lycaons growled as Klara was interrupted.

"I am as lenient as a queen can be, as I'm sure you have come to see. In return, I expect honesty."

Silence fell amongst the witches. There was only a finite amount of time before the veil between night and day closed, and she sensed their increasing unease.

"I have scouts in every corner of the Forest, so I already know the answer, but I want a confession. A demonstration of penance."

A willowy witch with pale skin and a round face had stepped forward. "We are only trying to keep our strength up. Without Eve's divinity we are lesser, and there have been... happenings within the Forest." She received an elbow to the ribs for speaking up, and Klara admired her courage, though she looked the most fragile amongst her sisters. *Happenings?*

"I'm sure her loss was great, but did any of you seek my guidance, *permission?* The creatures whisper about your defiance. If you are free to disobey the treaty, what's to stop the vampires from draining creatures at will or the warlocks from forfeiting their healing duties?"

A cloud covered the moon and sun as she spoke.

"We're sorry, but please let us finish. We've already used a great deal of magic to carry out the ritual." Klara wasn't sure who had spoken from within the tight group.

"How many?" Klara rose from the log. "How many of my demons have you sacrificed?"

There was a long, tense pause.

"Three," the crone admitted.

"Since the last full moon?"

"On this night." The willowy witch from before spoke up, and the others cursed her under their breath.

Klara heard the snarl of the demon guards behind her, but she couldn't intervene in who the witches sacrificed. They had moved on from creatures to demons because they were richer in dark magic than a mere creature.

She took a deep breath to rein in her own anger. "From this night, you are allowed two sacrifices a fortnight, one more than previously stated, to make up for Eve's loss—but you will have to make up for the seventy-seven you have sacrificed this week alone by forgoing sacrifices until I say so."

It was written in Lucifer's blood that the covens were allowed to make sacrifices, but it was an oversight to say who they could or couldn't. The lycaons had the same right to eat the heart of a human once they matured to seal their transition to a mature lycaon, thus granting them more control over themselves. Klara had no

26

authority to define which human. *I can enforce new laws, but I can't break what was written in blood when Kalos and Malum were divided by Aemella and Lucifer, or I'll have an uprising on my hands.*

"Not even Lucifer cares for the lesser demons; why shouldn't we make use of them?" the crone said, and a few demons stepped forward—a move the crone obviously wanted.

"Don't be upset; remember that there will be fewer demons to compete with for souls," Klara said to them, and the realisation made their yellow eyes glow.

"Don't leave me with them, Your Majesty," the demon child begged, and the witch kicked them into the mud.

Klara held a finger to her lips before the child could speak again. Standing so close to the pyre had caused sweat to form on her brow. She wiped her forehead, stepping forward anyway.

"You cost your king souls, and you will pay the price," she said, and the crone sneered.

"More demons can be created," a portly witch countered, shaking her fist in Klara's direction.

"And more witches can be born. Only the loss of demons causes strain on our king—unless you are suddenly in the soul-purchasing business? I'm sure you wouldn't want to tire King Lucifer."

The crone bowed, accepting defeat. It wasn't that much of a strain for Lucifer, but Klara didn't need the witches growing too strong and challenging the warlocks.

"Right, everyone satisfied?" Klara was making her way from the circle when she felt the sigh of relief emanating from behind her and stopped. "Ah, yes—a punishment. Lilith would have beaten me for forgetting such a thing." She tapped her fingers together, making a show of thinking. "Free them," she ordered, and a lycaon stepped forward and removed the twine that bound the demon child.

"Thank you, Your Majesty," the demon hissed before joining her guard.

There was a rumble of disagreement from the witches.

"I can feel your frustration and it is completely unwarranted. Three corrupted souls in one night should easily sustain you. For your breach in my trust, you will hold no sacrifices for seven full moons."

There was a gasp. "Seven moons! There will be nothing left of us."

The response thrilled Klara. It was a petty punishment, but it wouldn't do them much harm. They would simply be a little emaciated, especially after wasting so much magic this evening.

"Lucifer won't be happy. He feeds on our sacrifices, even if they are demons," someone said.

Threatening me with my own father! My goodness, how I love the fight in the witches.

"That is true, but he hardly relies on you." Klara felt their hurt at her words. They loved her father almost as much as they had loved Eve, and many wished to take Eve's place as his mistress.

A bad taste filled her mouth as she thought of her father with a mistress. *Let's not think about that again.*

"We need magic to maintain our protections," a witch argued, and Klara shrugged.

"I'm not stopping you from making potions or casting. You will have to ration, unless you wish to sacrifice one of your own." Klara didn't mean it; she was merely curious to see what they would do, but she was disturbed by the silence that followed and the way their eyes drifted to the witch who had ratted them out. "So much for sisterly love," Klara said. "No, I take it back. Rationing will teach you to appreciate the magic you have." The air was thick with tension. "Am I clear?"

"Yes, Your Majesty."

"Perfect. It's been a lovely evening—thank you for having me." *Not going to win me any points, but they won't get greedy again anytime soon.*

She hoped.

"How did it go? Were the witches mad? Did it get bloody?" Lottie came bounding down the steps as Klara stripped off her axe. The venom and peeling back the witches' protections had taken a chunk out of her.

She let out an exhausted breath as Lottie slammed into her. Clearly, the night's rest had recharged her—Lottie's little arms were almost strangling her. The lycaon was still unable to grasp her own strength. They worked on it together, but Klara sometimes wondered if Lottie would love someone to death in a moment of excitement.

"Henny made me get up super early. Can we have breakfast? Did you kill any witches?" Her questions grated on Klara's growing headache.

"No, it didn't come to that." Klara noticed the hint of disappointment in Lottie's eyes. "I can't kill every creature who breaks the law. They are to be punished, and they won't do it again."

"How do you know they won't?"

"I don't," Klara said, motioning the lycaon towards the dining hall for breakfast.

"Then why not kill them and know for sure?"

"The witches would seek revenge, and that would lead to more bloodshed. The creatures aren't quick to forgive or forget. You will learn that when you are alpha."

"I'll challenge those who oppose me like you did with Abadan." Lottie was still too young to understand what had really happened, and Klara wasn't in the mood to explain.

"I'm sure your breakfast is getting cold. Go find Henrietta to eat with."

"But it's no fun! The doomed don't eat."

"Lottie, I'm tired," Klara snapped as the pain crept behind her eyes, then immediately regretted it. "I'm tired. I'll see you later, and we can go running."

"Promise?"

"Go on. I'll see you then." Klara ruffled Lottie's hair and headed up the staircase. *Promises to make lip balms, promises to go on runs… keep breaking promises, and she'll start to resent you.* She closed the door of Lilith's study and kicked off her boots.

Taking the pen from the open grimoire, she prepared to spend a few hours writing down the evening's events. It was essential to write down the history of Malum under her reign as she saw it. At least if it was in her words, it couldn't be twisted. She took the heavy leather-bound book and collapsed into the armchair.

"That's better," she sighed as she placed her feet on the plush cushion. The candlelight dimmed, and the pen grew heavy.

Klara jumped, her headache intensified from lack of water and food. The grimoire was still open on her chest, and Henrietta was standing over her.

"I'm sorry to disturb you," Henrietta said, "but the lycaons will be arriving soon, and Lottie is refusing to get ready."

Klara picked up the jug on the small table beside her and drank it down, not bothering with the glass beside it. She sighed, wiping her mouth as instant relief washed over her. *I slept through most of the day? When have I ever had that privilege?*

"Your Majesty?" Henrietta said, and Klara snapped to attention.

"I'll take care of it. Make sure the dishes are prepared." *The listening! Shit!* "Have the creatures been waiting long?" She winced when Henrietta wouldn't meet her eye.

"Would you like me to postpone today's listening?"

"No, they've been waiting long enough. The creatures deserve a few hours of my time." Before she could ask, Henrietta handed her a bowl of porridge topped with berries from the human world. "What would I do without you?" Klara sighed, and Henrietta chuckled.

Klara was glad to see that the girl she had met in Hell had grown into herself in Malum. *When she first arrived she could barely look at me.* Now she commanded the rest of the doomed in Klara's service and stood tall, never afraid to show her face or scarred hands.

"Starve?" Henrietta joked. "I will escort those who have waited longest into the throne room while you finish that."

3

The scents of many creatures collided in the crowded throne room. The smell of salt from the port market on the eastern coast and the stench of the heated swamps to the south fought against each other. The mismatched scents of all those gathered along with the heat of their bodies made the listening almost unbearable.

Klara rested her head in her hands when a demon came forward to air their grievance. Her legs were going numb after sitting for so long, but she didn't want to stand since it would only worsen the sensation of pins and needles, and she couldn't exactly shake out her legs and stretch in front of her wary citizens. The most she could do was flex her feet in the boots she wore. *How much longer can this possibly last?*

She couldn't help but stare at the never-ending queue of creatures waiting; it ran the length of the throne room and into the corridor. Some waiting even made up the time by talking with the portraits on the walls—not that the portraits, who loved all forms of suffering and gossip, would complain. Last night many had partaken in the festivities that ran throughout the Forest in imitation of the Gathering the elders and envoys had attended at the castle, yet the creatures had risen early to wait for an audience with their queen to complain about their woes. Some hadn't bothered to wash or change, as evidenced by the additional smells of ale, venom and fungus syrup that crowded Klara's senses.

The demon squawked at the bottom of the steps to her throne, regaining her attention. "The crossroads demons have been overstepping! Now that Abadan is gone, they make deals when they haven't even been summoned. It isn't fair! I want something done about this. How am I to earn souls when the crossroads are lurking around every corner?"

The demon's smoky appearance made Klara dizzy. *Why did I have to indulge in so much venom?* she thought, cursing the luminous green beverage that was a favourite among Hell's finest and the elders. However, when the elders offered her a goblet of the pungent stuff, she could hardly refuse. It wasn't often she could get them all in one room, so she did her utmost not to offend them and their delicate egos. *Or maybe you were trying to drown out the touch of a particular intruder,* her subconscious chimed in, but she quickly pushed that thought to the back of her mind.

"Don't start," she muttered, and the demon frowned in confusion. "What I mean is, what would you have me do to resolve this issue? Surely there are enough souls to go around." Klara straightened on her silver throne and plucked a daisy from the woven armrest.

"Bind the damned things to their crossroads, so they only prey on those who summon them!" There was a murmur of agreement in the queue.

"Have you ever made a deal at a crossroads? Have you impeached on their territory for the sake of a soul?" Klara asked. Demons loved to steal souls from one another. When a crossroads was in the process of being summoned, on rare occasions, demons would appear from the Forest line and poach the soul. It had been a practice since well before Klara's reign; this complaint was utter nonsense.

The demon bowed its head reluctantly. "I... may have. As is my right! Many who travel to and from the market like to make a deal from time to time."

"If you deal on their roads, then a crossroads has every right to deal off the paths. Unless you wish to forsake the roads altogether, and then I will discuss it with the crossroads demons."

"No, Your Majesty, that won't be necessary," the demon hissed.

"So you do not wish for me to punish them? To bring this to their attention?" Klara asked, leaning forward.

"No, no. I was merely bringing the matter before you. I know you like to be kept informed on the comings and goings of Malum." The demon clearly didn't want to lose out on the many souls travelling the roads daily and nightly for food, shelter or work.

"Very well then. I will inform the crossroads you quarrelled with that the issue has been resolved."

"Yes, Your Majesty." The demon bowed, its yellow eyes glaring up at her before disappearing in a cloud of black smoke.

"How many are left for the day?" Klara asked Henrietta, standing behind her. Henrietta looked at the sheets of parchment in her scarred hands.

"Under a hundred," she said, scanning the names.

"Why did I think these listenings were a good idea again?" Klara groaned quietly.

"Because you wanted the creatures of Malum to have a chance to voice their troubles, so they wouldn't come to your door with pitchforks and torches." Henrietta had to remind Klara of this every listening.

"I couldn't just place a ban on pitchforks and torches?" she asked with a rueful smile.

Henrietta shook her head. "I'm afraid they would only resort to other means."

The Forest had ticked along in some semblance of peace since Klara had taken the throne. The ogres had been the last to bow, but had done so once the giants had made peace with them. Each side had promised to stick to their own land, and a line had been drawn through the past. Klara didn't want spies to tell her about the Forest; instead, she allowed all creatures to speak freely about their grievances. That didn't mean she didn't have the trees listening to the whispers and stirrings, though.

Still, Klara hadn't realised what a pack of moans the creatures were. She might have a young heart, but she was still Lucifer's daughter, and listening to petty nonsense wasn't her speciality. The lit torches on the walls dimmed as Klara's energy did.

"If they are talking, they aren't plotting—and it shows that you have an empathic side," Henrietta told her as the next creature stepped forward.

"Ah yes, caring and all that shit," Klara said, and Henrietta smirked. If she had dared to smirk as a handmaiden in Hell it would have been lashings for a week, but Klara had promised to never lay a hand on her in Malum.

"I'll hear one more case..." Klara started to say when a Hell-hound bounced through the doors, knocking over many creatures in its path. Shock and confusion filtered through the throne room, since creatures were unable to see the excited hound that ran to Klara and circled her throne.

She stroked the black fur, thick and full thanks to overindulgence from Lottie. Her touch revealed the hound to the creatures, and they took a great step back from their queen for fear of what the hound could do.

"Why are you not with our ward?" Klara asked the hound, who responded by jumping up and licking the length of Klara's face, knocking her silver crown from her black hair.

"Down!" Henrietta barked as the creatures in the queue watched in amusement and terror. Klara pushed the hound down as its red eyes gleamed with excitement.

"I see Lottie has been forsaking your training," she commented, and the hound barked. As if on cue, Lottie came bounding into the throne room, her ice-white fur and blue eyes shining. There was a gasp about the room when Lottie shifted effortlessly into her human form; that was one thing she had mastered. Her clothes were filthy from her run. She was supposed to shift before she left the castle to spare her clothes, but she had obviously forgotten.

"I told you no chasing while we have guests," Klara said. Lottie winced at her scolding gaze and made her way to the throne.

She didn't want to scold the child in front of the creatures; she didn't need to give them anything to gossip about. As a young ruler, she needed to show she had absolute control. *If I can't control a young lycaon, how can I possibly lead the courts of creatures?* They would rise against her at the smallest hint of weakness. Klara faked a smile as Lottie's sad eyes caught hers.

"I have heard enough for one day. Your concerns will be dealt with accordingly."

There was a rumble of disappointment amongst the creatures, and Klara let out a clap of thunder from the glamoured ceiling. The threat quickly stopped the hushed whispers, and though their grimaces unsettled her, the creatures promptly shuffled out of the room. The thunder tore through her head—the venom had got the better of her. She rubbed her temples as Lottie circled her with excuses.

"Sorry, we were practising tracking in the gardens and he got away from me—I shifted to try and catch up so he wouldn't get in." Lottie panted, out of breath. *That explains the dirt.* The hound lay at Klara's feet, exposing its tummy, waiting to be rubbed.

"Practising your tracking is important, but you can't disrupt the listenings."

"I'm sorry," Lottie said.

Klara hated when Lottie pouted. "Dismissed. Take the mutt and get ready for the packs to arrive."

Lottie's head shot up. "They're coming already?"

"They've heard of your alpha eyes, and they want to see them for themselves. They also wish to pay their respects to their future alpha. This meeting has long been put off, and since they didn't attend the gathering, you need to make a good impression. There will be nothing to distract them." Klara had been through this conversation a hundred times, but Lottie was too young to understand the gravity of the situation. *She needs to get to know them whether she likes it or not. They won't come to gatherings, and*

I can't put off meeting them any longer before the lycaons start to think I'm trying to isolate her from them.

"I don't want them to pay their respects. I've already met them," Lottie said, calling her hound to her side. Klara had brought her to the lycaon territory to the west of the mountain so that she could see the rebuilding of her former home, hoping it would help Lottie heal.

"You've met them in passing; this is a formal acknowledgement. I've put them off for as long as I can. Your tenth birthday approaches, and they need to know their alpha. Matthias will hold your place until you come of age, so all you need to do is wash and put on a brave face. These are your people, and you need to greet the new alpha—show your respect for their current position."

"Is that what Lucifer said to you when he wanted you to rule Malum?" Lottie argued, and Klara clenched her fists.

"No, he set the Forest against me and took Arthur from my life. Trust me, there are easier ways to learn where you belong. Don't be stubborn and go change. You're covered in muck and Lucifer knows what else."

"No." Lottie glared, standing firm. Her hound behind her paced, sensing the tension.

"Excuse me?"

"If I'm the alpha, then I *don't* have to listen to you and I *don't* have to go to the meeting."

"I swear, Lottie, if you don't get up those stairs right now, I will take your roaming privileges for a week."

"You wouldn't dare," Lottie said, and the hound growled as the two stared each other down.

"Wouldn't I?" Klara backed Lottie up to the portrait on the wall. Before her ward could argue, Klara pushed her through the portrait that led to Lottie's room.

"That's cheating!" Lottie's shout echoed through the castle.

"Make sure she gets changed," Klara said, stroking the hound's head before it leapt through the very same portrait.

Frendall had gifted Lottie the hound for her protection. For months, Lottie had been unable to sleep in the castle because it was so close to the caves where she had experienced the burning of her pack. Transitioning so young had wreaked havoc on her emotional development, but having a hound seemed to balance her out. Klara had doubted the gift when Frendall had brought the pup; hounds and lycaons were natural enemies, due to the hounds' demonic essence and the fact that lycaons were descendants of a god. But this one had kept Lottie's nightmares and fits of anger at bay.

"Am I being unreasonable?" Klara asked Henrietta, the only other person left in the throne room.

"She is young, and there is so much on her shoulders—give her time."

Give Lottie time, give Lilith time. The Forest doesn't allow for time. It just takes what it wants, when it wants. "By her age, I had been starved, beaten and trained within an inch of my sanity."

"How did that work out for those who raised you?" Henrietta said, looking at her ravaged hands, clearly reliving some of her own harsh memories.

"Fair point. But all she has to do is meet with them, shake their hands and show her face. She can hardly expect them to accept her when the time comes if they barely remember what she looks like." Klara gripped the back of her neck, trying to knead out the tension, only to feel more knots form.

"All *you* had to do was put on a dress and smile,

remember?" Frendall commented with a smug grin, walking into the throne room.

"Do I look like I know how to smile?" Klara said, her eyes running appreciatively over the length of him.

"No, but you look damn good in a dress."

Now, this is the real deal. The black coat that stopped just above the knee emphasised Frendall's tall stature and broad shoulders. His form had changed since he'd begun to spend all his time training his new legion. Where he had once been lean, he was now broad, and Klara certainly wasn't complaining.

Henrietta bowed. "General Frendall." There was a strict balance of civility between them; Henrietta tensed in his company. Klara figured it was because he remind-ed her of the decades she had spent serving in Lucifer's manor at the centre of Hell.

"The queen is keeping you busy?" Frendall asked her, wrapping his arm around Klara's waist.

"Happy to be of service. Should you need me, I'll be seeing to Lottie," Henrietta said, before excusing herself.

Klara heard the clinking of claws at Frendall's feet and glared at him. "Please tell me you didn't. I just cas-tle-trained the first hound you got her."

She knelt down and stroked the tiny ears as the hound appeared. It was much smaller than most hound pups.

"The Breeder was going to kill the runt. It's also blind in one eye," Frendall explained.

Klara picked up the puppy, who greedily chomped on her arm, poking tiny holes in her flesh. "Feisty," she said as it snuggled into her chest, and she felt sorry for the runt.

"Thought it would be a perfect fit. It will give Lottie more responsibility," Frendall said, before kissing her.

Klara pulled him closer. It had been many moons since they had seen each other, and she didn't want to send him back to Hell. However, there had to be a reason for his visit. She considered telling him about the fae's trick with Jasper at the Gathering, but she didn't want to spoil the mood of their reunion.

"Lottie will be thrilled to have another to run around with," she admitted. Klara thought of her own lost hounds as she noticed the white tips of this one's ears. She hoped Lottie would never have to feel the heartache of losing them. She wanted to protect Lottie for as long as possible. *It will only be a matter of time before someone or something lusts for power that doesn't belong to them and we're all thrust back into chaos.* Jasper came back into the forefront of her mind.

"Mila sends her best; Head Torturer suits her well," Frendall said, and Klara shook her head.

"I highly doubt that, and can you please refrain from discussing my half-sister during these happy moments?"

"Not another word will I utter," Frendall said as she ran a finger through the single vertical scar that now ran from above his eyebrow to just below his left eye. She peeked into his mind, needing extra reassurance that it was him, and there they were in bed in each other's arms. She sighed in relief as her mind flooded with memories of them together: the good, the bad and the sensual.

"How was the Gathering last night?" Frendall asked, and Klara put down the small hound, who lay happily across Frendall's black dress shoes.

"The creatures agreed to the lower market taxes, and the warlocks have agreed to renovate the Beanstalk as a food kitchen." She informed him of the other deals made throughout the night after and during the cups of ale and venom. Hearing all she had accomplished spoken aloud made it worth the still-throbbing head.

"How you managed to get them to see eye to eye is a miracle," Frendall said, his amber eyes wide with amazement. It was the one part of Wolfgang, his lycaon half, he had decided to expose. He no longer had to hide his nature, and she was glad to see the familiar eyes.

"I wouldn't call it a miracle. It's a lot of deals and back-scratching—but if it keeps them from slaughtering each other, I'll make as many deals as possible," Klara said.

There had been a few growing pains upon her succession of Abadan. Some of the lycaons had returned from hiding and decided to offer her fealty in thanks for saving and raising Lottie. They hadn't wished to return to the newly formed pack under Matthias, and she had needed a guard. There was no reason to question them, and they were happy to be of service to both Klara and Lottie. The demons Frendall had sent to replace Abadan's guard, however, weren't happy about working alongside lycaons. Klara and Frendall had broken up more than a few brawls between them; a few lycaons and demons had even spent a few days in the dungeons beneath the castle cooling off. Once they'd gotten the fight out of their systems, the tension began to ease, and it had only taken a single gathering of drinking venom and singing war songs from the past to bond them.

It hadn't been all roses, though; when one problem was solved, another appeared. Not three nights into her reign, the vampires had challenged the witches to create a second underground settlement in the south. Luckily Klara had arrived in time to stop the vampires from attacking. It was one of the reasons Elder Langda liked to visit; Klara knew the vampire hoped she would change her mind or gift her lands for a new settlement. She hadn't even known why the vampires would want a settlement in the south, where there was more sun and the temperature was higher, until Elder Langda had told her that after the lycaons had been burnt out by Abadan, the vampires needed somewhere to evacuate to.

Klara respected Langda; she spoke her mind, and Klara always knew where she stood with her. She had assured the vampire that it wasn't necessary, but they both knew that wasn't true. Tides turned quickly in Malum, and it was smart to have an escape route. Unfortunately, she had been unable to approve the settlement in the south. The witches' Redwood was ancient land and threaded with their ancestral magic; they would never allow even the underground to be tainted and dug up by vampires.

The vampires were buried so deep under the surface of northern Malum, it was near impossible to be granted an audience; they didn't want anyone revealing the paths through their structures. However, thankfully Lokey had some connections since he supplied barrels of fungus to the vampires. Eventually, they had struck an agreement to expand their current settlement.

Only a moon after it had been settled did the elves try to raise the taxes on the southern coast of Malum. Klara had travelled with her guard of lycaons and demons to the coast to stop the elves, and they had quickly reduced the tax on the creatures who wished to visit the glorious beaches on the coast of Malum. She had been surprised at how effective simply meeting them and hearing their side of the story had been. Gatherings of the elders and the listening of the creatures seemed the most efficient way to sort out grievances without bloodshed.

"How are Abadan's guards settling into your legion? Any grudges?" she asked Frendall, though truthfully she cared little. Klara had spilt the blood of many of Abadan's allies, and banished many Crimson Guards who dared to make attempts on her life to the realm of Hell.

"Adapting to legion life. There aren't as many perks in Hell as there are in Malum."

She didn't doubt it. "Still better than the Maze; they should be grateful you allowed them to serve," Klara said, trying to hide the scorn she felt towards those who had hunted her and Frendall.

"Some served Abadan for hundreds of years; you can hardly blame them..."

"For trying to take my life?" she snapped, and he lifted his shoulders in defeat.

"Pretend I didn't say that last part." His hands rose defensively, but he retained his devilish smile, exposing his dimples. Klara hit him playfully, and he wrapped her in his arms once again.

She watched Frendall stare at the chandeliers that now matched those in Hell, and the once-blackened stones, now a pale grey.

"I see you've been redecorating—again."

"Every corner still reminds me of Abadan. Sometimes I swear I can still hear her heels on the stones." Klara did wish to hear Lilith's heavy footsteps again. Abadan's, however, could remain wherever the hell she had ended up. "No news on Lilith? I know Father was hoping to find her soul," she added, wondering if her father had any hint of her survival.

"She's gone, Klara. He had Lokey search every realm and plane of existence. No sign of her," Frendall told her.

"No harm in asking," Klara said, instantly feeling guilty about not telling him the truth. Secrets spread as fast as flames in Malum, and one less person knowing kept her guardian safe. If she told Frendall, he would be honour-bound to inform Lucifer, and the last thing Klara wanted was for Lilith to be taken away from her. She had decided to tell Frendall when Lilith woke up. *If she ever woke up.*

"Lord, how I missed you. Maybe I'll just give up my legion and become a kept man," he said, pulling her tight to his body, and the guards in the foyer averted their eyes.

"Don't say that, or I might not let you leave again."

"Is that a promise or a threat?" He winked.

"I think I have some chains in the dungeon," Klara whispered into his ear, her hands flat against his chest, and she felt his heartbeat quicken.

"Don't make promises you can't keep," he challenged, and she rolled her eyes.

"We both know you'll be back to your legion in a heartbeat; you enjoy your new command too much," she argued. He loved his role as general and she refused to keep him from it, even if it hurt every time they had to say goodbye.

"I'd much prefer having you boss me around," he said, his lips against her neck, and she blushed.

"Frendall!" Lottie shouted, breaking the moment as she slid down the bannister. The hound pup at their feet cowered in the presence of the older hound. Lottie landed on her feet and quickly got between Klara and Frendall.

"How's the little beast?" Frendall said, ruffling the blonde fringe that Lottie refused to have cut. Klara had the impression she was trying to conceal her fate—those telling blue eyes that only true alphas bore.

"I'm not little anymore, and I'm not a beast!" Lottie protested, and Klara rolled her eyes.

"I told you to change," she said, looking at Lottie's muddy clothes. Frendall frowned questioningly. "The lycaons and their new alpha are arriving this evening to formally meet Lottie and discuss the territory," Klara informed him.

She spotted the nervous look in the guards who stood at the doors. Those in Klara's guard had officially severed ties with Matthias's united pack when they had taken their place in the castle. Klara hadn't asked them to make the choice, but Matthias had—so they gave up the right to ever join the pack in order to protect Lottie, their future alpha, and a queen who wouldn't slaughter them. It hadn't gone down well with Matthias.

"I was about to when I heard his laugh," Lottie said, rolling her own eyes, and Frendall laughed.

"I see she has developed some of your stubbornness."

"She had that long before I met her," Klara pointed out. "Lottie, upstairs now! Don't make me send Henrietta to watch you."

"Are you staying for long?" Lottie asked Frendall, ignoring Klara.

"I have some matters to discuss with the queen, and then I have to get back to Hell."

Klara was disappointed to hear he wouldn't be staying longer. She watched as Lottie squeezed him tightly, and Frendall wrapped his arms around her small frame. She only reached his waist. Klara knew how much Lottie missed Frendall when he was gone. Both a brother and father in one.

Lottie glanced at the pup on the ground and could hardly contain herself. *Here we go.* Klara motioned for Frendall to tell her.

"Look after this little one, will you?" Frendall said, picking up the submissive hound, and Lottie beamed.

"He's blind in one eye, so you need to take special care, okay?"

"I can do it," Lottie said proudly, taking the hound in her arms. Its bright red eyes looked up at her, and Klara wished Lottie cared about her lessons as much as she cared about hounds.

"Go on," she said, and Lottie headed for the stairs.

She lingered on the staircase. "Can you bring more? I don't want them to get lonely."

"As many as you like," Frendall promised.

Lottie smiled, and Klara tossed a small fireball in her direction, knowing it would send her ward racing up the stairs.

"Losing patience?" Frendall asked.

"She has so much to learn about her own kind, the Forest, our realm, the other realms—and as much as I want to teach her, I don't want her to lose her innocence."

"She's going to discover everything in her own time; the Forest will see to that," Frendall consoled her.

"I know, but I've enjoyed the peace." She rested her head on his chest, allowing her hair to fall over her face, and he kissed the top of her head.

"Speaking of peace..." he started.

"I knew it was too good to be true." Klara's words were muffled against his shirt.

Frendall delivered the blow. "Your father asks for your presence in the manor."

"It can't be that time already?"

"A year. It was part of the deal."

A year in Malum was different to one in Hell—but when Lucifer decided a year had passed, a year had passed. Klara had agreed to rule Malum as long as the border between Kalos and Malum granted access to those who held no dark magic or had never murdered an innocent.

Creatures would be able to move freely between the two lands and make a new life for themselves among the fae in Kalos or in Malum, if they wished. A yearly meeting made sure everyone kept their part of the bargain. Lucifer was the appointed mediator between Klara and the fae queen, Aemella, who often tried to back out of her end of the deal. Aemella hated the thought of dark creatures corrupting her precious Kalos. She also wanted Klara to rule at her side and forsake Malum, along with her future throne in Hell. Without Lucifer's mediation, Klara often feared the fae queen would back out of her side of the deal, whether she had cause or not.

Perhaps Jasper's presence last night was meant to provoke violent action against a fae in my own castle, the heart of Malum. Hurting him would give Aemella cause to break the treaty. But tossing him in the dirt is hardly a violent action, and the blade didn't even break his skin. Klara considered all that had transpired between them.

"Klara?" Frendall asked, interrupting her train of thought. "Where did you go?"

"Sorry. My head is throbbing from the venom, and I've barely eaten. What were you saying about Hell?" She frowned, trying to concentrate.

"I can't tell you much, but Aemella has requested mediation. It's certainly early, but I'm afraid she has as much right to call a meeting as you do," Frendall was saying, when Klara noticed a creature pacing outside the castle through the new glass panes that ran from floor to ceiling in the stone walls. Another detail she had stolen from her father—but she enjoyed being able to look out on the Forest from such a great height.

"Give me a moment?" she asked, and he sighed, following her gaze to the window.

"Trying to make another break for it?" Frendall winked again, and she kissed him gently.

"Wouldn't dream of giving all this up," she said, motioning to the grand foyer. "Try and convince Lottie to get ready?"

"Because I had so much success with you?" he said, raising his eyebrows.

"Please. I won't be long."

Frendall nodded and disappeared upstairs. Once he was gone, she straightened herself up.

"Open the doors," she ordered her guards in their blackened armour. They obeyed with their heads slightly bowed. The chill of the Forest drifted into the castle, and Klara smelt the salt of the sea in the air.

"May I help you?" she asked the elderly witch standing there in her full skirts. The jars and poultices at her belted waist told Klara what she was.

"I'm sorry, Your Majesty. I did not mean to linger after the listening, but I feel like I'm running out of time," she said breathlessly. Her voice sounded familiar.

"If this is about mercy, I have already shown great leniency." It was unusual for the coven to send a lone witch to grovel. *They're more likely to poison the food that comes into my kitchens from the market than beg.*

"It isn't about the punishment. They would burn me for coming to you, but they won't help me—or at least they can't." Her teeth chattered in fear. "But I had to do something."

"No harm will come to you. Speak your mind," Klara assured the witch, who backed up, making it clear she didn't want to make contact with the queen. Her youthful voice only confirmed that the elderly appearance was a disguise.

"I have heard rumours. I wished to see you at the

listening, but we were dismissed before I had the chance to speak with you."

Klara finally placed her voice; the witch who had given away the number of sacrifices. "You have my undivided attention," she promised. "Whatever you need to say, I will listen."

"My sister-witch, my twin—Frieda, a white witch. She left for Kalos, and I haven't heard from her. She committed no sins to bar her entrance, but she has not written as she said she would." A sister-witch referred to someone within the same coven, but if Frieda was her twin, they were also related by blood.

"Maybe she is merely finding a place to settle?" Klara suggested.

"No," the witch barked, before bowing her head. "I have felt her energy fading for some time." Klara could see the fear in her eyes, sunken from lack of sleep. "I overheard dark fae at the fungus den talk of settlements for powerful creatures. They aren't allowed to leave once they pass through the Neutral Lands to Kalos," the witch continued frantically.

Klara struggled to keep up. She had never heard of such settlements at her gatherings of creatures, and they had their ear to the ground for anything related to the fae. *Any creature could have taken advantage of the witch.*

"All creatures are questioned upon their arrival. She could have been taken somewhere for questioning—" she started, and the witch took a necklace from her pocket. A dark ruby hung at the end of a thin gold chain.

"Frieda wears its twin, and this is how we let each other know when we are in danger. The light has been fading since the last full moon. I don't think my sister has much time; I can feel it in my bones," she insisted, holding out the ruby.

Klara took the necklace in her hand, feeling the white magic within, and knew that Frieda would have been granted access. *There is no dark magic in either of these witches.*

"You can drop the disguise," she said. "I know who you are."

The witch stilled, and then became a young woman.

"Why, may I ask, did you choose to remain in Malum while your sister ventured off alone?" Klara wasn't going to investigate without knowing the full story.

"I'm a Healer. I find peace in helping here, but Frieda... she thought she would be able to find some herbs and new medicines in Kalos—" The witch cut herself off.

"So she went to steal?" *The ill-intent could have been picked up by the fae, and they might have detained her.* Klara was trying to find the truth, but she sensed no malice.

"What comes from the Earth cannot be stolen!" the witch said defensively. She shook her head. "I knew this would be a waste of time. I was told you would help, but it seems the leprechaun was mistaken."

"Hold on," Klara said as the witch tried to descend the mountain. "Who sent you to me?"

"Glaudine. The lep at the den, the one with the babe on her back? She told me you could help."

Klara knew Lokey's wife wouldn't have sent just anyone to her for help. "How long has your sister been gone?" she pressed.

"Since the last full moon or so, but you know how the Forest plays with time."

"I will be meeting with the fae queen soon. I will ask about your sister, but I can't make any promises; she chose to leave of her own free will. There is only so much I can do on the Kalion side of the border," Klara said, wanting to make her position clear and not give her false hope.

"Thank you, Your Majesty. Please do what you can, and I will return the favour in whatever way I am able." The witch clasped her hands under her chin in relief and gratitude.

"Return home now before the moon is at its highest," Klara said softly, and the witch bowed in acknowledgement.

Settlements… What is the fae queen up to? Klara was about to step back inside when the witch called after her.

"My sister isn't the only one. Many have not heard from their loved ones once they made the cross-over." *Some may not have even crossed of their own will.* The witch projected the last part into Klara's mind.

"Return now, and don't speak of our meeting." Klara didn't want anyone knowing she was looking into the fae queen or Kalos. The witch nodded before disappearing down the mountain.

Frendall was waiting at the bottom of the stairs. "Everything okay?"

"She offered me a poultice in penance for the sacrifices they made." Klara didn't want to burden him with the details of the Forest. If she told him every single event, they would never get any time just to be together. Frendall did the same when he returned to her; they rarely discussed his role and all that it entailed.

"You were gone a while," he pressed, and she shook her head reassuringly.

"Merely getting some air before the lycaons arrive."

"I must return. The king has sent word that the fae queen wishes to push the meeting up to dawn."

Klara groaned, craving her bed, not even caring whether Frendall was in it at this point. Tonight she would meet the alpha by proxy and tomorrow she would be facing her mother. Even the thought wore her out.

"I'll see you at dawn," she said resignedly, kissing his cheek.

"Be careful with the alpha," Frendall said, the crease in his brow telling her of his worry. The castle doors opened and he was gone. She wondered if Frendall had met the alpha. He'd spent some time helping to rebuild the interior of the lycaons' caves and the surrounding territories before Lucifer had promoted him.

She dismissed her guard for their evening meal and sat on the staircase. After pulling her boots from her feet, she took the witch's necklace from her pocket.

"What could anyone want with a white witch? Please tell me this isn't your doing, Mother," she murmured to herself, watching as the crystal dimmed a little more.

4

"Lottie! Open the damn door, or I swear I will remove it!" Klara said, suddenly regretting having given Lottie her old sky room in the castle tower. She could use a portrait to get in, but she wanted Lottie to let her in herself.

She took her hand off the doorknob when a crash sounded from inside, followed by a bark. Klara moved away from the door, ready to kick it in, but there was very little space on the landing atop the steps that led up to the sky room. *Next time I'm using the bloody portrait.*

"If you destroy that room, you will be fixing it by hand without a single spell to help you!" She tried the doorknob again, but it was no use. Lottie had blocked the door with something heavy—Klara guessed it was the wardrobe or the desk.

"I'm not meeting them! You can't force me!" Lottie

shouted, and Klara heard something hit the wall. Lottie had the hormonal instincts of a fully grown lycaon in a ten-year-old's body. She had a long way to go until she would be able to control her abilities and emotions.

"Stop throwing things!" Klara ordered, resting her head on the doorframe. *Time to change tack.* "I'm not mad. Please open the door, and we can talk about the meeting, okay?"

A long silence, followed by a shuffle and the soft click of a key turning, told her it was okay to enter. Klara took in the overturned wardrobe and the desk, then the smashed crystal jug and bowl by the bedside table. *At least she was smart enough to use two heavy objects.* Surveying the damage, she whispered an enchantment, and the crystal jug pieced itself back together and returned to its place on the dresser. The clothes littering the floor filled the wardrobe back up as it found its position against the wall. *That's a start.*

Lottie sat cross-legged on her bed with her head on her knees. Klara suspected she was waiting to be yelled at, but she could feel the anxiety stifling the air around her ward.

"You scared the hounds. You don't want the pup to be frightened of you. He's only a little thing," Klara told her softly.

Lottie snapped her head up in concern to see the older hound backed in the corner against the wall, its paws protecting the runt.

"I didn't mean to scare them. I got mad again." She sounded ashamed of herself.

Klara went to the hound and stroked its ear before taking the pup from its paws.

"Nothing a cuddle can't fix," she said to her ward. Lottie dropped her knees, and Klara placed the pup in her lap. "Feel better?" she asked as the hound curled against Lottie.

She nodded, but Klara could still sense waves of sadness radiating from her.

"What upset you?" she asked, taking a seat beside her ward on the soft cream blanket that lay over her pale pink sheets. Klara hardly recognised her old room; while she had lived in the tower it had been cold and bare, but now it was warmed up with colourful rugs and torches on the wall. She wanted Lottie to feel at home in the castle, while Klara had always been made to feel like a hostage.

"If Mum and Dad were alive, I wouldn't have to meet with them or learn all this stuff. I just want to run."

Klara knew exactly how that felt—the longing to be free and not weighed by the realities of one's fate. "Missing them is completely natural, but if they were still here, you wouldn't have me and Henny, or Frendall and the hounds. Try to focus on what you do have, rather than what you don't."

"But *you* ran, and got all the way to Kalos." Lottie frowned.

"I did, but I realised that running away doesn't achieve anything and there is no real peace in life. There are challenges, no matter where you go. Peace is for the dead."

"Unless you're a doomed, or end up in the Maze, or can't pay Kharon," Lottie said, using Klara's lessons against her.

"Okay, smartass. For the majority, there is peace." Her mind drifted to Lilith beneath the throne room, wondering if she was at peace or trapped in a nightmare. She hoped it was the latter.

"I wasn't meant to be the alpha. Mom and Dad

were smart and strong; they weren't afraid of anything. I'm afraid of everything without them. The united pack doesn't even know me. What if they don't like me, and I have to fight a bigger lycaon? I'll die."

The fear in Lottie's voice pierced Klara's heart. Challenging a rival alpha was a rite of passage, and it usually meant the death of the less experienced lycaon.

"Listen to me. You have years before that might happen, and you will drive yourself demented if you keep focusing on it," Klara said calmly. Lottie buried her head in her hands, and Klara could hear her laboured breathing. "Until you reach maturity, you can't be challenged, and that gives you all the time in the realm to study and train. Become someone your parents would be proud of. You were born an alpha, the same as your mother and father before you, the same way as I'll have to take my place in Hell. Malum is my training, as the next couple of years are yours."

Lottie glanced up. "But they aren't here to help me. They're nothing but ash," she sobbed.

Heart clenching, Klara wiped away her tears, knowing Lottie still had dreams of them burning. When she had first shifted, she had gained access to the memories of her ancestors. It was a gift and a curse—years of knowledge, combined with years of oppression and abuse from the rulers of Malum. That was why lycaons didn't shift until they were fully grown; those memories could twist the purest of hearts.

"They're here, even if you don't see them. They'll watch your every step as I will. Do you know how proud they'll be to see how much you've developed?"

"You think so?" Lottie sniffled.

"I know so, and when you're challenged—many, many moons from now—I'll make sure you're ready to take down anyone who dares to stand against you."

"Promise?" Lottie said, and Klara was glad to hear her breathing had levelled out. *This is one promise I will keep.*

"Promise. Now, what are we going to name this little one?" she asked, frowning at the little red-eyed beast. Lottie stared at the sleeping hound as the other rested its head on the bed. "Hyde?" Klara looked at Jekyll, whose eyes perked up.

"It suits him," Lottie agreed, while the pup tried to hide in the crook of her arm. Naming the hounds was a privilege only Lottie was allowed—such a thing was forbidden in Hell. Naming anything gave it life, a personality. Handler demons would grow too attached and the hounds too soft. Jekyll padded over, resting his snout on Lottie's knee.

"Castle-training is up to you this time. No help from Henny or me whatsoever. Think you can handle it?"

Hyde pawing at Jekyll's long snout made Lottie smile. "Definitely," she said proudly.

Confidence restored. The hounds circled them before disappearing through the door as banging at the castle doors signalled their guests' arrival.

"Good, because if you can handle two Hell-hounds, then the lycaons will be a piece of cake."

Lottie paled a little, and Klara tossed her some clothes from the dresser. "Put on a clean shirt; you smell like the outdoors," she said, putting it politely and also trying to make light of the situation. *We don't have time for another freak-out.*

"Are you saying I smell?" Lottie demanded.

Klara took the pup and placed him on the stone

floor. "Yes. Wash, dress and be down in five minutes, or I will send Henrietta to escort you."

"Why not order a guard to take me by the hair?" Lottie's pale cheeks blotched as her temper rose once again.

"They merely want to meet you. You don't even have to speak if you don't want to," Klara said, knowing she would never have been allowed to act with such disrespect.

"Fine. Then I won't say anything."

"Good. It's now four minutes."

Lottie pushed her out the door. "Get out, I have to change!" she whined as Klara leant back into Lottie's hands. She struggled to kick her out, and Klara laughed, much to Lottie's displeasure.

"You are so annoying!" Lottie slammed the door as Klara passed the threshold, and the door hit her back.

Klara looked at Jekyll, who was already panting halfway down the winding tower staircase. "Does she speak to you like that?"

5

Alpha Matthias waited in the foyer under the grand chandelier with a few lycaons standing nervously at his back. Klara sensed their unease as she joined them. *Understandable, considering the last high queen who walked these halls burned their people alive and destroyed their caves in the West Mountains searching for me.*

"Welcome. I have looked forward to our meeting." Klara smiled, extending her hand. Matthias was smart enough not to take it. She suppressed a smile; touching her hand would have allowed her into his mind, so the refusal told her that he most certainly had something to hide. The alpha clasped his hand behind his back, which was a tell in itself.

Matthias's eyes shone a deep blue, highlighting his alpha status, although the brown threatening the iris told her he wasn't a natural-born alpha. He was taller than the others with him and built of pure muscle, though his stomach protruded from his shirt. He was older than she had expected: the thin lines of grey in his dark hair put him roughly in his late thirties, though what he was in lycaon years she couldn't know. Her guests all wore simple brown leather boots and loose cream tunics, tucked into their trousers and belted. The three buttons unfastened at the neck revealed their sun-scorched skin from hours of being outdoors. Lycaons always opted for simple, practical clothing, which was nothing compared to their transformed bodies with lush furs of varying colours, their battle scars symbols of honour. Terrifyingly beautiful, one might say.

It was possible to guess what form a lycaon would take by their stature in human form; some were lean and small, which made them faster and more agile, while others were tall and broad, making them slower but harder to bring down in a fight. Matthias's stature would make any lycaon think twice about challenging him.

"Klara Lucifer," he said, dragging out her last name as if she were a creature to be studied—or as if simply reminding himself of her parentage. Either way, his tone unsettled her. "The pleasure is ours. We have been looking forward to this meeting for some time," Matthias declared.

"I'm glad we were finally able to find some time to sit down," she said, not believing a word. She also took note of the fact that he hadn't referred to her by her formal title, a subtle insult she let slide. When those around him bowed to her, she nodded briefly, watching the guards in the hallways. Klara needed to ease the tension between the lycaons in Matthias's pack and those who served in her guard. She was raising their future alpha; she needed them to see that she was nothing like Abadan.

"This is my second-in-command, Ceylon, and her brother, Percy. They will be present during our discussion." Neither said anything.

"Both of you are welcome to stay; I will look for you at the next Gathering." Klara offered the olive branch, though she didn't miss the sneer that followed from both lycaons. "Lottie will be joining us shortly. If you will follow me through, I have food and drink ready for us."

No blood could be spilt once bread had been broken and drinks had been consumed, as written in the original treaty between Malum and Kalos. It had been written so envoys from the two lands could meet without either party fearing for their life. Now the law was used by many in Malum too; it was a good excuse to feast, and digestion was a little easier without the fear of death.

"Thank you, we would be delighted. The rebuilding and the burying of our fallen has taken much of our energy," Matthias said.

It was a loaded statement, and Klara ignored the barb as she led them through the corridors. She still felt a dull sense of responsibility; Abadan's burning out of the lycaons had been for their fealty to her when she had fled. But whether she had run or not, it had been inevitable that the high queen was going to make an example of them. Abadan had loathed their strength and sense of community, and how they wouldn't break no matter how much she pushed them.

"The past is behind us. You all deserve to rest and recover."

"I'm not sure something so horrifying can ever be behind us, but we will grow stronger from it. Some of our young still hear the screams of their kin in the caves."

I offered many demons to help with the rebuilding of the lycaon territory, and yet he continues to insult me. I wonder if it's his wounded pride because he isn't a true-born alpha that causes him to stay away from the Gatherings... or he simply hates my guts. Neither option can lead to anything good.

"If there is anything further I can do to make amends for the actions of my predecessor, I will do my best. I have seen the trauma you suffered through Lottie's eyes."

"Perhaps your ward is suffering the same visions as our young?" Ceylon said, moving to stand beside Matthias.

Klara didn't want to portray Lottie as young and scared. "She has her own memories of the night in question," was all she replied, and Matthias nodded sympathetically. They walked through the brightly lit corridor to the dining hall, and he stopped to stare at the portraits hanging and watching them pass.

"On to more pleasant subjects—we have much to discuss before the night wears on," he mused, exposing his enlarged canines. She could taste his eagerness to prove himself. That need was more dangerous than a starving vampire, and undoubtedly led to more deaths. He was intelligent, tough and bold from what she had already seen. The divided lycaons had grown into one united pack to make the most of what was left of their numbers.

"You have made the place your own, though I see you decided to keep the former high queen's eyes," Matthias went on.

They all looked to the portraits. They had indeed been Abadan's spies in the castle, but they also paid homage to those who had fallen. Klara wanted to destroy them, and yet she couldn't bring herself to do it. *Who is he to comment on my décor? His ego would challenge that of my father. I think I would quite enjoy Father's reaction to his tone...*

"Unfortunately, the portraits must remain. The King

of Hell insists upon it, and I'm afraid they are as much part of this place as I am. Who hung them up is of no consequence. I have done what I can to make repairs; there is nothing to fear here for those who seek peace."

Matthias raised his thick eyebrows at the word. He said nothing, which only made the hairs on her neck stand on edge. Klara had no memory of him being in the castle during the reign of the Three Queens. In fact, she had never heard of him until he took his place as alpha. One of the crossroads demons had informed her of his rising upon her succession; little was known of him other than that he had been a rogue, a lone lycaon, before the burning. And now here he stood, their leader.

How far you have risen? And, I wonder, just how far will you go to retain your status? Klara kept the thought to herself.

The elegant table was set with a modest banquet—long gone were the days of the former queens' gluttony. Candles lit the room and the open ceiling allowed the stars to shine in, the full moon gleaming through the high beams.

"Please be seated," Klara said as the lycaons stood behind the chairs. Percy and Ceylon's eyes drifted around the room. Their eyes were marking the entries and exits. The velvet-lined chair to Klara's right remained vacant for Lottie; she hoped her ward wouldn't keep them waiting long, as she could feel the tension thickening. Henrietta came and served the venom, but Matthias covered his crystal goblet with a tanned and calloused palm.

"I want to see the girl before we dine," he stated coldly, and Klara cocked an eyebrow. He was twice her age, but to speak to her as an inferior was a dangerous road to travel. She forced a smile, wondering herself what was keeping her ward; when she said five minutes, she meant five minutes.

"Lottie will be along soon," Henrietta said, drawing attention to herself. The doomed placed the jug of venom at the centre of the table. It was a favourite drink amongst the finest in Hell's society. Lucifer had gifted Klara a few barrels containing his favourite variations of the green liquid upon her succession.

"Thank you. That will be all for now, Henrietta."

Matthias watched Henrietta leave through the archway to the kitchen. "You keep doomed?" he asked, his upper lip curled in disdain. He downed the venom in his cup, clearly perturbed by the way Henrietta had spoken to him directly.

"She is free to leave whenever she pleases, as are any doomed who serve me. Once they have served their time in Hell, they make a choice whether to come to me or be put to rest." Klara didn't need to justify the presence of doomed in her castle, but the distrust on Ceylon and Percy's faces forced her hand. *I might not be able to win over their alpha, but there are many others who might take my side—and who better to start with than his betas, his most trusted?*

Ceylon, with thick curls and scarred forearms, chuckled behind her palm.

"Do the doomed amuse you?" Klara asked curiously.

Matthias glared at the lycaon, who shook her head.

"Speak freely," Klara urged.

"You are the daughter of Lucifer, and yet you would let your trusted servants leave you? Surely you need as many loyal to you as possible during these times. Won't new faces only feed paranoia? Doesn't your father maintain his servants for that very reason?" Ceylon said, resting her elbows on the table.

Remarking on my father's famed paranoia and refusal to

dismiss his servants? Slighting me is one thing, but going after the King of Hell only shows how bold and naïve she is.

"Henrietta has served her time for her sins in Hell. She was only a young teen when she corrupted her own soul with sin, and has long since served her sentence. I trust her, as she trusts me. I do not doubt that there will always be those willing and ready to serve me. What my father does is not my concern—neither is it yours to comment on," Klara said firmly.

"I meant no disrespect to you or your father."

"No disrespect noted. My father's paranoia is almost as famous as he is. However, paranoia does have its benefits." Klara lightened the atmosphere with a smile.

"And what would those be?" Matthias said, pouring himself some more venom.

"I can sense my enemies before they even consider moving against me."

This time his smile travelled to his eyes, but he refused to look at his queen.

Behind them, Lottie made her way through a portrait and Klara stood, showing her respect. The lycaons were smart to follow suit.

"Sorry to keep you waiting," Lottie said, but offered no excuse. There was no sign of weakness in her voice, and Klara's chest warmed with pride. She was clean and dressed; Klara was surprised to see that she had even put shoes on. The little lycaon hated shoes with a passion—she loved to feel the earth beneath her feet.

"Lottie, this is Matthias, his second Ceylon, and her brother Percy," Klara said, and the lycaons bowed deeply. *A lot more than I got.* Her eyes fell to Percy, who had yet to speak. His curls matched his sister's, but his skin was darker, and he was leaner than his alpha. Klara guessed he was a tracker.

"We are honoured to be in your company," Matthias said, taking a knee in front of Lottie. *Quite the display for a man dripping with disdain for authority.*

Lottie stilled, clearly unsure of how to respond. She wasn't used to being bowed to. Klara wasn't used to seeing it either.

"I was friends with your parents, as was Ceylon," he said but Ceylon only offered a nod, looking as though it would pain her to speak.

Lottie looked over Matthias's broad shoulders to Klara. It was apparent she didn't recognise this 'family friend', but when her eyes drifted to Ceylon, Lottie threatened a smile. *She knew Ceylon?* It made sense, if Ceylon had been part of her former pack.

"You have your mother's eyes," Matthias continued, drawing the attention back to himself. *Of course she does—an alpha's eyes.* Klara didn't voice the jab. Matthias ruffled Lottie's fringe, and Lottie took an instinctive step back. Clearly, she was picking up the same distrust Klara sensed in this new alpha.

"Come and sit; we can get started," Klara said, and Lottie took her seat beside the queen. Once everyone was seated around the modest amount of food prepared, Ceylon was the first to speak.

"Let us raise a glass to a united pack. We eagerly await your return. We have seen that the remains of your parents were buried under their favourite tree."

Lottie's head snapped to her. "Thank you, they would have liked that," she said quietly. Her voice cracked on the last words, but Klara couldn't blame her. There was only so much emotion a ten-year-old could suppress. They all took a sip of the luminous green venom.

"How are you finding living with the queen?" Ceylon

continued. *Clearly, she isn't afraid to speak her mind. Maybe she doesn't see Matthias as much of an alpha.*

"Ceylon, please, this isn't an interrogation," Matthias said to the curly-haired lycaon. She took another sip of venom, and Klara sensed her annoyance at being silenced. *To know Lottie's parents' favourite tree, she must have been an acquaintance of the family.*

"She is the sister I always wanted." Lottie smiled softly, and Klara's heart warmed—a sensation she wasn't used to.

Ceylon gave a small sigh of relief, but Matthias only scoffed. "You need your pack, not a sister. The sisters in your pack are eagerly awaiting your return. There are some children your age in the reserve. They will want to see you—"

Klara took a loud bite from the apple in front of her, breaking Matthias's speech.

"Sorry to interrupt." She wiped her lips with her napkin. "It sounds like you are suggesting that she return with you."

"I'm not suggesting it. She will come with us back to our territory."

Why do lycaons insist on creating tension at dinners? Awful for the digestion. Not a single lycaon had touched the food, either.

Lottie began to protest, but Klara placed a hand over her small one.

"Lottie is under my protection for the time being. As the last true alpha, I can't risk her safety. We share the same mountains; she is not far from you," she said.

Matthias's nostrils flared.

"We are sure you would do an excellent job in raising her," Ceylon interjected. "You yourself were raised and trained by Queen and General Lilith, but Lottie needs to be amongst her own, learn our traditions first-hand."

"I have every intention of allowing her to visit the territory, with a guard."

"She doesn't need a guard to protect her from her own kind," Matthias said, but Klara didn't need to touch him to know it was a lie.

"How many alphas have been lost due to jealousy and false politics? Lottie is a child—a born alpha, but a child—and I won't allow her to be used as a pawn."

"She has already shifted. She needs to carry out the ritual to earn her place amongst our people, or we will never accept her heritage," Matthias said, his voice raised. The guards positioned at the door turned their heads towards the table. Klara was pleased to see their reflexes and that they were paying close attention, should she need them.

Lottie had paled, and Klara knew what ritual Matthias was talking about.

"My family didn't believe in the old traditions," Lottie said.

Matthias pushed back out of his chair, and Klara felt for her axe, levitating it under the table.

"Your father believed in the old ways!" Matthias shouted down at Lottie.

The guards stepped forward, ready to defend them, but Klara motioned for them to stop. Percy had caught on to their approach, and she watched his claws appear.

Klara rose, her fingertips on the table. "I suggest you lower your voice and take your seat, if you wish for these talks to continue." *You might be the alpha for now, but I'm still your goddamn queen.* "All of us," she added, looking directly at Percy. He scowled briefly before retracting his claws, and Matthias motioned for him to sit. Ceylon, however, remained where she was, as though the tense moment hadn't even happened.

"Apologies, Your Majesty."

Klara hated the way Matthias said *Your Majesty,* like she was a child in need of pacifying. He was trying to be charming, but it came across as arrogant.

"I merely wish to see our tradition through. We have had so much taken from us; we must regain our strength. Surely as our future leader you understand this," Matthias added to Lottie, before he made a sorry attempt at a bow and reclaimed his seat.

What he wants is to stop Lottie from having the ability to move freely from Malum into Kalos. The ritual of consuming a human heart would seal her fate in Malum and twist an irreversible part of her soul.

"We all must go through the rite of passage, and it will help Lottie control her emotions. I can sense how much she is trying to control them as we speak," Matthias explained, pulling a piece of rolled parchment from his tarnished jacket. "Sign this, saying that you accept our traditions, and we can accept you into the fold," he said, offering the scroll to Lottie, who refused to take it.

Klara wondered what other rituals this new alpha was preaching. Unfortunately, she couldn't prohibit traditional ceremonies, no matter how much she objected; every creature had the right to choose their path. Still, creatures also couldn't be forced by their leader or alpha to complete acts that would corrupt their soul, though many would fear being cast out if they disobeyed. If there was one thing you needed to survive Malum, it was allies.

"If Lottie chooses that path, so be it; but if she wishes to respect her parents' wishes, then she's well within her rights to object," she said calmly.

"I won't disrespect them by consuming human blood," Lottie said. *I don't know this alpha's face, and my dad would have thrown him out of the pack for saying such things,* she projected to Klara, who was impressed that Lottie had made her stance on the subject clear without losing control. "If you were a friend of my parents, then you would know that my pack hasn't consumed a heart for generations. My mother would have ripped out your claws for suggesting it. You may have belonged to a distant pack, but it certainly wasn't mine."

Matthias went silent, scorn riddling his face with lines. "There is no 'your' or 'my' pack anymore. If you wish for a place amongst us, then you will honour my wishes as your current alpha."

Lottie laughed. "Alpha? You drain your pack of strength to grant you those eyes and tell me to respect you? No alpha would risk the pack for self-gain."

Klara regretted telling Lottie that piece of information. But when her ward had asked how someone had taken her place, Klara had had no choice but to explain that a bonding ceremony similar to a coven's bond allowed one lycaon to feed off the many. It was rare that such ceremonies took place in packs.

"You are too young to understand. The pack needs an alpha, now more than ever, and I would do it again if it meant uniting what's left of us," said Matthias dismissively.

Now more than ever? Klara thought. *What's that supposed to mean?* Her mind drifted to Jasper's intrusion on the gathering, and the witch's warning and missing sister. *Maybe the lycaons know something I don't.*

"No alpha hurts the pack for self-gain," Lottie reiterated.

Klara watched Lottie's nails lengthen under the table. *Calm down. Letting him see your anger will cost you the others,* Klara projected. She could feel Lottie's resistance, but her breathing evened out after a moment and her nails returned to normal.

This was why Klara would never let her leave with the delegation. Lottie wouldn't last one night in the pack before Matthias found her and snapped her delicate neck.

"We aren't getting anywhere, Matthias; we should discuss this another time when everyone has had a chance to think it over," Ceylon said, suddenly playing the mediator. Matthias sat back from Lottie.

"This child has some fight, but I can smell the queen's influence. She is not one of us." Matthias scratched his bearded face.

Klara's stomach dropped. If Lottie was cast aside, she would lose any claim as alpha and would have to fight her way through the ranks to regain her place amongst her pack. A lycaon without a pack could go savage; rogues rarely maintained their self-awareness, and usually ended up remaining in their lycaon form for the rest of their lives. Frendall had told her this when she had questioned him about his lycaon half. He'd explained that was why Lucifer allowed him to visit the territory, to run with other lycaons, and how he had met Lottie's parents.

Frendall had also thought the hounds would give Lottie the sense of a pack and help cull her instincts. She needed constant stimulation, or her senses would overwhelm her.

"We will take our leave," Matthias said. "There is nothing for us here."

Klara noticed the panicked expression on the other lycaons' faces as their eyes darted from Matthias to

Lottie, unsure whether to follow their power-hungry alpha or a child.

"You can't kick me out of the pack," Lottie snapped.

Matthias chuckled, enraging her further. "As acting alpha, yes, I can. Since our practices disgust you so, I don't think this will burden your heart for too long." He gave a cold smile, obviously enjoying every moment of Lottie's distress.

Matthias called his lycaons to his side, and they quickly fell in line. Klara watched Ceylon and Percy's reactions. They didn't seem happy about it, yet she sensed the fear they had of their alpha. Beneath that, though, she felt their distrust—and that bred unrest.

Lottie opened her mouth to argue, but Klara placed a hand on her small shoulder, letting her into her mind. *They wouldn't have come here without the chance to negotiate; he could have sent a messenger to cast you out or to order you back to the caves. The unsigned parchment would have been his proof that you denied their traditions—that's the only reason he wants your signature. However, coming here means he wants something... Something only I can offer.*

"I'm sure we can come to some sort of arrangement," she said aloud.

It wasn't a moment before he spoke. "One united pack takes up a lot of land. Our numbers are strong, even if some did desert to your guard, and we have rebuilt our homes and settlements—but much of the land was too burnt to do anything with, and it will be years before the earth heals." He leant forward into the table, his hands gripped together.

There it is. That's the real reason why he agreed to visit; he wants to expand.

"More land to regrow?" Klara asked, raising an eyebrow.

"We have been stuffed into those caves long enough. We want what Abadan took from us," Matthias said firmly.

"And with that, you will allow Lottie the freedom to choose? Forget this whole signing issue?"

"A lycaon shifting so early without the control of our bonded tradition is a threat to the rest of the pack, but if she shows some semblance of control and learns to control her tongue amongst her elders, we can discuss it," Matthias said.

Klara knew it was a crock of shit. The only part she believed was the control element. A bonded pack might be stronger, but it also made it easier for them to be influenced by the majority.

Lottie tried to pull away from Klara, but she dug her fingers into the younger girl's shoulders. *They could still fight and take you by force! None have eaten from the table.* Lottie stilled.

"I will draw up the scrolls for further west of the territory. The trees will need to be cleared, but I think you can handle it. You will have them by tomorrow," Klara said. Gone were smiles and pleasantries.

"You have been a most gracious host," Ceylon said.

Klara wished she could strike the grin from Matthias's face, but she needed the lycaons. A revolution on her doorstep wasn't going to benefit the Forest in any way. *A little land never hurt anyone,* she told herself.

"The pleasure is all mine," she replied with a feigned smile.

Ceylon offered Klara a sympathetic look, but she didn't need it. *It won't be long before Matthias is gone and Lottie in his place.* Klara knew a truly dark soul when she saw one, and it wouldn't be long before the rest of the lycaons saw it too. Matthias wanted land, power and, as he'd said himself, *control*. Lycaons might live in packs, but they were founded on respect and honour. If an alpha showed neither, it would be a hard and violent fall. Klara only hoped she would be there to witness it.

Guards appeared in the archway as Klara summoned them to escort the lycaons back down the mountain. She wasn't going to leave them alone for a moment.

"Why did you give in to him? He wants me to eat a heart!" Lottie finally pulled herself free from Klara. "I wouldn't ever be able to travel to Kalos, not even just to see it!"

"You would," Klara said. "You have my permission to pass through the border."

"How is that possible?" Lottie asked, her eyes wide in bewilderment.

"My mother's blood helped build the divide between our lands—a blood we share." Klara had learnt this when she had signed the amended treaty; she couldn't break her mother's protections, but she could pass through. However, her mother would sense it when she did.

"Then I still have to eat…?" Lottie cut herself off in horror. Klara took a step back in case she shifted in a rage.

"No, that's not why I told you about the protections. You won't ever have to eat a heart," she said. Her head throbbed, though she had hardly touched her venom.

"They tried to take me, and you barely argued," Lottie said, her eyes filling with tears.

"The last thing he wanted was you running around with the children of those you could influence. Growing up with them would bond you just as much as a heart would. Trust me—I know from experience. He knows you are far away from the lycaons' eyes and ears in the castle, thus putting him in a stronger position. Or so he thinks."

"Why didn't you tell me he was after something from the start?"

"I knew you were safe, and I'm proud of you for standing your ground. I don't want him to be the one to challenge you. Your challenge and my leniency will play to your advantage."

"I'm sick of your games! Why can't you say what you mean?" Lottie stormed out through the archway and into the portrait to Eve's expansive conservatory.

Lucifer, grant me the strength not to kill this child. Klara followed her ward through the oil painting. "Leave us," she said to the doomed spraying the enchanted flowers and plants, but Lottie was off the marble bench, shifted and out the glass door before Klara could call after her.

"I wouldn't follow her," Henrietta said, appearing out of nowhere, her arms folded on her chest, covered by her long flowing sleeves. "A run will do her good, and she is angrier at herself for losing control in front of the others than with you."

Klara waited on the marble bench for a few moments, watching the brightly coloured fish swimming in the large pond, hoping Lottie would see sense and come back. *Arthur always knew what to say when I was being a pain, yet all I do is add fuel to the fire. Why couldn't you have been here to help me?*

"Maybe I should take a page out of Lilith's grimoire and throw her into the ice pits for a week," she said to Henrietta, who looked unimpressed by the option. Probably not the best person to discuss harsh punishments with, considering that she had spent decades in Hell being tortured.

"How did that make you feel?" Henrietta asked, taking a seat beside her.

"Cold," Klara admitted, "but I didn't forget to leave without a dagger again."

6

Klara eyed the large maps that outlined the lands of Malum laid out on the desk in front of her.

In need of the maps, she had opted for the castle library, with its high ceiling shelves made of dark varnished wood and equally tall ladders of gold that leaned against them, fitted with small wheels so she could move around the concentric rings of shelves with ease.

Eve had been in charge of organising the library, which meant that books had been left unattended in corners in stacks that were taller than Klara. She stared at the grimoires still open and left on the stone floor. Eve seemed to have thrown the books from the shelves so she wouldn't have to carry each one down, which explained why they all looked like they had been through their own personal war.

Klara's doomed had tidied up as best they could, but

the library spanned shelves upon shelves. At the centre sat a large desk and plush armchair, perfect for long reading sessions. Eve had liked her comforts; even the deep blue and purple rugs were extra luxurious. Klara—or Eve—could have used a spell to organise the library in seconds, but there was a sense of organised chaos that she liked about it. Though Eve had clearly known where everything was, it was nearly impossible to find something in a rush, so Klara organised as she went along when she found spare moments. Hence why, after a year, it was still a mess.

Klara scrunched her toes against the rug, letting the sensation ground her. She finished a small plate of fruit, vegetables and pastries that Henrietta had brought in to keep her going. The silence was almost too good to be true, and she knew it wouldn't last. She began to write out the new land agreement, careful not to offer too much land but enough to soothe Matthias's ego.

After writing *thereby* and *agrees to* far too many times, she grew exceptionally bored. She took a moment to rest her head against the desk, only for sleep to take her.

A few hours later, she was awoken by a drip of hot candle wax from the chandelier above. The quick, sharp sting brought her attention back to the map before her. A blob of black ink had dropped from her silver-tipped fountain pen onto the parchment. The moonlight drifting in through the stained-glass window in the ceiling of the castle told her that night had fallen.

I can't give them any more of the mountain, or the goblins will feel threatened, and I have to rule out eastern expansion or it will threaten the vampires beneath, she thought, peeling the wax from her forearm. She eyed the vacant plot of the Forest. It was mostly made up of dense trees further west, but it had always been an essential escape route if the castle was invaded.

"Not looking like I have many choices," she said to Jekyll, who had padded into the library, followed by the pup. I shouldn't have let Lottie run off without them, she thought, even as she enjoyed their presence. They lay under the desk at her feet.

"She left you, too?" she said, patting Jekyll's head on her knee. The soft whine told her so.

Klara left her signature off the scroll; she wanted Matthias to sign first so that she would be the last to see the scroll, just in case he felt like adding something without her knowledge. It was a paranoid thought, but judging from his superior attitude, it was best to err on the side of caution.

The hounds suddenly stood and ran from the room. Klara watched the pup try to keep up. Before she had time to consider what had drawn their attention, a piercing scream ripped up the mountain.

Lottie!

Klara abandoned the scroll and ran through a portrait that led her straight to the mountain pass. By the time she had followed the howls of pain, she found Henrietta already at Lottie's side on the edge of the Forest, while the guards from the pass surrounded Lottie and kept an eye out for anyone approaching them. Gone was Lottie's white lycaon fur. *I told her not to shift back while still in the Forest!* Klara was about to scold her but then she saw Lottie's ankle clamped by a snatch—metal jaws meant to maim creatures.

No one would dare lay a trap this close to our home, Klara thought, but she didn't have time to hunt for the culprit as Lottie cried out in agony. Her eyes ran over the rest of Lottie's small, shaking body: nothing, not a scratch, other than the angry jaws wrapped around her exposed ankle bone. The leaves and earth were absorbing the blood that flowed freely around her small foot.

Klara placed a hand on Lottie's leg and absorbed as much pain as she could, until Lottie traded the howling for soft sobs. The pain settled in Klara's own ankle, and she gritted her teeth until it dissipated. *If I don't get her out of here, the lycaons could hear her and come to her aid, and it would only prove Matthias's point that I'm not capable of raising Lottie.*

"That should buy us some time," Klara whispered to Henrietta, removing her hand from Lottie's thigh.

"How do we remove the trap?" Henrietta asked, panic muffling her words. They didn't have snatches in Hell, and this was her first time experiencing their disgusting nature. They were used to force creatures into making a deal for their soul in exchange for freedom, or by the fae in the Neutral Lands to stop creatures from trying to pass through to Kalos.

"There's no pretty way to do it," Klara told her. She gripped the jaws, slicing her fingers trying to get into them. Once she had a good grip on its razor-sharp metal teeth, she tore the snatch apart. Her biggest concern was the state of Lottie's ankle. Once the jaws were free, her foot might go with it.

"Don't look, Lottie," Henrietta warned, but Klara couldn't take her eyes off what remained of her foot. It was the job of a snatch to maim. Even in the dark, she could see the dislodged bone, but the muscles and tendons were desperately holding onto the small foot. *Still attached, but barely,* she thought in relief.

Henrietta caught Lottie's upper body as she fainted.

"Take her to the infirmary," Klara ordered. Henrietta disappeared back to the castle with Lottie safe in her arms.

Klara paused to examine the destroyed snatch; it was identical to the ones she had seen in the Neutral Lands. *The fae laid those for the fleeing creatures, but there's no way fae would dare to lay them here. A demon could have...* Klara eyed the empty trees and noticed they weren't too far from the market road. *This close to the castle, though? No demon would run the risk of me finding them.* She held the sharp half of one of the two jaws in her hands and closed her eyes, trying to pick up any trace of what had set such a trap. *Nothing. How is that possible? It could have been laid a long time ago, and yet it wasn't rusted or overly covered in filth. If there's one, there could be more...* She dropped the snatch's jaw and rose, knowing she didn't have time to check for them.

Instead, she placed her hand on the earth and summoned the demon who worked this path. Within seconds it appeared in a haze of smoke.

"See that?" she said, not bothering with pleasantries. The demon shifted towards the destroyed snatch.

"I would never, Your Majesty," its deep voice argued, and she rose from the mud, silencing the creature.

"I want to know if there are more. If there are, destroy them immediately and report how many you find back to the castle." The demon vanished without a word. "Stand down," Klara told her guard, who were still watching out for anyone approaching the pass.

"You should return to the castle, Your Majesty, in case this was an attempt to lure you out from the castle," one of them said. Their black eyes revealed their demonic nature, while the others' exposed claws told her they were lycaons. She was relieved to know they were working together with ease, both focused on a common goal—protect and serve.

"I won't hide in fear of my forest. Report to the next guards; I want eyes open until this matter is resolved," she told them, not a lick of fear in her voice.

"Yes, Your Majesty," they said in unison.

On her way up the pass, she was still taken aback by the statue of Abadan's form marking the passage way. She had considered destroying them, but they marked the past—monuments to what had been—and history was to be remembered so that mistakes would not be repeated. She examined her fingers. The cuts healed while she paced in front of the castle, contemplating all that had transpired in the last two days—that, and she didn't want to stand before Lottie shaken.

The witch, the fae, Matthias's words... Too much is happening at once for it to be a coincidence. Matthias could have set the snatch to trap Lottie, but he would have to know it would immediately put him at the top of the suspect list.

7

The smell of disinfectant crowded Klara's senses as she darted down the spiral metal staircase to the infirmary one level beneath the castle. Last year, in the filthy beanstalk kitchen where she had lost her heart, she had been reminded of her vulnerability. Since she now had a young ward to care for, she had decided to commission the warlocks—the healers of Malum—to build an infirmary within the castle.

Most of the time they got by on their own. Eve had left enough spells and potion books to cure many injuries and illnesses, but Klara was still learning how to brew specialised potions. One wrong ingredient and it would result in miserable side effects or death. Thank Lucifer for a functioning infirmary. *Much better than the few baskets of spider's web and other concoctions that were set aside for me when I was the three queens' ward.* Lottie had advanced healing, or she would be forever bandaged and bruised. A warlock only came when absolutely necessary, when Klara or Lottie's natural healing abilities weren't capable of doing the job or Lottie's shifting brewed a fever that could swell her brain and a special poultice was needed to soothe her.

Torches kept the infirmary brightly lit, and the walls were decorated with translucent amethyst and white stone for maximum healing and visibility. Klara let out a sigh of relief when she saw that Henrietta already had a spider's web weaving Lottie's ankle back together. The rest would be up to Lottie's lycaon blood.

"Should we call a warlock? She hasn't woken up! I fear the trap was laced with poison," Henrietta worried, releasing another spider from the jar. Lottie's own healing abilities would need as much help as they could get.

"Try not to panic. The shock has probably worn her out. I would have sensed any poison when I touched the trap," Klara told her. Her words did nothing to ease the worry from Henrietta's dark eyes. "We should keep this to ourselves. She will be healed and running around soon enough." Klara sighed, standing beside Lottie, who looked so small and fragile.

"Who would lay a trap so close?" Henrietta asked as she stroked Lottie's hair where it fell over the edge of the marble slab.

"It could be my mother playing a cruel joke. Snatches are usually kept to the Neutral Lands."

It was unlikely. *If my guard caught a creature or demon laying a snatch so close to the castle, they would be shredded in mere moments. Who would want to risk getting caught for such a minimal trap?* Her heart was racing again. She had to get a grip. *Maybe whoever set the trap—or traps—wants my attention,*

or is trying to distract me, which only leads me back to Matthias.
Klara rubbed her temples as she went around in circles.

"I have to be in Hell by dawn; there's no getting around my father's orders. Make sure she doesn't shift while she's healing, or the web will tear," she said.

Henrietta nodded in agreement. "And the traps?" she asked, her eyes never leaving Lottie.

"I've ordered a demon to search for other snatches. They'll report here on what they find."

Henrietta stared at her, clearly noting Klara's cold tone, but getting emotional would do nothing to help Lottie heal.

"Shouldn't you send some of the guards to check the Forest as well? A single demon isn't reliable." Henrietta had served in Hell for so long that there wasn't a shred of her damned soul that trusted the demons.

"The guards need to be here while I'm gone, and too much movement in the Forest will stir gossip. They'll keep to the pass and the forest line and report what they see, but that's all I can do for now," Klara said, and Henrietta didn't argue further. Klara placed her hand on her ward's forehead. Lottie's skin burned as she healed.

"Maybe you should wake her up before you go."

"She'll want to come, or be too freaked out to see me leave, and I can't have her there injured—it would raise too many questions." Klara bent to Lottie's ear. "Listen to Henrietta," she whispered.

"Don't let her out of your sight, no matter how many portraits she hops through," she added to Henrietta, anxiety weaving through her voice in spite of herself. She pulled herself from her ward's side.

"Good luck in Hell," Henrietta offered.

Klara climbed the steps to see a guard in a black uniform waiting with her axe, encased in its harness.

"Your Majesty, a demon reported to the guards at the mountain pass." The lycaon bowed.

Klara took her axe. "What did they say exactly?"

"It didn't make much sense. All they gave was a number."

"Which was?" she pressed, fastening her harness over her shirt.

"Zero."

No other snatches. How is that possible? The odds of Lottie getting caught in the single snatch are too small. She clenched her fists so tight that her knuckles threatened to crack. *Unless the rest are glamoured. Once I return from Hell, I can find out what is going on.*

"Make sure the Fall from Lottie's sky room is sealed. She is not to follow me to Hell. Let the others know so she can't hoodwink them," she ordered, running her hands through her hair as she tried to think of anything else Lottie might use to follow.

"It will be done," the lycaon said.

She was about to leave when she remembered her pact with Matthias. "Also, the scrolls on my desk in the library need to be delivered to the lycaon territory by the western caves." The lycaon's eyes flashed amber with nerves. "I suggest you take a demon with you," Klara added. She didn't want her allies to be harassed for their choice not to return to the caves.

"I will see it done before dawn breaks."

"I will be back by tomorrow's moon," Klara said.

Klara found herself staring at the flowers in the conservatory, which had blossomed under the night's sky.

She made her way to the twin fountain of Medusa that linked the castle to her father's lifeless garden in Hell—a present for surviving his trials, so she wouldn't have to experience the soul-shaking Fall to Hell each time she visited her future domain. Originally it had only been meant for her personal use, but she had removed the restriction spell and granted Frendall, Lottie and Lokey the privilege of using it.

She stepped into the calm waters. The water in her father's Medusa only sprayed a mirage to taunt the doomed who served in his soul-consuming garden, but Klara's contained real water, enchanted to maintain what remained of Eve's plants. Furthermore, she had no doomed she wanted to torment with thirst. Taking the knife on her belt, she reopened the thin cut on her fingertip caused by the snatch. One, two, three droplets of blood turned the waters black.

Before Klara could say 'Hell', the scorching heat hit her like a wave and her hands slammed into the ledge of her father's fountain as the force of the portal closing threw her forward. She raised her head to see the familiar dull grey flowers and a doomed only a few feet away, cutting every individual blade of dead grass with blunt scissors.

Good to be back.

*J*ust *the welcome I was looking for.* Klara smiled to herself, having caught Frendall studying his hands while sitting on the marble bench by Medusa's fountain.

"Perfect timing," he said, looking up at her.

She climbed from the fountain, taking his hand for support. What water had come with her evaporated from her trousers and boots in seconds. She was glad for her loose shirt, already feeling the beads of sweat on her back—but in Hell you didn't have to worry about sweating through your clothes, because the heat would evaporate it as soon as it appeared.

"I figured you would choose the fountain over the Fall," Frendall continued.

She wanted to forget the meeting with her father and lose herself in his arms. The familiar scent of his cologne made her feel at ease.

"Much softer landing," she confirmed, careful to keep some distance between them. They couldn't embrace as they did in Malum; there were too many eyes in Hell, waiting to sense weakness in their general and Klara, their future queen. Their relationship wasn't a secret amongst those who dwelled in Hell and its Maze, but discretion was the key to survival. So, they kept a reasonable distance as they ascended up the stone steps to Lucifer's manor, though Frendall's knuckles brushed hers every dozen steps or so. The hedgerows on either side of the wide steps shielded them from the Maze below.

"Lottie didn't come with you?" he asked, his dark eyebrows pulled together in concern. His raven hair was slicked back in his usual style, and his buttoned hip-length black jacket was without a crease or stain. *The image of perfection*, she thought. *Should I tell him about the snatch and the new agreement with Alpha Matthias?* She shook the thought away. *It's my problem, not his.*

"She was hurt running in the Forest. I might have rushed her meeting with the lycaons... it may have brought up some memories that are best left forgotten, but I have Henrietta watching over her," Klara said, and Frendall paled. "Don't worry, I wouldn't have left her if I thought she was suffering."

"Meeting the alpha was always going to bring up the past, but in time she will heal from those wounds," he assured her, and she wondered if he truly meant it. "I worry about you both. Anyone would be a damned fool to try and attack the castle, but I wish I could be there to support you. My demons, along with a lycaon, reported that Alpha Matthias left in a hurry, though they failed to grasp his mood." Frendall hesitated on the step, studying her reaction.

"Your place is in Hell. Wandering around the castle waiting for something to happen would only drive you crazy. If you gave up your position here, which we both know my father would never allow, you would quickly grow to resent us."

Frendall sighed softly and continued up the steps. "It's disturbing how well you know me."

"Did they mention anything else?" she asked, wondering if the demon had witnessed the snatch clamping itself onto Lottie.

"No, but then again they weren't looking for anything in particular; Bromwich was merely on their way back to Hell. They got a little sidetracked after the gathering. Told me they came upon some quarrel between a lesser demon and a crossroads," he explained.

Klara remembered the petulant demon from the listening. *If only I could pull souls from thin air to stop the quarrelling—but then the dealt souls would lose their value.*

"Bromwich didn't come to me?" she said, wondering why they would interfere in the quarrel.

"I had already communicated to Bromwich that you were on your way to Hell—no need to concern yourself with a petty squabble. If every scuffle was reported, you would never get a minute of peace," Frendall reasoned.

"And you are close with this demon?" Klara asked, a stem of jealousy growing. *There's so much I don't know about his time in Hell and who he spends it with… but if he trusts the demon then I should too.*

"We trained together when I was a commander. Loyal to a fault," he said simply. It was clear from his relaxed stature that the demon held his implicit trust.

"Why was Bromwich wandering through Malum? Loyal or not, I don't like the idea of a legion demon dealing with issues in the Forest without my say-so. Their

91

place is in Hell—I don't want the creatures to think I'm bringing in one of Hell's legions to handle matters."

"I let Bromwich indulge in the fungus den, let a bit of steam out of the pot. On the way back, they talked down a fight between demons. I'll tell them not to intervene in the future."

"I'm obsessing, but peace is hanging on such a fine line… I can't risk it."

"And one of my demons wouldn't do anything to jeopardise that," Frendall said, no hint of concern in his deep voice.

"Let's not think any more of it. Who am I to get in the way of a demon and some fungus?" she said, her thighs aching from the climb. She missed the days when she could have run up the steps with ease. Her new heart had held up well over the year since her father had replaced the one the ghouls had ripped from her chest, but she had noticed some pesky side effects. The more magic she used, the quicker she felt pain and weakness. Rest was quick to restore her strength, but it was weakness she didn't need anyone to witness.

"Are you going to tell me why the lycaons left so swiftly?" Frendall pressed, looking at her flushed face. It wasn't his concern, but Lottie would tell him as soon as she saw him.

"The alpha wants Lottie to consume a heart in order to take her place in the pack," she admitted as they reached the top.

Frendall stopped on the last step. "I had an inkling that Matthias was going to challenge her. Anyone can smell the ambition on him," he mused, closing his eyes for a second.

"Lottie refused outright, and safe to say I needed to appease him."

"What else could he want?" Frendall asked, his jaw clenching.

"Land, for now, and I've sent a treaty for further west of the territory into the Forest. The lycaons will have their work cut out for them, but we'll make a nice profit if they sell the timber to the elves for the ships. He'll waste time and energy, and I'll gain the tax from both parties."

"Why give him any land at all?" he asked.

"I could always take his head, mount it on a spike— what do you think?" she joked, but his eyes seemed to light up with the idea. *What happened to my peace-loving commander?* Klara raised her eyes to the blood-red sky and answered his question minus the sarcasm. "Because Lottie needs to survive long enough to challenge him. I don't want to have to lock her up in the castle as the queens did to me. If I show favour to the lycaons for a while, then he can't preach to the others that they suffer under my rule. I don't want him stirring up an uprising."

"Protecting and teaching Lottie is not locking her away, and she has the hounds to help her learn social skills when she shifts. You can hardly compare what the queens did to you to your current situation," Frendall countered, folding his arms across his broad chest.

"Yes, it is. A cage is a cage no matter how well it's decorated," Klara snapped, careful not to raise her voice in front of her father's manor in the centre of Hell. *He is in no position to comment on my decisions. He might be my companion, but he's still of a lesser rank.* She hated thinking about rank and position, but she questioned herself enough for the both of them. She didn't need to hear it out loud. Turning her back on him, she strode to the skull-encrusted door of the manor.

"I shouldn't question your judgement. Matthias is yours to handle alone," Frendall acknowledged.

Klara felt a dull pinch when the pitchfork shield on the doors tasted her blood. "I appreciate your advice, but I'm doing the best I can," she hissed as the thick needle withdrew from her palm and slid back into the shield.

The door cranked and clunked, her blood granting them access. They were both surprised by a doomed waiting for them on the other side, their face shielded by a white cloth.

"Your Majesty, welcome home."

Klara breathed in the familiar scent of her father's manor: rich cinnamon and varnished wood.

"Thank you," she said, motioning for the doomed to rise. They held out their arms for jackets and weapons.

Frendall removed his jacket, leaving him in a simple white shirt and exposing the sword belted at his side. The pillars with their shining faces stared at them while they stood under the shining grand chandelier.

Klara took her axe from her back and handed it to the gloved doomed, and Frendall removed his sword. Usually, she would have felt exposed without weapons, but there hadn't been an attempt on her life since she had taken her place in Malum. However, the quiet could also suggest that her enemies were merely plotting, waiting for the perfect moment...

Klara had made an effort to visit Hell more frequently over the past year to ease the tension with her father. It helped that the King of Hell also enjoyed spoiling Lottie, something he had never done with his own child. They were cordial, and Klara trusted him to some extent, but she knew they both had their doubts about each other.

"Is my sister home?" she asked.

"I'm afraid she is busy with her duties," the doomed

replied, not meeting her eye. *They clearly fear Mila more than me.*

Klara asked after her half-sister every time she visited, and no matter the time of day, she received the same answer. Mila refused to meet her after Abadan had left her to fend for herself and suffered a humiliating defeat. She had lost both her standing in Hell and her mother, Eve, in mere hours; it would have been a hard pill to swallow.

"Tell her I asked for her," Klara said.

"As always," the doomed said meekly.

Klara tried to get around them, but the doomed blocked the path to her father's throne room.

"Yes?" she asked, and the doomed began to shake.

"There is no need to tremble. Deliver your message," Frendall said, his voice tight with impatience.

"The king asked me to inform you both that the fae queen has delayed the meeting until tomorrow morning." Their voice was barely audible, but Klara had heard the message loud and clear. *Bringing me here only to keep us waiting—remind me to thank you for that, Mother.*

"Really?" she demanded. The doomed stood slumped, their head bowed. "I have never known the fae queen to reschedule. Have you, Frendall?" Klara stepped closer. *More likely he wanted me here early, because God forbid I be late and he end up alone with Aemella.*

"Please, Your Majesty, I am only the messenger."

"Was there anything else expected of you?"

"I am to escort you to your room." The doomed tried to steer them towards the grand stairs.

I am no child to be escorted anywhere. "I didn't come all this way to stay in my chambers." Klara brushed the doomed aside, and Frendall followed close at her back.

The portraits lining the dark navy walls whispered

as she passed until they reached the doors to her father's throne room. Two doomed blocked her from taking the doorknob when they didn't automatically open them for her.

"I'm sorry, Your Majesty, but the king is not to be disturbed," one of the doomed said, not meeting her eye.

"Move aside," Frendall ordered, and the doomed obeyed.

"So much secrecy. What could he possibly be doing?" Klara asked, and threw open the doors.

"Father!" she shouted. "Your child is here—" She stopped short. A demon was on their knees in front of her father, and Klara gagged at the look of ecstasy on the king's face.

"Sweet Judas," she exclaimed, covering her eyes. "What the hell are you doing?" She didn't actually want to know the answer, and wished she had listened to the doomed when they'd told her the king wasn't to be disturbed. She had never been more grateful for the dim lighting.

"I was not to be disturbed," the king roared, and the demon disappeared from the room as the king readjusted himself.

"Really? I was expected." Klara kept her eyes on the glass ceiling and the blood-red sky above it.

"A king has needs, just like every other creature," Lucifer scolded, while Klara resisted the urge to gag again. "I told the doomed no one was to disturb me!"

The doomed quickly closed the doors to the room, afraid of being discovered. Frendall cleared his throat and nodded to Klara, telling her the king was decent once again.

"At least it wasn't Queen Aemella. I would never have recovered," Klara muttered.

Lucifer descended from the steps to his throne. His black suit, embroidered with gold floral motifs, was undisturbed.

"Unfortunately, Aemella prefers the fairer sex this millennium." The King of Hell sounded disappointed.

"I think I should visit the torturers to get that image stripped from my mind," she whispered to Frendall, who suppressed a smile.

"I'm sure your sister would take great pleasure in doing the honours," Lucifer said, his red irises flashing in warning for her to show some respect, and Klara chewed her tongue.

"If Mother wanted to reschedule, you could have sent a messenger before I fell. I can't just leave the Forest and Lottie," she pressed, trying to conceal her annoyance. They moved to the impressive fireplace, where a long table was positioned. Lucifer picked up the crystal whisky decanter as if to offer them a drink, but Klara shook her head in refusal.

"If I had informed you of the change of plans, then how was I to get you to come to tonight's soirée? The court of Hell and my council are gathering to celebrate the anniversary of Abadan's fall—may that traitor rot, wherever she is," Lucifer said, tossing a decanter of whisky into the roaring fireplace at her name.

The flames soared with the toxic levels of alcohol and poured more heat into the insufferable room. Klara wasn't sure what had happened to Abadan once the fae queen had turned her into a pile of blackened roses. However, she wasn't sure that the Demon Queen would be that easy to get rid of.

She rolled her neck at the thought of being in the court's presence. She hated seeing the faces of those who had stood on Abadan's side in the Neutral Lands, only to bow and run to Lucifer when Abadan fell.

"When will your court be joining us?" she asked.

Lucifer shrugged. He stared at the blood-red sky, and a dark cloud submerged them further into darkness. The chandeliers were quick to brighten, making up for the loss of light.

"We still have a few hours to catch up," Lucifer said.

"I'm sorry, Father, but I have to catch up on some rest. The journey has exhausted me, and I'm in no way prepared to entertain your guests. I thought I was here for a meeting, not a party."

"How can one so young be tired? Did you not come by the fountain? Don't tell me you lost another heart," Lucifer said, raising a dark eyebrow.

"Nothing of the sort—and yes, I came by the fountain, but I have been busy as of late. Dealing with the new alpha, who is determined to have Lottie return to the pack, and the many other nuisances that come with ruling Malum."

Lucifer sat on the steps to his throne, pulling up his trouser legs.

"Ah yes, Matthias. I have heard whispers about him since his youth. Always snapping at the heels of his elders, roaming from one pack to the next. Do you not know him, Frendall?"

Klara watched Frendall stand taller. "I have seen him in passing, but I can't say that I know him."

"Didn't you help with the rebuilding?" Klara asked.

"Yes, but the alpha was dealing with the witches at the time. They are still unsettled since Eve..." Frendall hadn't even finished the thought when Lucifer tossed the second decanter at his feet. Klara hadn't expected him to mourn for Eve; he had often forgotten and discarded her when she was alive, but with Lilith gone, it had occurred to him that Eve wasn't around to console him. *It's only when we need them most that we appreciate those closest to us.*

"I'm sure you will meet him soon enough," Lucifer said. Klara could feel her father plotting. "If Lottie needs a place to stay while you smooth things over, she can come here for a time," he offered.

I would rather chew glass for a decade than hand Lottie over to him. "That won't be necessary. He has been dealt with," she informed him.

"Excellent. That's what I like to hear."

He never wants to hear about a problem, only that it's been solved. Explains why he has so many commanders and generals.

"Will Aemella be joining us for the soirée?" Klara asked, her hands clasped together in front of her.

"No; she sent word last night. As you were on your way here, I thought, why waste an opportunity to mingle? It's not as though you can leave now—Aemella should make her appearance in the morning."

I hadn't left yet. There was plenty of time to cancel. She thought of Lottie lying injured—and her father had taken her from her ward's side to *mingle*.

"She didn't give any further explanation?" *It's not like her to rearrange once a plan is in motion, but considering that I threw her fae out of my castle, she might be embarrassed and looking for some excuse.*

"Yes, Aemella explained all the inner workings of her land and then we shared a lovely cup of tea," snapped Lucifer.

Doesn't hurt to ask. Then she heard the distant screams echoing up from the tunnels beneath them. Actually, in Hell it could hurt a Hell of a lot. "Sorry I asked," she quipped.

"Apology accepted." Lucifer failed to understand

her sarcasm. "I'll send a doomed to your room when our guests arrive," he said.

Klara headed for the door with Frendall at her back.

"Before you go, how is my dear Henrietta?" Lucifer asked.

Klara froze. To free Henrietta from her father's manor, she had handed over a third of what had remained in Abadan's vault, and she still couldn't be sure whether her father would take back one of his most trusted.

"Settling in nicely—she was trained exceptionally well. Malum and Hell are very different, but she is Lottie's closest companion, and she keeps the other doomed in order. I don't think I could run the place without her," she said, in hopes the praise would be enough to soothe his ego.

"So hard to part with such excellent staff... the manor hasn't been the same without her buzzing around," he mused.

"I'm sure you have managed well enough without her."

Lucifer's eyes flashed black. "Don't overstep, daughter. She is still a doomed."

"And that's exactly why Klara needs her. Who better to serve her than one so loyal to you?" Frendall interjected, trying to ease the tension.

Klara bowed her head in apology. Lucifer didn't like being challenged when it came to his playthings. Her freeing Henrietta had only made her that much more of a treasure.

"I'm tired of this conversation. I expect you both to be dressed and prompt for our guests," Lucifer said firmly.

"Will Mila be joining us?" Klara asked as she watched her father twisting the immortal ring on his finger—the ring that would be placed on the hand of his chosen heir when it was their time to ascend to the throne. The day he handed it over would be the day it was time for her to rule Hell, and even the sight of it made her nervous.

Tonight will not be that night, she thought and hoped, looking at the ring.

"I'm afraid she has too much work to attend to. So many to torture, so little time." Lucifer winked, giving her the small bright smile they shared.

"I see. Tell Mila I was asking for her." *I don't have a burning desire to see my sister, but if she did attend, I would know if her plotting and scheming towards me had stopped. As long as Mila remains hidden in the shadows of the tunnels, I can never be sure.*

"I will. She will be sad to have missed you once again." Klara could hear the genuine concern in her father's voice. From the whispers of the doomed, Lucifer had quickly forgiven his daughter for her part in the uprising. Mila had lost her mother, after all. Klara hadn't told him how Mila had treated Eve in the dungeon, and she had no intention of adding fuel to that Hellfire.

Passing through the foyer, Klara noticed the almost smiles in the marble faces that made up the pillars of the manor. There was a sense of ease in the place that made her blood chill. *He likes peace on his own doorstep, but that doesn't mean he'll leave the humans alone.*

"He seems in a better mood," she said to Frendall once they reached the second floor.

"There is peace, so I don't expect him to stay much longer; the calm gives him an excuse to make trouble in the human world," Frendall warned, confirming her thoughts. "He has Mila torturing round the clock in hope of uncovering some plot."

The portraits in their gold oval frames bowed to her as they passed. She was a queen now, and they respected that—although she was fully aware that the souls contained within them would still report anything they overheard to the king in an instant.

"I doubt he'll be gone long. I can feel something coming," she said as they cleared the last portrait and the gold brackets that held candles in the hallway dimmed.

"Even if that's true, let's enjoy the peace while it lasts," Frendall said, kissing the side of her head. His arm reached around her to twist the doorknob, and Klara smiled as he closed the door behind them.

Alone in her room, there was no need for them to keep their distance. Klara was relieved to see that her room remained unchanged; it was cast in red from the skylight until Frendall began lighting some candles. She walked over to the carousel on her dresser and ran her thumb over the ruby on the base of the spinning antique. Soft music filled the room as it began to chime, and she smiled as she felt Frendall's hard chest at her back, his arms wrapping around her middle, hands against her stomach. A sigh escaped her as she leant against him, her hands on his forearms, muscular from hours of training.

"I should go check in on Captain Darley before the court arrives," he said, breaking the moment, and her eyes sprang open. Captain Darley oversaw her father's manor guard, and right now he was the last person she wanted to be thinking about. Disappointment flooded her as Frendall moved away.

"I'm sure he can handle welcoming a few guests," she said, kicking off her shoes in the middle of the room.

He leant against the closed door, watching eagerly as she unclasped the harness crossed over her chest and began unbuttoning her shirt.

"Are you trying to get me tortured?" he asked, the corner of his mouth turned up in a devilish smile.

"Only if I'm the one who gets to do the torturing," she countered, removing her shirt entirely.

"You sure know how to tempt a general," Frendall said, and crossed the room without any hesitation.

Her breath caught as he swept her up in his arms and tossed her onto the bed. She laughed as she sank into the soft mattress.

"Shh! You want the doomed or the portraits to hear us?" Frendall whispered as he kissed her hungrily. She returned the kiss with just as much enthusiasm until his lips travelled from hers to her neck and shoulders. She gasped as his tongue ran the length of her collarbone and pulled his jacket from his shoulders, suddenly aware of how overdressed he was.

"We should put this on hold—we have to get ready," she tried to reason, knowing that once they started, she wouldn't want to leave this bed.

He laughed between kisses and slipped the thin straps of the lace that covered her chest from her shoulders, kissing where it had been. Klara bit her lip to stop herself from making noise.

"We have some time before the guests arrive. Do you really want me to stop?" he asked, looking down at her, his thighs on either side of hers and pinning her to the bed.

"No," she confessed.

He pulled his shirt over his head and she marvelled at the sight of his sculpted body, her hands trailing over his toned chest.

"How the roles have reversed. What happened to the ever-early commander who threatened to dress me against my will?" she said playfully.

"He got promoted." He winked and shifted down the bed, pulling her legs around his waist. "Sweet Judas, how I missed this," he breathed, tossing the rest of her clothes to the stone floor.

Klara pressed closer, needing to feel his skin against hers and giving herself over to the feel of his hands on her body. They wouldn't have much time together before her throne and his duties separated them again for God knew how long.

9

The heat in the room startled Klara; she had forgotten where she was. She lay back on the pillows, lighting the candles beside the bed, as some around the room had gone out. She settled closer to Frendall.

Would he really want to stay in the castle with me? He has his duties here, but he would never be far with the fountain, and I wouldn't have to be so alone.

You really are weak, you know that? Think he can protect you from the big bad forest? her inner voice scolded her.

It's not weak to have someone by your side, she told herself.

No, but it's weak to need them there.

Shut up! She didn't want to let her inner demons ruin the moment.

The ache in her chest dulled as Frendall smiled in his sleep; it was a rare sight. Usually he slept fitfully, his nights full of terror, but now he lay calm, breathing softly. Klara's fingers gently traced the pitchfork that scarred his back as he slept on his front—the one her father had given him. Frendall had tried to escape to the Forest as a child when she had been sent to live with the Three Queens of Malum.

"Isn't this precious?" Lucifer whispered, suddenly standing at the end of the bed.

Klara yanked the sheets higher on her chest and covered more of Frendall's exposed skin. He continued to lie undisturbed.

"Get out," she hissed, trying to keep her voice low.

"Relax; I saw nothing of importance," he said, pacing back and forth at the end of the bed.

"Get out!" she said again, louder. She didn't want her memory of this moment being tainted by the king's intrusion.

"What? You can barge in on *my* private time, but you demand privacy?" Lucifer said.

Klara picked up a large candlestick from her bedside table.

"Fine, I'm going." The king headed towards the door. "I came to tell you the court has arrived. I suggest you both hurry and get dressed. You know how I don't like to be kept waiting."

"You mean you don't like leaving your court alone to gossip," Klara said.

He laughed, startling her. "How well you know me. I do love it when you visit; no one else dares to talk to me as you do." Lucifer picked up their discarded clothes and tossed them over the bed, startling Frendall from his dead sleep.

"It's okay," Klara said as Frendall jumped, ready for a fight, only to see the King of Hell and change tack.

Instead of reaching for a weapon, he covered himself with the blanket.

"I'm sorry, Your Majesty," he said, scrambling with his clothes.

Lucifer waved his hand. "I'd rather you share my daughter's bed than some lesser demon or creature attempting to elevate their status."

"I'll take whomever I like to my bed. That is none of your business," Klara snapped, ignoring the hurt in Frendall's eyes.

"Ah, well, I've realised I don't give a shit whom you take to bed, so long as they keep their eyes off my throne." Lucifer's eyes narrowed in on Frendall, who paled. He made to speak, but Lucifer snapped his fingers and disappeared from the room.

Klara let out a breath as Frendall sat on the edge of the bed. "Talk about killing the mood."

Frendall kept his back to her. *What's his problem? It's not like the king is going to put his general's head on a spike—not tonight, anyway.* She placed her legs on either side of him and kissed his back, only for him to stand abruptly.

"You can take whomever you want to your bed?" he asked coldly, the muscles in his back rippling as he tensed.

She winced as he repeated her words. *One minute I want him in the castle with me and the next I'm pushing him away. What is wrong with me?* The candles brightened the room as she pressed her hand to the one on her bedside.

"Do you want him thinking we're something serious? We would be bound by the next full moon," she reasoned. Her father loved any reason for a party.

"Would being bound to me be so awful?"

She found it impressive that he could sound so pissed off and hurt at the same time.

"We've barely lived. We have centuries, millennia ahead of us—provided one of us doesn't lose their head. Can you honestly tell me that you want me and only me?" she asked, trying to reach for him, but he shrugged from her embrace.

"If Lokey can be bound then I think I can," Frendall said, putting on his shirt.

"Lokey has been around forever, and I'm sure he will tell you that he had many great loves until he found Glaudine."

"So you need centuries to be sure you want me?"

Klara thought of her father's many lovers since Creation. She was terrified of betraying Frendall. *I can't lose you*, she thought, unable to voice how she really felt. She was still plagued by the memory of seeing his lifeless body on the field. *If we were bound, I would feel everything he felt, our souls fated to find each other for eternity.*

"I already gifted you part of my soul. Is that not commitment enough?"

"Life-and-death situations don't count. You did that because you thought you were going to die, not because of your love for me."

Love. It was the first time they had ever let that word fall between them. *What do we know of love?* she thought, supporting herself on the pillows. She loved Lottie as a mother would love a child, but to love another person as an equal… she didn't know.

"It's not about love. If I'm bound, it speaks to my rule: will you be king? Will the creatures support you at my side? Will the fae queen? The realm is easily thrown off balance. I can't make a decision like this on a whim."

The hurt she felt emanating from him made her regret that last word.

"Understood," he said simply. "I suggest you get

ready, Your Majesty." Frendall pulled his tailored suit jacket from the wardrobe. He had left some clothes in her wardrobe upon her last visit, since he spent most of his nights in her room.

"Don't leave like this. You know how important it is that I appear strong on my own before I'm bound to anyone," Klara said.

"I will do as you command." Frendall stopped in his tracks, which only infuriated her.

"Can you please stop being a general for one second? I'm trying to protect you," Klara exclaimed, dropping the sheet, but his eyes failed to find hers.

"But isn't that what I am—someone who keeps you warm until you find someone more suitable? Protect me? I think you're only protecting yourself."

His words cut through her, and she folded her legs beneath her and knelt up on the edge of the bed so they were more level with each other. "That's not what I meant. Of course I'm protecting myself. It's a political statement—one that needs to happen at the right time."

"With the right person," he finished, his eyes never leaving hers.

Klara leapt off the edge of the bed, bringing the sheet with her. She didn't have the energy or time to argue.

"I barely get to see you. I don't want to fight," she said, pulling on a deep grey, almost-silver dress that fell above her knee and lacing a dark grey corset over her waist.

"Understood," Frendall said, and Klara gritted her teeth.

"We will discuss this after the court has left," she clarified as she tied the straps from her black stilettos around her ankles.

"As you command."

"I swear to Lucifer, if you pull that *Your Majesty* crap again—" Klara shouted.

Frendall blocked her path to the door. She folded her arms across her chest as he took something else from the wardrobe.

"If I may, Your Majesty," he said, but there was a hint of mischief in his amber eyes ringed with black.

"What?" she snapped, unable to see what was clasped in his hand.

Frendall stepped dangerously close and brushed her raven hair behind her shoulder.

"What are you doing?" she asked with a frown.

He dropped to one knee. Slowly, his hand travelled from her ankle to her knee, then up under her dress. Her breath caught when he stopped mid-thigh, and he chuckled as his eyes met hers.

She watched him secure a small leather sheaf to her thigh and slid a small blade into it.

"Safety first. I would hate for anything to happen to my queen," he said.

He dropped his hand and stood tall, his nose inches from hers. She hated the conflicting emotions, the desire he brought out in her.

Opening the bedroom door, he was the first to break the spell.

10

"**G**ood evening, Captain," Klara said.

Captain Darley had his hand raised to knock on her bedroom door.

"I didn't mean to interrupt," he said, his yellow eyes not knowing where to look. His hair was slicked back to match his general's. "I was to escort you to your guests—I wasn't aware you had company." Captain Darley blushed, embarrassed to interrupt the Heir to Hell with his superior, and bowed. "General."

Frendall cleared his throat and changed the subject as Klara closed the door behind them. "All weapons have been stripped from the guests?"

"Y-yes, sir. All clear," Darley stammered. "It's a pleasure to have you back home." Klara noticed that his teeth were no longer sharpened to match her half-sister's. Clearly, his loyalties had changed since their failed coup.

"Always good to be amongst friends," Klara replied,

and his eyes went wide at being referred to as her friend.

"Since I'm not required, I should make sure everyone is prepared for your arrival." Darley quickly disappeared through the right wing of the manor.

Once he was clear of the hallway, they could speak freely.

"Come to my room once this night is over. I want to finish our conversation," Klara said.

Frendall finished buttoning his jacket. "I don't think I'll be able to get away from the king; he'll want me by his side until the last of the guests have left," he said, not meeting her eye.

Now who's trying to push away whom?

"I don't want to leave without—"

Klara was cut off by a round of applause as they reached the top of the staircase. She looked from Frendall to the manor foyer to see the court gathered in all their finery. With their piercing black and yellow gazes aimed at her, she swallowed, thankful for the blade at her thigh. They were dressed in finery and jewels which spoke to their standing in Hell.

At least in Malum the creatures had grown to accept her, but in Hell, she never knew where she stood. Demons were forever plotting for the throne. In the Forest there was a combination of good and evil in every creature, but in Hell, there was nothing but greed and lust; there was no compromise, only outright defeat. To rule over Hell and the Maze, you needed a twisted heart— one that could kill without hesitation and take instead of give. Klara wasn't sure if she could do it.

Frendall offered his arm and she took it, realising she was still frozen on the top step on the stairs. The applause continued until they reached the last step.

"To your victory," the higher demons cheered, and

some dared to kiss Klara's cheek. With so many so close, she couldn't reveal any hidden secrets as they came at her in a blur.

She caught a glimpse of purple hair in her mind's eye and stilled in the crowd, only for a higher demon to congratulate her on the increase in souls coming from the realms of Malum and Kalos. *The increase in souls?* Before she could ask, she was distracted by someone lurking by the ivy-lined windows.

Goodnight, sister, echoed in her mind.

Klara went after Mila's shadow, but she was gone by the time Klara made it through the demons. Silence surrounded her, and she realised she was being rude to her guests—a dangerous thing when one was surrounded by higher demons and Hell's finest.

"It's a pleasure to have you all here tonight, and I'm honoured that you have welcomed me back with open arms. Let's not keep my father waiting, shall we?" she said, and the demons murmured in agreement.

How long is Mila going to hide from me? Klara asked herself as she led the court through to the throne room. Frendall's arm slipped from hers as he talked with a demon beside him. She had to suppress her fears that they would want Frendall to rule instead of her. *They adore him; you can see it.* She tried to ignore the thought as the portraits greeted her and the demons.

The doomed opened the doors to reveal the king on his throne. He was dressed in a dark grey suit, and he let his black eyes shine.

"Welcome, welcome!" Lucifer cried out to his guests as they gathered in the middle of the room to get a good view of him on the steps. "It's been many moons since this court has been brought together. Before we start the celebrations, I want to clear the air."

Fear snaked down the back of Klara's neck. Clearing the air could lead to the removal of heads, and his cheery mood was not reassuring. However, she noticed no guards lingering in the corners of the great room. It was bare of furniture, and a line of doomed with trays waited in front of the scorching fires with drinks at the ready.

"High Queen Abadan took advantage of many of you, and I know some of you still have concerns about the future of Hell. But I assure you that I intend for the peace amongst the realms to last many decades, so please bring your issues to my Council. No issue is off-limits. I wish to know every happening in Hell and the human world—as I'm sure my daughter, Klara, would appreciate being informed about any happening in Malum." He took a glass of whisky from a doomed at the bottom of the steps.

"Never forget that you will be rewarded for your loyalty," he continued, and there was a round of applause as Lucifer motioned for the doomed to serve the drinks to the crowd. "But though I reward loyalty, I also urge you to remember what happens to those who rise against myself or my child." His words dripped with threat, and Klara could almost taste his bloodlust. The higher demons went silent as his dark expression reached them, but it was soon replaced with a cheery smile as he raised his glass. The demons followed suit, and together they drank.

Klara hated the court, and she feared she always would. *Could I rule something I despise so much?* It was a court of whispers, not a court of allies.

This was the most demons she had ever seen in the

manor at one time. It was a test to see who spoke to whom and who currently wasn't speaking. Lucifer was smart to gather those most important and those who felt excluded from his Council. Before Abadan's fall, the gatherings had been much more intimate; that they had bred resentment, she had gathered from the number of higher demons who had stood with Abadan.

Klara would rather have seen him take the heads of those who had tried to kill her on the battlefield than wine and dine them. The lesser demons had paid for their crimes against the Daughter of Lucifer, but the higher demons were much too important to kill. She found herself standing in a small circle of demons she didn't recognise and tried to keep up with their conversation about how the decline in the Catholic Church meant possession was much too easy to get away with in the human world, but her mind was elsewhere. On her argument with Frendall, Lottie's recovery, the witch's warning. She longed for the night to end and for the meeting with her mother to be done with so that she could get back to Malum.

"Your Majesty, how well you look!"

"Malum's air must be doing you well."

"How is that sweet pet of yours? I hope you remember to beat the lycaon often—they won't learn without a rough hand."

Klara nodded at the comments as she worked her way through the crowd with a glass of glimmering venom clutched tightly in her hand.

"You must visit the human world in the spring; everything is being birthed and blooming. There is so much hope to destroy." A crossroads demon squealed at the thought of tormenting the humans. *How did a crossroads make it into the inner circle?*

"I will have to visit when I have the time. Unfortunately, I'm kept busy in Malum," she replied, knowing that the only way she would have time to visit the human world was when she had passed to the other side.

"You work too hard in that forest." The voice came from a top hat bobbing through the air, pushing demons aside to get to Klara.

"Some of us have to work." She smiled as Lokey appeared before her, his long and lean body wrapped in his signature waistcoat and pocket watch. His snake-like tongue slithered between his lips as the half-demon, half-high-warlock smiled back. *He has a handsome face, but that tongue!* Lokey took her hand and kissed it. He had nothing to fear in her revealing touch, although she noticed that the 'trustworthy' court always kept a reasonable distance when addressing her personally.

"How's the baby?" Klara asked him quietly, in the private corner of the busy room. No one outside their inner circle and the warlocks knew of Lokey's child. Son of a high warlock, Lucifer's trusted advisor, the child would be an easy target.

"Growing quickly. Poor thing almost set the den on fire, but at least I know he can protect himself," Lokey said proudly, though Klara noted the dark circles under his eyes.

"I'm sure the little guy will be terrorising the other young warlocks in no time," she said, offering him a drink.

Lokey frowned. "I'm afraid the warlocks won't let him study with the other children."

"Why not?"

"You know how the warlocks can be about mixing blood. They feel the leprechaun magic running through his veins will make him unpredictable." He sighed. It wasn't like Lokey to let anyone disrespect him, but with a new family he couldn't exactly make waves.

"I can take it up with them. I won't have any creatures discriminated against."

"I don't think you will have much luck. If they won't listen to me, I doubt they will appreciate your interference."

He had a point. The warlocks had backed her rule from the outset; offending them would do her no favours, especially with the witch's current predicament.

"He can study with Lottie when he comes of age. I'm sure I can find a tutor who can assist him. Your child always has a place in my home." *I'll figure out a way to convince them; there must be something the warlocks want.* She kept the thought to herself.

"Glaudine will be happy to hear you say that. She's terrified of the day she has to explain it all to him," he said, visibly softening at the mention of his wife.

"We have many moons before that day comes, and you never know what might happen."

"Spoken like an optimist. Has the crown made you soft?" He laughed.

"I can still shed blood when I have to."

"Speaking of..." Lokey drawled, and Klara heard gasps throughout the crowd as Matthias walked in with Ceylon at his side.

Well, aren't you brave? Klara downed the rest of her venom. She was preparing to greet the lycaon when she followed Matthias's eyes to Frendall.

"Brother." Matthias gripped Frendall's shoulder, and Klara wasn't sure if it was the embrace that made her stomach knot or the glass of venom. *Brother? He's just greeting a fellow lycaon, right?* There was surely no way they could be related by blood. Either way, she found herself beside them. Gone were their simple clothes, replaced with fine fabrics. Ceylon looked almost pretty in her fitted suit with her pinned-back curls highlighting her strong features, though her expression remained sour.

The room watched the new arrivals closely. The demons didn't look fondly on lycaons, and Klara couldn't help but wonder why the hell Matthias was here in the first place.

"How good it is to see you again so soon," he said, clapping Klara on the back. Her new glass of venom sloshed onto the marble floor.

"I'm delighted to see that you received my father's invitation." Klara didn't want him to know she was surprised by his arrival; she needed him to think she harboured no ill will for the sake of the Forest.

"The lycaons serve in your very castle. It's only right that we visit when an invitation is offered." His arrogance forced her to smile.

"I'm sure it's nice to have a change of scenery; every day in the caves might prove tiresome after so much work," Klara offered, and Matthias's sudden laughter garnered the attention of the other guests.

"Unlike some, I have no desire to leave Malum or its people, no matter how tiresome," he replied pointedly.

She clenched her fist, her long nails digging deep into her skin as she tried to suppress her temper. "How grateful the lycaons must be to have such a dedicated leader."

Leave my people? She desperately wanted to ask him how he had managed to survive the flames—because the truth was that any who had escaped Abadan's fires without a single scar, as he had, had been the first to run and hide, leaving others to burn. The burns that painted

Ceylon's chest and the side of her neck told Klara that she, at least, had remained behind to help her people.

Frendall handed Klara another glass of venom. She needed something to keep her hands busy, or she would be tempted to smash the empty crystal glass over the alpha's head.

"Nice to see you again, Ceylon." She addressed the beta of the lycaon pack, noticing how she surveyed the room.

Ceylon nodded but offered no feigned civility. Klara clenched her jaw at the public slight. She sensed no danger in the beta, only distrust, but she wasn't sure whether it was meant for her or the room in general.

"I would have met you at the gate had I known you were coming," Frendall interjected, to Klara's gratitude.

"No need for my little brother to escort us. We found our way just fine," Matthias said.

Klara felt the heat of the room increase as the words sank in.

"You must visit us more," Matthias went on to Frendall.

"I'm afraid I have been busy overseeing the Maze. Humans seem determined to die in vast quantities."

Klara had lost all ability to speak. *'Little brother'? What happened to 'we have never met before'? He judges me for not wanting to commit, and yet here he is, lying about having a sibling! A sibling who is a threat to both myself and Lottie!* She couldn't wait to get him alone. Her eyes bored into the side of Frendall's head as he replied.

"The king despises tardiness—I'm glad it escaped his notice."

"The scrolls the queen sent over had to be signed before we arrived."

Matthias opposed the lycaons serving in her guard,

and yet here he was using it to his advantage. Lucifer had clearly invited him thinking he was Klara's ally.

"I'm sure you didn't want to waste a moment before claiming your new land." Klara struggled to hide her distaste for him.

Matthias tapped his head with a smug grin.

"What did I fail to notice?" Lucifer asked, appearing by Klara's side. Clearly he had been listening in.

"Pardon our late arrival, Your Majesty. We had some urgent matters to see to; as you know, time works differently between our two lands," Matthias smarmed. Klara suppressed a sneer.

"Think nothing of it. We are grateful to have you with us. The fae queen is eager to meet the alpha that has pieced back together the pack the late high queen burnt to the ground." Lucifer's comment garnered a swig of venom from Ceylon.

He can't be serious. My own mother wanted him here for our talks? Klara asked, "You are joining us for tomorrow's meeting?"

"Wasn't it your idea to solidify the relationship between Malum's creatures and Kalos?" Lucifer asked, as though he had aided their relationship. Instead, he had allowed her enemy to be seen and heard.

"Absolutely. I only want what is best for my subjects," she replied, taking a long drink.

Matthias's eyebrows rose on the word 'subjects'. *Yes, you are my subject, and I will break you in two if you force my hand.* The glare in Matthias's eyes told her he was thinking a similar thought.

"Let's have a toast, shall we?" Klara took two glasses from a passing doomed's tray. Ceylon downed the venom before the toast was even raised.

"To new friends," Klara proclaimed. Lucifer was eating up the civility.

"To the king and queen. May your reigns be eternal," Matthias finished. Lucifer cheered, and the room followed suit. They followed Lucifer in smashing their glasses on the black marble tiles once the venom was downed.

Klara ignored the next glass of venom offered; she could already feel its tingling effect softening her restraint. *One more and I might attack Matthias for my own satisfaction.*

"I hope I'm not late to the party."

The delicate voice echoed throughout the room, and everyone went silent. Before anyone had a chance to question its origin, a high-pitched shrill echoed, and the ivy-lined windows smashed inward, coating them all in shards of glass. Many of the court covered their ears as the keening pulsed through them and faded out to silence.

"For the love of Judas!" Lucifer shouted as the crowd brushed glass from their clothes. A spiral of shimmering white formed in front of the grand fireplace, blocking out the flames, and the guests quickly backed away.

"I ask for a delay, and here you are having a party. I'm hurt not to have received an invitation."

Klara didn't need to guess who spoke as she brushed the glass from her shoulders. Small cuts decorated her neck and forearms, but they quickly healed.

"She really does love to make an entrance," Klara said to Frendall as the spiral cleared. Through the portal they could see, sitting on her floral throne beneath a waterfall in her glistening white palace, Klara's mother, Aemella, fae queen of Kalos.

"Aemella, we meant no disrespect; it was merely a

celebration of our victory. Since my daughter arrived early, I thought why not have a small gathering? Try not to be too hurt," Lucifer said, but there was no hint of apology in his tone.

"And was I not part of said victory, and is she not *our* daughter?" Aemella asked, pushing her ice-white hair behind her shoulder.

Klara moved through the crowd to stand with her father in front of the portal.

"There she is! My young queen." Aemella leant forward on her throne, her white eyes trained on Klara.

How patronising, she thought, offering a faint smile. "We thought you were busy due to your wish to postpone," she said.

The court was silent. Many, if not all, of the demons present had never set their eyes upon the fae queen; she was exceptionally beautiful, with delicate features and deep brown skin that almost glittered. Judging from their expressions, they were captivated. Darkness can't help but be drawn to light, even if only to extinguish it.

"I had some minor issue to deal with, but had I known there was a gathering in honour of *our* collaboration, I wouldn't have dreamt of postponing. In fact, since we are all here, why don't we have the meeting now?" Aemella asked.

Lucifer cleared his throat.

She doesn't seem angry. Perhaps Jasper hadn't been the reason for the postponement. Klara wondered what had kept the fae from reporting back to his queen immediately. *But if he isn't going to tell her, I'll keep it to myself for now. It might come in handy.*

"We've all had too much to drink; perhaps dawn is more fitting." The king's tone told Klara that it wasn't a suggestion.

"I'm afraid that if we wait, something else might force me to postpone," Aemella said, leaning back in her throne and plucking a flower from the woven vine armrest.

Klara watched her father stare at Aemella, who didn't even offer the satisfaction of a blink. Silence held the room, and no one dared to breathe as the ancient rivals stared at each other, neither wanting to be the first to break.

"I don't have all evening to discuss this," Aemella threatened at last, trying to force Lucifer to yield. Her image went fuzzy as she started to close the portal.

Klara's heart quickened. The rulers might have their own issues, but she needed to ask them about the creatures going missing—ask whether the fae guard was keeping their word on allowing the creatures to live in peace in Kalos. She wouldn't get any answers if her mother left in a huff.

"Everyone out!" she ordered, and the court quickly filed out of the room.

The portal between Hell and Kalos became clear as glass once again. "I'm glad *someone* is making the decisions in Hell," Aemella mused.

11

Klara's gaze went to the doomed cleaning up all the glass, but with a simple incantation from Aemella, the windows were replaced and shining even more than they had before.

The throne room cleared of guests and doomed, and all that could be heard were the flames snapping at the wood in the fireplace. Only Lucifer, Klara, Lokey, Frendall, Matthias and Ceylon remained, as well as Aemella, sitting comfortably in her own domain.

"With the others gone, we can talk freely amongst ourselves," she said.

A long table formed before them at Lucifer's summoning. Klara was taking a seat when she felt her father's hot breath on her neck.

"We will discuss this later."

The pleasant hum of the venom in her veins disappeared, and she was suddenly incredibly sober. She knew she had overstepped by commanding his court to leave. *What was I to do? Leave the rulers to embarrass themselves in front of those who are meant to follow them?*

Klara and Frendall sat on one side of the table, with Matthias and Ceylon staring across at them. However, Lokey remained standing at the king's back, facing the portal to Kalos.

"Where would you like to begin?" Lucifer said. "Since you are so desperate for this meeting to take place in such haste." He wanted this meeting over as quickly as Klara did.

"I wanted to discuss the border," Aemella said, her elbows resting on the armrests of her throne.

Klara resisted the urge to roll her eyes. *Every time like clockwork—but it will give me the opening I need.*

"More and more creatures have been coming through the Neutral Lands, and I have nowhere to put them." Aemella sighed, as if she were the wounded party.

"We both know that isn't true. You have more than enough land for every creature and then some," Klara countered. "The agreement stands. So long as they can pass through the border wall's protections, they are to be offered shelter. It's not my fault if many are deemed worthy of a place amongst your fae."

"Perhaps I should strengthen the border, then," Aemella said.

When they had first made the agreement, it was clear the fae queen hadn't expected so many dark creatures to pass through her protections. If they hadn't spilt innocent blood or used dark magic, they were able to enter and seek a new life in Kalos. To remain, they only had to follow those same laws.

"If you are reforming Malum, with your reduced taxes and improved potion factories, then I don't understand why they need to come here. I think it speaks to you as a ruler rather than the quality of my lands."

Aemella was obviously trying to bait her, but Klara resented being called a weak ruler in Matthias's company. "It's not our place to question why they wish to leave, and I could say the same about the dark fae who land on my doorstep. Neither of us is responsible for the choices creatures make."

Aemella's expression turned to stone. "There has to be another clause to protect my people. I have been much too lenient."

"Once they pass through the wall, they are *your* people." Klara couldn't count how many times they had had this conversation.

"Perhaps a fee—a small token to show they are willing to contribute to Kalion society," Aemella began.

"You already tax the businesses the creatures establish twice as much as those that are run by the fae," Klara snapped, tired of petty bartering.

Aemella pouted. "Daughter, you do not play fair; we agreed no spies."

And yet you send a fae to my Gathering disguised as a general in my father's army! Klara wanted no one but her mother to hear the thought. She knew she had heard when a small smile danced in the corner of Aemella's mouth.

Where is your sense of humour? No harm was done. That was apparently all the explanation she was going to offer.

"Only if you remove yours from my lands first," Klara countered, returning to their public conversation. She didn't want her father knowing about their private interaction. There was no question that her mother had spies in Malum, just as she had her demons who made sure the fae guard weren't abusing their power in the Neutral Lands.

"I'm offended by the accusation," Aemella stated, hand on her chest in feigned shock.

"I feel we are at an impasse," Lucifer said, thumping the table.

Klara noted that her mother couldn't confirm that she didn't have any spies in Malum. Sometimes not being able to lie came in handy. Klara's hair slid to a calming faint blue, allowing her mother to see that she was unaffected by the goading.

"Fine. I will remove the demon scouts from the Neutral Lands if you remove the excess taxes—"

Aemella opened her mouth.

"—but the border protections remain the same," Klara finished. She was careful to specify scouts and not 'spies'. *I can play word games too.*

"Fine. I'm not one to be unreasonable," Aemella conceded, to Klara's surprise. If there was one thing she had in common with her parents, it was their stubborn streak. "But how can I be sure that they aren't committing crimes once they pass through the wall?"

Klara gripped her thighs beneath the table in frustration. She should have known her mother would never give up so quickly.

"I'm sure your fae guard is capable of handling whatever comes their way," Matthias interjected at the vital moment. Klara tried to hide her irritation.

"And what about those who wish to leave your land and return to Malum?" she added.

From the set of Aemella's jaw, her mother hadn't expected her to ask. *If the fae are stopping creatures from leaving in fear of what they might reveal, she won't be able to lie about it. Maybe that's why the witch's sister went missing—she tried to leave.* Klara was careful to keep her thoughts guarded from her mother. She felt her father staring at her, but she ignored him, waiting for Aemella's answer.

"I know some of the lycaons that have decided to leave Malum have found great peace in your land. I don't know what you mean to insinuate by talking of those who wish to leave, Your Majesty, but who would want to leave Kalos after going to such lengths to gain entrance?" Matthias leant against the table, insinuating himself once again where he wasn't wanted.

"I thought you preferred Malum above all else," Klara hissed.

Matthias grinned. "As you said, it's not about how we feel about our lands. Who are we to judge those who decide to leave?"

What a kiss-ass. She resisted the urge to roll her eyes.

"I'm delighted that I can give them a home after what the late High Queen Abadan did to your home." Aemella relished his praise.

Is she kidding right now? He gave her the perfect out for my question! Considering how open they were with each other, Klara guessed that this wasn't Aemella and Matthias's first conversation.

Frendall's eyes fell to the table as they talked of his fallen mother. He never discussed Abadan's demise, and Klara wondered how the loss had affected him. *Evil or not, a mother is a mother.*

Still, even if Matthias backed her mother, Aemella's own concerns gave Klara a perfect chance to make sure the queen was holding up to her side of the bargain.

"If you suspect the creatures are corrupting your land, then allow me access to your capital. I will examine whether the creatures' behaviour is befitting of your lands. I'm talented at figuring out when creatures are being deceptive," she suggested, watching Aemella's face fall.

"Why go to all the trouble? Surely you can send someone in your stead?" the fae queen replied.

"I'm the one who demanded the clause to grant them access to your land. I must make sure you have not been wronged. I wouldn't be able to sleep at night," Klara said sweetly. "You must not miss me as you claim, Mother?" She feigned upset.

"I would like nothing more than to have you at my side, but I wouldn't want to delay you in all your great reform."

"It's no delay—but if you truly do not wish me to visit…?"

"Come tomorrow if you wish it. I will show you the capital myself if it's so important to you," Aemella challenged. Klara felt triumphant. She didn't want to give the queen a chance to get rid of any evidence.

"Can Malum spare you?" Frendall asked with a frown, glancing at Matthias.

Leaving the Forest without a proxy is a risk, especially with the alpha snipping at my heels. However, if creatures are going missing and snatches are appearing on my doorstep, it's a risk I'm going to have to take.

"I'm sure Lokey can manage for a few days," Klara said, and all eyes went to an open-mouthed Lokey. "If I name you as a proxy, will you look after Malum in my absence?"

"Heiress, I respect any and all orders, but a hat suits me much better than a crown," Lokey said, resting his fingertips on the table.

"Don't worry. I will be back before you know it, and who can I trust more than you?" Klara said, not giving him a choice. *He is the only one I can rely on not to take full advantage of the situation.* Now she knew that Frendall had lied about his connection to Matthias, Klara wasn't going to leave the Forest in his care. She didn't care about his motives, she was too hurt to trust him with this, especially since she had confided in him about handing over extra land to the Pack.

"I don't know… I have many responsibilities," Lokey said, silently reminding her of his family.

"I'm sure you will be able to manage within the castle. Plenty of doomed to help you and guards to keep you safe." Klara knew it was his family's safety he was worried about.

"Are you questioning your queen?" Lucifer asked, evidently not wanting to be seen divided before the fae queen. "I see no reason why you can't take over for the time being. I don't need you here, and I'm sure that den of yours will survive just fine for a few days."

Lokey bowed his head towards Lucifer. "As you wish, Your Majesty."

"It's settled, then—and do bring your half-breed with you; I miss his company. We worked so well together in the past," Queen Aemella said, looking at Frendall, whose eyes flashed amber. The last time he had been in Kalos as himself, the queen had stripped him of his identity and forced him to bring Klara to her.

Asking for Frendall to accompany her alarmed Klara. Such a request would only play in her mother's favour, since he was Klara's weakness and they both knew it.

"It would be an honour to be able to see your lands," Frendall offered before Klara could prevent him or question it.

"Can you spare your best man?" Aemella asked a quiet Lucifer, while looking at him like he was something to take a bite out of.

"I'm sure I will manage, and I couldn't possibly send my daughter without any protection," Lucifer said, clapping Frendall on the back.

"Our daughter," Aemella corrected for the second time.

Klara sensed a grilling in Frendall's future. Lucifer would pry every bit of information from him upon his return from Kalos, and Aemella would look forward to Frendall's suffering at both rulers' hands.

"I can hardly wait. I will have to throw a ball in your honour, since I missed out this evening," the fae queen said. Klara noticed that her eyes never left Matthias. They had all gone many moons without a plot, and Klara suspected that it had been too long for the rulers. "I grow bored of this conversation. Klara and Frendall will visit, and Lokey shall act as proxy. My mind is at peace, knowing you will look into the creatures on my behalf," Aemella surmised.

The only thing I will be looking into is you. Klara kept the thought to herself.

"And you will put an end to the taxes," she reminded Aemella.

"How could I forget? Consider it done." Aemella rose to stand in front of her throne, her clear wings, veined with an array of colours, appearing behind her.

"All agreed?" Lucifer said, a gavel appearing in his hand. He always liked the dramatics.

There was a muttering of agreement, and then a loud smack on the table echoed about the room.

"It is agreed," he said formally, and the gavel disappeared in a puff of smoke.

Fae Queen Aemella gave a small bow before she disappeared back into her spiralling portal. The room felt frightfully dark without the bright shine of the Kalion

Palace. Klara felt Frendall's eyes on her, but she wouldn't meet his scrutinising gaze. She might have agreed to leave the Forest and with that, Lottie, but he had lied about knowing Matthias.

"I'm sure you will sign over my lands before you depart?" Matthias asked Klara, not hesitating for a second as Ceylon pulled the scroll from the inside of her suit pocket.

Better to get it over with before I leave. "Pen?" Klara asked, and her father was the first to conjure up a weighted gold pen. She pricked her finger with the fountain tip, and her black blood sealed the deal. A part of her hoped Matthias would try to break into the castle tunnel to challenge her and suffer the paralysing shriek of the Seekers.

"Excellent," Matthias said, taking the scroll and handing it to Ceylon. "We shouldn't outstay our welcome," he added as Lucifer yawned.

"I do love a lycaon who knows when it's time to leave," Lucifer said, and Matthias paled slightly. *So there is fear in him*, Klara thought as he bowed deeply to her father. She had to figure out how to inspire that same level of anxiety, since her generosity had clearly done nothing to diminish the disdain that oozed from his pores.

"I hope we meet again soon," Ceylon said with a hint of civility that Klara could feel pained her. Matthias said nothing to his queen. Instead, he turned his back and left with Ceylon and a deed to more land. The bitterness she felt for conceding to him gnawed at her insides.

Maybe I should have turned him into a rug and let the lycaons live without an alpha.

"I hope you have a pleasant stay with your mother. Be sure to pass on my greetings," Lucifer scoffed, rising from the table. Klara approached him, wishing to talk of the snatch discovered on the edge of the Forest and what she should look out for in Kalos, but before she could ask for his advice, he gripped her arm painfully tight. She almost yelped.

"Dismiss my court again while I am present, and I won't have an heir or a daughter," he seethed through his teeth, his irises flaring.

"Got it," Klara agreed. For a second, his grip tightened, threatening to break the bone before he released her. She let out a sigh of relief. She was glad her sleeve would conceal the throbbing bruise she felt forming on her upper arm. Lucifer embraced her with a smile, but she knew how genuinely he meant the threat.

A whisky decanter appeared on the table before the king, who quickly filled his empty glass. Klara could sense his unease. The fae queen had been able to portal into Hell without so much as a warning.

"What an eventful evening," he said, draining his glass.

Klara pushed Frendall's hand away from her lower back as he moved beside her. "Lie to me and then you think you can put your hands on me?" she snapped, keeping her voice low.

"Let's talk about this in private," Frendall whispered, keeping some distance between them. Lucifer looked amused.

"I don't know what we could possibly have to discuss, since you are always so honest with me," she bit back.

A laugh broke into the exchange, and she looked to her father, drowning his sorrows.

"Lovers' quarrel... how I miss the way Eve used to poison me. Such divine elegance and sheer rage wrapped up in a floral bow." Lucifer downed another drink.

"If you will all excuse us," Klara said. *I think I've had*

enough of everything and everyone this evening. I need to prepare to leave if Mother is to show me the capital herself. Can I bring my axe? I should... but should I?

"Before you retire for the evening, may I have a word in private?" Lokey asked. Klara didn't think she ever heard Lokey ask for anything politely—and then she remembered how she had just trapped him in her castle until she returned from Kalos. *He'll protect Lottie and my interests, but I have put his own family in danger.* She could tell from the pleading look in his serpentine eyes that he was going to seek a way out of the arrangement.

"I suppose we have to discuss the matter of you taking over for a while," she agreed, looking to others in the room and hoping they would excuse themselves.

"You may have the room," Lucifer said, taking a decanter and glass with him. "I'm off to see your sister. Hopefully there is something more entertaining happening in the tunnels. Tell your mother I said hello, and don't forget to come back." Lucifer disappeared into the fireplace, and the flames roared around him before residing into a faint flicker.

"He does love a dramatic exit," Lokey hissed, removing his outer jacket. It was impressive he managed to wear so much in Hell. A waistcoat, an outer coat, a top hat—she was sure his blood boiled beneath it all.

"I do have to ask you to give us the room, General," Lokey added, resting his hands on his narrow hips.

"I will see you later," Frendall said from Klara's side, not attempting to touch her.

Once they were alone, Klara started to speak, surprised when Lokey held a finger to his lips. His hands danced, forming a glass seal around them. *Being a high warlock has its moments.*

"Now we can speak freely. I don't trust your father

not to be lurking in those flames." Lokey hadn't survived for as long as he had without extreme caution. They stood so close together, only taking up a small fraction of the great room, that Klara could smell the musk and cinnamon on his skin.

"I'm sorry for naming you proxy. To be honest, you're the only one I could trust to leave in my place, and I can't leave Lottie without protection."

Lokey removed his hat. "I understand. I could smell Matthias's ambition the moment he walked into the room. The warlocks won't be happy about it, though; you forget I am half-higher-demon and your father's advisor. Many creatures won't want to see a half-breed on the throne."

"If they are capable of stomaching a fae-angel with demonic tendencies then I'm sure they will resist revolting for a few days," she argued, but Lokey's eyes remained cold.

"You come from royal, divine blood. I do not. My family comes before your Malum. Even with the protection of your guard, it will be tempting for many to usurp you."

"Nothing will happen while I am gone. I'm merely visiting across the river, which will only benefit the elders in the Forest."

"I used to think your naïveté was sweet; now it serves to remove my head," Lokey said with a light shake of his head.

"No one need know you are proxy while I'm gone. Stay in the castle with your family, and if anyone appears at the doors, tell them I am off visiting another elder."

"Darling, Matthias will have messengered half the Forest before I even step foot in a portal."

"Give me three nights," Klara pleaded, "and I promise to keep you out of my future schemes for as long as you like."

"I see your bribery skills have certainly improved. Three days and no other favours?" Lokey said thoughtfully.

"There has been a change in the air in Malum. Too many coincidences weighing on my chest. It might be an elder within my own Forest, but I need this time in Kalos to make sure my mother isn't up to any tricks."

Lokey hesitated as she pressed her hands together, begging him to do her bidding. He groaned, pulling at his waistcoat.

"I can tell you right now that she is. Glaudine has overheard rumours in Tapped. The toadstool den has been flourishing as of late."

"What rumours?" Klara wondered if he could confirm what the witch had warned her of. Clearly, the den was a hub of information.

"I can't confirm anything; mostly the ramblings of some drunken dark fae. Talk of creatures going missing." He shrugged.

I need more than hearsay. Klara placed her head in her hands, frustration welling up inside her.

"Before you go and interrogate your fellow sovereign, remember that creatures go missing in Malum all the time. They leave the realm through other portals, through the ghost ships at the port. There is no way to link the fae queen to missing creatures unless one returns," Lokey warned her.

She took a moment to consider.

"That might be true, but I was warned of those going through the border never being heard from again. How can it not be connected?" She didn't want to give away the witch that Glaudine had sent—she worried it would create a rift between the couple, and since Lokey hadn't mentioned it, she doubted he knew about his wife's involvement.

"If you left Malum, had decided to forsake the darkness, wouldn't you want to cut any ties?" Lokey asked.

He has a point. When I planned my escape to Kalos, I didn't intend on thinking of Malum again.

"The creatures of Malum make their own decisions; what comes after those decisions are made is not on you. I know you won't listen to me, but if something is happening in Malum or Kalos you need to keep a level head, or you might be the one to lose it." He placed a hand on her shoulder, and she knew he was being sincere.

"I have no intention of losing my head. I will go to Kalos and see for myself if the queen is hiding something."

"Everyone in the realm is hiding something—but please, for my sake, think before you rush in. The fae queen is cunning, and the fae will do anything for her."

Klara suspected he knew more than he was letting on. Of course he did; he had eyes, ears and tongues in every corner of every plane of existence. As devious as he was, she could sense he wanted no part in whatever was happening between Kalos and Malum.

"I'm not looking to start a war. I just need you to make sure the Forest doesn't erupt into one while I'm gone."

He didn't look convinced.

"Relax, or you'll put yourself in an early grave," she joked.

He shook his head slowly, rubbing his brow. "As you command, Your Majesty."

"That's what I like to hear. And try not to destroy my

home while I'm gone; I don't need the little one burning down the castle after I just finished redecorating."

Lokey held his hands up. "I make no promises. So many little fingers and so many candles."

Klara regretted not switching to electricity, but she loved the smell of the fragrant candles that filled each room of her home, and she didn't want to give them up. "Henny will look after him, and it will be good for Lottie to have some company while I'm gone."

Lokey tutted. "I have a bad feeling about this." The glass bubble popped, exposing them to the listening walls. "I shall count the minutes until your return."

"Try not to get used to the crown," she said, suppressing a smile as he grimaced.

"The mere thought makes me want to retch."

"Tell Glaudine I'm sorry for the inconvenience."

"Getting her away from the den will be no small feat, but she will secretly be delighted to have the doomed at her beck and call. I can't risk them in our estate. Too easily bribed."

I don't even know where his estate is. He's never even mentioned it before… Like the smuggling cabin concealed by the towering toadstools, his home was probably shrouded in enough protections to make a high warlock dizzy.

Lokey evaporated with a wink, and Klara took a deep breath as she stared up at her father's throne. She worried the demon would repeat their conversation to her father. Lucifer would love to hear she was poking around Kalos for information, but he wouldn't look kindly on her taking action against Aemella.

The black throne, with its raised back and velvet cushion, mocked her.

"Why do you insist on making my life hard? I couldn't have been a doomed?" she said to the inanimate object. She craned her neck. One day the seat would be hers. *All I have to do is survive long enough. Malum I can rule, but Hell? I don't know if I would survive the politics.*

She turned her back on the mocking throne and found her way to Frendall's part of the manor.

12

Klara stepped through an enormous oil painting of dead animals and screaming faces which Lucifer must have recently stolen from the human world. The canvas took up an entire wall, depicting the atrocity of war.

Frendall's room was much starker than her own. Small torches on the navy-painted walls lit the room, creating shadows in the corners of the spacious quarters. Only one small arched window looked onto the Maze below: a structure of interchanging hedges and stone filled with creatures that would haunt even Lucifer's nightmares. It had been created to torture souls for eternity, and was something no one would wish to see first thing after waking or before a night's rest. Then again, the view would also serve as a reminder of where exactly a person didn't want to end up.

The bed was made with extreme precision; the dark

sheets looked as if they had never even been slept in. Klara noticed the sword leaning on the end of the bed's carved base, then the shirt on the simple grey armchair by the window, before she was greeted by Frendall's bare back as he washed himself in a sink. She watched him in the full-length mirror hanging on the wall in front of him as droplets dripped from his face to his bare chest.

"Are you going to stand there and stare all night?" he said, his smile exposing his dimples as the cloth in his hand stilled on his tight stomach.

Klara forced a smile as she lifted the side of her dress, amused by the lift of his eyebrows. *I wouldn't get too excited.* She took the blade from her thigh and tossed it at his reflection, shattering the mirror. "That answer your question?"

The stunned look on his face, frozen in the mirror before it had cracked, brightened her mood somewhat. He stood rigid, then pulled the blade from the now exposed wood backing of the mirror. Shards decorated the floor around his bare feet.

"I think you need to work on your aim," he said, dropping the knife onto the dresser beside him and picking up a white folded towel.

"If I had wanted to hit you, I would have."

"I know you're frustrated with me, but throwing knives isn't going to solve anything."

"It certainly made me feel better," she snapped as he stepped over the shards of glass and dried himself.

"I thought you might at least pretend to have a shred of remorse for lying, but here you are acting like nothing happened!"

"You're going to resent me for washing? I had to wash the gathering off me. I can still smell the venom,"

Frendall said, closing the gap between them. He rubbed the towel through the wet hair that hung around his face.

"You lied about not knowing the alpha," she said plainly, placing her hand out to stop him from coming any closer.

"I didn't lie. When I met him he wasn't the alpha yet," Frendall answered, tossing the towel aside.

The next question made bile rise in her throat. "And the *brother* comment? Please tell me that's a lycaon term of endearment?"

She watched as Frendall chewed the corner of his bottom lip. That was all the confirmation she needed.

"Wow," she said, taking a step back. He tried to follow. "You simply *forgot* to mention that you have a brother who wants to take Lottie away and—from what I gather—isn't too fond of me?"

"I was looking for the right moment to tell you. It's not like I know anything about him. He's a stranger, and you don't exactly have a leg to stand on; your sister did kill me."

Half-sister. "Actually, she killed a lesser demon who was glamoured to look like you." Klara paced, wanting to get rid of the adrenaline seeping through her veins. "How long have you known him?"

"My father had a son before me, but I never met him until he appeared during the rebuild. He was claiming the right as alpha under my father's name. Since he was a rogue, I never thought he would take over the pack."

"How old is Matthias?" Klara asked, wondering how far back his history—and potential connections in Malum and wherever else he had been—went.

"I can't be sure. It's not like I was around when Lucifer took my father's head."

My father killed his, and I ended his mother's reign. It's a curse to be around the Lucifer name. Not that Abadan hadn't deserved to be overthrown.

"He's never asked for an audience with you? Never asked you for information?"

"This is the second time I've been in his company, and I have no interest in granting him an audience. He respects the old ways above all else, and if that is true, he has no love for Lucifer. It doesn't help that the king killed his father, either. I never knew him, so I can't exactly hold a grudge. The only thing I *can* tell you is that even before Matthias was alpha, there were rumours of his preaching about losing our strength and traditions. Then he appeared during the burying of the dead once the caves were cleared. He was making allies, talking of a united pack. I had to leave before a lesser demon saw me amongst the crowd, and I haven't seen him since."

"Why didn't you warn me before they came to the castle? You knew about the meeting."

"I thought Ceylon was the new alpha. I never expected him to walk through the doors of the castle, or I would have," he said, stretching his arms out in front of him, frustration creasing his features.

"If that's true, then why didn't you explain once I mentioned Matthias was the alpha when I arrived in Hell?"

"I didn't get the chance. We both got a little distracted," he pointed out, a smile dancing on his lips.

"You can't use *that* as an excuse," she argued, trying not to blush.

"You didn't seem to mind at the time," Frendall muttered, and she wanted to slap him.

Her feet were aching in her heels, and she rested on the edge of the bed. More minor aches ran through her joints. She had used too much power trying to figure out the intentions of those at the gathering.

"Would you have told me about having a brother even if he wasn't the alpha?" she pressed, gripping the edge of the bed, feeling the soft sheets under her palms.

Frendall hesitated, running his hands through his damp hair.

Everyone in the realm has their secrets. Lokey's words replayed in her mind.

"No. He's no brother to me; his existence is inconsequential." His voice was cold, but Klara, considering her ever-evolving relationship with Mila, knew that blood relations were hard to cut ties with. "He will be alpha for a time, and then Lottie will take her place amongst the pack—and if he knows what's good for him, he will concede peacefully," he reassured her.

"I don't think concession is in his repertoire." Klara groaned, trying to wrap her mind around this new information.

"This isn't about him or me. This is about the fae queen. I saw how you were looking at her. What are you looking for in Kalos? You would never leave Lottie with Matthias sniffing around if there wasn't something else going on," Frendall insisted, standing over her. His sculpted body made for a tantalising view, so she forced herself to look up at his eyes.

"You want me to tell you, after all you've kept from me?"

"Now who's the one keeping secrets? The crown has made you paranoid. If you can't talk to me, who can you talk to?"

"Don't talk to me like I'm beneath you," she snapped, rising to her feet.

"You *have* been beneath me." Frendall smirked.

It felt like a stab to her heart. She could forgive his lack of honesty about Matthias, but mocking their time together? He was the only one who had ever seen her in her most vulnerable state, and he had used it against her.

"For the love of Lucifer, I was trying to make a joke," Frendall said, leaning over her with his arms braced on either side of her, but she refused to meet his eye.

"There are some missing creatures, I think. Nothing has been confirmed." She had to tell him something. She brushed him aside and strode for the door before she said anything she would regret.

"I'm sorry I didn't tell you about Matthias," he said, grabbing her arm and pulling her towards him. The heat of his body seeped through her dress, and she didn't want to leave him, but she had more significant issues to think about than his feelings. She unclasped his hands from her waist, her touch revealing a crowd of lycaons hanging on to every word Matthias barked from a small stage in a cabin. The conviction in his voice was captivating; Klara didn't blame the lycaons for falling for his passion.

"I'm staying in my own room tonight," she said calmly. Even knowing the truth didn't ease her mind.

She missed his hands as soon as they were gone, and she knew she had to leave the room before she ended up in his bed.

"I messed up, but don't leave," Frendall begged. "We have to discuss what we're going to do in Kalos."

"I'll see you before we leave," Klara answered, and quickly closed the door on his reply.

She rested her head on the back of the door to his chamber, only to hear a loud crash inside. Placing her palms on the door, she felt his anger and upset, but it wasn't at her, it was at himself.

13

Back in her own quarters, Klara let her shoes slip to the floor and crawled under the cool covers, not bothering to change. She ripped the corset from her body and threw it across the room, trying to release the pent-up frustration she felt. Constant tossing and turning tangled her in her sheets until she settled to stare out at the arched ceiling.

All I want is sleep, she thought, praying for her mind to keep quiet so she could get a few hours. She touched her fingertips to the headboard, stripping away the ceiling to watch the passing clouds, and thought about the witch who had lost her sister. *How do you live knowing someone you love is out there, but you don't know if they're alive or dead? Suppose Aemella is up to something, she won't want witnesses—yet she wants me to bring Frendall. He's sure to report everything he sees, so she must want him for some reason.* Klara thought of Frendall's body on the Neutral Lands turned bloodied battlefield and resented how she could be both angry at him and terrified of losing him. *Maybe she hopes he can stop me causing any trouble for her, or perhaps she hopes to use him against me as she did before.*

The more she thought about it, the less she wanted Frendall to accompany her. *He's expendable in her eyes; bringing him to inspect Kalos will only put him in harm's way, and at least if he's in Hell, I can report back to Father without worrying about a messenger.*

The weight of the covers added to her anxiety, but she could only stare at the ceiling for so long before she drifted off.

Klara woke to a raven's scratchy caw; the light of Hell's sun drifting into her room told her morning was dawning. She rolled over and watched the bird perched on her window sill. *One of Father's messengers*, she thought, and it was gone.

She rose with a yawn and removed her dress, hoping the soft sheets and sleep had relieved some of her stress, but her mind continued to race about all that lay ahead. *The sooner you get to Kalos, the sooner you can put this issue to rest and return home.* Part of Klara couldn't believe that she now considered Malum home.

She scraped her nails through her tangled hair; feeling oil coat her fingers, she decided to opt for a shower in her private bathroom before leaving. Once she was washed, she dressed in a pair of light tan trousers, a cream shirt and a pale grey bodice. She hated corsets, but at least her bodices weren't boned so she could still fight. They had proved useful in helping to protect her organs during a fight, now that her year-old heart didn't heal her as quickly as her first. Plus, in such clothes she would easily blend in with the citizens of Kalos. She knew Aemella would expect her at her palace at first light, so she had time to visit the capital—or at least the outskirts—and see if the witch's concerns were founded. *If I convince Aemella the creatures are no threat, she might stop whatever she's plotting. A crack doesn't always have to lead to a break. If she is even planning something. Ugh, I sound like my father.*

"This is as good as it's going to get," she said aloud, rubbing the dark circles under her glamoured green eyes. Even she got sick of her all-encompassing white eyes, gifted to her from her fae half. Once her boots were laced, she clasped the buckles across her chest to secure her axe to her back, its weight making her feel whole.

Klara crept down the hallway. The small ball of fire in her hand flickered as she tried to conceal it from the sleeping portraits. The manor was silent at this hour, but she could still hear the faint screams of Mila's torturers at work. The oval paintings hung with their eyes closed, and some snored lightly as she opened the door to her father's office. She backed in slowly, closing the door with a soft clip, and closed her fist, extinguishing the small flame as the chandelier in the office lit.

She turned round and almost jumped out of her skin. Frendall was standing behind the dark mahogany desk, dressed in the same Kalion clothing she was, except with a loosely hanging brown waistcoat instead of her bodice. His sword strapped to his side gave away who and what he truly was.

"Trying to run again?"

Klara shushed him, afraid his voice would travel into the hall and disturb the portraits. "Keep your voice down!" She walked to the bookshelves.

"Your father destroyed the First Edition after you used it to escape," Frendall told her as she flicked through the hardbacks.

"I wasn't looking for that," she said, though she was saddened that her father would destroy one of the only keepsakes they both shared memories of. Keeping her back to Frendall, she added, "It wouldn't bring me to Kalos anyway."

"Us. Bring *us* to Kalos," he corrected, standing behind her.

"I'm ordering you to remain in Hell," she said coldly.

"Ordering me?" His hand rested on the end of the long sword.

Her gaze danced over the editions and titles, searching for the right one. "I need someone in Hell to report what I see in Kalos, not some random messenger who might decide to report my findings back to the queen."

"Queen Aemella is expecting my presence. If I don't appear, don't you think she'll suspect something?"

"I need to be able to move around discreetly before I make my appearance at the palace. I can hardly do that with you," Klara said, motioning to all six-foot-something of him. "You're as subtle as Lokey on Execution Day."

Frendall smiled as they both remembered Lokey's sulphur-yellow suit on the day Lucifer had passed judgement on the lesser demons, and a rare higher, who had sided with Abadan.

"That may be true, but what happens if the queen decides to hold you? A queen would never go anywhere without an escort for her own protection. If someone sees you skulking around and reports you, she will be well within her rights to detain you. You'll be a foreign ruler in her land, and if you intervene in the handling of the creatures, she'll treat you as such. You think the fae queen doesn't have higher fae to answer to?"

Klara placed the book back on the shelf and noticed a simple strand of ivy growing across the back wall, only to stop at the fourth shelf of grimoires.

"Are you listening to me?" he snapped.

"Yes."

"Don't you care about being imprisoned?" he demanded, hands raised.

"It's been a while since I spent time in a dungeon." She smiled at him, then felt the split in between the two bookshelves.

"Can you stop looking for whatever it is you're looking for and look at me?"

She ignored him and pressed the shelf inward. It sprang back and opened, almost hitting her. A puff of dust accompanied the opening of the dividing shelves. Klara coughed as the particles found their way into the back of her throat. She fanned the dust away from her face with her hand until it cleared.

"Knew it was here," she whispered to herself. She walked into the secret room, leaving Frendall to follow.

"How did you know about this?" Frendall asked, his eyes wide in surprise. Clearly, Lucifer hadn't shared this secret with him. The narrow room was walled with shelves containing dimly glowing potions as they aged, and above a small steel sink was a glass cabinet containing leather-bound notebooks and grimoires. A year's worth of dust coated everything.

He hasn't even let the doomed clean... maybe he's grieving more than I suspected. There was a pale pink chaise-longue in the corner surrounded by books, very much Eve's style, and as Klara ran her hand over the satin fabric she knew Lucifer had been here recently. She sensed his sorrow on her fingertips.

"I found one of Eve's notebooks in her room. She listed all the potions she had created, but I couldn't find them anywhere in the castle, and there were too many with too many variations for them to have been for her own personal use."

"This is a brewing room," Frendall realised, staring into the empty cauldron in the centre of the room. Klara noticed the room had no ceiling; you could look straight up to Hell's red moon. *Perfect for harnessing its energy. Eve did have her talents.*

"There's another room identical to this in Malum, hidden under the conservatory. I only discovered it when Lucifer gifted me the fountain. It's a mirror room; what happens in here will be replicated to that in the castle," Klara told him, looking at one of the walls. It was taken up with a mirror, and in it wasn't this room reflected back but the twin room in the castle of Malum.

"The king has never spoken of it, not even when Eve was alive. It must be how she came and went from Hell in private. I had no idea this existed," Frendall said, studying the potions on the shelves.

The cauldron in the centre of the small room was dirty, and cobwebs lined the walls.

"This was her way of brewing potions for the king without ever having to leave the castle," Klara said, running her hand along the shelves, searching for the right potion. "Easy to see that he hasn't allowed anything to change in here since her fall." She selected one and wiped the round bottle on her shirt, removing the dust. The liquid within began to glow. It was exactly what she was looking for. The almost black liquid had separated from the herbs at the base of the glass bottle.

"He doesn't talk of her?" she asked, wondering if Lucifer knew what Eve had sacrificed to heal his daughter.

Frendall shook his head. "Not once, or not in the way you mean."

"Hopefully the potion has kept," she said, ignoring the pangs of uncertainty in her gut. Taking the cork from the bottle, she was about to drink it when Frendall placed a hand on her arm.

"What are you thinking? That potion could have been sitting here for God knows how long," he exclaimed, panic raising the veins in his neck. Many of the brewing-room potions contained similar ingredients and were so similar in colour that it was hard to differentiate a poison from a cure—a curse from a blessing.

Klara held the bottle to her nose. The mugwort gave off a sage-like odour, while the blue vervain gave no scent, though small purple flakes gave it away. Finally the caraway seeds, which had long since settled, had been added for safe arrival.

"It will bring me to Kalos without being detected. Lilith used it in her smuggling operation to check on the daily patrols in the Neutral Lands," she told him.

He frowned. "When did you find that out?"

"There were countless vials of it in Lilith's chambers. Once I figured out the ingredients, I was able to find its use in Eve's journal. I couldn't believe that Eve was the one making it for her, but then again, she probably didn't think to ask what Lilith was using a portalling potion for."

"How do you know it's the right one?" The anxiety in his voice gave her enough pause to double-check.

"It's the right one." *I hope… or I'll probably be too dead to care.* "Eve left more journals than I could get through in this millennium, and I know what these ingredients can do once combined. Stop nagging me."

"I'm not nagging, but she isn't here to teach you now—she could have written lies in case someone read her journals," Frendall argued.

"She might not be my tutor anymore, but that doesn't stop me from trying. I only wish she had taught me half of what she knew; this was her true love," Klara said, holding the potion up to him. "As to lying, I think I'll leave that to you," she added, and he glared at her.

"Going alone is dangerous, and judging from the fact that you're willing to drink what could be an ancient potion, I don't think you're thinking clearly!" he said, running a hand through his hair and sticking back the few strands that had fallen in front of his face. "Are you doing this out of spite for last night?"

"This has nothing to do with us. I'm going alone because Aemella is likely to take your head to punish me for my *skulking,* as you so kindly put it. She will want a fae patrol to escort me if I go to her palace first. I don't want the creatures to think they're being interrogated and refuse to talk with me. I don't even want them to know it's me they're talking to."

"I think you're playing with fire." Frendall sighed and began to pace.

"Then call me the daughter of Hell," Klara said, and took a swig from the bottle.

He reached out to stop her but he was too late. The piercingly bitter taste burned her tongue, and she dropped the bottle, which shattered. The mugwort had clearly intensified after being so long in the bottle. Her vision clouded, and Frendall went blurry in front of her.

"Are you okay?" he demanded as she sank to the floor.

"I'm fine. It's stronger than I thought—" She coughed as she felt the air in the room thin. The feeling in her tongue returned.

"Tell me what to do!" Frendall was frantically searching the shelves, but she barely heard him.

Shit, that was strong. Remind me to bring a dropper next time. She wanted to say it aloud, but when she opened her mouth no sound came out. She tried to steady herself by placing her hands on the floor; only then did she notice that her limbs had become transparent. The potion's effect travelled up her arms and legs, and before she even realised what was happening, the room slipped away from around her.

The last thing she heard was the anguish in Frendall's voice as he called her name.

14

Klara felt every one of her cells being torn apart and put back together as the potion pulled her through to Kalos. Golden particles rushed around her; something lay crushed and jagged underneath her back.

That's the last time I drink an aged potion, she thought as pain radiated through her limbs. She seemed to be in a wheat field. The broken strands of wheat stabbed and poked at her, but she was still too stunned by the instantaneous travel to do anything about it. She coughed and rolled to her side, hearing the crackle of the crushed crops surrounding her. The wheat field told her she was on the outskirts of Kalos.

It couldn't have brought me closer? The last time she had been in the outskirts, she had been wounded, Frendall had been Wolfgang, the false Frendall had been dead, and Lottie had been crying. The sun blinded her as it ran through her clear palm. *Why in the hell am I still transparent?* As soon as she thought it, the burning in her gut subsided and her body returned to normal. *That's better,* she thought, clenching and relaxing her now very real fist.

"Let's never do that again," she said to herself as she successfully blocked the sun this time, grateful for the gentle breeze that drifted through the golden crops. Her axe dug into her spine as she stared at the pale blue sky. *Not a single cloud to be seen.* She was almost transfixed by the beauty of it, but her position was increasingly uncomfortable, and she opted to sit up before she did any permanent damage to her spine. She stood, noting the dent she had left behind. *I doubt the fae will notice; it's not as if they'll walk through the centre of the field. But I'm going to end up leaving a path. At least Frendall couldn't follow, or we would have left an even greater impression.* She felt a pang of guilt about leaving him behind. *It's for his own good,* she reassured herself.

She tried to step carefully so as not to disturb the crops more—she wanted to leave as little trace as possible if she were to convince her mother that she had portalled into the palace as agreed. Though potions didn't carry much of a magical scent, her arrival would still cause a shift in the air, thus alerting those patrolling the area to her presence. The downside of magic was that it demanded to be seen and felt. The fae patrol would know someone or something has forced its way in, but they wouldn't know it was the daughter of Hell herself.

Klara had almost reached the cobbled road when she saw a patrol at the edge of the field and ducked down into the wheat. They stopped walking right by where she was crouched. *Was Mother expecting me to do this?* Their sapphire uniforms were devoid of silver threads, so at the very least they weren't palace guards. *Has Aemella put on extra patrols because she knew I was coming?* But no sooner had the thought crossed her mind that the patrol continued on their way, their tranquillising spears on their backs.

She smirked, noticing that she had dropped to one knee. *How proud my mother would be to see me bow to her kin.* The fae queen saw Klara's fae blood as superior to Lucifer's and was determined to make Klara see the same. However, Aemella loved to ignore her inherited angelic nature, for it was the fae who served the angels.

Klara rose slightly, following the fae with her eyes as they disappeared into a watchtower further down the path. *Now I have to figure out a way to get past them. I could disguise myself as fae, but they would ask what I'm doing all the way out here, and I figure whoever owns these crops would be known to them.* She glared at the high tower of carved wood with an outwatch post that allowed them to see for miles into the orchards and crops that fed Kalos in all directions.

Her train of thought was disrupted by the sound of wheels trudging against the stone and mud path. A leprechaun approached, pulling along a wooden cart three times its size. She was surprised to see the lack of strain on the older creature's lined face; the cart looked like it weighed a ton. The vehicle stopped suddenly, and she pushed back into the wheat, afraid of being sensed. The leprechaun dropped his hands from the metal rail he was using to pull the cart and removed his hood.

Move along, she begged silently as he peered into the crops.

"If you stay still, they will find you," the leprechaun said suddenly with a toothy smile.

Klara cursed internally. She considered that it might be a trap, but she needed to get past the watchtowers without being stopped. She moved into sight. *If the tower watch spots him talking to thin air, it might pique their curiosity.*

"Hop into the cart, and I'll pull you through," he said gruffly. His voice was thick and rough, as though he had smoked a pipe every day of his life.

"Why help me?" she asked, her hand on the axe's handle at her back.

"Because someone once offered me the same help—and if you use that weapon, you will bring the fae down on both of us." She dropped her hand to her side. Would he recognise her? Her axe was famous in the Forest, since its elements could take down any creature it came across. *Why would he risk helping me if he knows who I am? Maybe he thinks he'll be rewarded.*

"Helping me could land you back in Malum," she warned, checking the path for any approaching fae.

"It's a good thing I don't plan on getting caught then," the leprechaun said. He pulled out a pocket watch, tapping it with his stumpy finger to get the dial moving. "I'm late; the missus will have my arse. You want the lift or not?"

"You can support my weight?"

"Sure. The cart practically pulls itself," he said. He lifted his hands over the rail, and the cart started to move on its own. *Handy trick.* "Now or never, love. Must hurry—I have to get these fruits to the market or the missus will have my gold." His eyes drifted to the watchtower.

"Thank you," she said, ducking under the sheet that protected the freshly picked fruits.

The cart shook as they moved along at a steady pace. Despite the discomfort of her current position, Klara tried to stay still; moving might alert those in the tower. She peered into the crate beside her as a sweet smell surrounded her. Golden pears in the dozens. She had never seen such a thing. The waxy skin glittering with gold speckles made her mouth water. *These must cost a fortune.*

"Not too long now," the leprechaun whispered as they pulled to a stop.

"What's in the cart, creature?" a fae guard asked, and Klara froze. She didn't dare take a breath.

"Some fruits for the market: the orchard was feeling generous today," the leprechaun replied without a hint of fear. Her heart was beating fast enough for the both of them.

A shadow moved over the sheet. Her eyes followed the fae through it to the end of the cart, and she feared she had failed to cover her feet—or maybe the outline of her axe was exposed by the thin cover. The silence was killing her. She saw the outline of a hand on the sheet just above her head, readying to pull it back.

"I must be getting to the market. The chefs are going to be buying for the queen's ball. You wouldn't want the queen to have dried-out fruit from being out in this sun too long, would you?"

The mention of Queen Aemella caused the fae's hand to disappear, and Klara's hand, that was clenched around her axe, relaxed.

"On with you," the fae said.

Klara almost laughed in relief as they passed the watchtowers.

"Hope you didn't shit your breeches, because I was certainly tempted." The leprechaun's laugh shook the cart.

Klara smiled. The leprechauns were known for their crass nature, but he had saved her from having to use magic to gain entrance.

The silence of the crops and orchards was replaced by the sound of busy streets and merchants' shouts. The sheet was pulled from her before she had a chance to react. She drew her axe as the leprechaun took up a tray of fruits.

"It's only me—you can put that thing away," he said. "Don't worry, everyone is too busy to notice you."

Another leprechaun, weighed down by layers of skirts, joined them. Her thick red curls had been tied back with a red headscarf. She stopped, hands on her wide hips, to glare at Klara as she sat amongst the produce. *I figure this is the missus he mentioned.*

"What time do you call this? I've been setting up the stall for the guts of an hour—even had to send away a few customers, because you were picking up strays!" she exclaimed. Klara assessed her deep scowl and waving fist. There wasn't a hint of fear in the creature, only annoyance.

"Don't be like that, pet. The poor thing got lost; it was the civil thing to do."

The leprechauns stared at each other, and Klara didn't like their questioning eyes.

"If you tell me your names, I can see that you are rewarded," she chimed in.

He opened his mouth, but his missus slapped his shoulder, and he grimaced in pain.

"What do you want our names for? Are you going to report us? You'll get nothing from us," she barked, standing right up to Klara.

I like her spirit. There's still some fight in the creatures this side of the wall. "I'll be going, then; thank you for your assistance," she said, not wanting to linger in their company in case the missus got the idea to shout for a fae.

"Here on the outskirts, I suggest you keep your wits about you. The fae guard aren't too kind to faces they don't recognise," the leprechaun warned.

They fear the guard, but that's to be expected. Doesn't confirm anything. Yet. She bowed her head silently in thanks and turned for the busy street.

"Good riddance—we have enough trouble as it is," the female leprechaun huffed.

Trouble? Klara wanted to ask more, but the look she received when she glanced back told her not to bother.

The market was not so different from that of Malum, except that here the cobbled streets seemed to gleam, there were no cart-destroying potholes, and every stand was wrapped in flowers. The produce was fresh without so much as a bruise or a spot. What surprised her the most was how many creatures and fae moved and talked together through the streets as stalls stood side by side. The dark fae in Malum held nothing but animosity for the other creatures of Malum, but here fae and creatures seemed to coexist peacefully after years of distrust and generational loathing. Klara worried her eyes were lying to her. She searched the buildings' corners and stalls for the slick skin of glamours but saw none. The market was real, and the peaceful nature of the market-goers and merchants rang true.

The lack of animosity unsettled her. She watched a fae sell a crystal to a young giant; she expected it to be made out of glass, that the fae would try to trick the creature, but as she moved closer she saw the faint shine confirming the crystal was real. The sweet smell of food cooking on the various open fires floated through the air, making her mouth water. *I wish I'd robbed one of the pears from the cart.*

"Excuse me." The leprechaun who had brought her here was suddenly at her side, surprising her. Her startled reaction caught the attention of the fae selling their wares, and the leprechaun ushered her quickly down a narrow alleyway. Lines of dripping clothes hung between buildings above them.

"I don't mean to pry, but you should consider taking this." His voice rang with true concern as he held out a light grey cloak. "Not many in Kalos carry such a fierce weapon. I fear it will give you away," he whispered.

Just as coloured clothing in Hell gives someone standing, it's obviously a weapon that makes you stand out in Kalos. "I forgot it was even on display. I'm in your debt once again," Klara said with a faint smile, taking the cloak that just so happened to match her bodice. *I'll have to be more careful.*

"It's an honour to be in a queen's debt." The leprechaun bowed, and Klara placed a hand on his shoulder, allowing him to rise.

"I figured you knew. My weapon gave me away, didn't it?" She sighed, ill at ease that someone knew she was lurking in Kalos.

"Rest assured, your secret is safe with us. My missus has a sharp tongue but she's all heart. Now, you'll be needing rest before long, and it will do you no good to be out once night falls. The fae are extremely suspicious of those who decide to hang about at night. There's a tavern only two streets over. Tell them Warloth sent you and you won't be questioned."

To tell me his name shows his courage—and his naïveté. Yet she respected him for it. She could count at least one creature in Kalos as an ally.

"May I ask you something?" she asked, not wanting to push her luck.

"Anything. My family and I were able to leave Malum thanks to you."

"How is life for creatures here?"

"Better now that you have the queen's ear. The taxes force us to tighten our belts, but we're safe."

Klara was relieved, knowing that the taxes would soon be amended, but as she placed her hand on his, she felt sorrow.

"The creatures are safe here? All of them?" she pried, moving closer in case Warloth feared being overheard.

He hesitated, looking the length of the alleyway.

"Speak freely. You'll never have to repeat what we have discussed."

Before the leprechaun could continue, his companion appeared at the entrance of the alley.

"I'm sorry; this is all I can offer you," he said, smiling through sad eyes.

She took the cloak. "It's more than enough. I won't ask any more of you." *Back in Malum, I would have already been turned in for gold.*

Still, Warloth's eyes had told her all was not right here. Their cart passed the alley as she wrapped the cloak around her shoulders, relieved to discover that the hood concealed her face from the crowds. Her eyes appreciated the shade; she wasn't used to the bright sun. Such bright rays were a rarity in Malum unless you visited the beaches of the Elven Coast.

The further she walked, the closer she got to the heart of the capital. The stalls grew further apart, and pale stone buildings with balconies lined with flowers and plants became more common. She couldn't help but notice an increased fae presence. She stepped aside as a fae guard in their silver-threaded uniform passed by carrying a tray of meats and fish. *Palace guard.* She dipped her head. The fae's skin glistened in the sun as if they had stolen the golden speckles off the pears in the cart. It was hard to pull her eyes from them.

"Watch it, missy," a pixie said as Klara blocked her path. The pixie only stood to her chest, and Klara moved aside as she noticed her arms were full of empty spell jars. Klara was about to continue on when she noticed that one of the pixie's wings was missing.

"Are you going to move, or perhaps you'd prefer to stare?" the pixie snapped, and Klara thought of the snarky pixies she had served in the Beanstalk.

"Apologies," she said, and the pixie continued to her small wooden stall made up of shelves of jars.

A pixie with one wing would easily be shunned by their group. They flew in groups in case their mischief-making turned sour. *If she can't fly or has been cast out, it explains why she would go it alone.* Klara wondered if that was what had caused her to make the journey to Kalos. She sensed no ill intent from her; the pixie was simply using the natural magic that would have remained in her, wings or not, to make a living.

A fae was watching their interaction from their own stall of crystal trinkets. Deciding not to linger, Klara kept her eyes down as she searched for the thatched roof the leprechaun had mentioned.

15

Just as Warloth had said, Klara found the thatched roof two streets over. The tavern made from layered logs reminded her of the toadstool den in Malum, though this one was able to stand without the support of a toadstool stalk. She spotted the black smoke that billowed from the chimney despite the warm air; she couldn't imagine why they needed a fire lit.

She clasped the door handle, and a rush travelled up her arm. The handle was made of iron.

"Wasn't expecting that," she muttered to herself. Weakness crept into her limbs as she stepped through the iron door frame. The iron wouldn't kill her, but it would weaken her both magically and physically.

Is this a trap? Did the leprechaun set me up? she thought, staring into a darkened tavern full of fae. The only light came from the candles on the tables and the torches on the walls. It looked like the whole place had been taken out of Malum and placed here; its structure was provincial but solid. *Nothing like the flower-and-plant-covered buildings and homes in the streets.* It was truly out of place, and yet the fae seemed to be enjoying themselves. Why were there no windows? It didn't make sense, considering that the sun outside could have easily lit the place during the day, and the torches only added to the heat.

She forced herself to move through the door, to ease the stares from those sitting on wooden benches at long wooden tables. They had goblets of what, from the smoky yet sweet smell in the tavern, would probably be venomed ale. The smell almost choked her, fear heightening her senses. Still, Klara walked with confidence, acting as though she belonged, until she almost stumbled on the cracked and uneven boards that made up the tavern floor. Judging from the muddy footprints and pale chalk from the outside paths, the tavern wasn't lacking in footfall.

"Looks like we have another to break the tie," a voice bellowed, followed by the smacking down of a goblet against one of the tables.

Ignoring the words, Klara noticed the vampire behind the counter, drying a goblet. Barrels of ale were gathered on either side of the bar, with bottles of expensive liquor and venoms at the vampires back. *At least the vamp explains the lack of windows.*

"Will you not join us?" a voice asked.

Klara looked around, waiting for someone to respond, only to freeze when she saw Frendall.

She realised he was the one who had called out to her. *I can't believe he would draw attention to us like this!* He offered her a lazy smile. His simple dark brown trousers hung low on his hips, and his loosely tucked in shirt was hanging out on one side. *He's either drunk or pretending to be. Please let it be the latter.*

He fitted in easily amongst the other creatures, though he was currently surrounded by a group of fae. Some sat at the long table while others were gathered around a wooden board nailed to the wall, marked with a bullseye and with small knives protruding from it. She reluctantly made her way to him.

"I told you all she'd be along soon," Frendall announced, and if looks could kill, hers would have.

How the hell did you get here? she projected to him.

Yours wasn't the only potion in that room, he projected back, spinning a dagger through his fingers. His usually slicked-back hair was dishevelled and hanging in waves around his strong jaw.

Are you drunk?! she demanded as he leant against her.

"Finally, darling—I was beginning to think you'd got lost. My friends and I have made a tidy wager; all I need is for you to make the final throw," Frendall said aloud. She didn't know how he could look so at ease while surrounded by so many fae. *It would take a lot more than cheap ale to get me drunk, but I figured I could make some coin out of these idiots,* he added, and she wanted to strangle him.

Klara studied the board. It was hard to make out who was winning; the iron lamps with severely worn-down candles braced on hooks on either side of the board offered little light.

"Get a move on. We'll be expected on watch soon, and I can't wait to get my hands on that gold coin of yours," a fae said, taking a gulp of ale. Klara watched the brown liquid drip through his beard. Thankfully, there was no silver in their uniforms, so they wouldn't have seen her in the palace.

"Sorry to keep you waiting. I would have come

sooner had I known coin was on the table," she said, trying to sound confident, and dropped her hood. Revealing her face was a risk, but concealing her face any longer would have only raised suspicion. The armed fae stared at her white eyes; they should believe she was just another fae. A moment passed, and she detected no suspicion from those gathered, but she was still careful to conceal her axe under her cloak.

"She's lethal with a blade; wouldn't have her any other way," Frendall said to the fae, before embracing her. She was about to scold him when he kissed her hard, and her breath caught as the fae whooped.

"Enough of that, let's get on with it," another fae said, smacking their goblet against the table. Klara could smell the venomed ale as it sloshed onto the floor.

Are you trying to get us killed? she hissed, and he laughed. She noticed he was exposing his lycaon amber eyes.

They think I'm a lycaon, not a general in Lucifer's army. Hiding in plain sight, he projected back.

She took the dagger from his hand.

"Win it for us, and they'll go on their way," he whispered while the fae were distracted by the vampire, who had brought over a tray of drinks.

Klara accepted a cup of venomed ale from the vampire's extended hand, noting the exceptionally long black nails, filed to a spike. She saw the vampire's cloudy red eyes and realised that he was blind. She had never seen a blind vampire, though it didn't mean he couldn't see them. Like a snake, he would be able to make out their positions by the heat of their bodies and the smell of their blood. Vampires' senses of hearing and smell were the highest amongst the creatures of Malum.

Klara took a gulp for courage, barely tasting the venom. The ale had watered it down significantly, which was surprising considering the smell that had emanated from the fae's spill earlier. If the vampire had served such a diluted drink in Malum, he wouldn't have lived to serve another night. She eyed the board again, feeling the snake of excitement and anger that came with betting in the room. They needed a direct bullseye to win.

If I win they could take it badly, she projected to Frendall. *They won't want to hang around after being defeated,* he reasoned.

Klara drew back her arm and tossed the dagger. Her bullseye knocked the faes' silver blades from the wall, and they landed on the stone floor with a clatter. There was a moment of silence as she waited for their response.

From the sudden cheers and laughter, the guard had been drinking for a long time. Frendall called for them to pay up, and she watched as they each dropped a silver coin into his pouch and left, one by one. Frendall was careful not to touch the coins, which would burn his skin on contact.

Klara glanced at the vampire, who winked in her direction, holding up a jug in celebration. Judging by the fae's staggers, he had clearly given them generous helpings of a potent venom, and if it had been from the selection of darkening green bottles behind the counter, he had opted for an aged one. The darker the colour, the stronger the venom. *Why would he help us?* She moved to the sticky counter.

"Well done—they'll go back to barracks with wounded egos," the vampire said, wiping the counter.

"And aching heads, from what I can smell."

"Only the good stuff for my high-paying customers." He smiled through his blackened lips and stained teeth.

"How is it that a vampire comes to own a tavern in the Capital of Kalos?" Klara leaned in closer, so the patrons wouldn't overhear her question.

"I don't think the Queen of Malum should be asking the intentions of others while she's hiding in their tavern."

"Fair enough," she said, not wanting him to declare who she was to the room—but this close, she could smell the blood on his breath. *How could he have got through the wall?*

"The wall dictates that I can't take the life of an innocent; you do not have to kill to drink from a creature's neck." The vampire's smooth, lyrical voice enchanted her, but that was their nature. A vampire could draw you in, and before you snapped out of the trance, you were dinner. Even if this one hadn't taken an innocent life, she was still wary of him.

"Your general is waiting for you," he whispered before they could talk further.

She looked up to see Frendall waiting at the top of the stairs to the open second floor. He met her eyes before disappearing into a corridor.

"I take it you won't be needing two rooms." The vampire smirked, and Klara glared, even if he couldn't see it.

"Your silence will be rewarded," she said stiffly, and the vampire laughed.

"I have already been compensated for my loyalty: you got me into Kalos."

Frendall may have been an unwelcome sight, but she was relieved that he had secured their lodgings and she hadn't had to give the leprechaun's name. She climbed the wooden stairs to the second floor and grimaced at the battered maroon carpet, stained with what—she didn't know. She put it out of her mind as she followed Frendall's scent to the last room down the hall. A key was in the door, and she twisted it.

"Son of a bitch. I can't believe you got away with that."

Frendall leaned back in his chair with a smile plastered across his face.

"Accurate but hurtful, and *we* got away with that," he said, tossing the full purse into the air. "For you," he added, and tossed it to her.

She caught it with ease, closing the door behind her in case they were overheard. Before talking further, she scanned the room for any listening charms, but she couldn't see the flicker of any glamours.

"The room is clean; I already checked it when I arrived," he told her.

She removed her cloak and tossed it onto the double bed. The crimson comforter reminded her of Abadan.

"What are you doing here? I told you to stay in Hell and wait for a message." *The potion bottle that brought me here smashed, so he couldn't have drunk it.*

"I thought you might need my help—and considering you walked into a tavern full of fae without a moment's hesitation, I think I was right," Frendall said.

"I didn't need your help. They wouldn't have noticed me if you hadn't called out to me."

"Agree to disagree. Nobody wouldn't notice you," he said with a wink.

She rolled her eyes. "Did Lokey make it to Malum?" she asked, wanting to make sure Lottie was taken care of.

"He left just after you did," he told her. "Right after he showed me which potion to drink." Klara began to pace. "Look, I tried to stay behind, but I couldn't think of you here without protection against so many."

"How did you find me? I didn't sense you amongst the crops."

"You ended up in the outskirts?" He frowned. "Interesting. The portal knocked me out, and I woke up in a Kalion cellar full of fermenting cabbage. The fae chased me out when they discovered me."

"And you happened to end up in the same tavern as me?" Klara folded her arms.

"When I left the cellar I was almost run over by a cart, and when it passed I sensed you in the back of it. So I followed. I overheard the leprechaun talking to you, but it took you longer to get here than I anticipated. I waited at the bar, thinking you wouldn't come at all, and then the fae made me a bet and I couldn't leave without raising suspicion. I was only minutes ahead of you; the fae had been drinking long before I joined them," he explained, resting his elbows on his knees.

"I was wandering around for a while, taking in the streets. I hadn't intended on taking the lep's advice of coming here, but then I caught the attention of a fae guard—didn't have much of a choice," she said, thinking again of the one-winged pixie.

"The vamp was happy to lend me a room once I gave him this." Frendall took his hand from his pocket, revealing gold coins.

"A creature with a pocket full of gold coins? You didn't think that would have set off some alarms with the guard?" Klara asked, wondering how he could be so careless.

"They didn't seem to mind so long as they had a chance of winning it." He smirked.

"When they expected to win, but you had me beat them!" she argued.

"What's done is done. The fae queen is expecting me to be at your side. If we're discovered, I can say I wanted to visit a lycaon who decided to cross over."

Klara considered it. It would make for a good excuse, considering that her scent seemed to give her away to some of the creatures like the leprechaun and the vampire.

She found it strange seeing Frendall without his general's uniform, his chest exposed in his loose shirt. She suppressed a smile as he undid his sword from his side.

"What?" He frowned, looking over himself.

"You look... relaxed. It's disturbing," Klara said as he moved in front of her.

"How do I usually look? Devilishly handsome?" he teased, running a hand through his loose hair.

"I was leaning towards uptight."

Frendall chuckled, exposing his dimples. Before he could kiss her, a knock on the door startled them. Frendall reached for his sword, but Klara sensed no danger. She opened the door a crack to find the vampire holding a tray out to her, and she took a step back before it hit her in the chest. The food on it called to her empty stomach.

"A high fae has arrived and will be here for the night. The queen is preparing for some grand event, so the fae guards will be busy preparing and their posts will be lax until shift change at dawn. I suggest you take this opportunity to do whatever it is you came to do."

"Thank you for informing me," Klara said, and Frendall tossed him a gold coin, which she was surprised he caught while balancing the full tray on the other hand.

"One small issue. The high fae that arrived has brought some of the guard, and I suspect it's because of the earlier display caused by that tall drink of venom of

173

yours," the vampire said, eying Frendall as though he was something to snack on. "It was enough that he nearly scared my kitchen maid to death—not that she can die twice—when he sneaked in the back; now he's agitated my patrons, and high fae don't take lightly to other fae being shown up by a creature."

"I apologise for any inconvenience caused. We don't wish to cause trouble between the fae and yourself," Klara said, taking the tray, while Frendall muttered about poor losers under his breath.

"Not many lycaons pass through my tavern, and the scent of his is something special. However entertaining it was to hear the fae panic at the prospect of being defeated by a creature of Malum, it was a risk. The high fae has requested a meeting with the creature who beat members of his guard," the vamp said.

A knot formed in Klara's stomach. *If they knew he was a general, they would really want to put him in his place. So much for laying low.*

"I'm sure you will be discreet about our remaining here—perhaps mention that we have already departed?" Klara suggested as the vampire smelt the air above her.

"Discretion is my middle name, but I cannot lie to a high fae, or I could be punished—and as much as I care for Your Majesty, I won't risk being tossed back into Elder Langda's settlement."

Klara glared at Frendall, who shrugged indifferently.

"I never asked your name," she said, hoping charm would win him over, but he didn't take the bait.

"Should you be tortured, I'd prefer you not to know. I would, however, recommend you depart before they realise you are still here and risk being sought after; or you can appease them and hope your secret isn't discovered," he advised.

He was right in saying they might be chased if they failed to meet the high fae.

"We'll talk it over, but I can assure you there won't be any trouble," Klara insisted, placing the tray on the table beneath a heavily curtained window.

"I don't think it will be you who decides that," the vampire replied, closing the door on them.

Klara's heart raced. *Would he out us to the high fae?*

"Something's off about that vampire. How could he have possibly caught my scent through the smells of the tavern?" Frendall said, leaning against the bed base.

Klara had sensed no ill intent in the creature. Anyone could be bought, but she'd spotted no concealing glamour; he'd had no fear in showing her his true self. An enemy wouldn't have risked it.

"He's blind."

"So his sense of smell is heightened? I get it," Frendall said, propping his sword against the desk.

"Or maybe he liked what he was smelling?" Klara suppressed a smile as he grimaced.

A multitude of fresh vegetables and seafood decorated the tray. She checked the food for poison but found no stain or scent of magic. Frendall reached for seaweed-wrapped rice and popped it into his mouth.

"I wasn't finished checking," Klara snapped, and he took another piece.

"Better my life than yours, Your Majesty."

She hated how little respect he had for his own life.

"We only have until dawn tomorrow before we are expected at the palace," she said, changing the subject and grateful that time ran slower in Kalos than it did in Hell.

She watched the sun dissipate, leaving behind an orange and pink sky. The night never truly came to Kalos.

The fae queen hated the darkness; that was why she had cut off Malum like a diseased limb. One of the reasons, anyway.

Klara ate as much as she could and climbed out the window to the small balcony outside, watching street lamps be lit as the sky barely greyed. *This is the dead of night,* she thought, wondering how the Kalions and creatures got any sleep. She regretted having wasted so much time already.

"You haven't slept, and the potion that brought you here will have weakened you," Frendall said, sitting on the window ledge.

"I can sleep once we reach the palace. We don't have much time, and I doubt the vamp will distract the high fae beneath us for long. Plus I can't sleep, knowing they could discover who we are at any moment."

"Then let's go. We can make a run for it, or see what this almighty high fae is made of; what's it going to be?" Frendall asked, heading for the door.

"We can't go through the tavern! There'll be too many eyes on us, and we don't need to be followed," Klara warned.

"We can't sneak out the back either—there might be fae blocking it. What about a cloaking spell?" Frendall asked.

"I would have to use too much fae magic. The high fae might sense it," Klara explained, climbing back inside the small room.

"Why is it that whenever you need to use your magic, you can't?" Frendall sighed, scratching the back of his head.

"I don't make the rules. Fae magic is tied into my born gifts; one exposes the other."

Frendall paused, then opened the door with a wicked grin that meant nothing good.

"I have a better idea."

He disappeared down the corridor, and Klara grabbed her cloak from the bed before chasing after him.

16

"How could you leave me here waiting for you?" Frendall roared, and Klara stilled in shock as the guests below looked up towards the balcony on the second floor.

"While you were with a warlock, I was here waiting for you like a fool!" he shouted, pointing an accusing finger at her.

Klara was too frozen to speak, and wished she could bind his lips together as the busy tavern became deeply engrossed in their exchange. *Hide in plain sight,* Frendall projected with a wink.

She glared at him. She would have picked any other route but this.

"I have needs," she shouted back, playing to the prejudice against the creatures. Fae would believe in the disloyalty of the creatures. *I hate myself,* she projected back.

"Needs? If I don't satisfy you, then why am I even here? I left everything behind for you!" Frendall marched down the steps, and Klara swallowed as he stood, arms raised, beside a table of fae. She recognised a few of them from earlier; he was playing up their earlier story.

"Don't blame this on me. *You* were the one that thought we would have an easy life here, but I'm still the same witch. I can't help that I'm part fae!" Klara followed him down the stairs. The tavern was lit up with more lamps now that night had fallen, and the heat only added to her anxiety.

"A witch! Please. This was just some fae trick. Your potions don't even sell. I can't call you a witch, but I would call you something that rhymes with it," Frendall yelled as he passed a guard, who seemed to be enjoying the exchange far too much to think about who they were.

Klara eyed the vampire behind the bar, waiting to be thrown out, and thankfully he took the hint.

"Both of you out. I won't have you upsetting my guests," he ordered, and Frendall reared up.

"I paid good coin! I can damn well stay where I like!" he argued from the bottom of the stairs.

One of the fae guards stood, her sapphire jacket undone after a long day's work. "I'm afraid all taverns in Kalos have the right to deny service, and if you continue to demonstrate such irrational behaviour, I will toss you back over to your side of the wall."

Klara noticed the fae's hand settle on her tranquilliser and knew she meant it. The weapon wasn't what worried her; it was the silver thread that ran through her jacket. *A Palace guard. They might report this to the queen, and one description would out us.*

"See what you've done," she snapped to Frendall. Pretending to well up, she hid her face in her hands as she turned her back to the guard, peering through her fingers.

"What's all this about?" a voice said. Frendall's eyes went to hers in warning, and she knew it was the high fae.

"Nothing that concerns you," Frendall said, but Klara felt the high fae at her back, towering over her. Familiar energy ran down her spine, and she knew exactly who it was.

"You have disturbed the peace and my guard; I think that concerns me."

Jasper. Klara shook her head slightly, telling Frendall to remain calm.

"Are you alright?" Jasper asked her. "No one deserves to be spoken to in such a way, not on this side of the wall."

Klara nodded, afraid her voice would give her away.

"I would suggest you treat your companion with a little more respect," Jasper said to Frendall. It suddenly dawned on Klara that he should recognise Frendall, yet he hadn't said anything to call them out. Yet. *Frendall might not look entirely like his general self, but I doubt it will be enough to throw off a high fae.*

"We didn't mean to disturb your evening," Klara said, walking to Frendall. "We can solve this in private," she said to Frendall, who frowned in confusion. Klara was careful not to stand directly in front of Jasper, as she felt his eyes studying her. Frendall looked between them, and Klara sensed he suspected something else was going on.

"Let's hope we don't run into each other again," Jasper threatened, but Klara felt the words weren't directed at her but Frendall.

Maybe he doesn't recognise Frendall… or he is toying with us?

I don't know which is worse, she thought to herself. *I threw him out of the castle, and now he's throwing me out of a tavern.*

"As if I want to stay in this filthy place. I've seen better taverns in Malum," she drawled, provoking the vampire to break the escalating tension.

"Out! Both of you!" he said, a long, pale arm extended from his black cloak and pointed to the door. Frendall pushed through some observing patrons, spilling some drinks along the way, and swung open the door.

"We won't stay where we aren't wanted," Klara retorted and pushed Frendall out, leaving Jasper behind.

They both felt a rush of energy as the iron-lined tavern released its grip on them. Out in the air, she could finally breathe. *Why didn't he reveal our secret? Did he truly not recognise my energy or Frendall?* The question gnawed at her, but it wasn't as though she could walk back in and ask.

Frendall rolled his neck. "Much better. That iron was like having a weight on my shoulders."

"The iron lining would greatly reduce in fighting back in Malum; Glaudine could use it at Tapped or the Beanstalk's new dining hall," Klara mused, wondering why she hadn't thought of it before. She was surprised to see that all the stalls with clothes, spell jars and trinkets had been left behind as the creatures and fae turned in. That level of trust disturbed her.

Frendall grunted in response. "I thought you wanted freedom for the creatures," he said as he pulled a cloak from a stall.

"Stealing? Really?" Klara scolded, not wanting to draw any more attention to themselves.

"Told you I don't belong on this side of the wall." Frendall winked, wrapping the cloak around his shoulders.

"And if it's protected by a spell?"

"Are you going to fight with me about everything while I'm here?" he muttered.

She didn't dignify that with a response.

"I don't think the creatures would take kindly to you weakening them with iron," he went on, "good intentions or not."

"Fair point, but it would make life easier." She sighed. Just because something was easier didn't make it the right path. "Let's get off the main road; we'll attract too many eyes." Klara turned down an alley devoid of lanterns. She wanted to get as far away as possible from Jasper and his guard.

"Who was that back there? The way he was looking at you, it seemed like he was studying you, trying to get into your head," Frendall said.

Klara ignored him as she walked.

"You didn't answer my question," Frendall pressed.

"His name is Jasper," she said at last, moving into the shadows and stopping. "He snuck into the last gathering glamoured as you. It was a dirty trick, nothing more."

Frendall's pupils expanded with a rage Klara didn't need to touch to feel. "He *mimicked* me? Did he touch you—try to get close to you? Tell me what he did!" He didn't give her a chance to respond. "I swear I'll go back there and rip his throat out!"

"Are you jealous?" she teased, closing the gap between them.

"Of course I'm jealous, but if he touched you without your permission and you thought it was me, that's not something I can ignore!" He sounded more concerned than angry, and it melted her heart. He wasn't just jealous; he cared that she was safe.

"I threw him out. I knew it wasn't you. I didn't tell you because it was inconsequential; he was just trying to get under my skin," she said calmly, resting her hands against his chest.

"I'd say that wasn't the only thing he was trying to get under," Frendall muttered, placing his hands over hers. Klara blushed in spite of herself. "That's one of the reasons why you're here? You think your mother sent him to humiliate you in front of the gathering?"

"I don't have proof, but too many things happened at once to be ignored. I had to come and figure it out..." Klara broke away as a hum in the air demanded her attention. Her skin prickled as she sensed discord, and her feet moved without permission, pulling her towards it.

"Where are you going?" Frendall asked, following.

"Something is calling me," Klara said.

"What?"

"Fear."

She stopped at the edge of an alleyway to see two witches trading spell jars. There was no one else on the street, and she considered that it might have been their fear of discovery she had sensed. But it was thick, and coming from multiple sources. Klara watched as they chewed whatever was in their jars.

"Witches trading? Hardly something to spike your interest," Frendall pointed out.

"It's not just them."

As soon as the words left her lips, the two witches disappeared through the alley wall into a small cottage.

"Not something you see every day—especially when there's a perfectly good door to use," he said, and Klara dashed to where the witches had stood. She ran her hand over the bricks to find they were damp. She felt the spell laid over them straining to hold its place.

"They clearly don't want anyone knowing what's happening in there. They've cast a silencing and no entrance spell, but it's barely holding. There must be a lot of creatures within," she told Frendall.

"Can you get through it?" he asked, his hand resting on his sword hilt. They didn't know what they were looking into yet.

"It would be easier to drop the glamour, but it shouldn't be too hard to peel back—but I have to be quick or the witch who cast it will sense my magic," she said. "I need you to watch the alley while I do this. I can look inside without them knowing I'm there, but I can't break focus, so I need you to stop anyone from approaching."

"Understood," he said, now that's the general she knew. He went to the edge of the alley and kept watch, his hand still on his sword, ready to protect her.

All thoughts of Jasper only one street over disappeared as she neared her first real clue. *Like peeling an orange skin,* she told herself. The bricks blurred under the weight of her revealing magic. The magic enveloping the cottage was relieved to ease even the slightest hold as she looked through the glamour. She was careful to leave some concealing properties so she wouldn't reveal those inside the cottage to anyone other than herself. They wouldn't be able to see her; she had merely made a window that she could peer into.

The crowded room was lit by a small hearth, and Klara spotted the two witches in the corner looking distressed. Her head began to ache as so many creatures argued back and forth that she couldn't make out what the issue was. *It has to be important for creatures of all shapes and sizes to gather in one place, especially with the fae guard only one street over.* She was grateful when an ancient warlock at the head of the room called for silence. Arthur had been elderly, but this creature looked like it was made of chalk.

Their skin was powdery, and the white beard stretched to the floor beneath a veined bald head—*No wonder the spell is straining.*

"One at a time, or we won't get to everyone," the warlock said, clearly the head of the meeting.

"We need to do something. My son was taken by the patrol last week, her mother this week in a night raid," a leprechaun began, motioning to the distraught elf in the corner of the room. "The streets are empty after the sky changes because we're all too afraid of being taken!"

Klara was surprised to see an elf on this side of the wall; the Elven Coast was one of the richest and safest places in Malum.

"We thought maiming ourselves would help, but it obviously isn't making a difference. The patrols are sensing the power of our magic, and all we do is make ourselves appear physically weak while our magic still runs strong. The fae queen and her patrol are going to catch on soon enough," a giant said, hunched in the corner.

Maim themselves? They loathe Malum so much they would rather disfigure themselves than return? Klara's heart felt like it tore in two as she noticed the giant was missing all their fingers.

"We are guests in this land; we earn our keep," the warlock said, and the crowd quietened.

The warlock would have been an elder by their age; maybe they came here before the first treaty. If the warlock is loyal to the fae queen, why are they leading a crowd of creatures?

"Once the fae queen has taken what she needs, they will be returned and no more will be taken," the warlock went on.

Klara wanted to tell them all not to listen, to defend themselves, but she couldn't without revealing herself.

"No one has ever returned in their senses or alive," a pixie said.

By the hearth, Klara recognised the leprechaun and his missus from the cart upon her arrival. No wonder Warloth's companion hadn't wanted her around; they had issues of their own to deal with, and angering the fae queen wouldn't help them. Klara tried to remain in control of her temper at this proof that her mother hadn't kept her word, but she still didn't understand why the creatures didn't leave. *If they had returned and told me about this, I could have intervened or negotiated.* She felt so blind.

"If you are truly dissatisfied, the wall will allow you back into Malum." The warlock took a seat, resting their hands on their lap.

"Provided we pay a fee. You're meant to be our envoy to the queen, and yet you do nothing to help us," the giant huffed.

The warlock rubbed their forehead. Klara noticed the crafted wood that took the place of their legs.

"Have conditions not improved for us in Kalos since the young heir took the throne? They will only continue to improve. I have been here many decades, since the divide of Malum and Kalos. I know that all things change with time, if we only have patience."

"There might be none of us left by the time that change comes," the giant said sadly.

Klara froze as the warlock's eyes found hers.

You are a long way from home, young queen. The warlock's voice echoed in her mind.

She wanted to close the window she had opened, but she needed to know the creature's reply. *If you want my help, then you will say nothing,* she said to the warlock, who tipped their head slightly in response.

"Yes, and Klara's reign only feeds more of us to

Aemella. The more the young queen challenges the fae queen, the more of us disappear, and who's to say the heir—to Hell, need I remind you—isn't in on it? She was raised by the three queens who drove us here, for that matter," the pixie argued. Klara recognised her from the market with her one remaining wing. *I'm glad she didn't know who I was, or that fae would have dragged me to the Palace by now.*

She didn't need to hear more of how poorly they thought of her and her rule. The warlock offered her a weak smile, and Klara dropped her hands. The window sealed and bricks barred the way in front of her. All she could hear was the faint hum of the warlock's glamour. *I have failed them.* Klara stared at the bricks and ran her hands through her hair, trying to get to grips with all that she had learnt.

Frendall returned to her side, clearly eager to know what had transpired.

"All Aemella had to do was let the creatures in if they passed the protections. Why does she insist on provoking me into action? Does she want a war? Because the creatures will rise against me if I can't protect them," Klara said, frightfully calm.

"I don't understand. What did you see?"

"She's harming the creatures, or at the very least taking them—for Lucifer knows what," Klara told him, trying to slow her racing heart.

"How? Why?" he said, taking her arms before she mindlessly walked out of the alley.

"I don't know, but she's taking them somewhere. I couldn't hear where, but I sure as Hell am going to find out."

Klara didn't want to get mad. She wanted to get even.

17

"**W**atch out," Frendall exclaimed, yanking Klara back into the alleyway as a barred cart clattered down the street. "That would have done some damage," he panted.

She barely even noticed that she had almost been run over.

"That can't be what I think it is," she breathed, afraid to look as she heard the distinctive sound of metal shackles. She peered around the corner to see a fae patrol driving a horse-drawn cart. In it, several creatures were caged together and shackled, silver chains around their neck, connecting one to another. Silver was toxic to most of the creatures in Malum; it was too pure and would prevent them from being able to defend themselves.

Klara noticed the light from window shutters slightly ajar in the homes looking over the street. Those safe from the patrol watched the cart move along, and she felt their dread. The creatures within the caged cart were clearly terrified, yet the others watched from the comfort of their homes and did nothing to stop it. A rage coiled in her stomach, watching them fail to intervene. Then again, fear could paralyse as much as any spell. She knew that from personal experience.

"We should wait for them to move on," Frendall whispered, his body pressed against hers in the small alley.

Klara watched as two fae flanked the sides and back of the cage, yet she noticed there was no door to seal the cage. She eyed the chains binding the creatures. If one tried to escape, they would have to bring the others, and from the varying ages and sizes of the creatures any attempt at freedom was sure to fail. She wondered if they had left the cage open just to taunt the captives.

"We follow them. They'll lead us to where they're being held," Klara said. Elation suppressed her rage; her paranoia had been confirmed.

"And if we get caught?" Frendall asked.

"This is the reason I came here. I'm not going to ease up now that I have a solid lead."

Aemella was imprisoning creatures, whether or not they deserved it, and she had to figure out why the fae queen needed their magic.

The cart trudged past, and she felt the fae moving closer to where they hid. She grabbed Frendall and pulled him close, putting his back to the patrol, her arms visible around his neck. All the fae who passed would see what was a lover's embrace and not their faces.

"I don't think now is the time." Frendall raised his eyebrows with a grin as she loosened her grip on him, and she gave him a playful whack on the arm before turning to follow the patrol.

They left the city of Kalos, sticking to the shadows until they reached the edge of the capital. The buildings and market were replaced with a vast wood, and at its centre, far in the distance was the fae queen's palace. Only the highest of the palace's three towers stood out.

At least in Malum, everyone knows they're in danger; here it creeps up on the creatures and steals them in the night. The thought made Klara ill. She had assured the creatures who had chosen to leave that they would be safe in Kalos, provided they followed the rules. Instead, who knew what she had sent them into?

"Don't overthink this; they may have committed a crime," Frendall cautioned her as leaves crunched underfoot. They were careful to keep their distance from the patrol—they didn't follow the road but hid amongst the trees, just far enough away so they wouldn't be detected.

"How can I not? I was a fool to believe my mother would treat the creatures with even an ounce of respect."

"They made the decision to leave Malum. What happens on this side of the Neutral Lands has nothing to do with you."

"If they wanted to be maimed and chained, they could have stayed in Malum and at least been given a fighting chance. Instead, my mother hides behind her disguises and glamours."

"We don't know anything yet."

The woods darkened as the branches overhead gathered together. A faint chill in the air reminded Klara of being in the thick of the Forest of Malum, but she soon saw something that would never occur there. She walked ahead, not caring about the patrol, to a tree with silver coursing through its bark. She glanced back to tell Frendall to watch how close he got, but he was already one step ahead.

"What in Lucifer's name is this?" he said, kneeling. He picked up a single silver leaf from amongst the yellow and orange leaves on the wood floor, then hissed and dropped it as it seared his fingers. Silver burned the skin of lycaons and vampires; it stripped them of their power, and if they were exposed to it long enough it would kill them.

"Don't see pure silver leaves every day," Frendall commented, looking up at the branches above them.

Klara eyed the way they had come and saw no trace of silver. But when they went on another silver tree appeared, then another, until they were surrounded by glistening trees. The moonlight reflected off the leaves and brightened the woods as Kalos drifted into its rare hour of darkness.

"Aemella created a silver wood to protect herself, or maybe her palace." Klara smirked to herself. *And I thought my father was paranoid.* Frendall chuckled as she allowed him to hear the thought. "Careful where you stand."

"Probably not the best place for a lycaon-demon to be..." He frowned.

"That's exactly why she created this. Who would dare to risk it?"

The trees weren't densely packed, so he didn't have to get too close to them, but she could see the strain in his eyes as they were surrounded. The silver would still have some draining effect as his body sensed a threat. Klara placed her hand on the ground, grateful to see the dirt was still dirt. Aemella might be able to feel her magic, but not her location. Sometimes magical loopholes played in her favour.

She let her mind sink into the soil and flow with the tree roots until she saw the silver and white palace in the centre of a great garden that rivalled her father's. A small moat flowed around the building, and Klara guessed that was what fed the waterfall in her mother's throne room. She could only see as close as the roots travelled to the palace; it was heavily protected at every entrance by palace guards.

"We're losing the patrol," Frendall said, watching for the fae.

"Looks like we won't be sneaking in as I planned. She has every entrance guarded." Klara was about to lift her hand when she noticed a haze to the west of the wood. Beams reflected off the mist, revealing the skin of a glamour to the far west of the palace.

What would Aemella need to hide this far into the wood? She already has the silver to protect her. However, she soon realised the glamour didn't actually encase the palace; it flowed in the opposite direction.

"I think I know where they're headed," she said, internally cursing the fact that she couldn't see through the glamour. A creature's glamour could be peeled back with ease, but a fae couldn't see through another fae's glamour unless they had permission. Since they shared the same blood, Klara would be able to get through the glamour, but Aemella would then be able to sense her and track her to where she stood.

Magic always came with a price. It might grant you entrance, but it told your enemy exactly where you stood.

Klara rose, wiping her hands on her trousers.

"She's altered the wood to protect the palace from the creatures."

Frendall sighed. "Makes sense; she despises them above all else."

"There's an area to the north-west that's protected by her own glamour. She must have known I would come, or at least didn't want to risk me discovering it by accident."

"Are you sure it's her glamour? It could be another high fae protecting their land."

"Maybe. I can't see through it without touching it up close, but it will mean risking our exposure," she said.

He dragged a hand through his hair in frustration, then suddenly snapped his head towards the trees. "Do you smell that—?" he began, only to be cut off.

"Stop where you are!"

The muffled shout in the distance startled Frendall. He had been focusing so hard on trying to hear who was approaching that Klara guessed the shout overwhelmed his senses. His hands went over his ears, and she pulled him aside to stop him crashing into the tree closest to him.

"I was too distracted to keep track of anyone else patrolling in the wood," she said, cursing herself for not protecting them.

"I can hear multiple pairs of boots. A patrol, but the fae won't be able to see us clearly through the trees. That'll buy us some time," Frendall said through gritted teeth.

"The patrol must have had a secondary protection following behind them; when we stopped, those in the rear closed the gap." Klara knew that if she fought, her mother would definitely know she was up to something—and Frendall hardly blended in with the other creatures.

"We should make a run for it. Fighting would break the treaty, and you would lose your head," Frendall said, hand on his sword as the fae guard approached. Their sapphire uniforms came into view as they stalked them.

Klara made a split-second decision. "Bear with me, this is going to sting," she warned, placing her hands on his neck. If my mother can alter someone's appearance, so can I.

"What are you doing?" he groaned as his eyes flared amber and his hair turned ashen blond.

Klara didn't answer, forcing Wolfgang's face to appear over his own. She felt his general scar burn as the symbol of his status slipped under his skin. Wolfgang was shorter than Frendall, though only by a fraction, and stockier. Her hands burned too as the magic rapidly flowed from her to him.

"Not again," Frendall grumbled. He patted himself down with a curse, feeling his new body.

"We don't have any other choice. I won't run," Klara said, stripping her hair to white and replacing her clothes with those of a fae guard. She lightened her olive skin and straightened her uniform's collar. Her magic clawed at her; it wanted to reveal who they really were. She tried to suppress her natural urges, but it was as though ants were trying to chew through her skin. She had never held an altering glamour for two at the same time, and now she knew why. Her heart raced at the strain.

"Can you hold it?" Frendall asked anxiously.

She pushed down the discomfort, reaching to grip Frendall's sword. It slipped from sight: the fae wouldn't be able to see or touch it, but he would still be protected. Then she let her axe warp into the fae spear. A three-headed axe would definitely give them away.

"Just try not to shift, or I won't be able to hold it," she whispered to him as the sound of boots slowed. "Stand down," she shouted, holding up her hands. "I got separated from the transport. This lycaon tried to escape."

The fae guards came out from the trees' protection; had they arrived a second sooner, they would have been discovered. Klara waited for them to spot a missing detail, a button in the wrong place or the scent of her magic. The fae at the front of the patrol stepped closer. She noticed that these weren't the guards from the cart, so they had to be back-up.

"The creature made it this far from the trail? Why did you not have back-up?" the guard, who appeared to be the youngest, asked, spear still in hand. *There isn't a scar or mark on him... not much of a threat.*

Klara hesitated. *I'm a fae—I can't lie, right? They have no reason not to trust me.*

"In the Silver Wood, how hard would it be to catch him? We found him on the way. I was just getting the chain on him when he bolted," Klara said.

The mention of the chains seemed to relax some of the young guards, but she needed to seal the deal. The patrol smirked as she planted a knee in Frendall's back.

"Easy," he growled. "I'm not going anywhere."

"Shut it," the guard told him as the rest of the patrol put away their weapons. "We'll help you to the factory," he added to Klara. "Where's the chain?"

"I lost it in the chase," she lied, hoping he would buy the weak excuse. *The factory? They're taking creatures to a factory?*

"There should be enough of us to handle one lycaon," a fae with bright blue hair that matched her uniform joked, and the others mumbled in agreement, their spears at hand. "But it's a good thing I always keep a spare," Blue continued, pulling a long, silver chain from a utility belt pouch. Frendall snarled as the fae wrapped the thin but deadly chain around his neck and clasped it.

"I haven't seen you in transport before," the tallest fae commented, moving through the others as Klara got Frendall to his feet. The silver chain was already blistering his skin, and she had to suppress the urge to take the end of it from Blue's hand.

She noted the silver-winged brooch on the tall fae's uniform. She didn't know what that meant in terms of rank, but from the way the others looked at him, he was their leader.

"I take my orders directly from Queen Aemella. I only hunt those she seeks personally," Klara told him.

"And yet you don't wear silver in your uniform?" he said, raising a quizzical brow.

Klara thought frantically. "I don't protect the palace—only the queen's interests."

She saw the young fae behind their leader whisper amongst themselves. *Aemella must be recruiting them young to keep up with the incoming creatures.* A fae's appearance didn't dictate their age, but their mannerisms did. She couldn't risk them not trusting her.

"Still, how are we to know she sent you and that you didn't free this creature?" he pressed, tilting his head.

"I cannot lie. Is that not proof enough? I'm to bring him to the queen." Klara shrugged.

The others circled Frendall, who was smart enough to keep his head bowed.

"And yet he was with the others? Is he to be processed before going to the queen?" the lead fae asked.

Processed? I need to see where they're taking the creatures, and if I say no, we'll end up in the Palace. But if I say yes, who knows what will be done to him? Can I even hold our glamours for that long?

"Yes," she said, and almost heard Frendall groan. "I can hardly bring him to the palace like this."

"Why him?" the fae asked.

She sensed his doubt, but he knew that his reward would be great if there was merit to her story. "He's nothing but a lycaon, but Queen Aemella is interested in their skills, considering the young queen across the River Styx keeps some in her personal guard. The rest is need-to-know." Klara told him, adding weight to her story. She got closer to the fae, encouraging them to believe she was letting them in on an important secret. "It's important she doesn't find out that he escaped. I'll mention those who helped me acquire him. I'm sure the queen will be generous in her thanks."

The fae's eyes glistened at the thoughts of promotion and reward. "It would be our pleasure to escort you."

"After you," Klara said. She didn't have a damn clue which way the trail was, and nor the magic to spare to find it.

The patrol moved off, and she followed without hesitation.

"Move it," Klara barked, grabbing the back of Frendall's neck. If she shoved him, Blue might not pull on the chain too hard.

Try not to enjoy this too much, he projected.

I can't make any promises, she replied. At least we don't have to worry about getting through my mother's protection. They'll walk us right through, and their presence should help mask me from her sight.

The leader locked eyes with Klara, and she shoved Frendall ahead. "Keep moving, lycaon." Her jaw clenched as she nearly sent him into a silver tree, but the fae turned back around as they kept to the back of the group.

It wasn't long before a trail of silver cobblestones divided the trees. The purity of the silver was sure to drain Frendall further, so Klara tried to pick up the pace without drawing too much attention.

"I'm surprised he was able to break from the chain," the fae leader said casually, but Klara knew it was a question.

"His father was an alpha, so that gave him an advantage. I underestimated his strength."

"Her Majesty is busy arranging a gathering in her daughter's name. I don't think she'll be seeing him anytime soon, so it will be factory work in the meantime. That will break his spirit before he stands before her." The fae turned to Frendall. "I'm sure you're used to hard work." He grabbed Frendall's sleeves and ripped the fabric, exposing the lash marks on his forearms that had adorned Wolfgang's body.

He's trying to confirm our story. A real lycaon who grew up on the territories wouldn't be without these marks.

"Heard the old queen, Abadan, liked to lash the mutts on the other side of the river. What a painful experience for those so young." There wasn't a hint of concern in the fae's voice.

"Like you're any better," Klara muttered before she could stop herself.

"Did you say something?" the leader snapped.

The other fae watched warily, and she noticed their hands were dangerously close to their weapons. She regretted her instinct to protect Frendall.

"Don't misunderstand. I meant, why should we treat this filthy mutt any better than she did?"

"Hmm... fair point," the leader said, and Klara relaxed as their hands drifted away from their spears.

"Are you invited to the gathering?" she asked, wondering if they would run into each other again. His pointed ears flicked a little, and there was a faint rumble of laughter amongst the group.

"We are kept rather busy. The queen's gathering is a good excuse for the high fae who wouldn't dare risk muddying their finery and jewels," the leader said, sounding bitter.

Aemella doesn't allow her guards to attend events? Surely that must breed some discord. But as she looked around the group, she found they seemed to have nothing but admiration for their queen. To be loved so much was a foreign concept to Klara. *What a great height to fall from,* she thought.

"Is the queen expecting you for the ball, if you're her private hunter?" Blue asked, yanking the chain around Frendall's neck. He almost lost his footing as he caught it on a cobblestone, then peered back over his shoulders. His pace had slowed as the silver drained his energy.

Klara struggled to keep her expression neutral, but did her best to focus on the question. "I wouldn't think so. All I was told was to report back to the castle when I found the lycaon."

"How could someone in the queen's inner court not know about her daughter's visit?" Blue asked, regaining Klara's attention.

Can't I catch a break? "I've been hunting down the creature for days; I've been too busy to listen in on palace gossip."

She sensed an emptiness in the path up ahead; the vibrations of the silver wood became muted, as if the realm simply cut off. However, the fae didn't seem to take any notice. They continued their steady pace until Klara caught the faint shimmer telling her they were on the outskirts of the glamour she had detected.

"The first part of our patrol passed through already, but we should be able to process him with the group," the leader said, as he waited for Klara and Frendall to pass through after the patrol. "After you."

The leader's distrust crept through Klara's muscles. Not wanting to leave any doubt in his mind, she quickly grabbed Frendall's arm and shoved them through the skin of the glamour as it opened for the advancing patrol.

The blood she shared with Lucifer sizzled in her veins as the glamour tested her, but she pushed through, desperate for her mother's protections to accept her. For the first time, she prayed she had enough fae blood flowing through her veins.

The protections awoke that blood, as evident by the cool wash that erased the burning as she passed the test. *Praise Lucifer! Our glamour didn't drop*, she projected to Frendall as the fae joined them with bright white smiles. *Two tests passed in one go*. She tried to suppress a triumphant grin, which vanished when she saw how pale Frendall had grown. *Now I just have to make sure we get out of here alive*.

She had been too busy ensuring their concealing glamour had held to notice what was happening around them. The other fae who had travelled with them scattered and went about their duties, and it took Klara a moment to notice the dozens of fae guards who covered their noses and mouths with thick strips of navy cloth as they roamed the smog-riddled land. The silver wood had been cut down, leaving no trace except for the few blackened tree stubs that broke through the hard-pressed soil. The ground was marked by hundreds of footprints, bare and booted, from the many creatures that had been brought here against their will.

Klara's senses were too overwhelmed to focus on one thing, but the hum of sheer terror slowly stroked its way to the forefront of her mind. She felt sweat coating her palms as her magic screamed danger.

This can't be real. The factories were destroyed. They don't exist...

18

A factory towered before them.

It was made of red brick, with three stone chimneys continuously pumping out a steady stream of black smoke responsible for the choking smog that surrounded them. Klara could have sworn she was back in the darkness of the Queen's Mountain in Malum.

The thick, smoky air coated her lungs as she tried to breathe, and the pungent, rancid smell of sacrificial magic threatened to strangle her. *A Gingerbread Factory.* Klara's blood drained from her extremities.

High Queen Abadan had used the Gingerbread Factories when she began her rule over Malum. She would take the children of the creatures who were against her rule of the Forest, or who didn't pay their taxes, then drain her victims of their magic to add to her own strength. After that she would kill them, or leave them with just enough magic to make it home, only to spread stories of the horrifying details of the inner workings of the factories. The name itself had been concocted so the children wouldn't be so afraid and would be easier to lure away from their homes. The creatures had quickly fallen in line.

When Lucifer had seen how Abadan's strength was growing—and since she only ruled Malum as proxy for him—he'd outlawed the use of the factories, though not before hundreds were lost to Abadan's thirst for power. Klara had only seen their haunting depiction in books or the mural on the wall of the Beanstalk Dining Hall; seeing one in the flesh froze her to the spot. *Why would Aemella go to such lengths? How is she able to do this without losing her light? The creatures are innocents.*

Before she had a chance to gather her thoughts, two fae with silver chest plates were leading Frendall away towards a group of shivering creatures, though it wasn't cold. The heat emanating from the factory rivalled that of the grand fireplaces in her father's throne room.

"We will keep him with those picked up, make sure there is no discrepancy in the final count of those collected," the fae leader assured her.

Klara struggled to find the words to speak as she watched Frendall go. His back was to her, so she couldn't see his expression.

"You have a list of those who passed through?" she asked at last, unable to peel her eyes from the monstrous factory.

He laughed, clapping her on the back. "What, you think we run a half-arsed operation? How else would we keep track of those in Kalos?"

If he has a list, then I can see if the witch's twin, Frieda, is here. It makes sense now why she hasn't been heard from, and it's no wonder the pendant dimmed—it was trying to get past the fae queen's own protection and glamour!

The enslaved creatures began to move in the corner of her eye. Frendall was attached to the end of the line, silver chains wrapped around his neck and wrists. They marched to a cluster of large cottages positioned not far from the factory. *Looks like housing… might be where they take them before they're brought into the factory.*

"I have strict orders to keep him within my sight at all times," Klara told the fae.

"It's ok; you don't need to keep an eye on him yourself. If we can see him, the queen can see him. Our eyes are hers," the fae said as he was handed a scroll from another fae. From his expression, it contained new orders.

"Our eyes are hers," the deliverer replied, and bowed before heading back towards the decrepit cottages.

"Still, he is not to be harmed. Or we will suffer the consequences," Klara insisted. I forgot some of the lesser fae share Aemella's eyes. Effective for routing out treachery but still creepy, she thought as the leader closed the scroll. Lucifer had used the same trick by replacing Arthur's eyes with replicas of his own, so that he could keep an eye on Klara while she was under the Three Queens' protection.

"How important can one lycaon be? At the rate they breed, we could bring the queen a dozen, and how is she to know the difference?" He laughed at the idea.

Klara ignored him. She kept going back to the same question. *Why would Aemella go to all this trouble to contain the creatures and to resurrect a factory of Abadan's making?* As sacrificial magic lingered in the air, a sinking feeling settled in her gut.

"How about we grab some venom? I'm sure chasing down that mutt has you all sorts of tired," the leader said, and she could sense his ease. *How can he feel so content surrounded by such horror?* It scared her more than peering into the vampires' nest when they hadn't fed in a moon.

Klara froze as he wrapped his arm around her shoulder. She'd forgotten others had no reason to fear her in this state. Frendall and Lottie had helped her get used to being touched, but she was still uncomfortable with strangers getting close.

"I should make sure he's processed correctly," she said, trying to get away from him.

"Don't worry; for now, they'll just get him all chained up and cosy—the next draining doesn't begin for a while. We have to let the creatures rest a while or the magic doesn't flow as well," he assured her.

"Very well, but my payment relies on his delivery, so if something happens to him you owe me," she lied. She was disgusted at the very thought of creatures being drained of their magic, but she had to grin and bear it if she was to get out in one piece with Frendall. The further he strayed from her, the greater the strain she felt on her magic, like a grip tightening on the back of her neck as she kept both their secrets safe.

"My humble abode is around the corner. I'm sure the queen's private hunter is used to finer things and not the standard mess hall. We can drink in peace and let the others do the work," the fae said, undoing the top button of his collar. The prospect of being alone with him made her nervous, though it would be easier to take out one fae than the horde she was sure to find in a mess hall.

"An offer I can hardly refuse," she replied smoothly.

The fae led Klara away from the factory entrance to a cottage made of the same brick as the factory. *He must be important to hold these quarters,* she thought, looking around the well-maintained cottage.

"Make yourself at home," he said, opening the door. *He's so sure of himself that he doesn't even lock the door. He might be easier to take out than I thought.*

The cottage had only one room, and she spotted a metal cot in the corner with a simple pillow and blanket. She would have thought a fae would seek greater comfort than that. No other furniture, except for the small kitchen at the back wall. There was nowhere to sit except around a small wooden table with a raised metal bar at its centre, attached to silver cuffs stained with blood she guessed were from interrogations. It was devoid of any comfort; the cottage screamed function above all else. Torches were fixed with cages on the walls, offering little light or warmth. Klara guessed the fae didn't want anyone who visited using the heavy torches as a weapon.

With his back to her, she took a seat at the table in the small kitchen. Resting her hands on the wooden surface only revealed the bloodstains and embedded nails. She removed her hands, and the stains disappeared as the fae opened the cupboard and retrieved two glasses.

"I only have diluted," he said.

Klara shrugged indifferently. She hadn't asked his name, but asking would reveal she didn't know the name of the person who, from the look of it, was in charge of the factory.

"My shipment from Malum was interrupted—some issue with the coven's magic," he went on, clearly annoyed by the delay. Klara suppressed a smile. The witches must have taken to brewing venom—that was one reason why they needed the extra magic.

"I heard the young queen is strict with the creatures. Do you think she knows of this place?" she asked.

"A little weak-willed, if you ask me. Aemella opened this factory as soon as her daughter claimed the throne. I say Klara must have struck a deal with Aemella; the more creatures that end up here, the less the young queen has to deal with. She must know what's happening—how could a ruler fail to see what's happening right across the Styx?"

Klara clenched her fist around the glass, trying to resist the urge to remove the fae's head. She changed the subject before her anger grew. "Forgive me, but I seem to have forgotten your name."

He grinned, making her uneasy as he leaned against the sink. "I wouldn't expect you to know it. Jasper, high fae of Kalos," he said, slipping out of the glamour like a serpent shedding a skin. His dark blue eyes were fixed on hers, while his ice-white hair was twisted back from his face, revealing his sharp jaw and faintly pointed ears.

"I wouldn't," he added as she went to stand. "You're much closer to the queen than you let on, Queen Klara."

She swallowed. She had been too focused on holding the strain of Frendall and her own glamour to check for anyone else's. Fae couldn't lie—and he hadn't; he had never offered a name, only an appearance.

"Let's talk for a moment. I have your companion, so don't force my hand."

Klara dropped her hand to her side and let her own glamour slip, careful to leave the ones covering Frendall and her axe in place even if the distance strained her.

"Isn't it so much better not to hide? Certainly much less exhausting," he said, rubbing his forehead, and she was glad to see him a little drained. He sat across from her, his eyes trailing over her. She had never wanted to blind someone more in her life. "Where to begin? I help maintain or oversee the factory, though not many last in this job long. I'm temporarily filling the position, as the queen has always thought highly of my family," Jasper told her, taking a gulp of venom.

"A high fae? I'm surprised to see you sink so low as a babysitter," she challenged.

His smile disappeared.

"Is this your first time seeing it?" he asked, gesturing to the factory just outside the barred windows of his cottage. He didn't let her answer. "I doubt your mother would tell you of this place, even if some of its guests believe you are complicit. Furthermore, the green look on your face when you saw the chimneys—I had the same look when I was first assigned here. The smell of the smoke really grips the back of the throat, doesn't it?"

"I would never have allowed this to happen. I didn't sign the treaty to send creatures to the slaughter," she snapped.

"The queen believes she is protecting her own kind—culling an enemy before it has the opportunity to strike," Jasper said, revealing no thoughts of his own.

"That might be true, but what's to stop the fae queen turning on you next? Maybe even a fae who grows too ambitious, too strong, could be considered a risk? Her motives reek of fear."

"Our queen would never do such a thing to her people. We are of her. Her children."

Klara knew first-hand what it was to be her child, knew how quick Aemella was to betray her word. "But you forget that Malum and Kalos were once joined. One land. You could even say the creatures of Malum were her children too, and yet she cut off the Forest as if it were a rotten limb. Now she taints this land with an evil that would rival the darkest time in Malum's history, and my creatures are the ones to fear?" She tried to keep her voice steady despite her rage.

"It's not our place to question the queen," Jasper sneered.

"Not the first time I've heard that sentence, and I believe I now wear the crown of that particular ruler," she pointed out. He looked like he was ready to strike, and she decided to reign it back. "Relax; I'm merely here for a visit, and on my way to the palace I couldn't resist the urge to pry," she said, taking a sip of venom.

How can he retain his light? How can any of the fae within this glamour? Draining others of their magic and lives is hardly a pure act. Maybe if you believe that what you're doing is just... it is?

Light was a gift from the angels. It ran through the fae like blood; it was their ancient reward for building the silver blades that had helped cut down Hell's army. The mines of Kalos were rife with silver and they had chosen to give it to the angels, to help maintain the balance between light and dark. Light was passed down through the generations for their continued loyalty to the heavens. However, if a fae corrupted their light or light magic—with sin such as murder, theft, or greed—they would be stripped of their light and become dark fae. They would no longer be permitted to remain in Kalos, as they had sullied their ancestors' memories and the light that connected all fae.

"If you're here for the gathering then why the charade?" Jasper asked doubtfully. He picked up the bottle of diluted venom and refilled Klara's glass; she wondered if he was trying to loosen her tongue.

"Her land, my land—we're one blood, and I was curious to see what her lands hold. I didn't want her to know I was curious. I can't change her ruling, nor can she change mine," Klara lied. She needed to feign disinterest if she were to escape his clutches.

Jasper slumped back in the chair. "Idle curiosity? That's all this is?"

"I know I broke the rules, but I was raised in Malum after all; it's hard to resist my nature to go where I don't belong."

"So you plan on doing nothing about the factory? You'll pretend as though you never came here or saw your precious creatures chained?" Jasper pressed, resting his hands on the table.

"They chose to leave. Who am I to intervene in another queen's ruling?" The lie tasted of ash and burnt her tongue.

"The thing is," Jasper said, leaning towards her, his face dangerously close to hers, "I don't believe you." He stood, straightening his jacket, and before she could form a sentence, he grabbed the dark brown bottle and smashed it over Klara's head, knocking her to the ground.

Did not see that coming, she thought, disorientated. Shards of glass had sliced the side of her head. Is it because he's a fae that I couldn't sense it? She blinked, trying to get her hands underneath her.

"Regardless of your intentions, I will arrange transport for you to be brought to your mother. Your pet, however, will remain—because you're right. The queen does have an interest in him," he said, crouching beside her. He pushed her hair from her face and sighed. "You really do rival your mother's beauty. If only you were as smart." He stood as Klara wiped the blood dripping from her forehead, trying to find the strength to stand. Holding Frendall's glamour had weakened her.

Jasper opened the door to reveal a young fae waiting. Their eyes went wide at the sight of her.

"Make sure she remains in this room, no matter what she says," Jasper instructed the guard.

"I hope the time we spend together in the future will be more enjoyable; maybe another dance?" he added to Klara with a wink.

Why does every movement hurt? She reached painfully towards the broken bottle and dabbed her fingers in the liquid. Tiny particles shone on her finger: iron.

I drank iron-lined venom. Naïve mistake. She cursed herself as she coughed up blood, her body forcing out what little she had consumed. To her horror, she felt the glamour protecting Frendall drop as her body fought to protect her.

The door closed as Jasper left. The other fae stood over her, spear in hand, the tip pointed at her. *This can't be good.*

"Don't suppose you'd take a bribe?" she offered, wiping the blood from the corner of her mouth.

A boot to the gut answered her as she coughed up the last of the iron.

"A no would have sufficed," she sputtered, clutching her ribs.

"Shut it," the fae ordered as she rose on her hands and knees, only to be struck with the end of the spear. "Stay down, or I'll be forced to use these." They took a pair of silver chains from their belt, and she could sense their fear.

"I think you're the one who's afraid of being chained if you don't follow your orders," she mocked, only to receive another polished boot to the gut. It knocked her back to the table, but she smiled through bloodied teeth as she felt her strength begin to thread back through her veins. Small iron particles lay in the small puddles of blood on the floor.

"Thanks for that. It would have taken a while for the iron to work its way out of my system without your assistance," she spat, finally getting upright. The fae stumbled back into the table as she craned her neck.

"What are we going to do about this?" Klara asked, taking her axe from her back. "Rather stupid of your leader not to check me for weapons, but I suppose arrogance gets to the best of us all sometimes."

"You won't make it out of here alive with your friend if you kill me," the fae said, moving back to the door.

She glanced at the iron-barred windows. She couldn't risk being locked inside.

"*If* I kill you? The fae really are an optimistic folk. Do us both a favour and drop the spear," Klara said as she stepped closer, twirling her axe in her hand. "Poisoning the venom... your leader is inventive. I didn't see it coming, and it takes a lot to surprise me."

The spear landed with a thud. She was just thinking, *Good at following orders. I might not have to kill them,* when she noticed their hand drifting to the wall.

"I don't want you reaching for whatever it is you're searching for. Hands off."

The fae raised their hands, but their eyes lingered on Jasper's cot. Klara backed up to it, not taking her eyes off the fae. She flipped the metal frame; there was no way to signal an alert, but there *was* an angel blade. A fae-crafted weapon that was lethal to any and all creatures, except fae. It looked like a long short-sword with a longer hilt wrapped in brown leather.

"This isn't your home. How did you know this was here?"

"I'm his personal guard—he trusts me," the fae stammered.

"Then I guess he'll be sorely disappointed in you

when I escape. Not the type of weapon to leave lying around…"

"I can help you," the fae pleaded through chattering teeth.

"Like you helped the creatures forced to come here?"

"I'll tell you everything. You won't get into the factory without a fae."

"Explain," Klara said. Placing a hand on their shoulder, she forced them onto the chair in front of the table. The fae looked to the door, and Klara tutted. "I wouldn't do something stupid now."

The guard darted for the door anyway.

"Why do they never listen to me?" she muttered, pressing the ruby at the centre of her axe. Her dagger shot out of the bottom and she tossed it towards the fae, pinning their shoulder to the wooden wall. Using the axehead would have done too much damage and caused far more mess than she wanted.

Klara rubbed her eyes as a shout of pain filled the cottage. She waited for the shouting to subside as the fae's adrenaline kicked in. "Are you finished? Good. Now hold still." She gripped the fae's head and forced herself into their mind.

Transports came and went from the factory. Laughter from the fae and pleas from the creatures mingled together. Klara felt the fae's joy as creatures begged for their freedom, and she wanted to rip their head from their body. Then the guard walked to the back of the factory. She saw a flash of cages and a steel walkway that oversaw the cages below: a perfect view for the fae to watch over the suffering creatures below. Klara skipped through scenes as the smell of sacrificial magic filled her senses until she saw the processing room.

But how do I get in? she asked, watching creatures be

stripped, searched and covered in awful brown cloaks. She felt the fae slump against the wall as they stopped resisting her invasion. They left the factory, and she noticed the winged blood seal on the backdoor. *Fae blood.* Klara took her hands from the trembling guard as their eyes rolled back in their head.

"How does it feel to be at someone else's mercy?" she barked when they came back to consciousness. "We both know my blood won't grant me access."

The fae's pupils dilated. "I can take you in."

"You enjoyed watching my creatures suffer—got off on it—so I think I'm owed reparations. Don't you agree?" she hissed. The fae's shaking intensified.

Klara removed their hand with a single swing of her axe.

It landed on the floor with a thud. Shock set in and the fae sat still, mouth agape, before a shrill scream escaped that she was sure could be heard in Malum.

"Stop wailing," she said, though they were far from being able to listen. "Ignis," she whispered, and a ball of fire filled her palm. It only took a moment to sear the fae's stub. Losing a hand was penalty enough. "You should be thanking me; you don't have to worry about infection. I hope you'll think twice about harming others from now on."

Heavy pants escaped the sweating fae as they nodded slowly.

I know I should feel bad about maiming someone, but sometimes a queen needs to vent. Klara placed her hand on the creature's cheek. "Sleep," she ordered, and the fae's eyes grew heavy until they slumped to the floor.

Jasper's going to get a pleasant surprise, but he shouldn't have underestimated me—and without my presence, there'll be no evidence I was even here. The maimed fae might give me away, but I doubt Jasper will want the fae queen to know of his incompetence. I wager that fae won't last the night. Klara took the hand from the floor, shivering as she felt the cooling flesh.

"Why can't things ever go smoothly? If I'm late to the palace because of you, the queen won't be happy," she said to the unconscious fae. *What a waste of time.*

She rolled her shoulders, disguising herself as the maimed guard. A group of fae saluted as she stepped out of the cottage, following the path that had been laid out in the fae's mind to the back door of the factory. There, she removed the invisibility glamour from the severed hand and placed it on the silver-winged seal in the centre of the black steel door.

The door failed to budge for a moment and Klara winced, but as she was about to drop the hand there was a clunk and swish, and the door popped open.

The smell of fear and sweat stifled her as she stepped inside the factory. A narrow brick corridor greeted her; torches hung caged from the low ceiling. Steam drifted through the hall, and she could have easily mistaken it for a room in Hell as a crimson glow emanated down the corridor. The door closed with a thud, and she grimaced as another fae from the patrol, blue-haired, walked towards her. She was preparing to defend herself when the fae stopped.

"I thought you were finished after the patrol?" she asked.

Klara scratched the back of her neck. "I wish, but Jasper needed me to look into that lycaon that caused trouble today."

Blue Hair frowned. "The lycaon? You're a little late to the party—he's already been taken to the private cells beneath the draining room for interrogation. I don't think he'll be up for much talking," she added with a grin, and Klara clenched her fists at her side. Without protection, Frendall would have been revealed as a general of Hell in Kalos. The fae would take great satisfaction in torturing him.

"Well, if Jasper was satisfied with the results he wouldn't have sent me. As a member of his personal guard, I don't think I would question his orders," she said, and Blue paled.

"I didn't mean anything by it. If he wants to push the lycaon further, I can assist you?" she offered, clearly afraid of having appeared disrespectful to the chain of command.

"No need. I'm sure I can handle a single lycaon," Klara said, mimicking the words of the earlier patrol.

"Enjoy yourself. I'm going to grab some food before there's nothing left," Blue said before leaving through the same door Klara had used.

Klara closed her eyes and took a breath, trying to steady her anger. She wanted to tear the factory down, brick by brick, with her bare hands, but that wouldn't help anyone.

When she opened them, she was blocking a line of creatures with sunken eyes and bulging veins. She stepped aside as they trudged past her. A vampire met her eye, and a faint smile appeared on his lips. *Burn this place to the ground, Heiress,* she heard him project, and she tried to suppress the stunned look on her face. She was about to reply when a fae tugged on the silver chain that bound them, and the line moved on.

The faint whisper echoed in her mind. It was just like a creature of Malum to ask for destruction rather than salvation. As she looked after the defeated group of creatures, Klara promised herself that she would deliver just that.

19

Klara followed the creatures towards the light at the end of the corridor. Suddenly the smell of sulphur filled the air, and she was forced to cover her mouth and nose with her hand. It was a stench she usually only had to suffer in the company of demons. However, something about this smell was different; it was the scent of corrupted magic which had been pooled from various sources.

She peered around the corner, making sure there was no sign of Jasper within. Her eyes followed the billows of steam cascading from great charcoal-coloured cauldrons to coat the factory floor. The expansive room's ceiling tapered into the three great chimneys, allowing the black smoke from the fires to escape as the cauldrons boiled and sizzled. The factory was more extensive than it appeared on the outside.

Klara's nails cut into the palms of her hands as she

watched the fae stir the liquidized magic drained from the creatures suspended in cages a foot off the factory floor. The prisons reminded her of the cages Abadan had kept her ravens in, with rounded tops and small doors, thin bars spaced closely together. She frowned in confusion as she noticed that the cage bars glowed crimson and the creatures within struggled to move or even breathe.

How could the fae queen have created draining cages? Klara had never seen them in the flesh before, but she remembered the disturbingly detailed mural painted on the Beanstalk wall. The Gingerbread Factory proved even more terrifying in real life.

She needed to blend in, so she dropped the fae glamour and copied the clothing of the vampire she had passed in the corridor. Adjusting the muddy brown robe, she placed the fae's hand inside the pocket at the front and pulled up the hood to conceal her face. She watched as the few creatures lucky enough not to be caged walked up and down the rickety planks to the mouths of the bubbling cauldrons. They took out buckets of corrupted magic, which looked like black ink and glistened like diamonds.

"You're here to work, not to watch," a fae said, planting a spear into the base of Klara's spine. Shoved forward, she picked up a filthy, dripping bucket from the pile beside the cauldron so the observing fae would stop watching her.

The creatures studied her as she moved to join their line, but the fae turned their back to scold another creature who had fallen from the plank and dropped a bucket on the already sticky floor. Klara moved around the cage closest to her, attempting to get a better look at the fae guards on the raised walkway watching over the factory floor to see if any of them had been with Frendall when he was escorted off. *If I can find someone who escorted him to the cells, I can get myself caught and get in without revealing myself,* she reasoned, but she didn't recognise any of the fae.

She leaned away from the bars when a wrinkled hand reached out and grabbed her sleeve.

"Get out, Heiress," a witch rasped. Her rags were worn out, and Klara could hear her slowing heartbeat.

"How do you know me?" Klara whispered, looking around to make sure no fae overheard them.

"I can smell Lucifer's blood in your veins, and I saw your general being dragged through by the guards. Everyone in the Forest knows General Frendall is your lover," she slurred.

Klara was amazed that the witch still held such strength, but as their hands grazed, she sensed her diminishing power.

Frieda? she asked silently, and the witch stilled. Though she appeared drawn and her skin was marred with veins, she bore a striking resemblance to the witch who had visited the castle. Klara also couldn't help but notice the dim ruby pendant around her scrawny neck. It looked out of place against her dirty brown robes and magic-stained skin. She was surprised the fae had let the witch keep it, but then again, they weren't after jewels; only her magic.

"You have a sister, a twin? Can you show me where they took him?" Klara asked, and the witch moved closer to the glowing bars. She had paled, which Klara hadn't thought was possible.

"My sister isn't here, is she?"

"No, she's safe in the Forest," Klara replied, and Frieda looked relieved.

"Your general is through the door at the end of this room. There's a basement with cells. It's not a place creatures return from," she warned, but Klara shook that off; she would have felt it if they had ended his life. The cage's glow intensified the closer Frieda came to the bars. She hissed as the glow burnt her outstretched arm, and dropped her hand from Klara's.

Klara gripped the iron bars, her muscles straining as she tried to remove the magic, but all she accomplished was seared palms.

"Son of a—" she muttered, holding her raw hands out in front of her. Luckily the groans and protests of the suffering creatures drowned out her failure.

"There's no use, the protections are too strong." Frieda panted, moving into the back of the cage. "Leave me. Stop other creatures from crossing over—more and more are arriving every day," the witch begged. Klara thought that was the most selfless thing she had ever heard spoken by a creature of Malum.

"Is that what you want me to tell your sister? That you gave up?" she asked, studying the bars. The lock was made of iron, and the more Klara tried to break it, the more it drained her. She examined it, feeling a hum she recognised, a lust for power threaded through the magic. *This isn't Aemella's magic. This is darker, riddled with hatred and desperation.* She felt a familiar chill run up the back of her neck.

Before she could get a read on who the magic belonged to, two fae walked towards her. Klara crouched, pretending to pick up the broken potion bottles from the factory floor. They only hesitated for a moment before moving on.

"You need to leave this place. Even if you free me, I won't have the strength to run," Frieda wheezed. The witch's heartbeat was getting slower and slower, and

Klara knew she was a lost cause; she had been here too long.

"I'm sorry," she said helplessly.

Frieda offered her a delicate smile. "I've accepted my fate; just stop the others from crossing the river, from coming here," she begged.

Klara felt someone watching them. A loathing, a joy spread through her, and her mind drifted away from the witch before her. *Only one person can create cages of this strength...*

Klara shook away the impossible thought, but the claw at her neck only grew stronger.

My child, it's been too long.

The hiss in the air dried Klara's mouth. Her gaze rose to the overseers walkway, and there stood Abadan, wearing a crown of black roses.

Klara went numb as her former guardian's black eyes stared down at her.

Join me, or I will call the fae—and leave the witch where she belongs, Abadan projected.

Klara looked at Frieda who shook her head slowly, warning Klara not to disobey, that it would be worse for everyone if she did. Klara had no choice but to climb the steel stairs to the fallen high queen.

Abadan waited for her at the top of the stairs. The lump at the back of her throat grew the closer she got to her fallen guardian. From the overseer's balcony, Klara could see the exit at the other end of the room and a set of doors protected by two fae, where the witch had told her Frendall was being held—though she couldn't understand why she couldn't sense his presence if he was so close.

I'll have to get past the fae to get to him, and I can't exactly use a hand in front of them, she thought to herself.

"Of all the factories you could have walked into, you walked into mine," Abadan said.

Klara looked her over. Her once striking crimson hair was now dull and lifeless; she was a shadow of her former self. Her simple crimson robe was belted at the waist—gone were the extensive embellishments of her high queen's wardrobe—and from the lines around her eyes and mouth, her youthful glamour was taking much of her magic.

Factories? Please let that be a figure of speech, because dealing with more than one of these places will take an army. Klara kept that realisation to herself.

Abadan mocked a bow. "Or did you miss me?" She clicked her long nails against the railing, the yellow talons no longer brightened by diamonds and crimson polish.

Klara remained silent. *Maybe this is a mirage—a trick or a spell to throw off intruders.*

Abadan raised her hand and slapped Klara across the face.

Nope, definitely the real thing. Leave it to Queen Aemella to use the Mother of Demons to her advantage. It makes sense, though; who better to run a factory than the person who brought them to fruition? Klara wiped her cheek, noticing a thread of blood on her fingers. The cut Abadan's taloned nails had left healed after a moment.

"Sorry, darling, had to make sure Aemella wasn't up to her tricks," Abadan explained, though Klara could feel that Abadan had taken pleasure in striking her. "I take it she sent you here to check on me," she went on, frowning as she studied Klara's robe, before covering her mouth. "Don't tell me you're spying on your dear mama?" Abadan laughed, high and shrill.

"I didn't allow the creatures to leave Malum so they could be used to resurrect your Gingerbread Factories," Klara sneered.

"I can hardly call them Gingerbread Factories anymore; mine only attracted the children, whereas Aemella has limits to her cruelty. But there really is nothing sweeter than the screams of the young." Abadan sighed. "These are just factories without the delightful squeals of children."

"I'm glad to see you've learnt nothing from your fall from power," Klara said, although Abadan's consistent cruelty was somehow comforting. She couldn't handle any more surprises.

"Seems Malum wasn't enough to keep you occupied—you had to come looking for trouble. You rose against me, and now it's your mother's turn? It's almost too sweet to bear. How disappointed you must be to discover her nasty little secret. At least I'm honest in my depravity," Abadan said.

Klara ignored the remark, not giving her the satisfaction of an argument that would only grab the fae's attention. She was already nervous about Jasper making an appearance.

"But it entertains me to see you so dishevelled. Let us walk; I feel like we have much to catch up on." Abadan offered her arm, but Klara remained still. "Don't worry! If I was going to hand you over to the fae, I would have done it already."

Fae watching over the cauldrons stared up at them, so Klara reluctantly took her arm.

"How long have you been here?" she asked, wanting to know when precisely Aemella had brought the factory back into existence. *She must hold some authority,* she thought as Abadan motioned for the fae to return to work. They did so, pushing along the queue of creatures carrying empty buckets.

"I can't recall. One minute your father was coming through the portrait, and the next I was chained in Aemella's Palace," Abadan said, nostrils flaring at the thought of her defeat.

"How does she keep you here? Surely you can't be drained of that much magic?"

"She created the factory from my blood; it stands as I stand. I am bound to it. Even if I grow stronger, I can't leave," Abadan said. She lifted her crimson robe, exposing raw, bloodied feet shackled with silver irons. "These keep me moving slowly, and I am drained just as much as the pathetic souls beneath me. I'm merely here to keep things running without the cost of fae magic. God forbid their light is tainted by their own actions." Her words dripped with disdain.

"So if I kill you then this place will fall?" Klara asked coldly.

"Don't get too excited by the prospect. No, it isn't that simple. I manage the cages and keep the cauldrons producing and the magic draining, but if I were destroyed, another would take my place. Maybe not someone as strong, but a creature like the witch you seemed interested in—not that they would last long," Abadan delighted.

Guessing she was after something, since she hadn't turned her in, Klara decided to play along.

"I like the new crown," she commented, drawing Abadan's attention from the witch. Klara didn't want Frieda tortured more than she already was.

Abadan's shrill laughter gathered the attention of the creatures below. "This damned thing?" she said, adjusting the nest of black roses. "Dear Queen Aemella forced

224

it upon my head. Can't get it off no matter how many of these damned creatures I sacrifice. The more power and strength I try to give myself, the more it simply drains back into the factory. Aemella trapped me here, knowing of my caging skills. I'm as much a prisoner as the rest of these savages, regardless of the false crown upon my head."

Aemella knows that Abadan is the only one who knows how to cage Lucifer. Instead, she has her cage a multitude of creatures. So Aemella's end game isn't Lucifer… and yet what could she want with all this corrupted magic? Sure, she's freeing Kalos of an influx of creatures, but killing them would be quicker than capturing, caging and draining.

"The fae queen's end game?" Klara pressed. *It doesn't hurt to ask.*

"My guess? Power. Why else would the fae queen risk sullying her precious light? It wouldn't surprise me if she reclaimed Malum. I can't say she isn't disappointed to have you as a daughter," Abadan said, patting Klara's arm, tucked into her own.

"Excuse me?" Klara snapped.

"From the whispers of the guard, you've been quick to make allies in Malum, fair and just. Eager to negotiate rather than execute," Abadan explained.

"And that works against me?" *How could my reforms have angered my mother?*

"Nobody wants a stone—but turn it into a ruby, and there will be those who will chop off the hand that holds it." Abadan eyed Klara's pocket and winked. *She knows about the fae hand.*

"I don't recall you being so poetic," Klara remarked, anxious to get to Frendall as time ticked by.

"Captivity makes one awfully reflective; it's almost sickening. You are trespassing on a foreign ruler's land, which means you do not live in awe of Aemella. She won't appreciate that after all the years of pining for you. She'll show you just how strong and superior she is."

"Why tell me all this? You could alert the fae. I'm sure you would be rewarded for handing me over. Tell me what it is you're after." Klara stopped walking. Abadan stumbled a little, and a curse escaped her lips. Klara sensed how much pain her bare feet on the steel grille floor caused her.

Abadan shrugged. "We could do with a little excitement around here, and I always hated that smug Aemella. I would take great pleasure in seeing her fall at my ward's hands."

"There's more to it than that, and I'm not your ward," Klara said, hating that they had ever shared the castle.

"No, but I did raise you—and without me, you wouldn't be here now, independent and strong. Lilith would be proud," Abadan said.

"The idea that you had any role in shaping my success only makes me want to get on my knees before Aemella and beg for forgiveness."

"Dramatic, as always—but speaking of my children, where's that general of yours? If you're here, he can't be far." Abadan's eyes glowed black. Using his correct title told Klara that the fallen high queen knew exactly where he was; Abadan was merely taunting her. She placed her hand on Abadan's bare wrist, hoping she was too weak to notice her slipping into her mind.

The queen interested in Frendall that Jasper had mentioned wasn't Aemella, it was Abadan! At first she heard nothing but the screams of creatures being stripped of their magic as Abadan barked orders, but as she pried open Abadan's mind, Klara saw Frendall chained to a wall. He was being hosed down with filthy water, the force from the hose smacking his head against the stone.

"Why would you want to harm your own blood?" Klara exclaimed.

Abadan smiled. "He meant more to you than he ever did to me. Surely you don't need my son to help save the day? I didn't raise you to be a damsel. However, he does make for interesting leverage," she added, finally getting to the point.

"And what would Lucifer say if I returned shy of a general? You don't think he'd come looking? I don't think you have any intention of killing Frendall. I think you want his capture to provoke the King of Hell," Klara scoffed.

"Just think. Lucifer cares for him. If you return without him, the king will gladly go to war with Aemella, thus keeping your hands clean. You are rid of a factory and I will be free, as will Frendall. He's a mere distraction to you; let me have him, and I will let you walk out of here and back to your castle," Abadan said casually, as though she wasn't juggling the fate of thousands.

"The king doesn't know we are here, doesn't know this place exists—and if he did, I don't think he would free you unless it was to free the head from your shoulders. I would never leave Frendall with you, not for a second," Klara seethed, and she felt her eyes flash white, readying for a fight.

"Your arrogance will be the death of you and Malum. I provide you with a perfect plot against Aemella and yet you refuse to compromise. I could bring an army down on you as we speak," Abadan warned, her pinched face mere inches from Klara's.

"Or you could use Frendall as evidence against me to gain favour with Aemella. Furthermore, I could tell them that you summoned me here to help you," Klara said, recalling the glamour in the woods—the glamour she had been fooled into thinking belonged to her mother, when it was in fact Abadan luring her in. She wanted Abadan to see that she was no longer a child in need of protection.

Abadan sighed. "How little you trust me. Since you won't see reason, how about a new deal?"

Klara waited.

"I'll help you escape, provide a distraction if you will, and you free me when you destroy this place?" Klara could feel Abadan's desperation.

"And how do you plan to help me do that?" she asked.

Abadan looked down at the steel grille they were walking on, and Klara saw that beneath their feet the metal was pitted and eaten away with rust. They had made it to the other end of the room, closest to the doors where Frendall was being held, leaving the other fae with the creatures at the top of the room.

"Now you only have two fae to get through," Abadan said, and Klara suppressed a smile. She might put on a good act, but this factory was eating away at her, and soon there would be nothing left.

"Your schemes never cease to amaze me."

Though her words were calm, Klara could feel Abadan's calculating mind as she eyed the guards protecting the steel door. Before Abadan had a chance to betray her, Klara kicked through the weakened section of the walkway. It gave way, and Abadan gripped the railing.

Klara fell through the gap as guards from either end of the room raced towards her, freeing the door to Frendall. She put her fist through the scalding cauldron beside her to distract them. Her flesh burnt as the corrupted magic tasted her skin. Klara grunted, fighting through the pain weaving through her muscle and bone. A fae evaporated as the corrupted wave washed over them, the sight causing the others to step back.

I expect you to make good upon your return, Abadan projected from the ledge above her.

Tell the queen nothing, or you will be the one who pays the price, Klara threatened, but was only met with Abadan's evil smirk.

She ripped the robe's sleeve and wrapped her burned hand with a strip of the thick fabric. With the corrupted magic blocking the fae's way to her, she pressed the severed hand against the seal. She glanced over her shoulder at the caged creatures, sensing their hope for freedom, but she couldn't help them.

Not yet, anyway.

20

The heavy steel door opened, leading down a flight of stairs. Klara knew a dungeon when she saw one. When she raced down the cement steps, a shrieking alarm echoed.

If that doesn't tell Jasper I've escaped his cottage, nothing will. Jasper would have to tell Aemella of the disruption. Klara hoped she would reach the queen first, and they could negotiate. She didn't want war between Malum and Kalos, but after what she had witnessed here, there was no way she was going to let the creatures continue to suffer and die in the factory.

"Frendall?" she shouted, looking down a corridor full of steel doors. *This is going to be impossible.* She banged on every door, afraid that he had passed out and couldn't hear her. "Answer me! Or I swear I'll leave you to rot," she called, pounding on each cell door. She could barely see into the small, rectangular slot high up on each door, made for the taller fae.

"Klara? Can you hear me?" She heard Frendall's faint pleading from the other side of the door. She was so close to him, and yet she had felt nothing. *Something is blocking my senses.*

The spare hand proved useless on the door, so she tossed it aside, crammed her fingers into the side of the door, and pulled. The bolts struggled under the pressure; she panted as she felt every fibre of muscle in her arms and legs strain. To increase her strength, she spread her wings. The force blew out the bolts on the door, and it landed on the ground with a crash.

"Lucifer have mercy," Klara said.

Frendall hung naked on the wall. His hands and feet were bolted with nails connected to thick silver chains.

"Angel to my rescue. Never thought I'd see the day," Frendall said with a forced smile.

"Glad to see they didn't beat the sense of humour out of you," she said, folding her wings within herself.

"It would take more than a few lashes," he muttered, but she noticed the wounds across his abdomen were still flowing.

"Why are you still bleeding?" She went to work on the chains on his ankles.

"Silver-threaded whip. Filthy fae are more than pretty faces," he spat, his voice strained. "Watch—" he started before losing the strength to speak.

Klara turned to see a stunned fae in the doorway, spear at the ready. She ran and planted both feet into their chest, sending them into the steel door across the hall, knocking the fae unconscious. She couldn't kill another, or she worried her mother wouldn't negotiate.

One limb at a time, she thought, trying to free him. *You won't get him out in time; there are too many nails.* Her hands shook.

"More fae will come. The queen can't know you have seen this place," Frendall said.

Klara thought of her confrontation with Jasper. *Too late to worry about that now.*

"I can't leave you with your mother," she barked back.

Frendall's eyes shone, suddenly alert. "Abadan is here?"

"She's running the place, about as chained to the factory as you are to this wall," she told him, freeing one of his hands. A silver nail pierced each wrist. *The real reason he isn't healing.*

"She sounded the alarm?" Frendall asked, muttering a curse as she went to work on the next chain.

"No, I have to admit I'm responsible for that one. I had to get away from her. She would have traded both of us, if it meant her freedom." She shook out her hands, refusing to leave him behind.

"How could you be so reckless? If I die, nothing happens. You die, and the realms are thrown into chaos," he preached.

Klara took some small delight in ripping the nail from his wrist.

"Sweet Judas," he roared, his eyes flaring amber. "Try not to enjoy it so much."

"Stop complaining. The pain will activate your lycaon healing so you'll heal faster," she said, making quick work of the others. Once he was free, he collapsed on top of her. Helping him to his feet, she took off the mud-coloured robe, revealing her own clothes underneath.

"You need that to protect yourself," he argued, refusing to take the cloak. Clearly, he wasn't fully aware of

232

just how naked he was in his depleted state. Klara eyed his naked body; even scarred and bleeding he looked like carved marble.

"As much as I appreciate your naked form, I don't think the fae will. Something is blocking my magic down here. I can't create new glamours," she told him, and Frendall finally pulled the rough robe around himself.

"My sword?" he muttered, reaching out as she supported him. Klara looked around the cell; his longsword sat on a table alongside the bloodied silver whip. She threw the strap over his shoulder and he groaned.

They moved as quickly as they could up the steps to the factory. There was only one way out, the way she had come, and that sent a chill through her bones. Fortunately the door was still open when they reached the top of the stairs to the draining room. Klara felt her magic thread back through her veins; the dungeon must be lined with iron as the tavern had been. She was surprised by the lack of fae on the factory floor. Even the creatures in the cages barely stirred.

"Can you run?" she asked, though she could feel how weak he was.

Frendall nodded. "The wounds are healing now that we're away from the cell." He looked as relieved as she felt.

The fae were waiting to ambush them on the walkway above the factory floor.

"Stop them!" Jasper ordered. He was supporting the fae with the lost limb at the other end of the room.

Frendall dropped his arm from Klara's, knowing she might need to fight. She kicked over the cauldron closest to the factory wall and prayed it would lead them out into the open. The fae filed down the walkway, preparing to surround them, but the corrupted magic ate clean through the brick in seconds. Frendall glanced back at the destruction with a hint of respect.

The smog-coated air choked them as they ran past the worn-down cottages. Creatures in various stages of recuperation stood in the street or peered from windows.

"Any idea how we're going to get through the protection?" Frendall shouted as they neared the glamour separating them from the silver wood. Chaos unfolded around them as the creatures watched them escape and tried to stop the fae. Klara was grateful to have some cover from the flying spears landing on either side of them. The thunder of boots behind them spurred them along.

"I'm working on it," she shouted.

An explosion roared behind them. They stopped, and so did the fae. Both sides watched black and red flames shooting from the chimneys before striking the protections above them.

"We've got to move—it'll give us a chance," Klara urged.

The glass-like protections cracked and fractured as bright white flashes fought the flames. The fae chasing them had stopped to stare at the extraordinary display. Abadan's flames began to dissipate, and Klara pushed her legs and Frendall harder as the protection started to rebuild. The silver wood shone on the other side of the protections, beckoning them, and the pair dived through just in time. The glamour sealed itself behind them.

"What the hell was that? Did you do that?" Frendall gasped as they lay on the ground.

"I couldn't have even if I wanted to. It was Abadan,"

Klara said beside him. "She's the only one who could have conjured that much magic."

"Aemella will make her pay for that," Frendall said, struggling to his feet. "But better she thinks it's an escape attempt than that her daughter is sneaking around."

"Abadan is on our side for now, but she wants her freedom in return," Klara explained, dusting herself off.

"What aren't you telling me?" Frendall brushed back her hair to reveal where Jasper had struck her with the bottle. The wound had healed, but the blood remained. She gently pushed his hand away.

"Jasper was leading the patrol. I couldn't sense him. I think I was too distracted holding our glamours. He struck me before I had a chance to overpower him." She sighed, disappointed in herself.

"I'll take great pleasure in tearing off his wings," Frendall said. They watched the protections strengthen and shine before disappearing behind them, and all that appeared in front of them was the silver wood.

"And I might help you do it, but they'll have subdued Abadan by now, and then they'll remember us," Klara said. "We need to do something about your clothes." The muddy robe would give them away to any passing patrol.

Frendall placed his hand on her shoulder, and before she could question it they were back in the centre of the Kalion capital.

"Watch where you're walking!" a centaur shouted, rearing up on its hind legs as Klara and Frendall appeared in the middle of the cobbled street. Klara pulled him into an alley before they drew any more attention from the early risers.

"Sorry. I was aiming for the alley," he panted, still weakened from the prolonged exposure to the silver.

"How were you even able to do that? You can barely stand," Klara exclaimed. Portalling was a skill few had.

"Lokey taught me one or two things. Just don't expect me to do it again anytime soon," he said, sitting on the ground.

"Stay here. We need to get ourselves cleaned up, and you need clothes," she ordered.

"I'm not in a position to argue."

Klara left him sitting in the alley. There was a clothesline at the end of the alley, so she stole a pair of trousers and a shirt for him, and down the street was an unattended stall crowded with shoes. *Serves them right for being too trusting.* She had to guess his size, but she found a brown pair that would match the rest of the clothes she had stolen.

There was a mirror on the stall, and she caught her reflection in it. Her own clothes had been protected by the robe and glamours, but her face was smeared with blood from where Jasper had struck her with the bottle. *Water,* she thought, looking for some. She slipped into another alley as a fae stumbled from what looked to be a brothel, from their undone clothes and flushed faces. Her back against the wall, Klara sensed the water she sought. She almost moaned when a fountain appeared around the corner in a small open garden. Quickly, she washed her face in the cool spray, took a small bucket from the pile she guessed was for collecting water, and brought it back to Frendall. She kept her head low as she walked through the busying markets. The dimming lamps signalled night's end. They were running out of time to get to the palace.

"Dawn is breaking," Frendall said as the orange beams reflected off the building.

"I'll need to open a portal," Klara said. "I need to get to the palace before Jasper does."

"One of the stalls might have a potion," he suggested, and she nodded, about to head back up the street, when he placed a hand on her shoulder.

"Wait!" He was holding a glistening white potion bottle in his hand.

"Where did you get that?" she demanded, thinking it was too good to be true.

"It was in the pocket of the robe. When I picked it up, it fell out," Frendall said, holding the bottle away from himself.

"Abadan. She must have slipped it into my pocket when we were talking," Klara said, not believing her eyes. How did she know we'd need it? She popped the cork and took a deep breath. A sharp smell of vanilla, peppercorns and the underlying sting of mugwort emanated around them. "It's not for drinking, but its intention is not to poison," she said.

"What do you think it is?" Frendall asked.

"One way to find out," she said, throwing the bottle against the wall.

"Why would you waste it?" Frendall barked, but before she had a chance to respond, the silver of the fae queen's palace shone before them through a grand spiral. He groaned. "Abadan will want something for this."

"Yes, she does—but in order for her to be freed, we need to survive long enough to destroy the factory." Klara shrugged, trying to look on the bright side.

"How do we know this isn't a deceptive portal and we won't end up in Purgatory?" Frendall reasoned.

Klara stepped closer, examining the delicate edges of the portal. "There is no fray of deception," she said, feeling the absence of threat in her bones.

"I still don't trust it," he argued, but they didn't have time to debate; the portal dimmed.

"Let's get to the palace first and see if we survive until tomorrow to worry about your mother," Klara said.

"What are you planning to say to *your* mother when we get there?"

"I'm going to punch her in the throat and force her to tear down the factory." She was joking... at least about punching Aemella in the throat.

Frendall gaped. "And you think that will allow us to see tomorrow's dawn?"

Klara forced her muscles to relax. She could still smell the blood and sweat of the factory.

"I'll do whatever's necessary. I made it easier for the fae queen to take them. I didn't bother to look across the river, out of a desire for peace and because I was too busy keeping the elders of Malum appeased." *Now I'm paying for my naïveté.*

"You aren't responsible for another ruler's actions."

'But I won't ignore them either. Creatures are dismembering themselves to stay out of the factory; I think the fae queen deserves to feel an inch of that pain," Klara said.

Frendall paced in front of the portal.

"Trying to force her hand isn't going to resolve any of that. If you go against her, she'll only push back—harder!"

"I can't pretend I haven't seen or felt that monstrosity. The least I can do is negotiate. We know how Aemella hates to get her hands dirty. That's why she resurrected Abadan to run that damn factory. If I cause a stir, she'll see it's not worth the effort." Klara felt she was trying to convince herself as much as him, but she was sick of politics. "I'll negotiate for peace; the Neutral Lands are still stained with the blood from Abadan's uprising. Malum is still finding its way, and war with Kalos would only lead to death and chaos on both sides of the realm. Despite what you think, I'm not going into this blind."

"You might want peace, but who's to say Aemella seeks the same? That factory has been running for who knows how long. Queen Aemella could be giving the magic to the fae to strengthen her army. We don't know anything at this point, only that she's draining creatures."

"Do you ever get tired of preaching at me?" Klara asked, searching his exhausted eyes.

"Do you ever get tired of jumping in head first?"

Silence filled the space between them. *He's right about the fae queen's strength. The whole court will be in the Palace, and if the queen is strengthening her court and her guard, we're damned before we even walk through the door.*

Before they could debate any more, Klara shoved Frendall through the dimming portal.

21

*A*t least the landing is softer than the Fall to Hell, Klara thought as they landed side by side in the fae queen's garden. They stared up at the crystal-clear sky from the soft bed of green grass.

"Do you think Lucifer copied her or she copied Lucifer?" Frendall joked, rolling to his side. There was no comparison between the two gardens except that they both surrounded the homes of the two ancient rulers. The fae garden was vibrant and full of life, whereas Lucifer's was anything but.

"Who the hell cares?" Klara said, cracking her back as she stood. Some of the fae queen's servants squealed and ran at the sight of them. It seemed not many visitors landed in a heap in the middle of the gardens. Klara grinned.

"These flowers are a lot less terrifying than Lucifer's,"

she commented, looking at the lilies and orchids that thrived around them. The water in the stream that cut through the gardens glistened like diamonds. Frendall gathered water from it in his hand and splashed the back of his neck to cool himself; the cloudless sky provided no protection from the Kalion sun. The bright, unyielding rays wouldn't harm them, but as residents of Malum and Hell they found it a strain.

They both looked towards the sound of hushed voices as a few young fae peered around a tree at them. Klara secured her axe to her back for all to see. The fae were quick to disappear.

"You sure you want to play it like that? Our arrival will be announced before we leave these gardens," Frendall warned as they walked through the perfect flowers.

"Never hurts to have a little fun. Plus, if she hasn't sensed me by now it'll be a miracle." Klara stopped to smell a dew-coated bush of red roses. *If Father saw these, he would die of envy.* "Let's not keep Aemella waiting," she said, dropping her hand from a blood-red bloom.

They wove their way through the hedges and bushes until they reached the drawbridge to the queen's silver palace. Klara shielded her eyes as the sun reflected off the towers and high walls. Two guards stepped forward, crossing their spears as Klara and Frendall crossed the drawbridge to the outer doors of the Palace.

"The queen is expecting us. We can't be delayed," Klara told them.

One of them eyed Frendall's simple stolen clothing. "Why would she be expecting such a Creature?" he asked, not moving his spear.

"I don't know—maybe we should ask my mother?" Klara looked to Frendall, who shook his head with a smile.

The fae guard were quick to drop a knee. "We're sorry, Your Highness," they said in unison.

"You—do not appear as we expected," one stammered.

"How am I to look? A pretty gown and a crown?" she asked.

One of the guards began to shake, but neither dared to open their mouth.

"Forgiven," she said, and the fae quickly rose. There was a series of grunts and the creaking of wood as they opened the carved doors in haste. A small courtyard appeared before them with servants in simple dress scurrying back and forth across it, paying no attention to their arrival.

I'll be weakened here; the walls are laced with silver. I can sense it, Frendall said as his hand made contact with hers.

Don't worry, I get the feeling we won't be here very long, she replied, dropping his hand when a servant in a pale blue dress carrying a large vase of flowers knocked Klara's shoulder.

"Watch where you're walking," the servant snapped, but it was too late; the large vase shattered against the stone courtyard. "One of Her Majesty's favourites!" the servant cried.

Klara grimaced at the mistake, stepping forward out of the doorway.

"I'll take responsibility for the mistake," she said as the fae knelt amongst the broken porcelain.

"And you think that will help me?" the servant shot back, not looking at Klara.

"I think it will. Tell us your name," Frendall said, and the fae's head snapped up as she smelt the air.

"A demon? I won't give a demon my name—you

could curse me," she hissed, turning up her small nose and seemingly forgetting about the vase.

"I ask that you hold your tongue and show respect to a general," Klara said calmly. "I believe the queen is expecting us."

The fae grimaced, and Klara sensed some unkind words were heading in their direction.

"It would serve you well to escort a Daughter of Lucifer. Good to have friends in high places." She smirked, and the fae's dark pink lips fell open.

"Your Highness, I didn't expect you to be so..." She looked them over. "Thamalia—my name is Thamalia. I didn't know... I can take you, please, just through here," she stammered.

Klara admired the rings decorating Thamalia's pointed ears, visible due to her short—almost shaved—lilac hair, but felt the fear radiating from the fae's pores.

Do I have three heads? If another fae says a thing about my appearance, I won't be so lenient. I might be a little dusty and dishevelled, but imagine if I hadn't washed the blood from my face—they might have fainted at the sight of me! she projected to Frendall.

"I think we've both looked better." Frendall laughed, offering the servant some mercy.

Thamalia led them through the busy courtyard to a set of doors carved from silver wood.

"Servants aren't permitted to use the main doors," she explained with a bow. The doors opened from the inside, allowing them to enter. Frendall moved on ahead, but Klara looked back into the courtyard, making sure there were no other eyes on them.

"For your help," she said. Thamalia frowned in confusion. "See for yourself."

Thamalia followed her gaze to where the vase sat on the ground, mended.

"Better get back to it—don't want to leave it unattended for long or someone else might break it." Klara winked.

Stunned, Thamalia ran across the courtyard to the vase and carried on with her chores.

"That was awfully kind and unlike you," Frendall teased, his hand on Klara's lower back.

"I'm about to spoil the queen's mood; no need to give her a reason to take it out on others." Klara studied the blue walls of the palace, decorated with sculpted white stems and leaves; she almost missed the portraits' eerie eyes. It was rather too austere for her liking. Grand but plain.

What means of escape does the fae queen use in case she needs to flee? she wondered, before realising that the fae queen had probably never had to run. The thought brought a new wave of caution.

Specks of reflected light danced over Frendall; she followed the reflection to the enormous chandelier, but there were no candles—only long, clear crystals catching the sun from the glass ceiling.

"Your Highness, the queen is expecting you in the throne room." A guard wearing the symbolic sapphire uniform threaded with silver had appeared before them.

Klara noted the spear in their hand. *The queen allows her guards to hold weapons here? Or is it just for present company? Even Lucifer doesn't allow his guard weapons within the manor.*

Perhaps she has no reason not to arm them? It certainly demonstrates her trust in them, Frendall reasoned.

"Lead the way," Klara said aloud, trying to start a conversation, but she only received a turned back. "The palace is sublime," she continued, following the guard through a corridor walled with real flowers and golden ivy.

"The fae queen enjoys all things beautiful. She had the walls decorated with the freshest flowers for tonight's ball. Filling the palace with beauty brings her ease when the darkness provokes her," the guard replied coldly as they came to a set of white doors.

Provokes her? What does that even mean?

Klara wanted to ask the guard to elaborate—after all, they wouldn't lie to her—but asking questions of those she couldn't trust not to report back to the fae queen was too much of a risk. The guard opened the doors and stepped aside with a deep bow. Frendall followed Klara as she walked through, but the guard held out their arm, blocking his path.

"Just Her Highness," the guard insisted. Klara sensed the threat in their voice.

Why insist on Frendall accompanying me if she wasn't going to grant him an audience? To put him in his place? She didn't want to delay; she rested a hand on his forearm before he could argue. *Take a look around, see if any of the servants have loose lips.*

Frendall bowed slightly, letting her know he understood. She continued on alone.

The last time she had stood before the fae queen's mirrored steps, there had been a pool of blood surrounding her. Klara's shoulders tensed at the memory. 'Josephine', the foreign name her mother had called her, came to mind. *Who would have thought the first conversation I had with my mother would include orders to kill the King of Hell?*

Her mind emptied as she came face to face with Aemella. Jasper stood beside the floral throne in a long navy robe, whispering in the queen's pointed ear. Klara saw her mother's eyebrow twitch, her eyes never leaving her daughter's as Jasper whispered. The queen gave a stiff nod, and Jasper bowed before walking down the steps and past Klara with a smug wink. *A pleasure to see you again* was projected into her mind as her arm brushed his on the way out.

"I would hate to interrupt anything. If you have business to attend to, I can wait," Klara said as she watched her mother rise from her throne. Aemella's lilac suit set off her brown skin and her tall, strappy gold heels clicked against the mirrored steps. She was taller than Klara remembered, but it wasn't odd for the fae to tower over other creatures.

"Just a small hiccup; nothing that can't be fixed with some hard labour," Aemella said, smoothing her trousers down her thighs. "How wonderful it is to see you in the flesh!" She wrapped her arms around Klara.

Warmth and light radiated into her, and she wondered how someone so pure could create such evil as the factory.

The fae queen pulled back and gripped Klara's shoulder. "So much power," she said, seemingly to herself.

"I'm happy we both had the time to do this." Klara smiled.

"I thought it was about time you visited without the blood and mess. It took my servants a week to get your blood off the marble!" Aemella laughed and Klara winced, forcing herself to maintain her smile. They both knew Aemella could have rid the marble of the stain with a flick of her wrist. She was glad to have cleaned up at the market. Without that and the glamours that had protected her clothes, she would have been both bloody and covered in the sticky slime of the factory's leeched magic.

"Let us go to the balcony. I think some fresh air will do us both some good." Aemella left Klara's side to open the glass doors that led to a great white marble balcony overlooking all of Kalos. Klara followed her mother outside and stared at the silver wood and the city beyond. After witnessing the smog and filth the creatures were forced to live in at the factory, it was exactly what she needed.

"I doubt you have air this clear in Malum," Aemella said.

Malum? How about in your own land? She kept the thought to herself.

"No, I can't say that we do. Perhaps on the Elven Coast or high in the northern mountains." It was the truth, but at least Malum was honest about its brutality.

"Well, this will be a well-deserved break then. Frendall is with you?" Aemella asked, her white eyes glowing.

"As instructed. I was surprised that he was denied access to the throne room." Klara frowned.

"I meant no slight; I merely wanted some alone time with my daughter."

"We have our portal meetings," Klara pointed out, resting her hands on the balcony.

"I know, but we aren't truly alone, and there's plenty of time later to get to know the commander who shares my daughter's bed."

The words filled Klara with frustration. *She knows of his promotion—why insist on belittling him?*

"Don't be bashful!" Aemella slapped Klara on the arm playfully, and Klara stared at her long, spindly fingers. "I forget how young you are."

"General."

"Pardon?"

"He was promoted after the uprising."

Aemella's lips pinched. "Commander or general, a soldier is a soldier."

Klara decided to change the subject. "The silver wood is undoubtedly an excellent choice of protection. Pretty yet lethal—a bit like yourself."

"Is that all the small talk you can spare for your mother?" Aemella snapped.

Klara looked to where the factory stood hidden. "I never learnt the art of small talk. Eve must have been off that day," she said with a shrug.

"Civility was clearly missing from the curriculum also." Klara barely caught the fae queen's muttered words. "My council thought the wood was an appropriate precaution, considering the number of creatures we have allowed through our border since our treaty was rewritten. Since the higher fae reside behind my palace, placing the wood in front made perfect sense. A creature should have no reason to travel so far."

"I think it's a bit more than a precaution," Klara stated.

"I have every right to protect myself, as you do on your mountain. Now, can we talk about nicer things?" Aemella said, waving her hands as though she was bored of the conversation.

"I'm sorry if my topic of choice disappoints you, but I have a Forest to run and missing creatures to find. I don't have time to discuss the weather and fine flowers."

"They're exquisite, aren't they?" Aemella agreed, her eyes drifting to the gardens below.

"Queen Aemella—"

"Referring to your mother by formal titles? My goodness, I will have to find a servant to remove that stick from your—" Aemella caught Klara's dark gaze. "Fine. Missing creatures? How *awful*." Aemella folded her arms, feigned concern dripping from her lips.

"Yes. A witch came to my castle, telling me her sister had been abducted. A white witch at that." Klara followed the fae queen across the balcony. A white dove perched on the queen's finger, and Klara resisted the urge to roll her eyes.

"Abducted from Malum?" Aemella asked, face devoid of any emotion.

"No; she crossed into Kalos," Klara said.

"So you think a fae took a white witch? Don't be preposterous." The dove took off at the queen's harsh tone.

"I don't think *one* fae took her," Klara said sternly, knowing it would have been a patrol. Fae were smart with their lies.

"I don't want to discuss this any further. I won't have you pointing the finger at my citizens." Aemella strode back inside, and Klara followed.

"Do *your citizens* not include the creatures who passed the barrier of the Neutral Lands and pay ridiculous taxes?"

"Of course."

"What about the creatures you have caged in the Gingerbread Factory?" Klara demanded of her mother's frozen back, unable to contain herself.

"Hmm. Why am I not surprised?" The fae queen's hands found her hips.

Klara stood at the edge of the balcony and pointed to the silver wood. "Right over there, dozens of creatures are being held captive. Are you telling me you know nothing about the harvesting of magic on your land?" Klara was careful to leave Abadan out of it. She didn't want her mother knowing she knew that the fallen high queen was alive. "Aren't you ashamed of what you're doing? Is that why you shield it with protections? It reeks of darkness!"

Aemella walked over to her daughter, and Klara moved away from the ledge. One small push, and she would go over the balcony and onto the drawbridge below. She flinched as Aemella brushed a strand of hair behind her ear.

"Ashamed? No. If I'm to have your creatures wandering my lands freely, then I need to be prepared. Their magic keeps my kingdom strong. A necessary evil."

"A-a necessary evil?" Klara stammered.

"If you don't like to think of it that way, then how about we call it a civic duty? The greater good, sacrifice the few to save... so on and so forth." She sighed.

"How you have kept your light is a mystery to me," Klara spat.

The fae queen pressed her fingers to her lips in contemplation. "The angels need silver blades, and since I altered my trees, supply has never been better. Some things can be looked over for the greater good." Aemella's smile was disturbing.

"The greater good?" Klara stepped away from her mother. *So the magic that's supposed to detect evil and darkness merely ignores wrongdoing so long as the fae justify it?* She was dumbfounded.

"You are young. I do what I must for my people and my domain, which is mine to rule as I see fit. If, by the grace of God, you inherit my throne, you will understand what must be done to maintain balance."

"The creatures have done nothing to harm your land or people." Klara pleaded for her to understand, but Aemella only stared blankly.

"They were given a choice to remain in Malum or stay in Kalos. Just because they chose Kalos does not give them the right to a blessed life. I do not force anyone to stay."

"No, you cage them and strip them of their magic until they are nothing but bones!"

"Only the strongest among them. You must see that if they decided to revolt, I would be at a disadvantage. I allow them to be among my fae. They could easily corrupt the minds of those loyal to me." Aemella sounded as paranoid as Lucifer.

"You're mad," Klara said, unable to believe what her mother was saying.

"This is not your kingdom; I owe you no answer. You had no right to inspect my lands. I could declare war for your breach of treaty law," Aemella stated plainly.

"You invited me yourself—I merely got lost. Have you not encroached on my land? What of the snatches that have been found close to my very own home?" Klara said.

They basked in the awkward silence.

"I don't believe you. Fae would never lay snatches in your lands without my orders. Sneaky, like your father, to come here and toss allegations at me without any evidence," Aemella countered.

Fae would never lay snatches in your lands without my order, Klara repeated to herself. *That wasn't a denial—merely a fact.*

"The factories were outlawed centuries ago. This enslavement is against the laws of the realms," she argued.

"Lucifer outlawed the factories in Malum to prevent Abadan from growing stronger. There is no clause that prevents my use of them," Aemella informed her daughter.

"I will see that damned place closed, and my creatures returned." Klara refused to submit.

"Are they your property? Do you decide for them?" Aemella laughed.

"I'm sure when they decided to stay here, they didn't know they would be forced into the factory."

Mother and daughter stood face to face, inches apart, neither backing down.

"Until it's ruled into the treaty, I will continue to do as I see fit for both my people and my land—and until you can prove I'm taking the lives of innocents, you have no right to intervene," Aemella said through a smug smile.

"I won't let this happen. You can count on that. All it takes is one vote—once I tell the elders of the factory, you'll have no choice but to concede."

Aemella's expression softened. "You have no idea what you're doing. I could take everything from you with a breath."

"And I could surround this place with demons in that same breath," Klara threatened.

"Call your vote. I will wait eagerly for your raven. I would be more than happy to attend a vote; how I love our treaty meetings in Hell. Though I think you expect far too much from your Elders." Aemella pulled at her sleeves in a show of reluctance, but Klara could feel how much she was enjoying this. "Well, I can see you are in no mood to meet the rest of my court. I will postpone the ball until we come to terms," she announced.

Klara turned, not wanting to give her mother that satisfaction. *If I leave now, how will she spin this? That I declared war, overstepped and ended up insulting the very people I need to make allies of?*

"If the prospect of a vote doesn't upset you, then

I think we should be able to separate business and pleasure for one night. After all I have seen the preparations in your hall and courtyard, it would be a waste not to proceed—unless you have urgent matters to attend to," Klara conceded with her best smile. *I can't risk looking like a fool in front of the higher fae.*

"Such matters have already been taken care of; they won't spoil our festivities, though you made quite the mess of my factory. I will need to gather more creatures to fuel its rebuild. One cell, in particular, was left an awful, bloody mess," Aemella said with disgust. "I pray that you will learn your place sooner rather than later. I would hate to see you suffer for your inferiors."

So Jasper did tell her I was at the factory. She knew exactly what I did, and in turn what the fae did to Frendall. Klara clenched her fists, her nails cutting into her palms.

"I'm pleased to see you can separate our personal relationship from our personal ideals as rulers. I will have the servants prepare you something to wear."

"How thoughtful of you," Klara said dryly.

Aemella wrapped her arms around Klara, crushing her uncomfortably.

"Mother, I will see you this evening," she said as the doors opened and Frendall stared back at her.

"I look forward to seeing you both," Aemella called.

Klara charged out of the palace and across the drawbridge. She was in desperate need of some air if she was to spend the night entertaining the highest in Kalos.

"Slow down or you'll end up back in Malum," Frendall said as he caught up to her in the gardens. "Are you going to tell me what happened or make me guess?"

Klara didn't know where to start. She cursed the sun for its glare as she raised a hand to protect her eyes, her mind running a mile a minute.

"As soon as we get back, I'm going to call a vote between Lucifer's council, the elders of Malum and the fae court," she began, when she felt eyes on them. She looked up to see her mother glaring down at them from the balcony.

"You want to alter treaty law?" Frendall asked, following her gaze, but Aemella was already gone.

"Yes. That factory will burn before the next lunar cycle," she declared.

"I take it, from your searing rage, that the fae queen would rather not see such a clause happen." Frendall ran his hand through his hair.

"She sees no fault in it." Klara paced. "She truly believes that it's for the greater good—that's how she's able to maintain her light."

"Light aside, how do you plan to get a clause passed? She has allies in every corner of the Realm and plane of existence. You'll need the elder creatures from every faction in Malum, plus your father's approval, if you're to stand a chance," he warned.

"I can't let her strangle the life out of the creatures every day. What's to stop her from going further when she grows stronger? It's a death sentence crossing into Kalos, when it was supposed to be and promised to be the opposite!" Klara exclaimed, placing her hand over her heart, trying to slow it's beat.

"Then close the border on our side," Frendall said. "Cut off the source."

"I can't," Klara said, knowing how much the creatures of Malum would resent her—and she couldn't abandon those trying to return.

"Why? You have a right to protect your creatures as much as she has a right to slaughter them on her side."

"The treaty forces me to allow them to choose. If I stop them, *I'll* be the one the creatures turn against."

"All because you had to go snooping," he muttered.

"Don't come at me! You wanted me on the throne—well, this is what you get!"

"I'm sorry. I'm with you in this, it's just... you're kind of damned before you even begin," he said with a half-hearted laugh.

Don't I know it.

Once Klara had composed herself, they made their way back to the palace in silence, ready to face whatever the night might bring; but when they reached the guards, they were once again denied access. Klara crossed her arms, teetering on the edge of madness.

"I thought we'd already been through this. I am expected, and if you don't move in the next five seconds, I will shove those spears in a place that will be extremely uncomfortable," she threatened. To prevent Klara from entering the palace as if she was no higher born than any other Kalos citizen!

A soft chuckle sounded as the doors opened behind the silent and still guards.

"You really do have a way with words, Your Highness," Jasper drawled.

Frendall's hand went to his sword as Jasper motioned for the guards to lower their weapons.

"I was sent to give word. The queen is rather busy, and has decided to cancel the festivities. I'm sure you can understand her lack of enthusiasm to be in your presence," Jasper said. He looked much more refined than the last time Klara had seen him, with a maimed fae under his arm.

"Don't you have a wormhole to crawl into, or are you too far up Aemella's arse to call any place home?" she snapped. *Perhaps the idea of the vote does scare her. Why else would she cancel? Without a set date for the meeting, it will give me time to convince the elders and my father to take my side. I'll force Aemella's hand if I have to.*

"I see you have no influence in calming her irrational behaviour," Jasper said to Frendall.

"It's not my place to influence anything the Queen of Malum does. Show some respect, or you'll see just how rational she is," Frendall said, with a glare that would freeze fire.

"I think I preferred you chained to a wall." Jasper smirked, running a hand through his immaculately groomed hair.

Klara watched Frendall's eyes flash amber. Jasper seemed to be trying to provoke a reaction so the queen would have an excuse to cancel the ball. Klara placed her hand on Frendall's back, trying to calm him as Jasper stood inches from the general's face.

"Or maybe being chained up is what you're into?" Jasper mused.

Klara punched him in his pretty nose.

His hands flew to his face as a stream of blood spilt from his nostril. Frendall grunted in amusement, and

Klara felt rather proud of herself as Jasper's eyes watered. The guards gasped, unsure of how to react.

"I think we both know you deserved that. Tell my mother that I look forward to seeing her soon," Klara said. She caught an amused look in the guards' eyes; they thought he had deserved it. "Let's go before we outstay our welcome," she said to Frendall.

"I look forward to our next meeting, but in the meantime, I have a factory to repair," Jasper shouted after them as they turned their backs on the palace. Klara ignored the barb.

"Did you have to hit him?" Frendall said once they were out of earshot. She heard the faint flapping of wings and looked up to see doves flying in all directions from the Palace. *The queen is gathering her allies. I'll have to do the same.*

"The most pleasure I've got out of this day." She grinned, watching the doves disappear, then rubbed her knuckles, remembering the crunch Jasper's nose had made on contact.

"I hope we can fix that." Frendall smirked.

She leant against him, and he kissed the side of her head as they headed back to the capital.

22

Klara rubbed the back of her neck as she sat at her library desk in Malum. She and Frendall had made it out of Kalos, but she needed some room to breathe before she saw Lottie. A chance to gather her strength.

I can't do this, can I? Can I take on my mother and win? I didn't defeat Abadan; it was my mother who intervened. There's no way to know how that day in the throne room would have ended had Lucifer and Aemella not interjected. Her self-doubt gnawed at her as she looked at the map of Kalos and Malum. *If Aemella won't agree to a new clause in the treaty, can I really bring war to Malum?*

Resting her head in her hands, she looked to the witch's necklace on her desk. It was devoid of any glow. *She's the one vying for war. If that's the way this has to end, so be it.*

"Klara! I thought you were never going to come back!" Lottie said, jumping through the portrait of Ethel the Deplorable with Henrietta following not far behind. Klara eyed Lottie's healed foot as she met her ward in the castle corridor.

"It was only a couple of days," she said, wrapping her arms around a sweaty Lottie. "You've been running?"

The portraits eyed their display with eye rolls and tutting. Physical affection was foreign to them.

"Yep! All better now, and Henny couldn't keep up with me this time! I almost made it to the witches' Redwood, but Henny said I had to come back. The hounds were with me, but she still wouldn't let me go," Lottie whined.

Klara felt her stomach drop at the thought of her ward crossing into the Redwood. *The witches would have revelled in taking Lottie since I forbade their use of magic.*

"Welcome back, Your Majesty," Henrietta said, bowing deeply. Klara noted that she looked tired, probably from having to keep up with Lottie.

"Good to be back, but I need you to call the elder creatures from each territory for a gathering," Klara stated. There was no time to waste.

"All the elders?" Henrietta paled, if doomed could even pale.

"I never thought I would have to use the council clause of the treaty, but I need them all in one room to discuss urgent matters regarding the border with Kalos."

"Perhaps visits or envoys would be a better solution?" Henrietta offered, picking at her nails, clearly nervous about the elders all in one place.

"I don't want whispers travelling before I reach each faction of Malum, and I don't want eyes on me while I travel. The trees spread gossip faster than any creature."

"But the ogres and giants at one table!" Henrietta argued politely.

"Just do it, Henny. I don't have time to debate with you." Klara regretted snapping, but she'd already had the same debate with Frendall before he had returned to Hell, and she didn't have the energy to go through it all over again.

"Perhaps if I knew what to tell them?"

"All will be revealed soon enough. For now, I need Lottie dressed and presentable."

"Are you leaving again?" Lottie asked, watching the exchange.

"I have to return to Hell to talk with my father, but I—" Klara was interrupted by a push from behind.

"You're never here anymore!" Lottie shouted. "Now you want to leave again, and I didn't even get to talk to you!"

Klara knelt in front of her ward, tucking a strand of blonde hair behind her ear. "Right now, there are others who need my attention. You'll understand when you're the alpha."

"How will I ever be the alpha if you're never here to teach me?" Lottie argued, moving away from her.

There's no winning with children. "Okay. I'll show you how to make one potion, and then you'll go to your room and get ready?"

Lottie nodded frantically. Klara figured she had just enough time between Henrietta sending out the ravens and the arrival of the elder creatures.

"Before you began your lesson, we were on our way to tell you that you have a visitor in the throne room,"

Henrietta said, and Klara bit the inside of her cheek anxiously.

"Go on ahead to the conservatory, and I'll be along shortly."

"Promise you won't leave?" Lottie said, mistrust in her eyes.

"I promise I won't leave just yet. Make sure she doesn't get at the poisons while I deal with this."

Henrietta took Lottie's hand, and the pair stepped through another portrait together.

"I'm so delighted to be considered worth dealing with," Lokey said, stepping into the corridor.

Klara let out a sigh of relief. "Thank Lucifer. I thought you were a fae waiting to take my head."

"And why would a fae want to take your head?" he asked, his serpent eyes narrowing.

Klara rubbed the back of her neck. "Long story," she muttered, walking alongside him. "What can I do for you? You don't usually grace me with your presence."

Lokey gripped his hands behind his back. "Trouble at Tapped. I was wondering if you could spare a few guards."

"Don't you have some demons on your payroll?" she asked, shocked that he would ask her for help.

"Many, but they don't come at the behest of the queen. The dark fae will react to your guards' black uniforms, whereas the dark fae will fight with my demons."

"I can send two to guard the doors," Klara said, considering the options. "Good enough?" Losing too many guards would put the castle at a disadvantage, but she didn't want Glaudine to suffer after she had sent the witch to Klara. *And she warned me about the creatures being taken.*

"Good enough. Glaudine has been trying to calm things down, but the dark fae seem to be looking for a fight before they've even had a drop of fungus syrup," Lokey explained, his brows knitted together in frustration.

"The guards should right the situation, and if not, I'll make my presence known."

"Most kind of you."

"What are friends for, especially since you took care of matters while I was in Kalos," Klara said, and Lokey laughed.

"Never friends, darling—have I taught you nothing? Allies are what matter most. Friends can be bought," he said with an exaggerated swing of his wrist.

"What's the difference?" Klara asked, amused by Lokey's political musings.

"An ally has skin in the game, a reason to side with you, whereas the love and affection of friendship can be bought, tainted and polluted by jealousy. You'll be wise to remember that," he concluded, pulling at the bottom of his waistcoat.

"I would never doubt your guidance," she said as they walked to the foyer. "Damien is with his mother?"

"No, the little rascal is with your father. We didn't want him around while we are dealing with the issues at Tapped."

"The King of Hell is babysitting? The day I see that for myself will be the day I die of shock." Klara laughed, and it felt good to feel some relief. Lottie loved Lucifer's tricks, but a baby in the hands of the king was a terrifying thought.

"Your father is quite taken with the little demon—anything to distract him from not being able to venture into the human world." Lokey sighed. Klara didn't envy his position as the king's advisor.

"In that, I can agree with you."

He kissed her cheek as the doors to the castle opened for him. "Always a pleasure," he said, bowing before her.

Klara dipped her chin and watched the doors close behind him. *Lucifer babysitting*, she thought, and a shiver ran down her spine. *Dark fae are being disruptive? They're usually too defeated in themselves to be a bother to any creature...*

The conservatory's glass ceiling allowed the moonbeams to illuminate what they were doing.

"Grab that cup from the shelf," Klara told Lottie, getting up from the large wooden table in the centre of the conservatory engraved with a worn, sizeable pentacle.

Lottie climbed the ladder to the wide cabinet shelf laden with potion bottles; beneath it sat cups and saucers of the most delicate china. The structure of the cabinet had almost grown to be a part of the ivy lining the wall, while the rest of the conservatory was made of a combination of clear and stained glass looking out on the Forest below them.

Klara watched as Lottie chose a floral gold cup and saucer, but the flapping of wings drew her attention. She looked up through the glass ceiling to see the ravens flying towards their destinations. At this moment, she was relieved that she had decided not to destroy Abadan's pets after her fall.

Hopefully the creatures will receive the ravens' summoning more kindly than if I had sent demons. I don't want the elders to arrive any more confrontational than need be. They already won't be happy with being in the same room together.

The clinking of cups interrupted her train of thought.

"Why are we using these for a potion?" Lottie asked, hopping off the ladder.

"Presentation matters," Klara replied, offering a half-truth as she flicked through the open grimoire on the table, picking the right potion. Lottie placed the cup and saucer carefully beside the cauldron. Most of the cups had chips and cracks, and a simple touch could cause them to break. Klara wondered why Eve had never used a spell to mend them, but she kept them this way in honour of the queen's passing. The flowers didn't bloom as brightly without constant sacrifice, but Klara fed them with enchanted waters.

Lottie sat on a stool as Klara looked over the plants. Gelsemium, a yellow plant, sweet-smelling, caused paralysis. Chamomile to soothe. Water hemlock for amnesia.

"Which one taught you all of these?" Lottie asked, already knowing the answer.

"Eve, as I've told you many times."

"Was she a good teacher?" Lottie's big eyes stared at Klara, who moved a plant pot from where they were going to work.

"Yes and no. If you wanted to learn, you had to find her and perhaps watch her work. At a safe distance, I might add." She remembered Eve throwing a plant pot at her head when she had failed to name all the plants and herbs in the room.

"Why couldn't you help?" Lottie asked, her little nose all scrunched up.

"She'd argue that plant life can pick up the intentions of those creating them. She said my intentions weren't good."

"Why not?"

"Because I would have much rather have learnt how to poison Abadan than how to cure Eve's mint plants of a slugworm infestation."

Lottie chuckled, and Klara forgot how angry she was at her mother and the creatures' suffering for a brief moment.

"Do you miss her?" Lottie asked, and Klara could see genuine curiosity in her young eyes. She was so pure of heart; sometimes Klara worried that she wouldn't last long in the Forest.

Missing Eve was an unanswerable question. "I'll always be grateful for what she did for me, but she had her own troubles."

The answer didn't seem to make much sense to Lottie, and she furrowed her brow. *You'll understand when you grow up.*

"Enough stalling! Name these three," Klara instructed as she plucked flowers from their beds.

"Gelsemium, water hemlock and..." Lottie frowned as she twirled the white petals between her fingers. Klara smiled at her confusion. Lottie had only been taught the plants and herbs she should fear. She'd noted early that Lottie was fascinated by the toxic and harmful rather than pure and healing.

"Chamomile. It soothes the nervous system." Klara put her out of her misery.

"I thought we were making a poison. Why bother adding it to the other two?"

"We are making a poison, but you need to learn how to disguise your intentions. That's why we're using a cup." Klara popped all three plants into the small cauldron of simmering water at the pentacle's centre on the table. "Allowing the pot to boil will only burn the leaves and destroy the richness of the plants' properties, sinister or otherwise, so you have to observe it. Poison-making is not something to do while distracted, or you might poison yourself in the process."

"Okay," Lottie said, staring so intently at the pot that Klara had to suppress a laugh.

"You could use this if you were in a sticky situation, and you wanted to escape. These three plants will allow you to paralyse the intended, soothing the convulsions brought on by the gelsemium. The chamomile will put them to sleep, and then the hemlock will force them to forget you were even there."

"How would I get them to drink it? And wouldn't that break the Malum breaking-bread clause if they took a drink?"

"So you have been paying attention," Klara said with a wink. The scent of almonds from the gelsemium travelled around them as she stirred the cauldron. "Once the bread has been broken, you *cannot* poison a guest; the consequence for breaking the clause is death itself. However, I hope you have no need to use this within the castle or at any other gathering, unless you plan on starting a war."

"No, I don't want there to be a war."

"That's what I like to hear. Take a vial of this with you on your runs, and if trouble finds you, or you need to escape a territory that you *shouldn't* have visited in the first place"—Lottie cowered slightly at her words; they both knew how she liked to wander where she wasn't supposed to—"and are discovered, you can use these plants to aid your escape. They can be found in the

Forest. You can smell them out if you didn't bring it with you."

"But how would I get them to drink it?"

"Play the fool; act as though you don't want them to have it, and sure enough your enemy will want to take it from you. It's the nature of the Forest. Or force them, pretend it's medicine. Only a witch or warlock would be able to figure out its ingredients with a sniff."

Lottie frowned, watching the steam escaping the simmering cauldron. "I don't really get it."

"Others want what others have, especially in the Forest. Act as though you don't want to give it and it will be taken."

"Oh. I think I get it."

"Everything you need is in the Forest. This is why you need to be studying each and every plant, not just the ones you think will do harm."

"Why? Doesn't it waste time adding others?"

"Creatures are suspicious, as they should be. If there are hints of almond and bittersweet from the poisoning plants, the creature will realise your intentions. However, the chamomile binds them as one plant, as it's also sweet in fragrance."

"What if they force me to drink it?"

"A potion will not work on its brewer unless desired," Klara said, seeing the fear in Lottie's eyes as she poured the potion into the cup. "Now smell," she said, and Lottie took the warm cup in her hands.

Her button nose scrunched. Klara could sense the danger in the cup; her magic wanted to toss it across the room, but she resisted the urge.

"It's really sweet, but I still want to drink it. Something is making me sleepy."

"That's the pure chamomile drawing you in. Can you smell the others?"

"Not really, but it's like I don't care." Lottie looked puzzled.

Klara took the cup from her and poured the potion back into the cauldron. "That's why you need to add good properties within your potions to draw in the drinker. Otherwise, the ill intent will reveal itself. Magic wants to be discovered; its ego demands recognition."

"But it's just a potion! It doesn't have feelings."

"Don't be fooled. Magic lives and breathes like the rest of us. It chooses a side and doesn't come without cost." Klara could see that it was too much in one lesson as Lottie yawned. "That's it for today; it's late. Go on up to bed."

"I thought I would see the elders! I haven't seen them all together yet, and the envoys at the gatherings don't count," Lottie protested, as Klara had feared she would.

She had considered and planned on letting her ward sit in, but she felt the disturbing nature of the factory was too much for someone so young, and she wanted to spare her a little while longer. But *if I don't make a small concession, she'll only use the portraits to listen in.*

"You can stay for arrivals, but you won't join us for the council meeting." She placed a lid on the pot. *I'll have Henny vial this later; no point in it going to waste.*

"But..."

"If you argue, you don't come at all," Klara snapped.

Lottie hopped off the stool. "Fine," she huffed, and Klara ruffled her hair. *Why does she have to be so eager to grow up?*

23

"Crown or no crown?" Klara asked Lottie, standing behind her at the dressing table in Lilith's rooms.

It had taken more than a few days for the elders to respond to her ravens —more days than Klara was prepared to wait, but she had to respect their need for time if they were to side with her.

"Always a crown," Lottie said, picking up Abadan's once gold and ruby-adorned crown. Klara had never liked the blood-red jewels, so she'd morphed it into a simple silver crown studded with diamonds that sat nicely in her hair. It would be a gentle reminder to others of her status without flaunting it.

Since Klara had given Lottie her sky room, she sometimes opted for Lilith's old chambers. Lilith had hated anyone in her private room so Klara had had her own quarters built, but once Aemella and Lucifer had left Malum with a newly signed treaty, she'd found herself at the centre of Lilith's room with a bottle of venom and a heavy head. It might have been the weapons on the walls or the smell of bergamot lingering on Lilith's remaining clothes that called to her. She had silently hoped that Lilith would spring back to life just to kick her out of the room.

"Your Majesty, the elders have begun to arrive," Henrietta said, coming through the bedroom wall while Lottie placed the crown on Klara's head. Lottie wore her mini commander suit—it was sure to irritate the lycaons, but it made her ward feel strong so Klara allowed it.

"Thank you. Now, how do I look?" Klara asked, running her hands over the black bodice that pulled in her waist. Heavy emerald fabric beneath it flowed to the floor but showed her skin-tight black trousers beneath. It was almost too similar to Abadan's style, but Klara liked the combination of feminine and masculine. It made her feel untouchable. The bodice pushed up what cleavage she had, while her hair draped over her shoulders.

"Good enough to kill," Henrietta admitted, with a faint wince. "Though something is missing."

Klara revealed her white eyes. "And now?"

"Like a queen worthy of the name." Henrietta smiled.

"Let's hope I can call myself one after this meeting," she muttered, and both Henrietta and Lottie looked worried. "Remain at Lottie's side. The lycaons will no doubt have their eyes on her since our last meeting."

"I won't let her out of my sight," said Henrietta.

Behave yourself, or you will not be allowed to run for a week, Klara warned, projecting the thought to her ward, who suddenly found her feet very interesting.

The doors to the castle remained open, with demons posted on either side. Klara noted the sneers they received as the elders from each faction gathered in the foyer.

Matthias and his beta had been the first to arrive. Klara followed the alpha's gaze to the landing, where Lottie and Henrietta watched the arrivals.

The warlocks had decided to remain concealed behind their white porcelain masks and painted red eyes, while the ogres remained closest to the doors, their overalls freshly pressed for the occasion. It made Klara miss her own dungarees. She felt a wave of anxiety; there was no sign of Gratide with his giants. It had been a long while since she had seen her friend, and she wondered if he was abstaining or merely late.

The witches wore their full skirts; some walked through the foyer with canes in hand as their magic waned. *The climb up the mountain must have been Hell for them.* Klara tried to conceal the joy she felt at the thought. *Then again, if it hadn't been for the witch who warned me, I would have remained ignorant of the Gingerbread Factory.* She was relieved to see that particular witch had not attended, or Klara would have had to break the news about Frieda's death, if she had not already felt it.

The vampires were the last to arrive as the second moon rose to its highest position, the whites of their eyes threaded with black and red veins. Klara watched over the elders from the staircase; they had each come with two of their own kind. She couldn't blame them for wanting back-up.

She cracked her neck for some small relief from the tension in the air. Since the divide of Kalos and Malum, they had never been together at one time. During the monthly gathering at the castle, it was mostly envoys, while each elder decided to attend only when another did not.

Klara tried to wait for the giants to make their entrance, but she couldn't stall any longer as the pixies and minotaurs grew restless. With everyone else gathered, she cleared her throat, and the small conversations halted.

"Thank you for coming at such short notice. If you follow me through to the dining hall, we can begin."

Before she even had a chance to move from the grand staircase, a voice from the gathered creatures stopped her.

"The Three Queens never summoned us like this. Lumping us together like we're yours to command—it's beneath us, and we deserve more respect," one of the vampire envoys said, their red eyes peering out from their black hood. Klara noted it wasn't Elder Langda who spoke.

"It's because I see you as equals that I call on you like this; I do not go to one faction before the other. Trust me, this matter affects all of us."

"Equals? Our settlement predates the Lucifer treaty. How can *we* possibly be equals?" the vampire muttered under their breath, but Klara heard it, as did everyone else in the room. Elder Langda removed her black silk hood and snapped the outspoken vampire's neck in a flash.

The silence threatened to remove the air from the room.

"I apologise for my envoy's sharp tongue, Your Majesty. Many of our kind have been underground and away from other creatures for too long," the elder said, revealing a fanged smile.

"Elder Langda, I take no offence." Klara offered a bow as thanks for the show of support. Not many creatures would have sacrificed an envoy at such a mere slight. "I understand that calling you all here is unorthodox, but all will be explained. Now, if you will follow me." The last sentence was a command this time.

Klara turned her back on the elders, her heels clicking as she made her way to the dining hall. The table was stripped bare and only gold goblets marked each seat. Klara had ordered her doomed to remove anything that might be used as a weapon. In the company of elders that meant anything, so they had done their best. The elders took their carefully distanced seats while their envoys stood beside them, protecting their flanks. Klara eyed the portraits on the walls; their yellow eyes watched on with great amusement.

"To peace," Klara said, raising her goblet, and they all took a sip, silently agreeing that no blood would be spilt tonight. They were waiting for her to lead the conversation. The torches on the walls shone brightly as the gathering commenced.

"I recently returned from the fae lands of Kalos, and it is with a cold heart that I seek your counsel," she started.

"Why should your trip matter to us? We have had no issue with the fae in the south," Elder Ogre Rathbrook said with his wart-covered fists on the table.

"Yeah, what's it to us what happens on the other side of the river?" Elder Pixie Mythola chimed in, and the minotaur elder, Turoc, grunted through their tusks in agreement.

Great start, Klara. "You might not take issue with those across the Styx. However, Fae Queen Aemella has taken it upon herself to restore a Gingerbread Factory."

Silence returned to the table.

Not the reaction I was expecting, she thought. "Perhaps I

shouldn't call it that name, since its intent is no longer to lure in children, but Aemella has no intention of luring; she has been taking. Kalos itself is the lure."

"Such a place has been outlawed by Lucifer himself," Centaur Phylix said in dismay, puffing out his bare chest.

"This is true; however, Aemella is enslaving the strongest of the creatures who pass through the Neutral Lands and using their magic and strength to empower herself and her guard."

Again silence. Morals they might not have, but Klara had been expecting some sort of reaction to the loss of their kin. Instead, the elders refused to meet her eye.

"Do you have nothing to say?" she asked, her palms flat against the table, trying to read her guests as best she could.

"How are we to know this is the truth? Aemella is your blood. How do we know you are not testing us?" Elder Rathbrook said, rubbing the eye-patch that concealed his missing eye. There was no love lost between Klara and the ogres, since they had sided with Abadan and she had been forced to remove them from the castle. They resented losing their position as protectors of the castle.

"I'm your queen and ally before I am anyone's blood. I don't want to see any creature drained of their magic and life, no matter who they might be. I plan on calling a vote to add a clause to the treaty forbidding the use of the factories, and I need your votes if it is to pass," Klara said.

"Still, this is not happening in Malum, so why should we dirty our hands? Such a vote will only anger the fae queen," Alpha Matthias said, and there was a mumble of agreement.

How is this their reaction? "Do you not care that your

kin is being stripped of their magic and mutilated, when a mere vote could stop it?" Her voice laced with contempt.

"How dare you question our loyalty to our kin? Such a vote could cause a war. Where was their loyalty when they left us for their precious Kalos? They think, like the fae, that we are inferior—so I say we let them be." Elder Elf Yadira rose from her chair, her long silver cloak causing the others to shift away. "Your Majesty, as you are well aware, the Elven Coast has a long-standing history with Kalos; we did not make war when Aemella decided to sign over this land to Lucifer, and we do not wish to get caught up in petty politics with Kalos now. If this is all that you have to tell us, I wish to take my leave."

"I was surprised you even accepted my invitation. The elves are renowned for their isolation on the coasts," Klara acknowledged. The elves held enough considerable power over the port and owned ninety percent of the ships that sailed the different lands; ordering them to remain would do her more harm than good. *If they decide to side with the fae, it will give Aemella access to their coast and port.*

"I would never disobey my queen, but given how we are so cut off from the Forest, I don't think the fae queen will take much interest in us, as I doubt any of my people would take an interest in leaving for Kalos. We have our own war with the mer-folk to consider; we cannot waste resources on those who now suffer the consequences of their own choices," Yadira continued, a few of the elders following along closely.

Klara herself had seen an elf in the factory, but she could sense the lack of empathy radiating from Yadira. The one thing the fae and the elves had in common was their superiority complex. There was a quiet grumble about the elves' self-importance and pompous nature before Klara's fist hit the table and silenced them.

"I understand you are already under strain; you are excused. However, if there comes a time when I need your ships and your people, I expect them to be ready."

"You never need doubt it, Your Majesty—but until that day comes, my people are to be left out of this." Elder Yadira bowed politely before vanishing from the room. *I might not have her vote, but at least I have her ships should war come.*

"I see there are rules for some and not for others," Matthias said.

"The elves will be my allies in war, should it come, which is more than the rest at this table have done— shown themselves to be my ally against the fae queen!" Klara barked.

"At least the elves showed up. What of the giants, your own allies against Abadan?" Rathbrook argued, the pixies and minotaurs nodded along.

"The giants are dealing with a separate matter at my behest." It was a lie, and she prayed they wouldn't question it. Klara wished to know as much as the rest of the table where they were and why they had failed to attend.

Rathbrook eyed her suspiciously.

"I have heard reports of some being taken from Malum by force. Can anyone second these rumours?" Klara asked. It was another lie, but she wanted to see how deep this lack of action would run. The witches had yet to speak, which made her suspicious.

"We would never allow that to happen," Elder Langda said, taking a sip of blood from her goblet.

"No, neither would we. However, I highly doubt Queen Aemella would go to such lengths," Ogre Rathbrook said, leaning back into the chair.

"She would," the Elder Crone said, her frown deepening. "We are paying the price for our strength, as Queen Klara sees fit; however, my sister witches started going missing the more sacrifices we held. Choosing to leave or not, they were gone. I thought it was our young queen until she visited us."

Klara stared wide-eyed at the crone. *Aemella is trafficking creatures out of Malum by force. The treaty might not allow me to shut down the factory for now, but trafficking creatures means the fae are stepping foot on Malum soil.*

"Your Majesty, do not pay heed to the crone's words. Nothing but lies escape her lips," the elder ogre sneered.

"The lycaons have witnessed no such thing, and we run the lengths of the Forest; we would have smelt the fae," Matthias argued.

The witch shook her head. *The witches and warlocks carry the strongest magic—it makes sense that she went after them first.*

"Warlock Osmund, have you nothing to add? Your warlocks travel the Forest with medicines; have they witnessed nothing, not even the presence of a snatch?" Klara asked. There was a mumble between the creatures as she mentioned the snatches.

"We shall remain neutral, as the warlocks have always done." Osmund's wry voice echoed from behind the mask, and everyone at the table groaned at the non-answer.

"Remaining neutral will only appease the fae queen. I negotiated for the border reliefs to aid our kin, not sign their death warrant."

"Creatures die every day in or out of Malum. Our young queen has a bold heart," Matthias mocked, and the ceiling's stars crackled with thunder as Klara tried to contain her rage. She noticed that his beta, Ceylon, was nowhere to be seen amongst the exceptionally long table of twenty-plus elders. Klara hadn't even met them all yet—she only knew their names, especially those from the smaller factions. *Ceylon must have slipped away. She's probably lurking in the castle, trying to find answers at her alpha's request... but the doors of importance won't open without the right blood.*

"My heart isn't the problem. One factory can easily turn to several, and if Malum lets a few creatures be sacrificed, then the fae queen will take more and more—until she thinks, why take one at a time? Why not take back my land?" Klara argued. That seemed to grab everyone's attention. "Do you not like the reduced taxes I have implemented, the freedom to sell human objects and trade personally with the Port? Do you think Aemella will allow such lenience? I turned the Beanstalk into a damned food kitchen. I can't be accused of not doing what is right for the creatures of this land!"

"What would you suppose we do?" Matthias put in with feigned indifference.

Klara pressed her knuckles into the table as she stood. "The vote will add a clause to the treaty, thus preventing Aemella from maintaining the current factory and resurrecting another. The creatures already held will be released once it passes."

"A vote? What fae nonsense. Why not slit the fae queen's throat and take Kalos?" Elder Langda hissed.

"The fae guard is too strong, and the fae court holds great houses that will take time to invade. There would be more losses to our side than theirs, and the magic they're harvesting will only make them stronger, which is why we need to act sooner rather than later."

"Where will this vote take place?" Langda asked, tapping her sharp nail against the table.

"Hell. Neutral land for both the fae and us."

"We can't venture to Hell; who's to say your father will not turn on us all?" Minotaur Turoc argued.

"If you are going to continue to argue, then maybe we should submit right now—send our youngest to the factory in good faith," the crone croaked.

Roars of outrage filled the room as the elders boasted their anger and goblets clattered against the walls. *Now that's more like it.* Matthias remained silent.

"If I can convince the King of Hell to hold the vote, and everyone at this table votes in favour of the clause, then the vote will carry. I suspect even some of the high fae will want the factory gone."

There was a mumble of agreement between the elders and their companions.

"She clearly has the support of the giants; who's to say others at this table won't turn," Klara heard Centaur Phylix whisper to Elder Goblin Kogamar, who was more fascinated by his gold goblet than the current conversation.

The giants? I can only pray they take my side.

"We stand with our queen."

Elder Langda said it first, and the rest followed in agreement, one after the other, but Klara could feel the hesitation in their voices. Their belief was not as steadfast as she would have liked, but it would be enough for now. *I'll bring them proof to seal the deal.*

With all in agreement, Klara signalled for the doomed. They refilled the elders' glasses with their drink of choice—blood, venom or wine.

"Then it's settled. I will send ravens when the time has come to depart to Hell. A piece of advice: my father hates delay, so please be on time. We all stand as individuals, but a threat to one of us is a threat to all of us," Klara said, rising with her goblet. Everyone raised their glasses and drank, except for Matthias.

One by one, the elders left, whispering amongst themselves as they went and leaving a sour taste in her mouth. When the doors to the castle closed, Klara let out a sigh of relief. *Step one complete.* She was about to climb the stairs when she saw Matthias lingering in the archway.

"I didn't realise you were still here," Klara said.

"Your senses have weakened." Matthias smiled, leaving the shadows.

"Or I'm simply tired, and if you don't mind—" She was about to have him removed when she smelt it: a faint sweetness in the air. Klara moved closer to the alpha and eyed the goblet in his hand as he went to drink.

"Matthias, you don't want to drink that," she yelped, stretching a hand over it, to his surprise. "It seems my ward bears a grudge from our last meeting."

Klara sniffed the sweet almonds emanating from the liquid. The little devil had mixed the potion into the venom, and from the strong scent of almonds, she had added enough gelsemium to kill the alpha.

Matthias put down the goblet, and a smile travelled to his eyes.

"The little lycaon has some fight in her; I can appreciate that," he said, smelling the poison himself.

"She will be punished accordingly, that I can assure you." Klara's eye fixed on the portrait behind Matthias as she sensed Lottie lurking behind it, waiting to see if her foolish plan landed. She gritted her teeth. *If another elder had succumbed to the potion, there would have been war.*

"I can forgive a half-hearted poisoning," Matthias said. Klara was surprised by his indifference. *Did he already know it was poisoned? A test to see if I would stop him from drinking it?* "You're really sure about making the fae queen your enemy?"

She was grateful he had changed the subject. "She is not my enemy. I understand she wants more power, but I will not have it be at the expense of Malum. My mother is doing this to test me. She loves games more than anything."

"Still, riling the elders like that can only lead to war."

"What is it you want? The night has been long, and I have no interest in your cryptic thoughts."

"To see Malum standing strong—and yet you can't seem to get a handle on a single lycaon child. I worry as you do about the creatures you seem to be leading into war."

And you don't think Malum is strong enough to defeat Kalos? Klara listened to his words, but sensed no hate for Kalos or the fae queen. *He's playing his own game. I'll be watching your vote on the day, you can be damn sure of that.*

"Then we both have the same goal: to see Malum thrive." The castle doors opened with a wave of her hand. "Now I ask you politely to return to your beta. I think she has waited long enough."

Matthias drifted closer, and Klara could feel the loathing emanating from him.

"Everything okay here?"

Frendall's voice surprised her. She had been too busy figuring out what Matthias was doing to detect his energy.

The alpha bowed and handed her the goblet. "Goodnight, Your Majesty." He winked before leaving. Once the doors closed, Klara threw the poisoned goblet against the wall.

"What did *he* want?" Frendall wondered from the shadows.

"To make my life harder." Klara ran her hands through her hair, removing her crown as she sat on the stairs.

"Heavy is the head," he said, watching her place it on the step.

"How was Hell?" Klara asked, trying to rid her mind of Matthias and the sinking feeling in her gut. "Did you manage to see my father?"

Frendall shook his head. "No, I didn't get a chance. There was a breach in the hounds' kennels; they destroyed a few souls in the Maze, but I managed to sort it out."

Klara sighed. *How many things can go wrong in one moon?* "No matter. Probably best we talk to him together, now that the creatures have agreed to a vote—although the giants were a no-show," she said, eased by having him close.

"He won't like that you talked to the elders before informing him. Gratide didn't show?"

"Better to ask for forgiveness than permission. I'll have to visit their territory tomorrow, find out where his loyalties lie." Klara rose on her tiptoes and pressed her lips to his, surprising him. He pulled back for a second before placing his hands on her hips.

Frendall pushed her against the bannisters, and she forgot about the vote, the imprisoned creatures, as he carried her to her bedroom. His lips never left hers.

"She will join the family," Gino said, and Klara felt the ghoul's hand plunge through her chest. She watched Gino's face slip away, and there stood her mother, a beating heart gripped in her hand.

"Son of a bitch!" Klara sat up, pushing the sheets off as she tried to catch her breath.

Frendall stirred and rubbed her back, his eyes still closed. Klara hugged her knees to her chest. *Get out of my head*, she prayed, but when she settled back down and closed her eyes, she saw Frendall lying dead on the battlefield, coated in blood, his cold eyes staring up at her.

"Nightmares?" Frendall murmured. She leaned against her pillows and nodded as he rubbed his eyes awake. "I didn't know they'd started again."

"Neither had I. I think my magic is trying to warn me," Klara said.

He patted his chest. She rolled to her side and placed her head on his bare skin, her racing heart steadying to match his.

"The pressure is getting to you, that's all," Frendall reassured her.

"How am I supposed to do this forever? I feel like I'm cracking at every hurdle," she admitted, tracing a recent scar on his abdomen. *His magical healing is usually quick, so it must have just happened. The injuries from Kalos and the prolonged stay in silver might have slowed his healing slightly.* Being a general came with more responsibility and hard choices. Unless she needed to know, she knew he wouldn't want to darken their limited time together.

"I don't envy you, but you're doing your best. The creatures have agreed to support you," Frendall said, brushing her hair through his fingers.

"For now, I can feel their plotting, and I don't know if it's real or if it's my father's blood making me paranoid." She looked up at his eyes.

"One step at a time. If they turn on you, we'll handle it. If you don't have the Forest, there's a whole legion of demons, lower and higher, that will go to war with you."

"To get Hell on side, I have to talk with my father, but only after I speak with Gratide." Klara sighed as he kissed the top of her head.

"Good—your being in Hell means I get you into my bed again. I beg you make it quick with the giants," Frendall said playfully, and she slapped his chest. "Oh, you want to fight?" He rolled over, his impressive frame pinning her to the bed. Klara struggled as he trapped her wrists above her head, then laughed as he brushed his nose against hers.

"Get off," she coughed as he pressed the delicious weight of his body against her.

"I would prefer it if we did that together," he whispered in her ear, and she moaned as his lips trailed down her neck to the faint scar between her breasts. Klara let the weight of her anxiety drift away, and lost herself in the sensations.

24

The guards opened the castle doors with a polite 'Good morning'.

Klara had left Frendall to sleep, since they had been up most of the night—plus, she figured that if she woke him he would have to leave, and even knowing he was in the castle brought her some peace.

She had had to pull herself from the warmth of their bed, wanting to leave for the giants' territory before the day began. The journey would be long, so she opted for a warm cream shirt tucked into trousers cuffed tightly at her ankles, an excellent feature for keeping out the vampire beetles that roamed the giants' territory. Her axe was harnessed high on her back.

Much to her surprise, when the doors opened Gratide stood before her, a sad look in his eyes as he waited at the top of the mountain pass. His flushed purple skin and sweat-stained shirt made it obvious that he had rushed here. Waves of uncertainty washed from him, and Klara sensed that bad news was coming her way.

"Before you start," Gratide began, "I need to be clear that my decision not to come before you and the other elders was not intended as a slight." He paused, catching his breath, and Klara allowed him to continue without interruption. "The giants have had no issues with the fae, and wish to be left out from this vote you talked of last night. I know you were on your way to see me, to convince me of their wrongdoing, which is why I made the journey to you. I wanted to talk to you in private, without the creatures interfering."

"Your kin is mutilating themselves so they aren't deemed fit for the factories, and you have nothing to say?" Klara asked, the cold mountain air whipping around them.

Her words seemed to pain him, yet she sensed no outrage. "Klara, I serve you first and foremost, but the factory is a small price to ensure peace. The giants have seen war between Malum and Kalos when the lands were split. There is no winning, only bloodshed felt through the generations. We have to learn to share this plane, or history is doomed to repeat itself," Gratide said.

Klara remembered that giant blood still stained the fields of the Neutral Lands from when they had stood with her against Abadan's army.

"Appeasing Aemella won't stop those she has taken from dying; it will only shield our eyes from it," she said. "I'm not asking for a war, I'm asking for a vote. To negotiate," she added.

"This vote could inspire war. If it does not go our way, will you stand by and allow Aemella to continue?"

he countered, and she could feel his sorrow bubbling beneath the surface.

"Sacrifice a few to save the many? That's what you would have me do? I'm willing to negotiate, to make peace, but if she won't see reason then I'm not left with much choice—or are you so deluded by your loyalty to the fae queen as to believe this is as far as she'll take it?" Klara demanded, folding her arms across her chest as the cold wind bit at her skin.

"For such allegations there needs to be proof—a witness other than you. One factory can hardly do us damage. The welfare of a few creatures is no reason for war if their loss means improved relations between our lands." Her challenge had angered him.

Klara couldn't believe what Gratide was saying. He was obviously in denial. Then again, he was protecting his own kin, as each elder would.

"I'm sorry you feel that way. I'll bring the proof I need to the vote, and I hope you'll make the right choice for your people—on both sides of the Styx," she said, placing her hand on his.

"The fae queen has done more for us than you can possibly imagine. She protected us with glamours against Abadan, gave us resources and food after the war with the ogres. How am I to repay that with betrayal?" Gratide said, shaking his head in dismay. *He's already at war with himself.*

"You didn't deliver the first blow. She took advantage of your loyalty, and will continue to do so until we stop her and diminish her thirst for power." Klara pleaded for him to see reason.

"I can make you no promises. My people are torn apart. They had heard rumours of the factory, and your raven only confirmed our doubts. The young want to rise, and now I'm dealing with a divided people and my loyalties to you."

"I don't care about your loyalty to me. The fae queen won't stop with one factory, as Abadan did not stop with one jewel. I've seen the horrors for myself, and she has no intention of stopping the draining of the creatures. I don't think it's a question of whether I want war or not," Klara said sadly.

There was a moment of silence, and Gratide let out a deep sigh of defeat.

"I'm sorry, Your Majesty, but I will side with what my people decide," he told her.

"Then I ask no more of you than to listen to both sides and make your choice in Hell," she answered calmly.

Gratide opened his mouth to speak, but there was nothing left to say. A line had been drawn between them, and only time would tell where either would stand at the end.

Klara watched the elder giant disappear down the mountain. *That saved me a journey, but I'd have happily made it to get a different answer.* But she suspected that if the young giants had heard her speak, Gratide would already be dealing with his own uprising, and that was the last thing she wanted. With a heavy heart, she wondered what would happen should she lose not only his support but his friendship.

"I thought you were leaving us for the day?" Henrietta said, greeting Klara in the foyer.

"Change of plans. The giants have decided amongst themselves. There's nothing more I can do to persuade them without provoking an internal battle. While I have you, could you brew me some black cohosh root tea?"

Henrietta blushed. "The general stayed the night? Shall I make breakfast?" The tea would help regulate

Klara's cycle and prevent the pitter-patter of little feet running through the castle. "I shall brew a cup and bring it right away. The usual place?"

"Yes, and since I won't be making a trip to the giants, I'm afraid I have to leave sooner than I expected. I'll accompany Frendall to Hell. I have some urgent matters to discuss with my father," Klara told her.

"Of course, Your Majesty."

"What would I do without you?" Klara asked, and Henrietta shrugged before disappearing.

"Still don't feel like getting up?" Klara asked.

Lilith lay motionless on the stone slab. Her face was expressionless, her skin ashen and dull, her body covered with a light woven dress that travelled to her ankles. Klara placed her hand over her mentor's, resting on her abdomen. She slipped into Lilith's mind.

Nothing. Just a blank sheet. Is this what death looks like?

"Should I let you go?" Klara asked Lilith's blank expression as she stood in the dimly lit room beneath the dining hall.

No answer.

"If you could just open your damn eyes and tell me what I should do! Am I wrong to call for a vote?" she begged, pacing back and forth. "I confronted my mother, the fae queen—but you already knew that, didn't you, that she was my mother? Almost a decade to tell me the truth, to warn me, to prepare me, but you decided to keep that truth to yourself." Klara leant against the slab. "Aren't you going to scold me for acting before thinking? Question my abilities as a queen?"

Nothing. Not even a flinch. Klara massaged her temples as she vented, losing herself in the surrounding silence.

"Abadan's alive, and her precious factory is back up and running. Aemella has decided to bring the harvesting factory back to life." She'd been sure that information would bring about a small reaction, but Lilith didn't budge. *The witch's potion factories might be considered harrowing, but at least they now offered food and shelter to their workers.*

"She set hounds on you! Don't you want the slightest bit of revenge?" Klara took a seat on the simple wooden chair beside Lilith. The torches on the wall flickered, and she wondered if it was a sign or just a draught. "I shouldn't even want your counsel. You only ever gave me half-truths and lectures."

She sat in silence for a moment, but the anger wouldn't dissipate.

"What if I hurt you?" Klara filled her palm with fire and threatened Lilith's skin, singeing the light hairs on her arms so that she would feel the threat of the incredible heat, only to toss it against the wall. "Damn you! If I end up with my head on a spike, I will find you, wherever you are, and bug the shit out of you for eternity—so wake up and save yourself that misery," she pleaded.

Save the creatures, sacrifice the creatures. Ignore the factory, burn the factory. If I burn that bridge with my mother, what will happen to the border? Kalos could shut itself off completely, meaning the fae guard would be able to go back to torturing those who dare to cross into the Neutral Lands. Since when have I cared about the just thing? The creatures did choose to leave on their own. Why should I risk war for those no longer in my care?

Klara could almost hear Lilith's preaching. *Because if it was Lottie, you would burn down every high fae house in Kalos. It's not about being morally superior, it's about not appearing weak to those who would gut you, it's about saving a village instead of gutting the person who caused the destruction in the first place.*

A smile threatened to appear on Klara's lips. "Why did you always have to speak in riddles? You couldn't have just said 'Defeat thine enemy'?"

If you know that's what you have to do, then shut your trap and spill some blood.

Klara's eyes widened as the thought emanated from Lilith. "So now you feel like helping?" she demanded, only to receive no reply. "Silent treatment—how very Lucifer of you." *Maybe if I brought my father, he would be able to force you awake?* Klara didn't know what damage a forced awakening would inflict on Lilith's soul; she would have to wait and see, as much as it pained her. *She thought something. That's progress.*

"Don't die while I'm gone. I know you'll want to see how this turns out," she whispered in Lilith's ear, before kissing her mentor's cheek. "Because I know how much you *love* affection."

Still nothing. Klara sighed as she dimmed the torches and made her way back through the portrait, leaving her mentor in her eternal sleep.

Klara stepped out of the portrait to find Frendall talking with Henrietta, and Klara eyed the cup in the doomed's hand.

"I thought you wanted to leave for the giants' territory first thing?" Frendall asked as she went to his side.

"Gratide came to me—he's on the fence," she said, and watched his jaw clench. Henrietta offered her the fragrant cup.

"At least he saved you a trip," he said as she took a sip and winced at the bitter taste. "Something to tell me?" he added in a whisper, and she elbowed him in the ribs.

"Unless you want a fae-angel-demon running around, I wouldn't joke about birth control," she told him, seeing Henrietta flush before dismissing herself. Frendall winked as Klara finished the cup's contents. "Now I have more time to punish that little runt," she said, placing the cup on the long table. Lottie sat at the other end, surrounded by pastries.

"What did I do?" she asked innocently, taking a small bite of snapper-fruit-filled pastry.

"Oh, you don't know?" Klara asked with feigned surprise, before her glare became menacing. "If you lie to me, Lottie, I swear on Lucifer—"

Lottie dropped the pastry, the pale green jam oozing out onto the table, and eyed the door. *I'll give her a head start.*

"You have to catch me to punish me!" Lottie locked eyes with her guardians for a second and then made a run for it. The demons posted at the doors attempted to grab her but she slipped between their legs, sliding along the stone floor before leaping into lycaon form.

Klara smiled at Frendall. "Don't you love it when they run?" She laughed sadistically, before chasing after her ward.

"Can we not have a civilised breakfast?" Frendall yelled after them.

"Keep running! I'd better not catch you," Klara called as they raced through the castle, up and down the varying levels and jumping through portraits, until Lottie reached a dead end at the double doors of Abadan's sealed quarters. She shifted back into human form.

"Are you done running?" Klara asked, and Lottie's shoulders hunched. Klara grabbed her by the back of the neck, not hard enough to hurt but enough to make her stop struggling. "I showed you that potion to teach you a valuable lesson, not to undermine me."

"You taught me to hurt my enemies! I tried!"

A few guards chuckled as they passed.

"There is a time and a place, Lottie—not in the middle of a gathering!"

"You said when their defence is down, and there was technically no bread on the table," Lottie panted as Klara dragged her down the stairs to the west wing and the ice baths. Freezing ocean water travelled through the mountains, seeping their way through the stone and into carved crystal baths there—perfect for teaching young creatures how to behave. Klara brought her to the one that Lilith had used to love dunking her in. It had been a way to speed up her recovery after hard training, but also a punishment.

"Get in." The torches reflected off the crystals embedded in the walls, so there was plenty of light to watch Lottie frown.

"It's so cold in there," she whined, dipping a foot in with a hiss.

"You almost started a *war* with the lycaons, and you're worried about a little cold?" Klara wanted her to know the severity of her actions.

Lottie stuck her tongue out in defiance.

"Get in, or I will force you in."

"Why am I being punished? You don't even like Matthias!" Lottie argued.

"If that goblet had ended up in another elder's hands, we would be lying in a pool of our own blood right now. Actions have consequences—now get in," Klara insisted, pointing to the water.

Lottie jumped into the circular pond, the sub-zero water steaming as it came into contact with the high temperature of a lycaon.

"Don't even think about shifting," Klara ordered when Lottie resurfaced, her once ice-blue eyes now roaring amber as she tried to stop the change. "Do you think I have time to stand here and punish you? That I *want* to punish you?"

"I c-can't swim, it's too c-cold!" Lottie's teeth chattered, her arms moving frantically as she kept herself afloat. Klara could see through the clear waters to the bottom of the crystal bath. She wasn't in danger of drowning even if her arms failed her or cold water shock kicked in; she would have to learn to float instead of treading water.

"Stop fighting the cold, and you won't swallow half the water." Klara's voice echoed off the walls.

"You never wanted me to be your ward—that's why you want to punish me!" Lottie spluttered.

"No, I didn't want a ward, but I've kept you fed and safe, and Henny teaches you everything you need to know in my absence. You're not beaten or starved as I was, and yet you defy me!"

Henrietta joined them at Klara's back.

"Help her out and see her bathed. She is not to step one paw out of this castle until I return."

"I can't even run? But it's a Full Moon," Lottie cried as Henrietta helped her from the water.

"Then it will be a great opportunity to learn to control the change."

"I hate you," Lottie said through blue lips, and Klara's heart constricted. She tugged a towel around her ward's shoulders.

"Good! Maybe that will toughen you up. Pull a stunt

like that again, and I will teach you to loathe me. Is that understood? Letting your emotions drive you will get you killed."

"Like you're any better," Lottie muttered under her breath, scowling, and Klara knelt in front of her ward.

"If the poison had been successful, the lycaons would have demanded your head as a traitor to their kin. They wouldn't have seen it as you defeating their alpha, but as the coward's way out. The lycaons would have rejected your claim in an instant." Klara gripped her shoulders. "Do you understand?"

"Yes. I wanted to make you proud!" Lottie sobbed, before pulling from Klara's grasp and running up the stairs from the underbelly of the castle. Klara buried her face in her hands.

"Don't look at me like that. A lot worse was done to me."

Henrietta picked up Lottie's shoes. "And where are they now?"

Fair point.

Frendall stood at the entrance to the cave with her sheathed axe in hand. "I thought you would need this," he said, and Klara secured it to her back. "Everything sorted with Lottie? I thought I heard her crying."

"She had a lesson to learn. I didn't get a chance to tell her we are leaving," she said, not meeting Frendall's eye.

"Probably best you two have some space for now. The baths were the best way to teach her?"

Klara felt he was too soft on Lottie. "A shock to the system will do her good. This isn't Kalos, and the quicker she learns that, the better. No one will offer her a helping hand. She's meant to be a leader, not a coward who hides behind a potion."

Frendall huffed, and Klara led them to the fountain in the conservatory. "Why are you looking at me like that? How else is she supposed to learn?"

"You're right, she could have got herself killed."

"So why the look?"

"You sounded awfully like Lilith." He shook his head, opening the glass door to the conservatory.

I'd rather hear Lilith's advice myself than sound like her. "I'm doing the best I can, and if you disagree with my teaching, then take her to Hell with you!"

"Now you sound like your father." He smirked, and she hated that he was right. Frendall gripped her shoulder and kissed the side of her head, but the weight of her recent choices only added to the tension gripping the back of her neck.

"You... you don't want me?" Lottie appeared from behind a tree, clearly having heard their conversation. Her face was streaked with tears.

Remorse gripped Klara's heart, but before she had a chance to explain, the portal pulled her and Frendall through to Hell.

25

"It seems you can't stay away from me," Lokey said.

He sat on the bench in Lucifer's gardens with an open book on his lap, his top hat resting beside him. Klara felt like she had stepped into open flames as they made it through the portal. No matter how often she visited Hell, she never got used to the scorching heat.

She didn't want to waste any more time with small talk. "I thought you were in Malum, helping Glaudine with Tapped?" She forced herself to put aside what had just occurred with Lottie in order to focus on the task at hand.

"The king called me back for a time, but not before I made sure the guards you sent had arrived. She is most grateful for their presence; there hasn't been a spot of trouble from the dark fae since their arrival. Not stirring trouble up again, are you?" Lokey raised his eyebrows as a scream echoed around them from the nearby Maze of tormented souls. Nobody took any notice.

"I wouldn't dream of it," Klara said.

Lokey shook his head. "Predictable as always, my darling." He kissed her cheek.

"The king's in his study?" Frendall asked, and Lokey shut his book. They were civil with each other, but there was always a chill between them. They didn't trust each other—Klara didn't need the power of revelation to know that much.

"Lucifer is around here somewhere," Lokey said, looking at the freshly trimmed hedgerows. "I don't tend to keep track of him, since I like my head where it is," he added in a whisper of mock fear.

"We need to see him as soon as possible," Klara said.

"You could have used the bowl to communicate, since you're in such a rush," Lokey commented casually, as if taking a life for a brief conversation wasn't barbaric. Klara sneered at the thought of slicing a throat. *Much too messy for my liking.*

A few doomed rounded the corner, trimming the greying rose bushes, and Lokey cleared his throat. "Let's go somewhere a bit quieter."

Klara glanced at his face, scarred by Abadan's torturers. Whatever weapons they had used had left permanent marks, but his bright, tailored suits detracted from the marks.

"Don't look so concerned, Heiress." Lokey winked, and in a flash the three of them stood in her father's empty office, the candles lighting as they appeared. "He's probably in the nursery."

"The nursery? Don't tell me: the King of Hell is still babysitting your child?" Klara looked outside the window to make sure the Maze hadn't frozen over. *I didn't even know the manor* had *a nursery.*

"Glaudine was ordered to return to Hell so that Lucifer could anoint Damien as one of his followers. One to be in his inner circle once he grows up into the fine high warlock he's sure to be. He noticed how tired my wife was. Raising a leprechaun-warlock is not for the faint of heart—your father discovered his hankering for gold and his innate ability to set things on fire. The two are now inseparable."

"And where is Glaudine? I doubt she was eager to remain here."

"Oh no, she went back to Tapped—had some business to oversee. Making sure the dark fae are maintaining their manners."

"And you're just sauntering around?" Frendall put in, his eyebrows raised in suspicion.

"Don't look at me like that; who else was going to do it while the heiress was blowing things up in Kalos?" Lokey winked. "Luckily, your father wasn't here when my fae friend arrived to inform me of that little tidbit."

"It's not a secret. In fact, I would much rather be filling him in on my mother's extracurricular activities than you."

"Touché. I can't stop you, but I will remind you that the king is in no mood for war."

"I don't care what he's in the mood for. The time for playing is over."

"You'd think sharing your bed would have loosened her up a bit," Lokey said to Frendall, who glared at the warlock, though Klara thought she saw a smile threatening the corner of his mouth.

She tossed her axe into the wall beside Lokey's head with a smile. "Don't forget who I am, Lokey. You're my friend, but talk of those who share my bed again and the next throw will land true." She yanked the axe from the wall.

"I love it when she's feisty," Lokey hissed, exposing his serpent-like tongue.

She raised her arm again, but she had no intention of killing him and Lokey knew it.

The manor was quiet except for the dull shouts of the tortured victims below. A humming caught their attention, and Frendall placed his fingers to his lips. Klara followed as he made his way to the kitchen.

"Breakfast, breakfast—what shall we have for breakfast? Bacon, beans or both?"

Klara opened the door, and Frendall put away his sword when they saw the King of Hell wearing a pink apron with an infant on his hip. The child was bigger, or at least older, than it should have been for the time that had passed; warlocks matured faster than most children. Klara saw that he shared Lokey's yellow serpent eyes but Glaudine's red curls.

"Have I died and gone to the Maze?" she asked Frendall, and her father turned, revealing the flour on his face and the burnt pancakes on the stove.

"Lokey must have used one hell of a spell for this shit to appear so real," Frendall agreed.

"Ha-ha," Lucifer said flatly, waving the spatula in his hand. "Can't the King of Hell make breakfast?"

"There are so many things wrong with this image," Klara chuckled as he placed Damien in a wooden crib and removed the apron. *Like a cage for the little guy.* Frendall removed the food from the stove before the king set the manor on fire.

'I take it that this isn't a social call," Lucifer said, picking Damien back up again.

"Can we talk? Away from the child?" Klara asked, not wanting the little boy to hear the expletives her father would roar when he heard what she had done.

"The last time I saw you, you were headed to Kalos; all went well?" Lucifer said, handing Damien to the doomed loitering in the corner, whom Klara guessed was there just in case Lucifer really did set the kitchen on fire. When her father left the kitchen, Klara waved goodbye at the infant, who was too busy chewing his fist to notice her.

"So, if this is not a social visit… what do you need from me?" Lucifer asked, leading them down the corridor and to a private sitting room hidden through a mirror.

The room was plush and clearly made for comfort, with high ceilings and expensive drapery on the tall windows that overlooked Hell. The carpet was decorative, the wallpaper textured, and the couches the kind one could lose oneself in, all in dark navy and rich gold. A private place for Lucifer to sit and contemplate. Klara was even surprised to see a portrait of Eve above the fireplace.

"I'm sure your dear mother bored you to tears with her garden," Lucifer scoffed, taking a seat in the armchair. Klara and Frendall remained standing until given permission to sit.

"Not exactly," Frendall said, eyeing Klara, who suddenly didn't know where to begin.

"What then?" he said, rolling his wrist in the air. "The ball wasn't as eventful as mine? I doubt she knows how to entertain properly with all that pomp in her court."

"I found Abadan," Klara said, the words tumbling out.

Lucifer sank back into his velvet chair. "Where?" he asked, his voice laced with contempt.

"In Kalos. Queen Aemella has used Abadan's power to resurrect a Gingerbread Factory."

Lucifer took it in, his eyes never leaving his daughter's. "Continue," was all he said, his red irises hinting at his anger.

"The fae queen is caging creatures who passed through the border to strengthen her standing," Frendall said. Lucifer held up a hand to stop him from continuing.

"Your proof?" he said, stroking his chin.

Klara frowned, looking to Frendall for guidance.

"Your silence doesn't exactly win my confidence. You can't come here with such a claim against another Ruler without hard proof," Lucifer said, clearly already bored.

"I'm the proof. We saw the factory with our own eyes. Abadan helped us escape," she said. *For God knows what reason.* "Let me touch you, and I can show you. The creatures are mutilating themselves for protection. You'll soon see that I have more than enough cause to call for a vote for the factory's destruction," she finished.

Lucifer looked appalled. "I won't have you using fae mind games on me," he exclaimed. "Words mean nothing; you should know this more than anything."

Klara clenched her fists, wishing she could touch him, let her see into her mind, show him all that she had seen—but she should have realised he would never let that happen; he had too many of his own secrets, and her touch would not only allow him into her mind but her into his. He would never let her be the proof she needed to condemn Aemella's actions.

"Did you have permission to travel through that part of Kalos and pass through her protections?" he asked.

"No..." Klara began.

"For the love of Judas! I need a drink." Lucifer shook his head. "You broke treaty law by investigating on her land without cause."

"I had cause," Klara said quickly, before the king decided to punish her.

"You did?"

"A witch from the Redwood came to the castle and informed me that creatures were going missing in Kalos. When I got there—on the queen's invitation, I might add—I noticed that some creatures were injured."

"A loophole, not a cause. You brought no proof, no creature to back your claim?" Lucifer tutted, pouring himself some venom.

"It doesn't matter, because I found Abadan and the factory and the caged creatures."

"Doesn't matter? If it doesn't matter, then what's to stop the fae queen from telling her people that you are murdering patrols?" he drawled, taking a drink. "I would ask her for the same thing—evidence. Without it, there would be anarchy."

"This isn't a claim. I was there," Klara argued, though she was starting to get a sinking feeling.

"I don't disagree with you, but I need proof if you are to go against Aemella to call a vote, as you so wish. Our peace has been short-lived, and I will not have the realm be thrown into discord over an invalidated dispute." Lucifer shrugged. Letting the creatures rot in the factories was no skin off his back.

"How am I going to bring you proof? Aemella isn't going to let me stroll back in and allow me to take a creature she has caged and drained to within an inch of their life," Klara snapped.

The manor shook as Lucifer's leathery wings expanded. "Don't you take that tone with me, Young Queen! You showed your hand to the fae queen, and this is the outcome. Had you used your senses instead of that beating thing in your chest, you would have been able to get everything you needed. Without evidence, you're wasting my time with squabbles."

"Aemella has agreed to a vote on adding a clause to the treaty," Klara said, not allowing her father to brush her aside. "Once I have the support of the Elders, I'm to send a raven summoning her to Hell."

"She has? Now that's interesting…" There was a moment of silence as Lucifer paced, folding his wings back within himself. "Why on this plane would she agree to that? She knows you have nothing that will harm her," he muttered.

"I saw—"

"YOU. HAVE. NOTHING," he roared, tossing them both into the plush couch with a wave of his arm. "I smell a bigger game. When is the vote to take place?" He looked almost enthralled now, his eyes wide in delight.

Before Klara could respond, a doomed interrupted, carrying a deceased white dove on a gold platter. Klara knew one of the queen's messengers when she saw one.

"A message from the fae queen," the doomed said, and Lucifer took the scroll from the dove's claw.

"It seems you haven't completely destroyed your relationship with your mother…"

Klara waited.

"She is inviting you to another ball in honour of your two lands."

"She wishes to make up for the one I ruined upon my discovery of the factory. I was determined to see it through, but she blocked our entrance to the palace at the last minute."

Lucifer reclaimed his seat, a glass of whisky appearing in hand. She could sense him weighing up his options. He leaned forwards. "Bring me a creature who will back your claim, and I will side with your vote. I can't be made a fool of, and the higher demons will want to be there."

"The higher demons have nothing to do with Malum and Kalos."

"They will act as a necessary buffer when the elders and high fae arrive. I must remind you, daughter, they *will* have a say in who they back as the next ruler of Hell, and I doubt they want a rebel who doesn't follow treaty law at the helm." Lucifer smacked the immortal ring onto the circular glass table separating them to further his point. Klara recalled when she had seen it in the Neutral Lands upon Mila's hand. She had almost felt relieved that her father had chosen someone else to rule Hell. In reality, Abadan had used it to trick Klara into thinking that her father was on the high queen's side.

"Kettle, black," Klara said under her breath, staring at the plain ring, and her father's eyes flashed red. She was instantly glad that he turned his attention to Frendall.

"You saw this place?" Lucifer questioned, taking his general's word into consideration.

"I did, Your Majesty. I was taken in lycaon form, and I can say that the creatures who enter that factory are never intended to leave," Frendall said, holding his head high.

"The loss of creatures is neither here nor there, but we can't have your mother growing any stronger; she already has the angels at her back." Lucifer swirled the drink in his glass.

"So you won't back the continued use of the factory?" Klara asked, wanting a clear answer.

"Daughter, I have no power in Kalos; I am merely the neutral party between you and your mother, as you both agreed when you took control of Malum." He sighed. "Bring a held creature before me and both sides to vote, and we will see where we land. But are you prepared for an answer you don't want?" He glanced between Klara and Frendall.

"I won't allow the factory to remain open without warning the creatures who intend to leave for Kalos. Allowing them to pass through makes me complacent," Klara said firmly.

"You have every right to inform the creatures, but I doubt many will listen. There will always be those who dream of greener pastures on the other side of the River Styx, and if what you say is true, some are willing to mutilate themselves to stay. They will see your statement as mere propaganda until they are forced to face it," Lucifer pointed out.

"And I'm supposed to allow it to happen anyway?" Klara asked, her nails biting into her palms. She had a horrible feeling he was right.

"Fighting for its closure is action enough, for now— but are you ready for war if the vote doesn't carry? Malum will suffer much more than Kalos, and the creatures on your side of the river will not thank you for it," Lucifer said, taking a long drink.

"The elders have already agreed to the vote," she said, glad she had gone to them first.

"But will they fight for your cause?"

Klara couldn't give him an answer. She hoped they

would, but the elders wouldn't go blindly into Kalos for a few creatures.

"Still so much to learn and so eager to fight. It will wear off in a few decades, as it has for many of those elders of yours, and for your general here," Lucifer said, laying a hand on Frendall's shoulder. "Find insurmountable proof that the elders can't ignore. Evidence that some of the creatures have not left of their own volition will add more merit to your cause; we will move on from there. No rogue moves, or it will be you the treaty sides against," Lucifer warned, getting up. "But if the creatures left on their own, and the elders vote against you, then I'm afraid you have no right to stand against Queen Aemella, just as it is written that she has no right to question your rule." He left the room.

No wonder Aemella didn't challenge any of the treaty clauses; I'd written myself into a damned corner. Offered up the creatures on a platter and then locked myself out of the feast. Klara resisted the urge to pull at her hair as frustration built up in her gut.

"We have to go back," Frendall said, weight behind his words.

"And they'll be expecting us," Klara realised, dread building within her. She felt like she would melt into the back of the couch under the weight of all that was to come.

He sighed. "Hungry?"

"What?"

"I think I want those pancakes. If I'm going to get my hands bloody, then I want to do it on a full stomach," Frendall said, offering Klara a hand.

Lokey smirked, taking a sip of venom, his legs thrown over the armrest of Lucifer's throne. "I feel like this is a *told you so* moment, but best not to rub salt in the wound," he said smugly as Klara paced her father's throne room. Lucifer had taken Frendall to deal with an internal matter and Klara had been left to simmer in the manor.

"If I was in his position, I would ask for proof too," Lokey added.

"If the king witnessed you sitting on his throne, you would lose those legs," Klara warned, and he shrugged.

"Trust me, the king is very much distracted at the minute."

"He'll be focused when the vote comes—I'll make damn sure of that."

"Even so, you still need to gather evidence, and that

could take decades. You'll need a creature to step forward, and how on this plane are you going to manage that? If what you say is true, the creatures who leave the factory can't exactly do much talking."

Klara didn't want to talk about that. "I think you would be happier to remain on that throne and have my father deal with your spawn."

"Have you heard the thing cry? He shattered all the windows in the manor only this week. When he gets going there's nothing that will stop him, except your father." Lokey trembled visibly at the thought.

This is why demon-warlocks don't make the best parents. High maintenance and they lack patience.

"I never knew he was so paternal," Klara muttered.

Lokey shrugged again. "He looked after you just the same way—you were too young to remember."

Klara wondered if that was true or if Lokey was trying to mend her father's image in her eyes.

"I'll get inside the factory and get someone out. With the damage I caused, they can't be running at full capacity. I'll need Frendall to go to my mother to offer an olive branch in distraction. If I had someone else to come with me, it would guarantee my success…" Klara paced, wondering if an elder would dare accompany her. *Elder Langda has taken my side. Convincing her might not be that hard, and her speed would come in handy.*

"I know someone who might be able to help," Lokey said, interrupting her train of thought.

"Who? The giants won't side with me and the others are hedging their bets. I held sway with the lycaons, but that's shot to shit now that Matthias has his claws in them." Klara rubbed her eyes, taking a seat on the steps to the throne.

"There's someone else."

Klara frowned. *Does he know about Lilith?*

"Your sister is quite apt at pulling the truth from those who do not wish to speak it, and getting in and out of places she shouldn't be. You should visit her before you return to Malum." Lokey circled her, and Klara wondered what game he was playing.

"I'm sure I'm the last person she wants to see."

"So she tried to kill you. What siblings haven't attempted to break each other's necks? I once had several siblings."

"And where are they now?" she asked, tilting her head.

Lokey squinted, not prepared to answer. "This conversation is not about my family tree."

"Since you're so eager to make suggestions, why not accompany me yourself? Portalling into the factory and snatching some unsuspecting fae or creatures would be easy for such a skilled warlock." Klara knew his strength—it wouldn't even be a challenge.

Lokey disappeared in a puff of smoke. "I much prefer to remain in the shadows."

"More like on the fence," she said, looking around the throne room from the fireplaces to the glistening chandelier.

"I have a son to think about," Lokey argued, reappearing behind her.

"And I take it that son is to inherit Tapped? Or maybe even become the high warlock of the Crest? Such events are unlikely to happen if the fae queen has her way. Your son is powerful; what's to stop her taking him for herself?"

Lokey's eyes shone yellow as she threatened his child.

"You have come a long way from the child who barked orders in my office." He smiled.

"If the creatures in the factories aren't worth thinking about, then I should let her take them. What's a mere few? Even let them take your wife. Is she at Tapped now as we speak? The dark fae would gain favour with Aemella if they brought her over the border."

Lokey lunged forward and gripped Klara's throat. "Try it, Heiress."

"See? Everyone is expendable until it's their family caged," she choked out as he threatened to increase the pressure, his face inches from hers.

"And yet it is your family doing the caging," Lokey hissed, before dropping his slender hand. "You will not trick me, Heiress. I will help you into the factory but that is as far as I go."

Klara was surprised by how far she had got under his cool demeanour. She had felt how much he truly loved and feared for his family when he had touched her. "Deal," she said, and the doomed opened the doors for her to leave.

"At least consider Mila. She should be lurking in the Maze at this hour," Lokey called after her.

Klara washed her face in the copper sink, letting the cool water run over her scorching skin. The bathroom on the manor's ground floor was large enough to house a small family of creatures in Malum. The fixtures were made of solid gold, with a tub she longed to soak in.

Pale blue threatened her dark roots in the mirror, revealing the worry within her.

"I don't need her," Klara said to her reflection.

"But you do," her reflection taunted. "Her heart may be twisted and her soul corrupt, but she respects power."

"I'll need to bargain with her." Dark circles framed Klara's eyes as her anxiety threatened to reveal itself. She dried her face with a towel, pausing to feel the soft fabric against her skin. Taking a moment to consider what she could possibly offer her sister.

I'd say she would do just about anything to get out from beneath the manor...

She tossed the towel in the small basket beside the sink.

"Where are you off to?" Frendall asked as Klara headed for the Maze.

The heat from the lava scorching through the rocks threatened to melt her boots. By the lack of screams running through the manor, she was sure Mila wasn't hard at work beneath in the tunnels. Klara had figured she might be picking out some souls from within the Maze to question.

Shit, why did it have to be him? Klara thought, the insufferable humidity of Hell's air making her sweat. She looked around to see Frendall standing with a group of demons at the entrance to the Maze.

"I was looking for you," she lied. A few demons disappeared as she approached. She almost smiled at inspiring such fear without so much as a boo. Two, however, remained behind Frendall at the entrance to the Maze, whispering and pushing each other forward.

"Larkin, Bromwich, this is your future queen; act accordingly. I left these two in charge while we were...

away," Frendall explained. Klara tipped her head, and the two demons bowed instantly, their smiles disappearing as Frendall glared at them.

"Sorry, Your Highness," the blonder one said, and Klara noticed the burnt skin on their neck. It looked old, perhaps from a previous life. *We take our scars with us in death; the marks on our souls are like badges of honour.* "Commander Bromwich, at your service." Bromwich bowed deeply with a dashing smile, while Larkin stood as still as Medusa's statue in the garden.

"I've heard good things from your general. You have served him well. What is your charge?" Klara asked Bromwich, who beamed at her question.

"The Maze. I oversee which beasts we set loose upon the souls daily, and keep track of which souls are in which section."

Klara resisted the urge to shudder.

"They are two of our finest," Frendall said, vouching for who were clearly his friends. *I didn't think real friends could be found in Hell.*

"Your name?" Klara asked the other demon, whose long curls concealed half her face.

"Commander Larkin doesn't speak," Bromwich interjected.

Klara wondered if the demon had once belonged to Abadan; the removal of tongues was her expertise.

"May I?" she asked, holding out a hand. Larkin offered a brief nod, and Klara placed her hand on the demon's arm. She flinched as Klara made contact.

She stepped into the demon's mind, and saw the moment that had turned her silent, followed quickly by the retribution that had turned the soul demonic. *Something no child should ever have to suffer. Was it worth it?* Klara projected.

Larkin smiled brightly. *Every second.* The demon's chest heaved as Klara disturbed long-buried memories. She broke contact with the demon before she unearthed anything else.

"Nice to meet you," she said aloud, looking into Larkin's obsidian eyes.

"Larkin is the Commander of the Kennels—one of our best trainers. She has taken them on since my promotion," Frendall said proudly, and Klara remembered that the hounds had escaped while they were away.

"We've heard so much about you." Bromwich winked and nudged Frendall. "I feel like we're already friends."

Klara smirked. She never knew what to expect from demons.

"Bromwich enjoys forgetting their place," Frendall said, smacking Bromwich on the back of their head. "Don't you have some beasts to release?"

"Trying to get rid of us—I get it, I get it. A pleasure, Your Highness. Please slum it with us before you go. A glass of venom on me," Bromwich said.

Larkin glared at her fellow commander and also smacked the back of their head.

"Why is everyone hitting me? Can't I get to know our future queen?"

Frendall rolled his eyes as Klara suppressed a laugh.

"Only if you promise to tell me all his secrets," she said, her eyes not leaving Frendall's.

"I have plenty of stories. You just wait." Bromwich beamed while Larkin rolled her eyes.

"Well then, the sooner you finish your duties, the quicker you can join us for dinner," Klara said, almost forgetting why she was visiting the Maze in the first place.

Bromwich bowed, and they and Larkin disappeared in a cloud of smoke.

"You keep interesting company. I thought the rest of the commanders would be as stoic as you are," Klara said quietly to Frendall once they were alone.

"I trained with them from the beginning; half of the scars we have, we gave to each other." He smiled, and she sensed peace within him. They were his family.

"Has Larkin ever spoken?" she asked out of mere curiosity as they headed back towards the manor. She silently hoped her sister had made her way back to the tunnels.

"Not that I've heard. That's why I thought the kennels would be a good fit—she doesn't have to interact with the other demons, and the hounds understand her just fine. Were you really looking for me?" Frendall asked, doubt in his voice.

"No. My sister." Klara kicked a stone, watching the hot lava weave through the rocks beneath their boots.

Frendall stopped still. "Mila?" he asked, furrowing his brow.

"The one and only, unless I have another lurking around that I have yet to discover. Lokey says she's good at getting in and out of places, and given her talent of convincing others to speak, I thought I would convince her to join me in the factory. I need proof, and Mila can get a fae or creature jabbering."

"She's good at getting others to talk because she's a torturer. If you bring a bloodied and beaten creature or fae before the fae and elder courts, they'll assume the confession has been coerced," Frendall pointed out.

Klara hadn't considered that. "I won't let her touch them, but her reputation might convince them."

"You can't trust her," he said coldly.

"I don't, but I have no other option."

"I'll help you get into the factory again."

"Brute strength and lycaon senses aren't exactly the stealthy skills I need. Plus, I have another plan for you," Klara said.

"I don't like the sound of that. I'm also of Abadan's bloodline—I have some magic in my blood. I can help," Frendall said.

How could I forget?

"Aemella will be expecting us to return together. I need her to think I'm coming around to her side. She's expecting us for the ball. I need you to go early and extend an olive branch. Tell her anything you need to, but keep her occupied and away from Jasper until I arrive. Though I doubt he'll be far from her side... Anyway, Mila might surprise us. The tunnels have a habit of changing people." Klara shuddered at the thought of being trapped beneath the manor.

"I'm supposed to play decoy?" Frendall groaned. "The only way Mila will surprise you is with a dagger in the back—or she'll sing like a canary and hand you over to your mother."

Klara dragged her hands over her face. "This plan is the best I have. The ball gives us a way in, and if you go, she'll doubt that I would dare go to the factory alone."

"Go alone then. Don't risk involving Mila for the sake of a second pair of hands." Frendall shrugged, walking ahead of her. "I'm not saying that to be an arse. I mean, if you can get in and if Abadan is still alive, you might be able to get her out."

"But it's her magic that's keeping the factory standing. If I remove her, it could fall. That wouldn't exactly be a subtle exit."

"Exactly." He smiled over his shoulder. "Take Abadan out of the equation, and there's no more factory to vote against."

Klara reached up on her tiptoes and kissed him in the middle of Hell. She hadn't considered removing Abadan from the factory and what that would mean. He froze at the public display of affection.

"She could resurrect another…" she reflected.

"One step at a time. I don't think Aemella would attempt it without Abadan. She would need a massive amount of power to make up for her loss," Frendall reasoned.

"This is why I love that brain of yours," she said, and he softened.

"Just my brain?" He smirked.

She pretended to think. "There are some other parts as well."

"Damn right." He flung her over his shoulder and made his way back to the manor.

Bromwich strode into the throne room with Larkin following behind, both dressed in crisp black suits. Bromwich's shaved head contrasted with Larkin's cascading curls. Klara recognised the indifference in Larkin's yellow eyes; she sensed the demon would much rather be in the kennels, undisturbed, than dining with them. But Klara needed allies in Hell, and if dinner could gain her at least two, she would put on a good show.

"How nice of you to join us," Frendall said, embracing Bromwich, but Larkin's eyes never left Klara's. The four all took a seat at the end of the long table in front of the fireplace, Hell's sun drifted in through the window and cast a red glow over them.

You don't need to do this, Larkin projected into Klara's mind. *We're on your side. Lucifer's blood is in your veins, our general loves you, and you took on the High Queen of Malum. You're our queen. My loyalty doesn't need to be bought—though Bromwich's can quickly be earned with venom and small talk.*

Klara was grateful for her brutal honesty. *I did not mean to insult you. I merely wish to get to know those who are closest to Frendall,* she replied silently.

Because you are bound to him? Larkin frowned. Bromwich and Frendall were too distracted with each other's company to notice their conversation.

We are not bound, Klara corrected, beginning to eat what was laid out on the table. An assortment of fruits and vegetables from Malum, and some she didn't even recognise.

But you gave him a piece of your soul. Are you not bound more than those who wear the ring? Larkin seemed confused, not touching any of the food or drink.

That would be fair to say. Should I not have done that?

He loves you as he can, but he loves Lucifer more. I hope you know where his loyalty will rest, should a choice have to be made. We can't help it; it's in the very fabric of our demonic nature.

The clinking of glasses disturbed their private exchange.

"To our queen," Bromwich said, standing on the table. "May your heart be strong, your mind cunning, and your blade forever sharp."

They raised their glasses and drank the venom. Klara tried to speak further with Larkin, only for her to leave without another word. From the look Frendall gave her, it had been expected. Klara almost rose to go after her, but her fingers dug into the chair. *If I follow her, it will only*

318

raise more questions. Do I even want to know what she meant about Frendall loving me?

She lost herself in the memory of watching Frendall sleep, a bicep covering his face while the bedsheet exposed the top of his chest. Leaning on the bedstead, she stepped closer, hearing his soft breath, watching the rise and fall of his pale skin. He had never looked more at peace.

Her fingers traced the edges of the sheet, moving them down his body to get a sneak peek. He groaned softly as her fingers grazed his stomach, causing his muscles to tense.

"Careful with those hands," Frendall said quietly, staring at her with lazy eyes, his arm no longer shielding his eyes but tucked behind his head.

Her hands made quick work of her own clothes until she stood before him in her undergarments.

"I thought you were busy?" he asked, but she would rather not think about the hours spent going through the treaty with her parents.

"Well, I figured if I'm to be the Queen of Hell one day I should learn of the sins." Klara moved to the empty side of the bed.

His eyes watched her as though she were his prey. "Is that so?"

"Mm-hmm." She nodded, bringing her face to his but not daring to touch him.

"Where should we start?"

"I think lust is as good a place as any," she said, leaning closer.

He pulled her on top of him, her thighs straddling his hips. "We'd better get started then," he said, sitting up so that his face met hers as her hands traced his shoulders.

"I have a lot to learn," she said, suddenly nervous as he kissed her cheek and then her neck.

"I'll be thorough." He smiled. "I wouldn't want my future queen to be ill-tutored."

"I'm safe in your hands?" she asked. Joking aside, in this moment she wanted to know she could trust him.

"Always."

Klara's lips found his, and that was all she needed to know how much he meant it.

"I seemed to have bored our future queen. I will take my leave," Bromwich said.

Klara snapped out of the memory. "My brain is all too focused on my duties—the life of a queen is never dull. I promise you did not bore me," she assured them.

"Nevertheless, I should take my leave. Too many venoms and I forget what monsters I've released on today's souls," Bromwich joked, their yellow eyes flashing in amusement.

"If you're trying to win the hearts of the demons, you aren't doing too well," Frendall said as the doomed sealed the doors behind Bromwich. "One leaves in the middle of dinner, and the other you couldn't be bothered to listen to."

"I have a lot on my mind," Klara said, smacking her glass on the table. The stem of the wine glass cracked.

"Still, it wouldn't be hard to make some allies—who would have happily helped you in the fight you are so determined to bring about." The hurt in his voice surprised her.

"I didn't mean to ignore your friends."

"Demons can never really be considered friends."

"You know what I mean. I can't win, can I? Between Malum, Lottie's adolescence, my mother's meddling and my father's sudden urge to become the realm's strangest babysitter, I'm just lost!"

"Well, if you feel like letting me in, let me know," he said coldly.

"You already know everything."

"Really? Then why did Larkin leave? Your private conversation?"

Klara hesitated.

Frendall huffed. "Thought so."

There was a long silence as she studied his features, the general's mark through his eye. *Where his loyalties truly lie...*

"The night is almost over. I'd better get going. I'll see you in Kalos," Klara said, and her axe appeared in her hand as she tightened the harness to her back.

"Fine. I don't know what she could have said to you, but we'll get through this together," he said, squeezing her hand, and Klara could feel that he meant it. "I'll meet you at the queen's Palace, open a portal inside to stop you drawing attention from the fae."

"How are you going to open a portal inside? The queen has protections to drain visitors of their power."

"I'll have Lokey worry about that."

"And how do you plan to explain my absence to my mother? You'll need to hold her focus."

"I have my charms." Frendall smiled, but Klara couldn't help but replay what Larkin had projected.

He loves Lucifer more. He's his king after all, and my father—why would he not love him as a surrogate father? At this moment in time, she couldn't doubt him.

Klara found Lokey chatting with a portrait on the second floor of the manor.

"How was your dear sister?" he asked, and the soul within the portrait disappeared, giving them some privacy.

"I decided against your advice," she told him, rubbing the back of her neck.

Lokey sighed, tapping his long fingers against his arm. "Well, I can't say I'm surprised. One of the things you have in common is your stubborn streak," he chided.

"I can't waste time wondering whether or not she will betray me," Klara said, though she knew he was right.

"It's not my place to judge you." Lokey looked down the quiet hallway at the portraits listening quietly to their plans. "No commander at your heel? Are you venturing alone?"

"General, and you'll help him through later. He'll be my decoy while I breach the factory and get the evidence my father demands."

"Risky plan, but I admire your guts. Just be sure to keep them within your body." He chuckled, a little too amused by the whole ordeal for her liking.

"I should slip in and out without attracting too much attention."

"Hmm. I didn't think you would want to go so soon, but since your mind is made up I suggest we get on with it," he said resignedly.

"If I delay, I risk the elders growing doubtful and my mother growing stronger," Klara said, fighting her anxiety about the journey ahead.

Lokey turned to the painting, who had reappeared. "You don't mind if I use your portrait, do you?" he asked the demon inside, who grinned a dark smile.

"A pleasure to serve, Your Highness," the painted figure said through bloodied, toothless gums. Klara didn't know what crime the soul had committed to have their teeth pulled, and she didn't want to know either.

"Since I have not seen the factory, I need you to lay your hand on me and show me what you have seen within. I would hate for you to end up in a wall," Lokey explained.

Klara closed her eyes, showing him every nook and cranny she could remember. "There are strong protections surrounding it," she warned as she felt his magic stirring beneath her hand. She revealed the bubble protecting the factory, and the building within.

"I'm stronger." Lokey chuckled.

That's what I'm relying on. When Klara opened her eyes, she watched the portrait warp and twist until the demon became unrecognisable. Its mouth stretched open, its jaw lengthening into a portal Klara had no desire to enter.

She took the opportunity to allow her touch to weave her way into Lokey's mind. She saw the birth of Damien, and the joy and fear he had felt at that moment. Then the hours of torture he had endured at Abadan's behest because he'd sided with Klara during the uprising.

"Be careful how deep you dig; you don't know what you'll find in there," Lokey warned playfully, and Klara stopped her search, unsure of what she was even looking for. Instead, she projected the image of the silver wood.

"The fae queen certainly went above and beyond," he said as his hands danced before the portrait. "It's been a long time since I saw a place like this. The brick is a nice change from the candied exterior the witches used to lure in the children on Abadan's behalf."

Klara shuddered at the thought. *Aemella may have taken creatures, but Abadan always went a step further and sacrificed children.*

"Much sturdier, but a lot less appetising," Lokey joked. Once the portal held its shape, he dropped his hands. "Be quick about it—the portal will only hold until the fae queen senses it," he warned.

Klara stepped through the open jaw of the demon, her axe secured to her back and spare dagger concealed at her ankle.

"Try to come back in one piece," Lokey advised, with a faint smile.

"Concerned about your future queen—or has a child made you soft?" she teased.

"No. I sold your father's hearts to refurbish Tapped, so try not to lose another." He winked.

Klara rolled her eyes, sensing no deception in his words. She couldn't wait to see what her father would do when he found out. If he found out. "Try not to sell anything else while my father is distracted."

"I make no promises." He smirked, and Klara slipped through the portal.

27

Klara awoke, her eyes fluttering open. She stared up at the metal beams above her. She could smell the pungent scent of corrupted magic.

The force of Lokey's portal cutting through the factory's protections must have knocked me out. Such was the cost of magic. She was in a room she didn't recognise. *It's recovered from my last visit,* she thought, sensing no disturbance around her as she placed her hands on the floor and wove her magic through the factory's structure.

How was Aemella able to harness so much magic in such a short time? Abadan would have been exhausted from the flames she had created as a distraction; she couldn't have mended the factory alone. The question plagued her. *At least Lokey portalled me inside, or I would have had to find another poor sucker's hand.* She was relieved that she hadn't ended up stuck in a cell or a wall.

There was a fae uniform hanging on the back of the steel door. Klara sat up and turned to see the crisp white sheets and spotless room. An oil lamp sat beside the bed, and she heard water running from behind a bathroom door. *There's someone here! I'd better get out.* She laid her hand on the uniform and told her clothes to alter. *Much better,* she thought as she stared down at the sapphire uniform she was now wearing.

She was reaching for the doorknob when she sensed someone behind her.

"What are you doing in here?" a voice said as a hand landed on her shoulder.

Klara flipped the fae onto his back. Her fist connected with his jaw before he had a chance to call for help or get a good look at her face.

"Sleep tight," she said, moving the body from the door and stuffing him into a trunk at the end of the bed.

She kept her head and eyes low as she slunk from the room. When she placed her hand on the factory wall, the cool brick contrasted with the cauldrons' heat. Her magic crept into the building as she sought Abadan. *If I need a witness, why bother going with a creature? Go straight for the top. At the very least it might bring down the factory, as Frendall suggested.*

Klara found her way to the cauldron room and watched fae playing cards on the second floor for a few seconds, then darted to the creatures protesting and crying out as magic was stripped from their veins and fed into the cauldrons. There was no sign of Abadan, and Klara couldn't pick up any trace of her presence, which only meant one thing. *The fallen high queen is in a cell. Couldn't she have been in her chamber eating bonbons?* Klara cursed, making her way past the cages.

"Abadan, where the hell are you lurking?" she said

to herself as she moved through the corridors. Her feet stuck to the factory floor, sticky with magic leaking from the bubbling cauldrons.

There were fae guarding the door, so she ducked back to consider her options, but there was really only one way she would get past them. Klara let the uniform slip away and allowed her wings to be seen at her back.

The crying in the room stopped as the eyes of those caged became fixed on her. Her expression turned to stone as creatures begged for her help; she strode past them and their outstretched arms. The mouths of the fae guards posted at the doors to the cell gaped open as she approached them.

"The queen sent me to talk with Abadan," she said with cold confidence.

"We have received no such indication of your arrival—Princess," a fae stammered. She sensed the guards didn't know whether to cut her down or bow.

Of all my titles, that's my least favourite. It sounded much too sickly sweet for Klara's liking.

"I don't have much time to waste, and wasting my time is wasting the queen's time," she snapped. She could feel their fear and their doubt.

"Still, we can't let you pass without orders from High Fae Jasper," a guard said, and Klara noted they were missing the tip of their pointed ear.

"Are you saying someone outranks your queen's daughter?" She flared her nostrils in outrage.

"N-no—we don't mean any disrespect—but we will need to check."

Klara tried to bury the sense of dread building at the back of her throat. "Check with whom you must, but I will see the prisoner now. Or do you wish to stop me?"

They eyed the axe in Klara's hand and the heavy white wings at her back. She smiled as their faces fell, and one quickly pressed their hand to the shield. The door popped open, and a rush of cold air surrounded them.

"Thank you for your service," Klara said, moving through them. She hesitated briefly, glancing over her shoulder to see one fae tip their head to the other before they rushed past the cauldrons. *Not going to give me much time before they return. The queen will receive word I was here... so much for getting in and out unnoticed.*

The bricks were marred with cracks, and the scent of unwashed bodies filled the air beneath the factory. Klara made her way past the cell doors as moans echoed in her ears, and she did what she could to block them out. Though the hopeless creatures begged for factions and families, she couldn't help them. At the end of the rows on either side of her loomed two double doors made of silver. There was only one creature who would need that much security. Klara observed that there wasn't even a lock on the door—the silver was enough to prevent any escape.

She paused as her hand landed on the silver handle. *Freeing Abadan from this place could mean unleashing a greater evil.* But as the walls sang with fear, her hand made the decision for her.

"How much you must have missed me to return so soon," Abadan said.

Silver hooks pierced her shoulders, hands, waist and hips as she sat cross-legged in the centre of the stone floor. There wasn't even a metal cot or bucket, Klara noted. Only her thin shift kept Abadan's modesty. Klara ran her hand over the door handle, glamouring it from sight to keep them in and the fae—who were surely on their way—out.

"Looks like it hurts. Can't say you deserve any less," Klara said, satisfaction creeping up her spine.

"Merely stings." Abadan sighed through a tilted smile. "To what do I owe this pleasure? Since allowing you to escape put these hooks in me, I can't say I'm happy to see you. I should have known you would be foolish enough to return without an army. I thought you'd make good on our deal, but it looks like I'm the bigger fool." Her voice was uncharacteristically low, while her black eyes followed Klara's every move.

"An army? No, there's no call for war just yet. But since I'm getting you out of here, you should be ecstatic," Klara informed her.

"Foolish child. You still have much to learn."

"Maybe I should tell the fae to use some bigger hooks," Klara mused.

"The only one in danger is you. Leave before you're discovered, and forget about this place!" Abadan reared forward, only for the hooks to pull her back.

"You want to be left here?" Klara frowned, taken aback by Abadan's lack of fight.

"Purgatory is a much crueller mistress. A lot of memories I would rather not revisit. I know I won't get out of here alive; I've been stripped of too much magic. At least here I had control over the creatures and was kept busy—until you showed up." Abadan glared, spitting the last few words in her direction.

"If you were so content to play Aemella's magical slave, why help me? What was there to gain?" Klara asked.

Abadan gave a sickly smile. "Because I want Aemella

to suffer at the hands of her child. To regret the day she birthed you, if she doesn't already."

"Be that as it may, my father needs proof that this place exists—and who better to bring before him? I need you to tell me whether Aemella is taking creatures from Malum or not."

"The king knows I'm alive?" Abadan's eyes went wide. She leaned forward again, but the hooks only ripped her skin, causing a hiss to escape her thin lips.

"That's not important." Klara wasn't sure if it was fear or relief that passed over Abadan's face. She didn't have time to care. "Is Aemella trafficking creatures for power? Not just going after those within Kalos?"

"Yes. She's using the dark fae to abduct small numbers of creatures. She promised the fae their light in return, but it's a lie; once their light has been extinguished, there's no getting it back. Once they bring enough creatures, she takes the dark fae, too, to silence them. In the beginning she had some of the creatures making snatches for a time, but they left a trace, so they stopped laying them. Aemella can't take only those who come to Kalos; it would be too obvious. If I leave, this place will fall, and then there'll be nothing for me to prove the existence of."

I was right. The witch was right. That's why no other snatches were found and the one that ensnared Lottie was rusted. Klara tried not to show her relief.

"We can't know for sure that the factory will fall if you leave. If you're alive the factory will continue to drain from you; it shouldn't matter whether you are here if it's your magic it's connected to," Klara said. She couldn't be certain if that was true or not, nor did she care.

"Always with an answer." Abadan hissed as she tried

to straighten again. Klara wondered what it would take for the fallen high queen to lose her sense of humour.

"Wasn't it you that told me the importance of posture?" she teased.

Abadan glared at her, but before she could speak, there was a commotion outside the door.

"We won't get out of here together," Abadan said with a sly grin.

Klara rolled her eyes. "Ever the pessimist." She yanked the hooks from Abadan's right side.

The fae guard outside began to rain heavy blows on the doors, creating dents in the silver. Klara followed a beam of moonlight from the ceiling to a small hole in the roof, but it was only big enough for one at a time—and Abadan could barely stand, let alone scale a wall.

"How quickly your plans fall apart. I knew it was too soon for you to inherit, but your father wouldn't listen, and then Aemella got her claws in him." Abadan took a hook from the floor and slashed her hand. Klara wondered what she was doing, but didn't have time to ask. The fallen queen chanted a series of words in a language Klara had never heard, and a glass vial appeared before her. Abadan's blood oozed into the clear vial before the glass sealed it within.

"This is all the proof you need. Place it in the seer in Eve's chamber, and it will reveal all that I have seen. Use your magic to reveal my recent memories," Abadan said, as if giving an order.

Klara considered it. A seer was a powerful magical glass sphere with the power to show you the past, the future, or the memories of those who held it. Or, in this case, Klara would drop Abadan's blood onto the seer's translucent skin and watch her memories come to life within.

"The courts could deem this a trick. I *will* get you out," Klara insisted, but another deafening blow to the door silenced her.

"Give it to your father. He will know the scent of my blood and know that it contains the truth," Abadan barked, gripping Klara's hand and closing her fist around the vial. When she touched her, Klara could feel how drained she was.

"If you like it here so much, why help me?" Klara asked, wanting a real answer.

"Because if I'm correct, this is the second favour you owe me." Abadan smiled, releasing her wrist.

The only freedom I'll give you is death, Klara thought.

Abadan's eyes turned black, and her head snapped harshly toward the ceiling. Bricks fell from the roof, crashing around them, as she tore a bigger hole in the ceiling.

"I'll see you soon. Next time, bring an army." Abadan grimaced, her limp crimson hair falling in front of her face. She collapsed onto the stone floor, the use of magic in the silver room having drained the last of her strength.

Klara put the vial in her pocket and allowed the glamour on the door to drop. *This better be enough to convince the king; I don't have time to take another creature,* she thought as she spread her wings. The fae burst through as her wings carried her through the crumbling ceiling. The guards were quick to follow, their transparent wings shining like panes of veined glass.

"Forgot they could fly," Klara muttered to herself. She soared into the sky, pushing herself hard, and looked over her shoulder as she weaved through the chimneys, trying to lose them in the smoke. All it seemed to do was coat them both in black soot, and she glanced up at the protective dome shielding the factory as the fae grew closer. *This is going to hurt.*

She tore through the glamour, grateful that Abadan had created it; if it had belonged to her mother, she would never have made it through only using the force of her wings. The protections shattered like glass on impact, and the frayed edges cut into Klara's wings as she soared high above the silver wood. She choked as the rush of magic ripped the air from her lungs, and plummeted into the silver wood below. The silver branches struck her painfully until she was finally greeted by the soft soil and sharp silver leaves.

She groaned, turning onto her back. A protective hand went to the vial in her pocket, and she sighed in relief. The vial had survived the fall, even if she felt as though her spine had not.

Klara staggered her way upright and leant against a tree as she concealed her bloodied wings. She didn't have time to check the damage, but judging from the searing pain travelling up her back, they would take a while to heal. Twisting from side to side, she heard her spine crack and pop, a groan escaping her lips.

She turned toward the palace, only for spears to greet her when more fae emerged from the trees. The two guards who had flown after her landed amongst the leaves, as filthy and angry as she had expected them to be. There was something highly satisfying about seeing the fae looking less than perfect.

"Maybe we can talk about this?" Klara asked, hoping to buy some time as she layered a small glamour over the vial in her pocket to stop Abadan's blood from being detected.

"Hands where we can see them!" a soot-covered fae ordered, a crazed look in their eye.

So much for Frendall creating a summoning portal. She raised her hands in defeat as they surrounded her. One swipe of a spear and she would be out cold.

"Is there really a need for weapons with so many of you against me?" She smiled, but the patrol only glared back, not daring to lower their weapons. "If I wanted to hurt you, you wouldn't still be standing."

"And it's for that reason I thought it best for everyone that I bring them," Aemella said.

Klara rolled her eyes as she heard her mother's voice. Her axe was suddenly gone from her hand as her mother handed it to a guard.

"Growing paranoid, are you?"

"I wouldn't call it paranoia, since you've breached my wood twice in one moon." The patrol surrounding her separated to reveal Klara's mother in a simple navy suit, a thick silver chain wrapped around her neck.

"Is that where I am?" Klara feigned surprise. "I got lost on the way to the palace. Still haven't got used to the flying thing," she explained, extending her wings. The fae jumped back in surprise, and Klara couldn't hide her smug grin when fear crept into their cocky eyes.

"Put those away. We're simply here to escort you home," Aemella tutted. The fae dropped their weapons to their sides, though some looked more than willing to take Klara in by force.

Home? She thought of Lottie and Henrietta back at the castle.

"To the palace," Aemella clarified.

"I returned to the factory, yet you wish me no ill will? Have you been tucking into the venom early?" Klara asked, confused by her mother's calm demeanour.

"Your wit fails to amuse. All you achieved was

harming yourself; Abadan remains exactly where I want her to. No one was harmed except for my roof," Aemella said.

Klara thought of the fae she had stuffed in the trunk, and silently hoped he suffocated for his crimes.

"Frendall already explained your reasons for visiting the factory; I'm glad my fae were able to stop you before you could carry out your plans."

"Frendall told you of my plans?" Klara felt herself pale, and Aemella placed a gentle hand on her shoulder.

"There is nothing to be ashamed of. Wanting to kill the high queen is something we both have in common," she said with the other delicate hand resting on her chest. Klara had to conceal her relief. "But she has work to do and will suffer in doing so. Her death will not bring you the closure you seek."

Klara made a mental note to kiss Frendall for his quick thinking. She bowed her head. "I apologise—I let my emotions get the better of me. It's not as though the factory would fall to ruin without her, would it?"

Aemella scowled. "Let us go. I think it's long overdue for us to spend some time together."

She gripped Klara's arm, and they zipped through the wood to the palace.

28

Klara bent over, spewing her guts onto the plush white carpet her boots were already doing a marvellous job at muddying. She wasn't used to all this portalling.

"Don't be so overdramatic. You take after your father in that respect," Aemella said, taking a seat on a spread of pale pink silk sheets. With a flick of Aemella's wrist, the vomit disappeared.

The room was too bright for Klara's taste—all whites and pale blues and pink, with threads of silver in the furniture.

"Whose room is this?" she asked, spying the bassinet in the corner of the room. The answering silence caused her to look at her mother.

"It was to be yours, though I made some recent changes." There was sadness in Aemella's eyes as she looked away from the small armoire clearly sized for a child's clothes. "Hand-carved by a mason. Such beautiful work—I thought it an awful waste to discard it," she added, though Klara sensed there was a much more emotional reason for her keeping it. "I had the servants bring in the new bed," Aemella went on, clearing her throat.

"Why not get rid of this stuff? I can feel that it upsets you," Klara said honestly.

"It reminds me of what's important," Aemella said. "I will have an outfit brought to you for this evening. To put it politely, your current smell would put my guests off their dinner."

"What's important? What would that be?" Klara asked, ignoring the comment about her smell.

"That everything can be taken if you don't act first."

"Is that what you did with the factory? Act first?" She didn't want to fight, she wanted a reason. Kalos was meant to be a place of good, and yet her mother had decided to go against her nature to bring life and take it instead.

"Here I was thinking we could have a civilised conversation without you bringing up your precious creatures," Aemella said, shaking her head slightly.

"I want to know why and how you thought you would get away with it. You hate my father for the evil he's done, and yet you strip creatures to the bone."

"Don't for one second compare me to your father. It's my right as a ruler to do as I see fit for my people. What he does is for personal gain. I do what I must to strengthen my people."

Klara let out an exhausted sigh; she was sick of having the same conversation repeatedly.

"I've seen your lands. You bring life and beauty to so much—why stain yourself with that heinous factory? A tradition even Lucifer despised!"

"To sustain life, some must fall. It is the circle in which we live." Aemella went to the balcony doors. "This room needs airing; it'd been ready for your arrival on your last visit..."

Klara remembered how the last trip had ended—with threats of destruction on both sides.

"Our guests will be arriving soon. I suggest you get ready," Aemella said, restoring her calm.

"I didn't bring—"

Aemella waved her hand over the bed, and some garments appeared that Klara found very odd.

"Some time with civilised society might show the importance of what I'm trying to do. I know that, having been raised by those three queens, manners were not a priority for you, but the fae court is easily offended, so please try your best not to insult my people."

"I thought they were *our* people," Klara challenged.

Aemella winked. "You're smarter than you look." Servants opened the tall double doors as the fae queen stood before them. "I will send that commander of yours to you. He has been pacing the foyer since the sun woke, and the sight of him is upsetting my servants."

General. Klara went to the empty bassinet and placed her hand over the engraved *'Josephine'*. A name for a girl who would never exist. *I might be her daughter, but I'm not the child she would have raised.* The bassinet looked like it belonged to the dead, and in a way, it did. That name, that child, had been killed the moment she was taken from Aemella.

Klara sensed no magic; it was a simple memory trapped in time. She took the blade from her boot, crouched under the bassinet, and made a small cut into the mattress's soft fabric. After removing the glamour from the vial, she slipped it inside the hard padding. *If you want to hide something, hide it in plain sight. This means a lot to her, so it's the last place she would think to look. I hope.*

"The queen forgot to give these to you," a servant said, entering the room holding a pair of deadly-looking stilettos.

Klara straightened quickly. "My own shoes won't do?" she joked, and the servant grimaced at her dirty boots.

"Though they may be stylish in Malum, I'm afraid the high fae would look down on you."

'Stylish' in Malum? Clothing was more about survival than it was about style there. Klara took the shoes from the servant's outstretched hands.

The fae bowed as Frendall walked through the open doors. Before Klara could greet him and the servant could take their leave, he threw his arms around her, lifting her off the ground.

"I saw the guard return with your axe and feared the worst. Sweet Judas, my heart stopped at the thought!" His eyes were panicked and his hands urgent as he checked she was still in one piece. "But how do I know this isn't a trick?" he said frantically.

The servant was clearly too afraid to move.

"Tell me something only you would know," Frendall ordered, stepping back, his hand going to the sword at his side.

Klara laughed as sweat gathered on his forehead. "You have a freckle on your—"

"Okay, that's enough," he said quickly, silencing her as the servant blushed and dashed from the room. *That's the quickest I've ever seen anyone move in Kalos. Then again, you don't have to move quickly when you're privileged enough to live a long life.*

"My axe?" Klara said, and Frendall handed it to her. "I didn't think you would be able to retrieve it so quickly."

Frendall shrugged. "I told them I would drag them to the Maze myself and feed them to the snafer beast." Klara grinned at his ferocity.

"That's why I love you."

He rolled his eyes, though he was obviously relieved. She considered telling him about the vial, but she couldn't be sure that the room or the servants outside weren't listening.

Frendall collapsed on the bed. Klara had never seen him worry like this before, and it warmed a part of her heart she hadn't even known she possessed.

"What's this?" he asked, arching his back and pulling the outfit her mother had created out from under him.

"The queen had it made especially for me. I've never seen anything like it before... How do the fae get into such things and wear them before others? Eve would have loved it."

There was a knock on the door, and two servants entered. Klara recognised one of them from their previous visit.

"Thamalia, isn't it?" she asked, and the fae bowed deeply. It was hard to forget her lilac hair; it reminded Klara of Mila's hair, though hers was a much deeper shade of purple. At least there was one person she recognised in the palace—and it was someone who owed her a favour.

"Yes, Your Highness. I didn't think you would remember. Sorry to interrupt you, but we are to see you bathed and dressed," Thamalia said, not meeting her eye.

Klara picked up the pale blue high-waisted shorts and matching top, made of light silk. There was a sheer white overlay covered in floral petals of every colour. *Where the hell am I supposed to hide a blade?* Klara thought. The two servants sniggered behind their hands.

"Not a lot to help with, is there?" Frendall smirked, clearly enjoying her distress.

"It's the latest fashion in the fae court. It's expected—bold colours and pastel are very in right now. Underwear is outerwear for the warmer seasons. There is no need to be embarrassed; all bodies are beautiful in Kalos." The younger servant, who had failed to introduce themselves, beamed as Klara eyed the pale blue strappy heels sitting beside the bed. *Not going to run far in those.*

"How can the fae hide their weapons in such clothes?" she asked in all seriousness, and the fae ducked behind Thamalia.

"They don't," Thamalia said, clearly suppressing a smile behind her hand. *Strange.* "If you will follow us we can show you to your bathing chamber. Your guest can get ready here in your private chamber."

Klara didn't want to scare the young servant by saying that it wouldn't be the first time they had bathed together, and from the smile reaching Frendall's eyes, he was clearly thinking the same thing.

"Through here." Thamalia extended her hand through the door to a vast room made of white marble threaded with silver and gold. A slow waterfall fell in the centre of the space into a shallow pool surrounded with crystals. Klara watched the continually flowing waters, waiting for it to overflow from the pool, but it never did. The bathing chamber contrasted greatly with the bathroom she had in the castle.

"There are towels on the bench. Take as long as you need," Thamalia added, before bowing out of the room.

Klara stripped off her trousers and shirt. She dipped her toe in the water, expecting the water to be freezing, but like everything in Kalos, it was perfect—not too hot, not too cold. It rose to her waist when she got in, and she dipped her head under the flowing water. As it passed over her body, she noticed one of the bruises from her latest fall: the outline of a branch painted across her ribs. She sighed, brushing her fingers along the mark, knowing it would disappear soon enough.

There were bowls of petals on the edge of the pool in a variety of colours. She picked up a bowl of yellow petals and brought them to her nose, then almost gagged as a citrus smell overpowered her senses. She nearly dropped the bowl in the water as she placed it back down. *You look safe enough,* she thought, reaching for some pale green leaves; a faint peppermint scent soothed her as she kept the wooden bowl further from her nose. She crushed the petals in her hand, unsure of what to do with them, but when she rubbed her hands together a lather developed. *Neat trick.*

She let the water fall down her back, embracing the silence, and her mind drifted to the pleading creatures in the factory and how she had left them. *Nothing has ever affected me like this before. Why can't I forget, or leave my emotions aside? Emotions will only get me killed.* Klara gripped herself tightly, trying to push out the helpless voices and their smothering despair, but she only managed to leave fingernail marks on her arms.

Once her hair and body were free from mud and sweat, she took a towel from the wooden bench and wrapped her body in it. Thoroughly dry and smelling of peppermint, she exchanged the damp towel for the robe hanging on a crystal hook. A shadow had filled the room, and she looked to the open ceiling; the sun was setting, and stars were forming. She snuck out of the bathing chamber before the servants came looking for her.

29

"Princess Klara?" a servant called from the other side of her chamber door. The title made her shiver, not the faint breeze from the balcony overlooking Kalos.

"For the love of Lucifer, leave me be," she ordered with a snarl as she slipped into the silk shorts and cropped top with tiny string straps. She studied the faint scar at the centre of her chest. It had never wholly vanished as she had hoped.

"It's strange not to hear you referred to as a queen," Frendall said, appearing from the private dressing room just off her chambers. It contained more clothes than Klara had ever seen, and she wondered if the fae queen had really thought she would come back to Kalos one day.

"In Kalos and Hell, I'm still only the heir. Tonight

I have to be cordial and on my best behaviour if I'm to make allies of the high fae."

"Is that all you're wearing? You look so fae—beautiful, but fae. And the day I see you cordial is the day Hell freezes over and I'm out of a job," he said, as she stood practically naked. "Just be yourself and they'll flock to you, like goblins on gold," he added.

She hoped he was right. "At least the shorts travel to my waist and cover the tops of my thighs. Apparently, it's all the rage here, and it's not *all* I'm wearing," she told him, taking the sheer white dress off the bed and slipping it over her head.

Catching her reflection in the full-length mirror, she found that the dress wasn't as sheer as it had appeared laid out. She could only see the outline of the pale blue garments she wore underneath, and the red petals helped conceal various parts of her body. Klara ran her hand down the sleeve, watching her reflection, but as her hand continued, the reflection's did not. Her reflected self stood still, staring at her.

This can't... Klara looked away, shaking off what she had seen. When she looked up again, she met her own eyes in the mirror. There she was—all wrong, her eyes blood-red, just like her father's when he succumbed to his rage. Her concealed wings were exposed in the reflection, but instead of white feathers her wings were tough and scaled, and her nails dripped with blood. When she looked down at her hands, she saw nothing, but in the reflection a bloodied smile terrified her.

What the...? She moved close to the mirror, needing to reveal its secrets. Her finger grazed her horrifying image, and Klara saw the snaking of black vines in her mind. They were wrapped around something glowing, something close within the palace, but Klara couldn't grasp what it was—only that it was evil, pure untainted evil. *What is Aemella hiding?*

She barely had time to consider it all when Frendall appeared, breaking the connection.

"Do you see that?" she asked as he stood behind her.

"All I see is how beautiful you look," he said, and she resisted rolling her eyes. "I think you should add some more clothes like this to your wardrobe," he added, and she felt his breath against her ear.

"In the chill of the mountain? I would catch my death," she teased.

"I'll keep you warm," Frendall promised, wrapping his arms around her waist as they stared at each other in the mirror.

"You don't look too bad yourself," she said, eying his slicked-back hair and freshly shaven face, but she almost laughed at the fae clothes that had replaced his general's uniform. The pressed white shirt brought out his tanned complexion and dark hair, but the pale blue trousers that matched her dress's undergarments and the coordinating long coat finished off with a white rose in the top pocket looked so wrong it was almost right.

"I look ridiculous," he corrected her, pulling at the long coat. As he lifted his arms, Klara could see his sword concealed at his side.

"Some things don't change. You think the guard will let you hold onto that?" she said, raising an eyebrow.

He winked. "Your mother would have to pry it from my cold, dead body."

30

Night was drawing in. Frendall remained close at her back as Klara walked through the expansive palace. The corridors were so wide and bright, she felt they might swallow her whole. Combine that with the overpowering scent from enormous vases filled with jasmine, and her senses were sharply on edge. She wondered if her mother was trying to throw her off on purpose. There were no portraits, only long mirrors in polished silver frames lining the walls, and after what she had seen in her room, the last thing she wanted to see was her reflection. She wanted to take Frendall's arm to ground herself in a foreign place, in foreign clothes, but she needed to show the high fae that she stood alone.

Aemella will try to push you. Don't allow her to make you look foolish, Frendall projected. They passed a series of servants dressed in pale blue robes, carrying trays of food down the grand white marble staircase that was twice as wide as her own in the castle.

Could we be any further from Hell? Klara thought, looking at the blinding crystal lights, and Frendall suppressed a smile. Voices reached them, and Klara rolled her shoulders.

The high fae stilled as she walked through the doors, unsure of whether to bow or not. Klara was almost relieved to see the waterfall behind her mother's throne; a sense of familiarity was what she sorely needed in this tense moment. She hadn't expected so many to attend.

"My guests, allow me to present my daughter," Aemella said from her mirrored steps at the end of the crowded room. A crown of silver petals sat on her head of silver hair; she looked every bit the fae queen.

Klara might be the fae queen's daughter, but she was a rival queen and the heir to Hell. Lucifer was hardly the fae's friend, and from what she sensed deep in her bones, she had as many enemies here as she did in the realm below. Unlike the dark and dull colours of those lesser in Hell, the fae—both higher and lower—wore bright colours, baffling Klara. Suits of patterned fabrics and dresses like her own moved around in front of them. The jewels that decorated the guests' pointed ears and necks would have made Abadan commit murder out of envy, and the floral headdresses worn by others would have been very much to Eve's tastes.

The fae took the introduction as a hint and bowed slightly, but others held her gaze, not lowering theirs. Klara made damn sure to stare back, offering no smile or scowl.

Well played, she projected to her mother, who sat on her throne.

Klara moved through the guests and forced herself to smile brightly as she was greeted by Elder Yadira of the elves and Elder Gratide of the giants, creatures of Malum with drinks in hand. Yadira raised her glass at Klara, but Gratide couldn't seem to look her in the eye. *Aemella has allowed elders to pass through her boundaries rather than give up her factory. She's trying to get them on her side; they could inform the other elders of her hospitality and lose me the vote.* Before she even had a chance to speak with them, they were swept up into the crowd and she caught sight of Matthias across the room. He bowed ever so slightly before turning away, and she felt Frendall's anger radiating at her back.

Try and talk to them—see if they are going to vote for her, she projected to Frendall, who was quick to obey, disappearing discreetly into the crowd of fae.

"I see you invited my elders. I didn't think they would be welcome in your land," Klara said under her breath, standing by her mother's throne.

"*Your* elders? Are they your property?" Aemella laughed softly.

"They are free to do as they please, so long as you don't toss them in your precious factory as soon as this faux show of solidarity has ended," Klara remarked.

"Since the vote is taking place sooner rather than later, I had to be sure to explain to them the reasons behind my decision. I think it's only right that they hear my side of the argument. They are much smarter than I gave them credit for."

"And I'm sure your side came with a great offering." Klara was relieved that only four elders had accepted

Aemella's invitation, even if they were among three of the strongest factions in Malum.

"Well, I do wish to make up for their losses. I have a conscience, after all." Aemella continued to smile for the crowd.

"Bribery is beneath you, and if you truly felt an ounce of remorse then you would reduce that damned factory to rubble." Klara's voice rose more than she would have liked. Aemella stood quickly, gripping Klara's arm to silence her in front of the watching guests, who quickly pretended to be engrossed in their own conversations. Such an action reminded her of her father; he too liked to silence those who spoke against him. She noted that it was only the lesser fae who talked with the elders.

"If your creatures were satisfied under your rule, they wouldn't crave such frivolity, and they certainly wouldn't have accepted my invitation with very little persuasion on my part. All it took was a single dove."

Klara opened her mouth to argue, but Aemella pulled her aside. "Let's not fight. This is your opportunity to make allies as much as it is mine. I talked with your elders, and they have decided that the vote will be held in the coming days, when Hell's sun is at its highest in your father's dominion. I think we can all agree that we want this over before the next full moon."

Klara clenched her jaw. *That was my job.* This barely gave her a couple of days to learn what Aemella had promised the elders.

"The king still needs to mediate, and I don't think he'll want to call for such a swift vote."

"Are you kidding?" Aemella laughed. "The king can't wait to get this over with. He looks forward to our little family being able to put all this nonsense behind us." She beamed as her guests looked on, waiting for any hint of discord between mother and daughter, queen and heiress.

"Your Majesty, I do apologise for my late arrival." Jasper's voice and heavy steps came through the room as he arrived with two palace guards at his back. *Smart of him, considering they're the only ones allowed weapons in the palace.*

Silence filled the room as both queens turned their heads. Aemella brushed her hand over Klara's hair. A belittling gesture, yet Klara allowed it; these were her people, after all.

"Jasper, how good of you to join us this evening," Aemella said. "I know how busy you are."

"The pleasure is all mine. When I heard your daughter was finally joining us for a gathering, I had to know if the rumours were true. We have had such rushed meetings in the past." Jasper smiled, and Klara remembered how the last time he had had a bottle in his hand, he had smacked it against her head. She eyed the pretty fae's high cheekbones and narrow shoulders. His long, trailing coat was threaded with blooming orange flowers she couldn't identify.

"Listening to rumours can be a dangerous game," she said, noticing the strands of blond within his white hair, which fell perfectly to his ears and curled ever so slightly—clearly styled by a servant. *Someone who likes to do the ordering and not the working,* Klara judged, taking two glasses of wine from a passing tray and offering Jasper one.

"And you certainly like to play, don't you, Princess?" Jasper smirked, and she desperately wanted to break his recently healed nose again. She made sure her hand brushed his, but all she caught was a grand house and flames so hot they singed her fingers. *Is he going to tell all those present about my recent trips to Kalos? Breaking into Kalos not once but twice, removing the fae's hand, almost starting a war?*

"I do what I must," she replied, not taking the bait. She wished Jasper would stop staring at her like an insect under a microscope and spit out whatever she could sense he was suppressing.

"During our last meeting, you were looking a little worse for wear. I can now say with full confidence that your beauty rivals that of our queen."

Klara was glad she hadn't eaten yet, because the latter statement was threatening to summon her wine from the pit of her stomach.

"Such a formidable pair," Aemella said, but Klara only saw it as an insult, and she was sure her own father had used the same words to describe herself and Frendall. "I knew you would be enamoured with each other. I wish you two had been raised together; such a perfect match." She clapped her hands together in delight.

"I'm afraid your daughter is out of my league," Jasper smarmed.

Disgusted, Klara looked over at Frendall, who stood with Elder Langda—from whom the fae kept a wide berth. Fae blood was coveted by the vampires, and judging from the bulging veins in Langda's neck, it was hard for her to resist those in present company.

"I think that's enough conversation for one evening. Let us dance," Aemella said, delighting in the orchestra as they began to play. Fae music was soft and threatened to lull you to sleep, whereas the music in Malum was loud and bold and held the listeners' attention. Klara didn't like it. "I will leave you two to get better acquainted." The queen winked, and Klara resisted the urge to summon her axe as Jasper moved closer.

"I hope we can move on from our past indiscretions," he said while fae couples began to dance.

"I would much rather move as far away from you as possible."

"You two should be dancing, so young and full of energy," a fae in an elaborate headdress remarked, motioning for them to join in.

"We would be honoured," Jasper said, taking Klara's hand and crushing her fingers in his palm. She attempted to pull away, but he leant in closer. "Cause a scene, and you will lose any allies you do have in this room."

The next dance began, and they began to move about the room. Klara watched in trepidation as the fae queen guided Frendall from the room, but Jasper gripped her waist tighter, pulling her body against his and distracting her from her mother. In that moment, she would have given her new heart for a blade.

"I'm not so bad, am I?" he asked as they danced, the fae watching them curiously. Their whispering made her feel like she was back in Hell.

"I'd rather be dancing with a minotaur with two left feet than have your hands on me," she said, sweetly so that the other guests watching them wouldn't notice her disdain.

"You didn't seem to mind my hands on you the first time we met," he whispered, getting a little too close. Klara trod on his foot, delighted to see the pain in his eyes as they broke apart. *Heels do have their advantages.*

"Was that your foot? I do apologise. Fae dances are a bit more complicated than I realised," she said, her apology loud enough for those dancing around them to hear.

"Nothing to forgive. May I?" Jasper said with a delicate bow, and offered her his hand once again.

"Do you want something from me? You threatened to kill me in the factory, and now you can't seem to get close enough." She didn't want to waste time keeping her calculations to herself.

He leant back to look at her, the white around his irises shining. "I think if you got to know me, you wouldn't hold such a damning picture of me in your heart. We are both ambitious and steadfast in our beliefs."

She tried to quell the fury he provoked. "You are nowhere near my heart, but if you think you can change my opinion of you in the next few minutes then have at it—because after this you will never put your hands on me again," she hissed, bringing her lips dangerously close to his. She felt his heartbeat quicken.

"Who knows what the future holds? You might loathe me in this century and love me in the next. Given the circumstances, our futures are destined to be intertwined."

"And what circumstances would those be?" she asked.

"My family controls the manufacturing of angel blades. We harvest the silver and pass it on to the forgers; we're the start of the great chain of fae in Kalos. I'm sure you know our match would be widely accepted, and indeed expected as the only daughter of our queen."

"Excuse me?" Klara pulled back, and Jasper stared at her outburst with wide eyes. He glanced at the other fae around them.

"No need to make a scene," he said, his grip on her tightening. "I saw the way you looked at that commander, but he's beneath you, following you around like a worthless hound. His birthright is inconsequential with Abadan having fallen. You would do better to cut your ties with him."

Klara smiled, but her tone was sharp. "I'd rather have that general beneath me every night than have your soft palms on me a moment longer."

He sneered at her crass remark. "Take a walk with me," he hissed.

Klara looked around the room. Frendall was nowhere in sight, and she could use Jasper to see more of the grounds. She refused to take his arm as he walked through the throne room to another balcony, this time at the back of the palace. The soft tones of the orchestra echoed out into the night air. The chill calmed her, reminding her of moments alone in the mountain air in Malum.

"I thought you would rethink your position once you saw them," he said, motioning over the balcony. She frowned, following his gaze, and her hands gripped the edge of the balcony as she saw them.

Legions. Legions of fae were camped behind the Palace, stone barracks for as far as the eye could see. An army, and a great one at that—one that looked like it was preparing for an invasion. Great fires lit the paths of the fae wandering around, and the sheer number made Klara's throat dry.

"The Great Houses have offered their guard to the queen, since you have stirred up some trouble," Jasper said beside her, taking in the view himself. She wondered how someone could look out at the sight and look so at peace.

"This is meant to be a threat? My demons could sweep your camp in minutes." *To summon this amount of demons from Hell's army, I would need my father's permission... and would he send his army to protect Malum? Lucifer would want something in return.* Her mind swam at this new revelation.

"Your demons? Are you the Queen of Hell? Would

354

you not need the king's backing?" Jasper asked, as though he had heard her thought.

Klara was taken aback by the familiar way he spoke to her. His patronising tone tempted her to toss his privileged arse off the balcony, but she couldn't risk it, not with a literal army at his back.

Jasper's handsome smile threatened to reach his ears. "Forget this trouble with the factory. You will not win the vote, and making me your enemy will not serve you well." He laid his hand over hers as it clutched the balcony. "Align yourself with me, and the fae queen will listen more attentively. There would be no blades for the angels without my house, and they will not tolerate a loss in production. A strategic alliance would benefit everyone."

So this is why he's changed his tune. He wants to bind himself to me, not kill me. Klara laughed at the irony. "Listen to yourself. You wish to bind yourself to the Heir to Hell— the future Mother of Demons bound to the maker of weapons that would destroy them!"

"Kalos and Malum would be united. Hell would be your domain. A unification like no other. With three armies, no one, not even an uprising from the elves, would be able to stop us."

Klara removed his hand from hers. "Don't take this the wrong way, but go fall on an angel blade. I'd be much more afraid of the demons rising against me than your pretty fae army, and you should be too."

Her rejection lit a spark in his eyes, but Klara turned her back on him and walked away.

"Enjoy your time in the Palace," Jasper called after her, his tone slightly threatening, "but I would hurry back to that commander of yours."

She quickened her pace.

31

Frendall, where the hell are you? Klara couldn't sense him in the palace, and she needed to show him the army Aemella had assembled should the vote not go her way. *If the elder creatures sided with her, would she take it as permission to invade Malum, to reclaim her land?*

"Where are you wandering off to?" Aemella said, appearing from behind a pillar in the starlit corridor. Klara could smell the fresh flowers emanating from her. *Has she been in the garden? What was she doing there when there are guests to grovel at her feet?*

"I fancied some air. Your palace has the most magnificent views, and I had an informative chat with Jasper," Klara said pointedly.

"The young high fae is rather intense, but his heart is in the right place," Aemella said, her hands behind her back. She betrayed no response to Klara's acknowledgement of the army. "He has great plans for his future; his heart is full of ambition. However, unlike your father, I nurture it rather than extinguish it."

"I wouldn't call invading Malum 'the right place'," Klara snapped.

"I have no wish to invade unless your actions call for it. You continue to concern yourself with petty matters—with the lives of those dark creatures—rather than thinking of *your* future, of *all* that could be," Aemella insisted, a mad look in her eye.

"As a queen who rules alone, I didn't think you would want your daughter bound to another," Klara said, wondering if this was Jasper's plan or her mother's.

"It wasn't my choice to be alone. Not all great love lasts, but if you have to be with someone, I need to know that it will help both our people. Align yourself with Kalos, not Hell; be the force that unites our lands."

"What gives you the right to dictate to me when you are the one determined to tear the realm apart?"

"What gave you the right to intervene in my ruling?" Aemella countered, inches from her daughter's face.

"We will never see eye to eye, will we? You want Josephine, the child who would bow before you and heed your word, even marry the high fae—but I'll never be her," Klara said, trying to get her mother to understand. "You talk of Malum's creatures as though they are nothing, but I was raised in that land. A general trained me, a witch lectured me, and the Mother of Demons taught me never to bow, no matter how strong the force. It seems both of us are a disappointment to each other," she finished, her fists clenched as she spoke.

"This never would have happened if your father hadn't corrupted you. I wouldn't have to resort to such basic instincts. They may have raised you, but I am your mother and you *will* learn to respect me," Aemella snapped, but Klara sensed the desperation in her voice.

"Resort to instincts? What does that even mean?" The image of Frendall and Aemella leaving the throne room rang out in her mind. *"Where is General Frendall?"*

"It seems he fancied some air as well. He wasn't feeling too well, if I heard correctly, but it was hard to understand him," Aemella said coldly, leaving Klara for her guests.

Klara sat on the grand staircase and tore off her heels. She ran from the Palace, feeling herself weakening. *What is that?* She panted, clutching her chest. *Frendall,* she realised. Her mother had protected the throne room against magic; Klara hadn't been able to sense his suffering, but as she ran through the glittering garden her chest tightened, and her breathing grew laboured. By the fountain, she froze as she saw Frendall's body on the grass, a goblet discarded at his side.

"What the hell happened?" she demanded, kneeling beside his body—an action that was all too familiar. Frendall's eyes wouldn't open. She slapped him across the cheek, hoping the shock of the blow would wake him, but he remained still.

Klara picked up the empty goblet lying in the grass beside him and ran her fingers over the rim. She could feel the dew of the poison between her fingers. *You can't leave me like this, okay? You can't let her do this to us!* She pressed her hands to Frendall's chest and pushed her way into his mind. He was alive, but barely. The poison had been slowed by his strength, and it hadn't reached his heart.

Klara tasted chamomile on her tongue and almond-sweet gelsemium. She watched as Matthias handed Frendall the goblet. Aemella hadn't poisoned him—*Matthias* had. *This poison...* she sensed her own magic. *This is my poison. Matthias has been in the castle?* She sank into the grass, dropping from her knees, the chilled air raising pimples on her skin. *Lottie? The same poison Lottie used to try to poison him.* It was Matthias's way of telling her that he had her, he had Lottie.

I'm so sorry. Breathe, please, I'll die before I let you leave, she projected into Frendall's mind as she pushed the hair from his forehead. *I swear I'll make this right.* Klara conjured what small portal she could to her room within the Palace, to get Frendall out of the garden and away from prying eyes. Just because her mother hadn't handed him the cup didn't mean she hadn't helped Matthias get close to him. Matthias wouldn't have dared to make such a bold move without her support.

She moved a pink satin cushion behind Frendall's head and undid the top buttons of his collar as his fever tried to burn off the potion.

"Hang in there." Klara moved off the bed and wiped the tear slipping down her cheek. Her hands shook as she tried to change into her old clothes, washed and hung up in the wardrobe. She pulled her harness painfully tight, trying to dull her rage as she gripped her axe.

"The queen wants you to wait in your chambers," Thamalia said from the door.

"Doesn't want me to make a scene?" Klara seethed, her face inches from Thamalia, who quickly stepped aside. "Good choice. Guard this door with your life, and if anyone gets past you, you won't see the next moon." She wished she could help Frendall, heal him, but there was nothing she could do in Kalos; he would have to hold on until they returned to Hell.

Feeling Thamalia's terror, and satisfied she would carry out her orders, Klara left.

Within minutes, Klara burst through the doors to the throne room. Her mother sat upon her throne; her confident smile disappeared as she saw Klara's state of dress.

Matthias stood with Ceylon and Jasper. Klara headed straight for them, and Ceylon averted her guilty gaze. Aemella stood to stop her, but it was too late.

"We were beginning to think you weren't coming back—" Matthias said, but before he finished bringing his drink to his lips, Klara had planted her foot in his stomach. He flew back through the crowd of stunned fae.

"Klara, please! You are making a scene," Aemella hissed as Klara removed the axe from her back.

"Think this through," Ceylon urged.

Klara ignored them both as her axe brushed Matthias's throat. "Where is Lottie?" she demanded, and Matthias smiled, exposing rows of teeth. He was satisfied by her reaction.

"She belongs with her own kind," he spat.

"I gave you the land you wanted," she roared. "Now you're marking your territory like the mutt you are!"

"Land that was already mine by right," Matthias declared. His skin stretching and snapping, he became the beast he indeed was. The fae gasped as Klara readied herself for a fight.

"If you spill blood on my land, you will be declaring war!" Aemella's exclamation echoed around the room. "This fight belongs in Malum," she continued. "This is why we must protect ourselves."

Klara knew Aemella was referring to the army. This scene would win the high fae's vote for the factory to remain. She could easily spill blood right now and feel no remorse, but Malum wasn't ready for war, and all those she would need to support her were drinking from the fae queen's cups. No doubt she had already scared them senseless with her army, ready and waiting for orders. She caught the eye of the other elders; some looked as though they would join her in the spilling of blood, but others didn't dare meet her gaze. *Now is not the time*, Elder Langda projected, and Klara knew she was right.

"My child, lower your weapon. There is nothing that can't be solved by civilised conversation," Aemella said, placing a hand on her raised arm.

"Malum has tainted her; she is as much fae as that lycaon," Jasper whispered ever so quietly to two high fae beside him, and they nodded eagerly. Klara glared at him, but that only seemed to gain him their further approval. She looked around the room to see the eyes of all the high fae and elder creatures watching her. *They don't know about Lottie or Frendall's poisoning; all they've seen is my attack without reason. A rogue queen out for the blood of an elder creature.*

She lowered her axe, and Ceylon blocked her path to the alpha, protecting him as he shifted back.

Lottie is safe. Ceylon's eyes didn't leave Klara's.

"There. Now we can behave with more civility. I do apologise, everyone; my daughter has some rough edges that are in great need of smoothing out." Aemella signalled for the orchestra to start up again.

"I did not mean to ruin the festivities," Klara said. "I should take my leave. I don't want to disturb you and your guests for a moment longer." She had no allies amongst the fae, and she would burn down every great house if it meant saving the creatures of Malum. Jasper tried to block her path.

Let her pass, or I will drink every last drop of fae blood in this room.

Both Aemella and Klara looked to Langda as she raised her cup with a bright smile that exposed her fangs. Aemella quickly motioned for Jasper to stand down. The confusion on his face delighted Klara.

Thank you, Klara told Langda, who winked in response. She was glad for the elder's interference—not that a single fae would have stopped her from returning to Frendall.

"Get some rest," Aemella said sweetly, and Klara walked away, feeling the eyes of the guests at her back.

So much for being able to convince the fae and the elders. I played right into Aemella's hands.

Back in her chambers, Klara heard footsteps approaching from the corridor and rushed to the bassinet to remove Abadan's vial. With her mother, Matthias and Jasper plotting, she had no intention of returning to Kalos anytime soon. She had tucked the vial into her pocket when the doors were thrown open.

"How could you do this to me? In front of my court, acting like a child and not the queen you are?" Aemella marched into the room with two fae guards.

Klara moved to the other side of the bed, putting distance between her mother and herself, and leant over Frendall to check his pulse. It didn't escape her notice that both the fae were armed with spears.

"Did you think this would stop the vote? Poisoning a general of Hell?" she asked Aemella, who folded her arms across her chest. "Did you not think I would be able to sense the potion of my own creation?"

"Oh, dear, you poisoned him?" Aemella asked, not a drip of sincerity in her mocking voice.

"Don't act stupid. You knew what was in the cup

when Matthias handed it to him, and you simply lured him out to the garden so I wouldn't be able to sense it," Klara said.

"I hardly have the time to keep track of everything my guests consume, and wasn't it one of your own creatures who handed him the goblet? My hands are clean," Aemella said smugly. "I can see you are upset; perhaps you should lie down," she added, feigning concern.

One of the two guards came towards Klara, who had a sudden inspiration. She needed a way out, and there was only one person who could bring her and Frendall back in one piece.

"You're right." Klara grabbed the fae, plucking a small dagger from their belt as Aemella made a step towards Frendall. Klara pressed the sharp edge to the fae's throat in warning and her mother stopped moving.

"This palace is riddled with fae. I would think twice about what you are about to do," Aemella warned, remaining on the opposite side of the room and chewing her lip.

"Go on—call your guard. I'm sure your guests would love to know that you were serving poisonous beverages," Klara said, delighted to see her mother's worried expression.

The guard attempted to take her arm, and Klara slit his throat without an ounce of hesitation. She had sensed the fae was no innocent the moment she'd grabbed him; nobody who carried out Aemella's orders was. The fae gasped, trying to breathe, while horror filled her mother's expression.

Klara grabbed the cup from beside her bed and placed it beneath the fae's gushing neck as he fell to his knees. Aemella watched, seemingly too horrified to move, the whites of her eyes boring into Klara. The other guard swallowed, his eyes on the blood gathering in the cup.

"Move, and you'll be next," Klara threatened as the guard made to step forward, and Aemella stretched out an arm to stop them.

Klara's heart throbbed as she quickly chanted, "Labraithir limm." The blood circled as she connected with Lokey.

"Klara? Not like you to use the bowl." Lokey's voice was distorted, but it would have to do.

"Lokey, I need you to open a portal where I stand," she ordered.

"I will never forgive you for this," Aemella muttered, watching the colour drain from her guard on the floor.

"I'm flattered that you think I'm that strong, but that would take—"

Klara didn't have time for excuses. "I know what it would take, now do it," she snapped, and the room vibrated.

Aemella took a step back towards the door.

"Hurts to see those you are meant to protect die, doesn't it?" Klara asked her, looking at the lifeless fae as blood stained the white marble. She wondered if her mother would keep this stain, as she had kept Klara's in the throne room from their first meeting. "I don't give a damn whether the creatures kill each other, but I won't let someone who thinks they're superior come in and slaughter them for no goddamn reason."

A faint smile rose to Aemella's lips. "You have no idea what you have started."

"I'll see you in Hell," was Klara's answer as the bed warped and stretched. She gripped Frendall and pulled them through before Aemella could seal the portal.

32

"And here I was thinking you were too *good* to use the bowl," Lokey said as Klara and Frendall shot across the floor of the king's throne room in Hell.

Klara gripped the side of her head as it made contact with the marble floor, pain radiating through her skull. Her eyes searched for the portal to Kalos to make sure no fae guard could come after them, but all she could see was the fireplace's flames.

"Don't let me do that again," she said as Lokey offered her his hand. Due to the lack of sensation in her legs, she took it. Travelling through the portal had numbed her magic, leaving her feeling empty and sore.

"Frendall has looked better." Lokey smirked, checking the general's pulse and eyes. Klara looked at him, still unconscious beside the flames.

"Is he alive?" she asked, supporting herself on the long table, her legs still numb.

"His pulse is weak, but I think I prefer him this way. I don't know what you see in him; he can be extremely dull. All that bowing and loyalty makes my skin itch." Lokey pulled at his waistcoat as he straightened up.

"Enough, Lokey. There'll be plenty of time for you to make fun of him later. Help me keep him alive for now." Klara looked to the doomed at the door.

"No, help me get him to his quarters," Lokey said, and hefted Frendall onto his back. *The doomed will sense how weak he is, and we don't need them spreading rumours about the general's health,* he projected, placing a hand on Klara's shoulder.

"I take it the night's events didn't go so well, considering that one of you reeks of poison," he said aloud, turning up his nose.

"It was my poison," Klara admitted, following him.

There was a hint of pride in Lokey's eyes. "I might not be an expert, but poisoning your lover does tend to be an awful turn-off for the affected party." He smirked, and she wanted to thump him.

"Matthias took my poison from my castle. He must have gained access while I was in Kalos. I need to get back there as soon as possible—I dread to think of what that beast has done to Lottie." She couldn't peel her eyes from the frightful portrait of decaying skin and exposed bone that Lokey had stopped in front of.

"I have to give the alpha credit for making a move. Even I wouldn't have dared to steal from the castle," Lokey said, and Klara raised an eyebrow.

"In my reign or my predecessor's?" she asked, knowing she would never be able to provoke the same bone-snapping fear the Three Queens had brought to Malum.

"Fair point. Nevertheless, he's growing bolder, which isn't going to benefit anyone—not even the lycaons."

"Matthias has Aemella's ear, I suspect, or he is at the very least one of her puppets."

"This should make him more comfortable," Lokey said, placing Frendall on the bed in the general's quarters. The torches on the walls lit as they entered. "What was the poison? It will take time to brew an antidote, and if he continues to fight it so hard, he'll run out of steam sooner rather than later."

"In equal proportions, it shouldn't have done so much damage, but Lottie tried to poison Matthias and added extra gelsemium. I don't know how much exactly—I never checked—but from the loathing in her heart, I know she wasn't light-handed." Klara winced, wishing she had thrown out what poison remained instead of asking Henrietta to vial it.

"How ruthless of you to teach her such a poison. I can see why the little runt was tempted by the opportunity." Lokey sounded impressed.

"I never intended for anyone to consume it. It was a lesson to teach her how to disguise your intentions with a mixture of harmful and helpful ingredients," she explained.

Lokey manifested a bowl of water and a cloth by Frendall's bed. Klara soaked the cloth and placed it on his forehead, trying to cool down the fever. He groaned as the cold water dripped down the sides of his pale face. *Any noise is good.* She didn't want him to end up like Lilith, frozen and deafeningly silent.

"He'll need a purging potion. It will take some time,

but getting it out of his bloodstream will take longer," Lokey said.

Klara turned to the doomed at the door. "I want this room kept as cold as possible. There should be ice blocks somewhere for the king's drinks; bring them here. I don't care if it takes six of you to carry it."

"Should the king notice, what are we to say?" the doomed asked, not daring to raise their head.

"Explain it's on my orders—something for when the elders and fae court arrive. You are to say nothing about the general," she snapped.

"It would be better to heighten his temperature. The lycaon in him will try to burn off the potion," Lokey pointed out, lifting Frendall's eyelid to reveal his blood-shot amber eyes.

"And if he keeps getting hotter with the poison in his system, there won't be a brain cell left," she countered.

"Not that he needs them…"

"Now is not the time for mockery!" Klara was glaring at Lokey when she heard shuffling behind her. "Why are you still here?" she shouted, and the doomed quickly dashed from the room.

"I'm sure he would be touched to see you so distressed," Lokey said.

Klara shook her head. *This is what Aemella wants: for me to waste time here looking after him.* "Cure him. His vote will count towards the treaty."

"Is that the only reason you want me to cure him?" Lokey asked, his arms crossed.

"I don't have time to stay and hold his hand. Aemella would take too much satisfaction in that. He's a distraction and, in this state, a useless one. My feelings are redundant," she said, trying to remain calm.

"I thought Matthias was the culprit?" Lokey frowned. A quill and parchment appeared in his hand and he wrote down the list of ingredients he would need to cure Frendall. Klara waited for the summoned doomed to take it and leave before she answered.

"It might have been Matthias who handed him the cup, but he's merely a face, a scapegoat. Aemella is going to make a move for Malum. She has an army at the ready—an army far greater than is needed to protect a single factory," she told Lokey.

Lokey paced, considering her words for a long moment. "I have long felt the stirrings of war. Now I know the source." He chewed his cheek.

"I need to prove it to Lucifer. I'll need his demons, should the time to fight come. The vote might go against me, so I need to be prepared."

"You have the evidence his majesty requires?" Lokey said, checking Frendall's pulse again.

"I wasted too much time in the factory with Abadan, but I have something. Whether it works or not, time will tell, but I need to get back to Malum and get Eve's seer," Klara said, rising from the side of Frendall's bed.

Lokey grimaced. "Why would you need a witch's relic? Seeing into the future won't help you."

"Because it's the only seer strong enough to reveal what this contains." Klara pulled the vial from her pocket, grateful once again that it hadn't shattered on impact. Then again, Abadan had made the glass. He sealed the door to Frendall's room so that no one else could enter.

"And what would that contain?" Lokey asked, following her through the manor.

"Abadan's memories."

He stepped closer, cocking his head to stare at the small vial. "The king will never allow you to use them.

You won't be able to tell what this might contain before it enters the seer, and then it'll be too late for the king to stop those in attendance from seeing what might be his very own private confessions to the fallen high queen."

"He'll have to," Klara said, stepping into the fountain, the snakes of Medusa's hair writhing as the portal opened.

"And why is that?"

"Because I killed a fae to get back here," she admitted.

Understanding dawned on his face, and he dropped his head.

"What have you done?" It was more of a quiet sigh than an accusation.

"What was necessary."

Lokey's serpent eyes bored into her as she slipped through the portal, only then realising that she had never said goodbye to Frendall.

33

Please be here. For the love of Lucifer, please let her be here, Klara pleaded, a reluctant hand resting on the castle door. She couldn't bring herself to step inside, afraid of what she would find there. The chill of the mountain air offered her nerves some relief.

"Lottie is safe." Ceylon's words in Kalos echoed in her mind. *But what does that mean? Didn't they take her? Will I find her covered in muck, exhausted from a run, or her bed empty and cold? Just let there be no blood.* Klara rolled her shoulders, ridding herself of the disturbing thought.

The doors clunked and creaked, opening before her. The castle was painfully quiet; the torches hadn't been lit, and the portraits slept. Her gut twisted. It's too peaceful, even for the middle of the night.

The torches lit as she stepped into the foyer and almost slipped on something. The light grew as she knelt, her breath catching as she smelt it: *blood.* Her breath caught in her chest, her heart pounding as her eyes followed the streaks along the stone floor until they disappeared under the shadow of the divided staircase. It's not Lottie's blood, she thought with relief, but as she ducked under the stairs, she came across a pile of matted fur. *Jekyll, what have they done to you?*

The young hound lay cold, his eyes closed as he lay motionless in a pool of blood. *I'm so, so sorry,* she thought, stroking the hound's ear. Her first gift to Lottie, gone. *Please tell me Lottie didn't have to witness this.*

The blood. The laying out of the body… *They wanted me to see this.* Klara ran her hand over the hound. *May you find peace,* she thought as she witnessed the creature's last moments, whining in pain, alone. At her silent command, the hound turned to ash before completely vanishing, leaving behind only the sticky, drying blood on the stones as evidence. She noticed something in the stains. Picking it up, Klara wiped blood from the small crystal, a chain running through her fingers.

They were smart not to let Lottie keep it, she thought; it would have informed Lottie whom to trust from its glow. Once it was clean, Klara clasped it around her neck, even more determined to bring Lottie back to where she belonged.

"Henrietta?" she demanded, rising from the floor. Usually, the doomed girl would appear whenever the doors signalled a new arrival. A moment passed, but she remained alone at the bottom of the stairs. "Lottie?" she asked the air quietly, but she already had her answer. Her magic didn't sense the young lycaon's youthful spirit. There was no quiet chaos stirring in her veins.

Where is my guard? Have the lycaons betrayed me? The demons fled?

372

She sat on the staircase and ran her hands through her hair. There was no shout of excitement, no rush of claws or pounding of feet. *Lottie is gone.* She longed to cry, to feel the well of tears and the great relief of letting them fall. Instead, she clenched her fists so tight she feared they might crack and rose. The pain silenced the sorrow she felt. *I freed myself and the creatures from Abadan and her minions. I won't let history repeat itself.*

As she fought the fear of failure, she spotted Henrietta watching her from the second floor. No words needed to pass between them; Klara saw the shame in her eyes.

They took her.

Klara closed her eyes as she felt the tears threaten again and took a slow breath. "When?" she asked.

Henrietta met her on the staircase, her head hanging. "Matthias and a few others came after you left." Her breath grew quick as she fought the memory. Klara could feel how much she feared punishment, but after a couple of hundred years in Hell, it was easy to understand why. "I know I shouldn't have let them in, but they said you sent them to clarify a few notes on the papers you sent about the land. It wasn't until I let them in that they started searching."

"It's not your fault. Lottie is an easy target without me here to protect her. Where are my demons?"

"Someone stirred up trouble—started burning areas of the Forest—and the demons had to put them out. The lycaons with your guard grew distressed by the flames, and they left. The demons went after them to bring them back," Henrietta explained.

"Lilith? Was she discovered?" Klara asked in a panic, wondering how much of the castle Matthias and his lycaons had searched. Taking her in such a vulnerable state would have given them a great advantage.

"Safe. All they wanted was Lottie. The beta made sure she wasn't harmed."

That was why Ceylon had told Klara that Lottie was safe; she had made sure the lycaons loyal to Matthias hadn't got carried away.

"Did Ceylon tell you anything else? Give any clue as to where they might take her?" They might have taken her back to the territory, but it seemed like an obvious choice.

Henrietta picked at her fingernails, already bloody around the edges. "No, she said nothing. There were too many other lycaons around, but she didn't seem like she wanted to be here, and when Lottie cried, she carried her out. She didn't tell her to shut up like the others. I don't think she'll harm Lots—do you think they will harm her?" Henrietta's words were fast.

"Judging from the distraction, Matthias must have convinced the dark fae to side with him and Aemella. He used fire, knowing it would draw those in the castle into the Forest. Most of the lycaons who took positions here lost everything and everyone in Abadan's flames. He didn't need to break in, he just needed to lure my guard out." *This is what I get for leaving.*

"I don't know if it was the dark fae. The flames were almost blue—it was magic that caused them to spread so quickly. I watched from the sky room. They took offence to your punishment; perhaps the witches are working with Matthias?" Henrietta offered.

"It's a fair point… The dark fae might not be able to use their light, but they can still summon dark magic. If the witches were involved, this wasn't because of the punishment. They've been pushing and scheming since

Eve died. Ironic, isn't it?" Klara smiled, and Henrietta frowned. "Eve sacrificed her immortal life to see me on the throne, and yet those most loyal to her want my head."

"That's Malum," Henrietta muttered.

Overwhelmed by the loss of Lottie and the violation of her home, Klara knew she needed to focus on finding the seer and getting back to Hell. She climbed the stairs.

Henrietta spoke up nervously as she lit the torches to Eve's wing of the castle. "There is someone who could turn them to your side."

"Who might that be?" Klara frowned.

"Mila." Henrietta went back to picking her nails. There was no doubt that she and Mila had crossed paths many times while in Hell.

Klara stifled a half-hearted laugh. "Have you been talking to Lokey?"

"Lokey? I would never discuss your affairs—" Henrietta sounded panicked. Klara placed a hand on her shoulder.

"Don't be distressed—it was merely a jest. I want ravens sent out to my guard. They're to return once they've helped those who were harmed by the flames."

"How long are you staying? Are you going after Lottie?"

"I need something of Eve's, and then I need to return to Hell. If Ceylon says they mean her no harm, they must mean it."

"How can you be sure?" Henrietta asked doubtfully.

"Because she would already be dead if that was their intention."

Klara sensed that the doomed was holding something back. She knew she could touch her and force the words from her lips, but Klara had promised Henrietta long ago that she wouldn't use her magic against those she trusted.

"Is there something else?" she asked, offering her a chance to say it.

Henrietta opened her mouth to speak, but the words fell short. "No. I won't delay you any further."

Klara watched as she made her way back through the castle. *Perhaps it's the guilt of not being able to protect Lottie?* she wondered, because guilt washed off her friend in waves.

The pup, Klara thought. *Where's Hyde? They wouldn't have let Lottie keep him. He must be hidden somewhere in the castle, or he would have been displayed with Jekyll.*

She opened the doors to Eve's study, down the corridor from the library, which had been used mostly for storing her brewed potions and poisons along with rare, personal grimoires.

As she stepped inside, she heard the faint whines of a hound pup. Klara went straight for the cupboard in the corner of the room, where the faint sound echoed from; she yanked the doors open, unleashing a waft of caked-on dust. The empty cupboard would have been dusty even when Eve was alive. She had much preferred her potions to studies, and that was precisely what the room showed: potions and grimoires on one side, and a wall of textbooks on the other. They were chained to prevent

Klara from accessing them. A vase of dead and wilted flowers was on Eve's desk, and cobwebs decorated the chandelier.

There, in the corner, cowering, was the frightened pup, making a sad attempt at baring its tiny, underdeveloped fangs.

"It's okay, little guy, it's only me," Klara said, reaching him, and the hound walked into her arms. Her bare skin became decorated with bloody paw marks; he had clearly witnessed what had been done to his sibling. "You're safe with me, okay?" she said in a hushed tone, and the hound buried its head in her chest.

The spiders must have escaped their jars, she thought, looking up at the threads of fine cobweb. Klara had used Eve's library as her sanctuary, but Eve's study only reminded her of the skeletal body and glassy eyes in the dungeon cell. There was no coming back from sacrificial magic. That was the price it demanded. She placed the hound on the floor as he struggled in her arms, and he disappeared.

Klara searched the shelves, lined with magical and possessed items. Tainted and corrupted objects were one of the many things Eve had loved to collect. She made her way down the line, only to find an outline of dust where the seer should have been. *Did Eve hide it during Abadan's uprising? It would have given the high queen an advantage…* Eve had only had one, but it held immense power due to centuries of sacrifice and use. Many witches had sought it after Eve's death, claiming it should be passed down to the covens. Klara hadn't wanted such a powerful object in the hands of her enemy, but she had never thought to search for it herself. *Probably another reason the witches don't favour my rule.*

"Looking for this?"

The voice stilled Klara, powerful yet soft. It was a voice she had longed to hear for many moons, but now that it rang out, she wasn't sure if that had been a wise desire. She was afraid to move in case it was merely a delusion.

"Are you afraid to look at me?" Lilith asked, and Klara turned to see her sitting at Eve's desk with the seer placed in front of her, a glass sphere on a crown-like stand.

She must have shielded herself from Klara's sight, because there was no other way she could have missed her mentor's presence. The chandelier shone painfully bright, and Klara's eyes struggled to adjust. She moved closer to the desk, needing to know that what she saw was real, and the hound reappeared at her feet.

"Clearly Eve failed to teach you not to stare," Lilith said, her feet up on the desk. Klara couldn't help the guilt that welled inside her, seeing the scars that painted Lilith's chest and neck. Her mind faltered as her mentor walked around the desk; Klara stepped back, knowing that many who returned from Purgatory were not the same. However, as they stared at each other, she sensed no threat of ill intent—only confusion and tiredness.

Klara rushed at her mentor, and she saw the flash of confusion in Lilith's eyes when she wrapped her arms around her. There was no armour in the way now, only a thin shirt and light trousers.

"I leave you for a few moons, and you go soft," Lilith muttered. "I know you suffered in my absence." And yet her mentor didn't remove her arms, and Klara felt reassuring hands on her back.

Klara released her. "Then why didn't you wake up?"

"I sensed nothing you couldn't handle. I was watching, though you could not see me. I told you I had a few tricks up my sleeve," Lilith said.

"Why did you wake now?" Klara asked, glancing at the seer on the desk.

"I didn't want to, but I heard the little lycaon's scream in the castle, and my body took over. Thankfully, your doomed girl stopped me before I wandered out of the portrait. I'm still regaining my strength. I wouldn't have been able to fight off any lycaons," she admitted, sounding disappointed in herself.

"How did you know about the seer?"

"I was already in here, looking for a potion to boost my energy, when you came in. Considering that this is the most powerful object in the room, it didn't take long to figure out that it was what you were after." Lilith shrugged, stroking the hound, who was currently brushing himself against her leg.

"He belongs to Lottie," Klara told her.

"Cute little devil," Lilith said, "but you'll ruin him without proper training."

"There's been a lot going on to worry about a hound's training, but at least he survived. Lottie will be devastated by the loss of Jekyll." Lilith and the other queens had cared little for Klara's emotional development when she had been Lottie's age. She would do anything to prevent Lottie's heart from hardening.

"How kind of you. Glad to see you're taking on the responsibility of another. The little lycaon has spirit; I'm sure it won't be long before you seek her return."

"Speaking of responsibility to another, why didn't you make yourself known when I came in?" Klara demanded.

"I had no intention of telling you that I had awoken." Lilith folded her arms across her chest.

"Why not?"

"Because you can't tell anyone that I'm awake." There was a hint of threat in her voice as she leaned against the desk. "I heard every word of your meeting with the elder creatures. If you announce that I'm alive, it will sway the vote in your favour."

"That's what I want!"

"Yes, but it will be because of the fear I project and not because of your abilities as an independent ruler."

"Do you doubt my leadership?" Klara snapped.

"No, believe me. Otherwise I would have woken up sooner," Lilith assured her. "But you need to finish this on your own, no matter which way it might fall."

"She's created an army!"

"Then she will only use my return to boost her justification for it, and see me as a new threat against Kalos. My return will not aid you in any way."

"And if it doesn't go my way? Am I to submit to her?" Klara asked, pacing in front of her mentor.

"Aemella might have handed over Malum when it was decrepit and ill-maintained, but you have already made great improvements, so she'll come for what she believes is her land."

"And when that happens?"

"Then I look forward to spilling blood on the battlefield with you," Lilith stated. She took the seer from the desk and handed it to Klara, who hesitated, afraid Lilith would disappear if she turned her back.

"I'll be here when you return." Lilith sighed, and Klara could feel her exhaustion. She suddenly thought of her father, how he had silently grieved for Lilith's loss.

If she kept this from him, he would be less inclined to support her cause against Aemella.

"What will I tell the king?" she asked.

"Nothing. Lucifer will want his general in these uncertain times, and if he doesn't know I'm alive, then he can't order my return," Lilith reasoned.

"Why not go back to commanding legions?" Klara asked, knowing how much Lilith loved to lead.

"Because I still have your behind to protect. My job was to turn you into the Ruler of Malum *and* Hell. We have one, and I want to make damn sure you live long enough to take the second."

Klara was about to respond when she remembered where they stood. *She knows Eve is gone.*

"What is it now?" Lilith asked, watching Klara look about the room.

"You know that Eve is no longer of this realm?" Eve and Lilith hadn't always seen eye to eye, but they had had more in common than they would ever have admitted.

Lilith sighed, resting against the desk. "Your doomed told me of her sacrifice. Eve was a spiteful little thing, but I have to say I miss her shrill voice around the castle. When she never came to me, I figured that Abadan had finally removed her from the equation. She never liked the bond between Lucifer and Eve. She worried that if it came down to them, he would pick Eve, the same way he picked you over the three of us." There was genuine sadness in Lilith's eyes, and Klara thought Purgatory might have softened her mentor. "Eve made her choice; at least she sacrificed what she must to carry out her duties. A very un-Eve-like thing to do, I might add," Lilith said with a faint smile.

Klara nodded. "If someone had told me she was

going to sacrifice her life for my own, I would have called them mad."

"You are Lucifer's daughter and Mila's half-sister. In her own twisted way, Eve wanted a family more than anything."

Klara had never looked at it that way.

"Since you insist on keeping your presence a secret, I will order Henny to keep the guards out of the corridors of the second floor. I don't need anyone sensing your presence. Neither of us would see the next moon if the king found out through another source."

"Good idea—I don't want to return to purgatory quite so soon. Get some rest before you return. You look worse than I do."

Klara closed her fist on the seer to shrink it to a portable size, then left her mentor behind. *Was Lilith's return what Henny was anxious to reveal?* It might explain the anxiety, but not the guilt, and she didn't have time to dwell on it.

After so much portalling, Klara slept like the dead for longer than she should have. When she woke, she was grateful for the food Henrietta had left in her room. She ate what she could, knowing that she needed to keep up her strength. Frendall's life and her own hung in the balance of the next few days.

35

If Klara didn't see a portal for a decade or feel Hell's heat for a century, it would still be too soon. During her climb to the manor, she went over the impact of what was to happen. Hell's sun above her told her the vote was only so far away, and she needed to get to her father as soon as possible.

I didn't expect to see you coming from the manor, she projected to Larkin as she passed her on the hundred-step climb. She knew she could speak to her aloud, but figured the commander would appreciate her more if she used her own way of communicating.

I was stealing steaks for some of the hounds, Commander Larkin projected boldly.

Klara respected that she was brave enough to steal from the king's kitchen. *And the doomed in the kitchens didn't stop you?*

I only take what is discarded, Larkin admitted, pulling at her collar.

Even what belongs in the trash is considered stealing in Hell.

What else could be done to me? Larkin asked. It was a fair point, though Klara would never be one to risk a visit to the torturers below Hell's manor.

So, you're the one responsible for the well-fed hounds, Klara said. *I need to ask something of you.*

A healthy hound is twice as effective, and many more souls return intact. I'm at your service, Your Highness, Larkin responded.

I need you to find Commander Bromwich and send them to Malum. They're to head my castle guard. No other demons are to enter the castle, only to surround the entrances and the escape tunnels. Klara was hoping she could trust Frendall's closest friend.

I'm afraid Bromwich already holds a higher position. It would be a demotion to serve in your—

Klara's eyes flashed white, and Larkin raised her hands. *The king will not like this.*

I will clear it with him, but I want Bromwich in Malum before the vote is decided.

I think you should reconsider, Larkin started, and Klara respected her candidness.

As much as I value a commander's opinion, I do not wish to discuss this matter.

I was simply going to inform you that the courts are arriving soon, Larkin said.

The courts are arriving soon? Has Lucifer called for the elders behind my back? I need to get Abadan's blood and the seer in front of him as soon as possible. Klara kept her thoughts to herself.

I have the hounds to return to, Larkin went on, *but Bromwich is never far. They will follow your orders without hesitation.*

I won't keep you then. Thank you for your help in this matter. I would also appreciate your discretion.

I don't think the hounds care much about our affairs, Larkin said with a faint smile, before leaving Klara on the steps to the manor.

"Did you have to pick such a volatile remedy?" Klara asked Lokey while she checked Frendall's pulse. *If the poison doesn't kill him, the cure will.* She was relieved to see the enormous, melting ice blocks in the corner to stop him from burning up again. His shirt had been removed and she could see the poison running through his veins, but his pulse was stronger than when she had last been here.

Frendall interrupted Lokey's response to vomit blood onto the plush carpet.

"Good thing you're attending a vote and not a dinner." Lokey smirked as Frendall lay back on the bed.

"What did you give him?" Klara demanded.

"You wanted a fast cure. The dried rootstalk, or rhizome if you want to get technical, will purge his system of the poison," Lokey said, tugging at his waistcoat. "Next time, don't be so heavy-handed with your measurements," he added.

Klara didn't take the bait. Lokey just couldn't resist the opportunity to taunt her.

"I need to be with you," Frendall grunted. "I've heard the doomed outside—preparing rooms. The vote will be—called soon. Lucifer has—arranged it in your absence—ravens have been flying all day." His body trembled.

"Don't be an idiot. You wouldn't make it more than

two steps," Lokey said, taking a small knife from the table and stabbing Frendall in the leg.

"What the hell?!" Before she could grab her axe, she noticed that Frendall didn't respond.

"Relax. See? He can't even feel his legs, never mind walk into a room of courts spying for weaknesses."

"Lucifer has been in contact with Aemella? Why did you not send word?" Klara asked Lokey, who shrugged.

"You were returning regardless, and given his current state, I figured you wouldn't be long."

"I haven't had a chance to talk with the king, and now he'll be in no mood to listen."

"And what has that got to do with me? I healed your lover, and now you are free to rid the cruel realms from those who wish to bring harm."

"I hate it when you're dramatic," Klara said.

"And I hate it when you play saviour," Lokey shot back, kissing her cheek. He was enjoying this far too much.

"Stay—rest. I'll need you soon enough," Klara said to Frendall as he tried to speak. She wondered if it was the poison or the cure that had exhausted him, but she didn't care so long as it worked its way out of his system as fast as possible. "Stay with him!" she ordered, and Lokey held his hands up in defence.

"What else would I have to do with my precious time? You should go; the king will want you at his side when you enter for the vote," he said, rolling his eyes.

"I thought they hadn't arrived yet." She suppressed her anger at her father calling for the Elders behind her back.

"My dear, the moment your father sent the ravens in your stead, they began arriving. Hell waits for no queen."

36

Klara caught her father coming out of his office with some demon guards.

"You're in a hurry," Lucifer said, frowning, as she skidded to a halt.

"Lokey said you wanted to walk to the vote together, and I didn't want to keep you waiting," she said, trying not to show how ambushed she felt. She couldn't risk arguing with him.

He narrowed his eyes. "What is it?"

"What's what?" Klara asked with a simple shrug.

"There's something about you that wasn't before," he said, his red eyes searching her.

Klara thought of Lilith—she'd never thought of Lilith's scent on her—but remembered that she had both showered and changed before portalling to Hell.

"The castle was broken into while I was gone," she admitted to distract him, and Lucifer's nostrils flared.

"How did you let that happen?"

She was taken aback by his response. He wasn't concerned; he was angry.

"Nothing was taken," she lied, walking with him. "I suspect some goblins got greedy and came down from the mountain. They probably snuck in through a tunnel, but I wondered if I could borrow Larkin or Bromwich? Larkin might be able to use the hounds to find those who dared to enter while I was gone." She knew that if she asked for Larkin, he would offer her Bromwich.

"On the eve of the vote, when you should be demonstrating your leadership, your very domain has been violated in your absence." Lucifer shook his head as he walked. "Take Bromwich and Larkin, if you must; the Maze and Kennels can spare them for a moon, but they must return to their posts once the intruders have been caught."

Klara didn't dare smile. "A moon should be plenty of time." The guard needed a leader, and two would surely strengthen her numbers, even if just to maintain control while the vote was being decided. She should have appointed one sooner.

Lucifer snorted as they came to the staircase. "Once this vote is over, I want you to stay away from Kalos. No visits until this ordeal is long behind us," he ordered.

Klara wondered if he suspected Aemella of taking her hostage. There was an unease to him that bothered her. She attempted to brush her hand against him to see something, but he read her mind and clasped his hands.

"Why you went to all this trouble is beyond me." He sighed, as if the whole situation was an inconvenience to him and not the creatures being taken against their will.

"What if demons were taken from Hell and the collected souls they had gathered were used to strengthen another Fallen Angel?" Klara knew he hated that term. It made him feel like he had lost the ongoing war, and not like the king he was.

"That would never happen; no one would dare. You need to show the same level of strength, of fear. It's not enough for them to love or respect you."

"I'm showing my strength by not allowing Aemella to continue her campaign against the creatures. I'm barely back, and I find that you've already called the courts together. Were you hoping I wouldn't return in time?" She watched her father's jaw clench.

"Votes may make treaties, but a single drop of blood is what breaks them," Lucifer said. "I knew you would return with General Frendall under my roof, and I called the courts together in haste to end this before a war is started," he added firmly.

Klara wondered why he was so afraid of war. He would never normally shy away from battle. If anything, he should be dying to get his hands around Aemella's throat. She stopped before they reached the doors to the throne room, knowing there was no going back once they went inside.

"I have the proof you asked for. If you wait for just a moment, you'll see the truth—a truth you might not want others to see," she warned him.

"If you have proof, then what does it matter who sees? It will have to be shown to the courts regardless, so there's no reason to delay." He dismissed the demons who had been walking with them.

He wasn't listening, and she knew it. Klara clutched the vial in her pocket, afraid that once he knew what it was, he wouldn't allow her to use it in front of the others.

"A moment won't matter to those already waiting for us," she argued.

The king came dangerously close. "You have forced my hand—forced me to bring fae into my home, something that has never been done before. I won't wait for a second longer," he said, his eyes flashing red.

"So you would prefer if I killed the fae queen?" Klara kept her voice low, remembering what Lilith had said. "You could have done that yourself, centuries ago."

"The only reason I haven't taken her head is that she has close relations with the angels, and she keeps the realm balanced. That means the angels stay away from my dealings with the Malum port, and don't come looking for trouble because I decided to kill their weapons dealer. So learn to get on with your mother, or I will spare another rib and make an heir who does."

There's the affectionate father I know and love. Klara felt like there was more to the story; there was a fear in his eyes that she had never seen before. Aemella had got to him, but she didn't know how.

Lucifer left her to walk after him into the sectioned and crowded throne room. Klara watched the fae fan themselves in the grossly heated room, beads of sweat running down their faces, something they had in common with the elders of Malum. The higher demons between the two halves of the realm were clearly comfortable and seemed bemused by the visitors' suffering.

Klara clutched the shrunken seer in her pocket along with Abadan's memory vial. *He wants proof? Then that's what he's going to get.*

"Let us all be seated," Lucifer said, addressing the Kalion fae to the right of the room and Malum's creatures to the left. The courts were separated by the grand fireplace, and the higher demons sat between them to make sure that peace was kept no matter the outcome. Klara thought it an odd sight; she had never considered that the day might come when the demons would be ordered to keep the peace in Hell.

Once Lucifer claimed his seat at the head of the long table, the rest of the room followed suit. Klara struggled to suppress her smile when she saw the fae grimace. They had to follow the customs of Hell, and could sit only after the king had given permission.

"A pleasure, daughter," Aemella said, dressed in a charcoal suit.

Klara tipped her head as she took her own seat across from her mother. *She holds no position of importance in Hell, but to wear no colour at all takes appeasing the king to a whole new level. Had I known the vote was happening mere hours after my arrival, I would have changed.* Her ordinary clothing made her look inferior compared to the overdressed fae.

She could feel the tension in the room. Animosity slowly worked its way up through the soles of her feet and into her body.

Lucifer brought the gavel down on the table, marking the beginning of negotiations; Klara was grateful that he wasted no time with pleasantries. She looked down the room and gripped the sides of her chair. *Where's Elder Langda? Elder Osmund? Not even Elder Rathbrook has shown up. Did they not receive their ravens? Without their vote, I'm sure to lose. The warlocks and vampires hold great sway.*

The clearing of a throat broke her train of thought. "As the ruler of Malum and bearer of the grievance, I think you should start your opening argument," Lucifer said.

Klara wanted to wipe the sly grin from Aemella's face. "Excuse me, I do not wish to delay, but it seems to me that some of the elders have not received their invitations."

"Did you not send them out?" Aemella said, rolling her eyes.

"They should be here, regardless," Klara argued. If her father had arranged this meeting at the last minute, she couldn't be sure what had been sent and when.

"We have gathered and given notice. I will not delay the proceedings—if they can't see a reason to attend, then I will not wait for them," Lucifer snapped.

Was this a setup? He knows what their absence will mean for me. They have no intention of this being a fair vote. Klara did the only thing she could, removing the vial from her pocket and placing it on the table in front of them. She almost felt the room lean forward to examine what evidence she had brought before them.

"What's this?" Lucifer asked, turning his nose up at the small vial.

"You asked for proof of the factory and how the creatures end up there. The fae queen argues that they know about the factory and are taken only if they have done wrong or their strength makes them a threat. Here in this vial are Abadan's memories. She herself is a captive of the factory."

The room went dead silent.

Aemella's jaw clenched, and her nostrils flared. *Talk your way out of this!* Klara kept the thought to herself. Even without the elders, if she had Lucifer's support, she could still shut down the factory.

"Memories of the fallen high queen? The very high queen who tried to end your life and cage the king who sits between us? This is dangerous material and should not be passed around so carelessly." Aemella turned to Lucifer. "Abadan was your advisor, after all; who knows what memories that small vial could reveal? It could be a trick to regain power—after all, there's no way to view what this vial contains without the memory dissipating altogether. I'm not sure if that's a risk any of us are willing to take. I'm surprised you would take Abadan's word, to be truthful."

Klara watched the doubt flash through her father's features.

"I think spending her days chained up in your factory has made her see the error of her ways," she said coolly.

Aemella scoffed. "That's nothing compared to what she deserves."

"Enough," Lucifer said, halting the conversation. "Aemella's reasoning is sound. This vial could contain anything."

"I can control the timing and only show the last moon; you'll only see what she's borne witness to. You can't discard this evidence!" *This is all I have.*

"But still, how are we to know that, with your incredible powers, you won't view whatever you please, or distort what is true?" Aemella asked innocently, knowing damn well that Klara couldn't alter a thing within the vial.

"Give it to me," Lucifer said calmly.

The elder creatures and high fae stared at Klara, waiting for her to hand over the evidence.

"You have brought the seer?" he asked, and Klara placed it at the centre of the three of them, putting the vial in her father's hand.

"Who would have thought that so many memories could fit so neatly into such a pretty vial?" Lucifer mused, cracking off the lid.

Klara didn't dare breathe. She closed her eyes and laid her hands on either side of the seer, ready to project what she saw to the others in the room, as the seer would only be visible to the three looking into the sphere.

Instead of a rush of memories, she heard a demeaning cackle echoing from Aemella and the hiss of flames. She opened her eyes to see her proof, Abadan and the creatures' last chance of freedom. The vial sat in the fire, glass cracking, and the memories turned the flames a damning shade of crimson. Klara's chest constricted while she watched her father return to his seat as if he had destroyed a simple sheet of parchment and not the lives of hundreds.

We make sacrifices. Lucifer's voice echoed in her mind.

"I apologise for the dramatics, but fire is the only way to extinguish drained memories. Furthermore, since we can't trust this source of such evidence, let's continue with the vote and end this discord."

Lucifer's words were sharp, his eyes never leaving Klara's—a warning that she was to do nothing. He was giving up on her before she had even had a chance. Lokey gave her a knowing look from across the room where he sat amongst the higher demons.

"Let us vote," Lucifer went on firmly.

Klara wished she had taken Lokey's advice, taken Mila and brought a creature back to stand before them. She sat back in her chair, defeated. Her allies hadn't shown up, and the room positively sang of her mother's influence.

"Those for the factory to remain in operation, because only those who pass through shall be chosen to serve?" Lucifer's voice boomed around the great room.

Klara watched the hands rise. Matthias, Elder Giant Gratide, who couldn't meet her eye from the end of the table, Jasper, Aemella, and many fae faces she didn't recognise.

"I see there is no reason for an against," Lucifer said, raising his gavel and smacking it. The treaty parchment appeared before him, words dancing across it in black ink. Not only had Klara lost, but now it would be written in ink that such a practice was allowed to take place.

Aemella winked. *This is what she wanted all along. She wanted to call a vote.* Klara's nails ate into her palms.

Aemella rose from her seat, took the quill from Lucifer, and pressed the tip into the end of her middle finger. Blood bubbled, and with it, she signed the treaty. The fae queen brought the parchment to Klara and leant over her daughter, watching her own blood dry into the parchment.

"If you want to blame anyone, blame yourself. I did try to warn you that you would not win this game," Aemella whispered in her ear, passing her the quill.

Klara held it between her fingers. *If I don't sign, it will mean war. If I do, nothing is stopping her from taking more creatures. She cut off Malum, yet now she wants the creatures eradicated.* She gripped the quill so tightly that she feared the long stem would snap as she wrote her name on the aged parchment, and she watched the blood settle.

She had been blindsided, ambushed by the sudden vote. She was furious at herself for not looking at the bigger picture, for not thinking of what her mother and father would be doing while she was busy gathering evidence.

"And so it is written," Lucifer said, and there was a weak round of applause. Klara could see the hands clapping, but after what she had just done, she heard nothing, felt nothing.

"I'm so glad to hear Frendall is feeling better. Do send him my love." Aemella kissed her cheek, and Klara suppressed her desire to take the quill and stab her with it.

"This is just the beginning," she warned, staring into her mother's white eyes.

"So young and with so much heart." Aemella beamed. "I hope the fight in you never dulls."

"Let us raise a glass and put all this behind us. Going forward, I hope that each queen will keep to her land, and there will be no need for future disputes," Lucifer said, before emptying his glass.

The queens faked a warm hug, and Klara didn't even need to access her magic to sense the bloodlust in Aemella's veins. Her mother was letting her in, taunting her. In her mind's eye, Klara witnessed the port burning, creatures chained to one another, and fae wandering freely through Malum.

There will be war. Not because I've caused it, but because the fae queen yearns for it.

If the heat hadn't stifled her, the company had. Klara left the throne room in desperate need of some air. Beside the leviathan mural, she found Lokey lingering.

"I can smell the defeat on you. Running away is only going to reflect poorly on you," he said, following her to her father's kitchen.

How she smelt was the last thing she cared about. "Frendall?" she asked, not needing to expand. Lokey raised his eyes to the heavens.

"Recovering quickly—or at the very least, your darling dearest has stopped projectile-vomiting blood all over the three-thousand-year-old carpets." Lokey grimaced in disgust.

As relieved as Klara was to hear that he was recovering, another weight landed on her shoulders. *He doesn't know about Lottie. How long will I be able to hide it from him?*

"Don't tell me you've lost all ability of speech?" Lokey laughed, and she shoved past him.

"Not the time to gloat," she snapped, rifling through the kitchen cupboards for something to soak up her crushing defeat. She supposed she should stay and mingle with the guests, but she couldn't muster up the strength or desire to remain in any of their company.

"I do love a pity party," Lokey said as Klara took a dessert from the cupboard.

"Is that why you're hovering?"

"I thought I should inform you that Bromwich and Larkin have left for the castle in Malum."

"I'm glad," she admitted, relieved. "The castle needs protecting—now more than ever, once news of the vote spreads." All she could think about was the uphill climb she had yet to face.

"I think it should be more than clear what you have to do now." Lokey's eyes glowed as she took a giant bite of cherry cake.

Klara stabbed her fork through the cake with such force that she broke the plate.

"Something you share with your father," Lokey commented, taking a jug of venom from the kitchen counter.

"What could that possibly be?" she muttered, scraping her fork through the icing.

"You both eat when you're stressed." Lokey laughed.

She glared at him, shoving the plate towards him, and he picked up a fork.

"You know, I thought the vote was going to be this big, climactic moment. The darkness winning over the supposed good—but life doesn't work like that, does it?

One moment just rolls into the next, and you spend half your time cleaning up what has already passed," she said, more to herself than Lokey.

"That's an awful lot to consider over a piece of cake," Lokey said, and she couldn't help but chuckle.

"You can finish it if you like. Probably not a good idea to eat before I visit where I'm going," she said, her mouth still full of delicious dessert.

"Best not," he said, pulling a shard of porcelain from the cake and eating it instead of the moist cake. Klara winced as she heard it crunch between his teeth and a satisfied look spread across his lips. "What you've seen upon your visits to Hell is nothing compared to what you're about to witness in the tunnels."

37

"You've had better ideas," Klara muttered to herself, travelling down the staircase into the lowest levels of the manor. She placed her hand over her mouth and nose as the smell of hot blood and sweat made her gag. The deeper she walked into the tunnels beneath the manor, the stronger the scent became. She stepped off the final stair onto the chalky ground of red clay.

"Mila!" she called into the darkness, reaching the arched entrances to the six tunnels spanning endlessly. The flames of the torches shone on the red brick, giving an amber aura to the space. "And this is how I'm never seen again," she joked to herself while she took one of the heavy torches from the wall, trying to get a better look into the dark voids of the tunnels.

"Sweet Judas!" She jumped as a torturer appeared at the opening of the tunnel in front of her, cloaked in bloodied grey robes and belted with an upside-down iron cross. She dreaded to think what state the demon, creature or soul was in on the other side of the door the torturer had just emerged from.

"Your Highness, this is not the place for you." The torturer's echoing voice emanated from the hood; their towering build blocked her from entering the tunnel. She sensed another appear at her back. Coming into their domain was a risk. They might work for Lucifer, but their bloodlust outweighed all else.

"I need to speak with my sister," she said, but they did not budge.

"Only the damned can enter these tunnels," one said, while the other circled her. Klara could smell their foul breath.

"That's bullshit. If Mila doesn't want to see me, she can tell me herself." She was about to force them out of her path when Mila spoke from the darkness.

"What can I do for you?" the demon said casually, appearing out of nowhere.

"We need to talk," Klara said.

Mila folded her arms. "Why would you want to talk with me, a humble servant? I wasn't even invited to the vote," she said, flicking her purple hair.

"Head Torturer is a high position. Trust me you missed nothing."

Mila scowled. "Second in line for the throne was much more to my taste." She turned for a tunnel.

"How would you like to claim that position again?" Klara offered hastily.

Mila stilled, her eyes narrowing in on Klara.

"Hmm... how desperate you must be. I like it. Leave us," Mila ordered, and the torturers moved behind Klara and into another tunnel.

"You will disturb my guests with that." Mila pointed to the torch. "I'm sure those pearly white eyes of yours will do the job."

Klara dropped the torch, the fire extinguishing once it made contact with the damp red clay under her foot. What it was wet with, she dared not to think.

"Follow me," Mila said, and Klara followed the sound of her voice out of the pitch-black tunnel. Her white eyes only allowed for outlines, so she prayed that it was actually Mila she was following.

Her half-sister opened a sealed door, and dim candlelight flooded the hall as if the flames were gasping for air. Klara walked through the doorway, eager to escape the darkness, only to land on her ass.

"Mila! I swear to Lucifer—" Klara grunted as she lifted her hands off the tiled floor, slick with blood. "Can't you get a doomed to clean up this mess?" she asked, averting her eyes from the bathtub full of limbs.

Mila followed her gaze. "Don't worry, I sewed on new ones. Poor creature won't be able to run from the demons this time." Mila sounded proud.

"I'll call a doomed," Klara said, holding her fist to her nose. "How can you stand the smell?"

"The smell? I think I've adapted to it. I hardly notice it—no need to waste a doomed's time. It's only going to get bloody again. Round and round we go," Mila said, motioning circles with her hand in the air. "I also like to have the next one I bring in clean it up. Perfect mental torture—gets their blood pumping, so there's even more to clean up for the next, and so on. Torturing is awfully mundane after the first hundred or so. Creativity is something I pride myself on, though I haven't had a fresh idea in two moons."

"I'm glad you're enjoying your new position," Klara muttered, while Mila helped her up.

"Not like there was much of a choice. I adapted, as I always do. I get results—which is more than I can say for your current cause." Mila spoke as she wiped her tools, covered in blood and Lucifer knew what else, on a rag by a steel sink: the only thing in the room that was immaculately clean.

"Oh, there was a choice," Klara said to herself, standing and wiping her bloodied palms on her trousers. Her half-sister didn't need to know that the king whom she idolised would have been just as happy to see her dead as he was to send her to the tunnels.

"What was that?" Mila said, tossing the rag into the sink.

"Nothing." She needed Mila's help, not resentment.

"So, what brings you to my part of the manor? I don't get many visitors, although I can hardly understand why."

Klara stared at the body parts hanging on hooks from the ceiling and knew precisely why no one would dare to come down here unless forced. Even if she hadn't been annexed to the tunnels, Mila's supporters were few after her fall.

"I need your help," she started, wanting to get out of here as soon as possible.

"Well, isn't this peachy?" Mila sat in the electric chair covered in blood stains without any hesitation. "I won't say I'm surprised. My guests have been singing about Abadan running the factory again. I suspect that is merely a rumour concocted by the fae, though. You need help slaying mother dearest? Aemella is far too conceited for my liking, and I would personally like to thank her for sending me here," she seethed, twisting a blade around her fingers.

"Your *guests* were telling the truth. Abadan isn't dead, and Aemella used her to resurrect a factory. I've seen her myself," Klara informed her.

"Really?" Mila's eyes went wide. "How thrilling that must have been to discover."

"I don't think thrilling would be the right word to use," Klara said, remembering Frendall strung up on the wall, bloodied and beaten in the factory cell. And now Abadan was trapped in her own cell, wasting away. "The vote was about the running of the factory. Queen Aemella takes the creatures to drain them; she sees it as the cost of letting in the many, but I want it gone. Most of my elders either failed to show or didn't receive Lucifer's ravens, which doesn't make sense, since he shouldn't want Aemella gaining power. Or perhaps they didn't show because Aemella poisoned Frendall in her own palace and threatened the elder creatures with an army of fae. Everyone that attended was on her side. I had lost before I even stepped into the room!" Klara ranted, glad to be able to vent.

"You could easily take down one factory," Mila said, as if the subject were beneath her.

"That would mean war."

"I don't like this new you, a saviour complex doesn't suit you," Mila said, leaning forward in the chair. "War? How dramatic! Why not destroy the army? You have legions of demons at your disposal. Your biggest problem is that you overthink. Creatures will die regardless of whether there is a war. What you should have done was brought down the factory when you first discovered it, reduced it to rubble. How could the fae queen have sought war over something that no longer existed?"

Obviously, she didn't understand the factory's sheer size or the lengths Aemella had gone to protect it.

"Aemella would only rebuild—it would only be a temporary fix," Klara pointed out. "Father won't get involved, so that rules out the demons."

"There'll be a banquet tonight to celebrate the vote? Father would never hold such an event without the chance of a soirée to follow it."

"Yes, I've already seen the doomed preparing." *Nothing like having your defeat rubbed in your face.*

"You know how our father loves some after-supper entertainment? The first time we were introduced, the duel between me and Frendall?"

"The one where you were knocked unconscious for the whole demon court to see?" Klara said, and Mila scowled at her. But Klara sensed where she was heading.

"You need to distract the fae queen while she's in Hell with her guard, away from Kalos. Challenge her to a duel." Mila leant back in the chair.

"I don't know… though the fae and the elders would probably relish the idea of a duel of such magnitude. I don't see how it would help me, though. She's already won the vote. Those who do support me will probably have already received word that I failed."

"My plan will only work if you get your creatures to take your side. Which they will if you win. Otherwise, you risk your crown," Mila added.

"My crown is the last thing I'm thinking about," Klara retorted. "If I lose again, which is more than likely, the factory will remain."

"You're missing the point." Mila sighed. "I will go to the factory while Aemella is focused on you; no one would expect me to be wandering around Kalos. Especially not to aid Abadan and some pathetic creatures who couldn't even protect themselves. You can sit here on your throne with your happy family and leave the dirty work to me."

Klara wasn't even going to argue about her dismissal of the creatures. Mila and compassion, like Lucifer and trust, were not exactly compatible.

"How do you plan to get in, having spilt innocent blood?" she asked.

"Innocent blood? Whose life have I taken that was innocent? Certainly not the souls who wander through the door in front of you," Mila said, gesturing to the bath of limbs.

"You expect me to believe that?"

"Believe what you like, but can I really be a monster if all I do is take joy in destroying other monsters?"

Klara thought she was making sense, which was a worry in itself. "Destroying the factory isn't enough," she said, going back to their earlier conversation.

"I'm not saying I'll destroy it. I'll remove Abadan; she's likely the source of power, or Aemella's light would be tainted."

Klara had to give her sister credit for figuring that one out. "I don't trust you to be alone with Abadan, or free to move around in Kalos."

Mila gave a mock gasp. "My dear sister doesn't trust me? I'm hurt." She faked wiping away a tear. Klara loathed her theatrics. Mila enjoyed the politics and bloodshed of the realms too much; to her, it was all a fun game. "Fine. I have an idea, but you won't like it." Mila exposed her sharpened teeth. "Use her own tricks against her."

Klara stared at her, waiting for her to explain.

"And they gave you the crown!" Mila tutted as she rolled her eyes. "You go in my place and accept the duel.."

"I can't be in two places at once."

"Yes, you can. Glamour me to appear as you. She can't see through her own blood magic. I'll challenge her in front of everyone so she can't back down," said Mila persuasively.

Klara paced, thinking it through, careful not to slip in any more blood.

"Aemella will kill you," she said. "She has her wings to protect her, and as much as I can glamour you, I can't give you mine."

"Like I'm living the high life right now." Mila gestured to the rancid room. "The duel will take place in Hell, so it will be up to Father to decide if it's a fight to the death or submission. You sneak away, like you're good at..." Mila winked.

Klara let that one go.

"And destroy the factory. Take Abadan or whatever it is you want to do, and by the time you come back there'll be no more factory to worry about and no evidence of you being there, hence no reason for war."

"There are too many moving parts," Klara said, and Mila rose from the chair.

"If you don't want my counsel, then why come down here? You wanted a plan that gave you an excuse to break the rules, because that crown and kid lycaon has made you soft. This is about power. It's not personal."

"Did Lokey tell you what was going on up top?" Klara demanded.

Her sister shrugged. "We share a cup of venom from time to time."

"I should have guessed."

"What? Not everyone in Hell holds a grudge, dear sister; life is too long." Mila gave her sharp smile.

Klara still hesitated. "How do I know you won't abuse my power as soon as I get to Kalos?"

Mila's high-pitched laughter pierced Klara's ears and reminded her of Eve. "I have nothing to gain if I go against you. The glamour won't last, and if I help you, Father will be pleased with our reconciliation."

"Always working an angle, aren't you?"

"If you worked more than one angle, then you wouldn't be in the dregs of Hell asking your fallen sister for help." Mila gave her a playful slap on the shoulder.

"I'll have to glamour something of mine to change you. So that it holds when I leave this realm…" Klara considered it.

"How about that?" Mila pointed to the crystal necklace that Klara had used to take Mila's life on the Neutral Lands that had become their battlefield. "No one would suspect me of wearing something that killed me."

Klara unclasped the necklace, and Mila handed her a knife. Klara was about to slice her palm when Mila hissed.

"Sorry, that one is blunt." Mila snatched it back and gave her one from her waistband.

Klara sliced her palm and squeezed the crystal. "Quid est, mea est ista." *What is mine is yours.* The words and blood would strengthen the glamour if challenged, and shield Mila from the queen's eyes. "I don't know how long this will last, so only put it on before you enter the throne room. I'll try and get back before the night ends. Allow her to win, and get injured enough to be taken to the infirmary. We can swap out there."

"My eyes will cover you while you leave Hell," Mila said, and Klara knew she meant the portraits.

A torturer dragged a soul into the room and thrust the soul into the chair.

Mila stared at Klara, holding out her hand for the

sharp knife. "Well? Get out of here. I have business to attend to."

Klara handed her the crystal and the knife, and Mila tucked them away. Klara was conscious of the torturer listening in.

"Mila?"

"What?" Mila snapped, strapping the doomed to the chair.

"Thank you."

Mila winced. "Sweet Judas, you *have* gone soft."

Klara laughed and closed the door behind her.

38

Walking anxiously through the corridor of Hell's manor, Klara shrieked as no ruler should when a hand reached out and grabbed hers. Before she could react, she was drawn into Lucifer's private sitting room—she recognised the portrait of Eve above the fireplace from her previous visit to Hell.

Her back hit the door, and before she could catch her breath, lips were pressed against hers. She was about to assault her offender when a familiar warmth crept up her spine. *Frendall.* She pulled him closer, feeling his smile against her lips.

"I've been looking for you. I was worried you went back to Malum after the vote," Frendall whispered, his forehead resting on hers.

"Well, you found me." She smiled back, noticing the two hounds at his back. *He must be feeling suspicious—which isn't surprising, considering what he's been through.* Hounds could smell out poison faster than any revealing spell. She was relieved to feel the steady beat of his heart beneath her palms, flat against his chest—a sign that the poison no longer coursed through his veins. "I'm glad you're feeling better. I was just about to check on you."

It was a half-lie; she had intended on seeing him before she left. The omission weighed heavy on her heart, but Klara didn't have time for sentiment—the crown came first. *It will always come first.*

"No need. Lokey did his job well. I saw Matthias with your father and I've never wished to wipe the smug grin off that bastard's face more," Frendall said through gritted teeth, and Klara could feel the rage radiating off him.

"I'm surprised you didn't rip his throat out."

"Considering how weak I am right now, I don't think I could inflict that amount of pain on anyone without injuring myself further," he admitted, not meeting her eye, ashamed. She thought he looked just as powerful as ever in his general's attire.

"I know you were really going to see Lokey," Frendall added, straightening up and releasing her.

Klara frowned, though she was pleased he'd changed the topic away from Matthias. She wanted to spare him the news about Lottie being taken for as long as possible, even if he would resent her for not telling him sooner.

He sighed. "I saw your path when I kissed you. It seems that surprising you is the only way to get past your defences at the moment."

"I was heading to Lokey's chamber before the night wears on and Lucifer calls me to the gathering to celebrate Aemella's win," she admitted.

"Why?" Confusion creased his handsome features.

"I need him to send me back to Kalos while the fae queen is in Hell."

"Care to explain?"

"Because I'm going to destroy the factory until there's nothing left but ash," she said coolly, the anticipation making her palms sweat.

"The vote didn't go the way you hoped, but there's still time to negotiate. Invading Kalos while she's out of the realm is just that, an invasion—it's a clause for war. The vote has given her express permission to maintain the same factory you wish to destroy. You swore by blood. Forget the fae and creatures and how they'll perceive it, the higher demons that support your right to Hell will see this as a lack of honour!" Frendall argued, and she could feel his concern.

"It takes a vote to make a treaty, but only a drop of blood to undo it. They won't support a queen who would roll over and play dead either." She was misquoting her father, but she was sure Frendall would get the point. "My mother is relishing in her victory, and my father won't let her or her guard out of his sight while she's here. It's the perfect opportunity." *Why does he always have to fight me every step of the way? Is this what our future holds?*

"And when they come looking for you? They'll know exactly where you've gone," he hissed, his face inches from hers. She could see the fear in his eyes.

"I already have that covered," Klara said, looking at Eve's portrait.

Frendall followed her gaze and squeezed his eyes shut. "Mila will betray you before you even step through the portal. You go to her before you come to me? You act before you think every time, and I don't want to stand by and watch you fall! It would kill me!" He picked up the decanter from the side table and downed the contents before hurling it at the wall.

Klara watched the liquor drip down the textured wallpaper.

"I knew you would react this way. You would want me to wait and bide my time, and I did that. I played the game, I went to the elders, to Kalos—and lost. Now it's my game." She stroked the head of a hound at her legs.

"And my opinion doesn't matter to you?" Frendall asked, running his hands through his hair.

"No," she said flatly.

"Because you're the queen and I'm a general."

"For the love of Christ. Yes. It's my responsibility, not yours. How many times are we going to have the same argument? Until you learn—" She stopped herself, her words running away from her.

Frendall turned on her. "My place?"

"That I love you, but your decisions don't affect the lives of thousands of creatures, don't upset an ancient balance." She gripped his shirt, trying to force him to look at her, to understand her, but his face was made of stone.

"She'll betray you, and I'll be the one who has to watch," he said coldly, removing her hands.

"No, she won't. I could feel how much Mila loathes being in the tunnels. The overkill I witnessed only confirms it." She thought of the limb bath. "She might betray me once I've destroyed the factory, but for now, it's working in her favour to do her part."

"Let things settle after the vote," he pleaded. "More rash action will only lead to war."

Klara paced, and the hounds backed up, sensing her unease.

"They think they can take anyone…" she started, knowing the truth would make him see.

"No, they don't," he scoffed, shoving his hair away from his face.

"They took Lottie." She hadn't wanted to tell him this way, to prove a point, but it was the only way to make him see that nothing would stop Aemella, especially not with Matthias in her pocket.

Frendall froze. Before Klara could stop him, he was out the door, the hounds following close behind.

"Stop! This isn't going to help Lottie," she ordered, stepping out into the hall, but he was already nearly out of sight. The portraits watched in amusement as she stormed after him. *Confronting Matthias will only screw everything up!* She attempted to project the thought, but he didn't slow down—he moved faster. His claws were replacing his fingernails. The doomed didn't have a chance to open the doors before he threw them open.

The throne room was full of laughter and chatter, which abruptly ceased when Frendall raised a partly shifted clawed hand and slashed Matthias's face. Klara was sure the growl that escaped the alpha would be heard in Malum.

Frendall grabbed Matthias by the collar, nostrils flared as he bared his fangs. Nobody in the room dared to move. *Everyone will see this as an unprovoked attack.* Klara was frozen by the door, searching for Lucifer, praying he wouldn't send his guard to subdue Frendall. Such a scene would severely reduce the general's standing amongst the hierarchy. She spotted Lucifer, but he appeared more amused than enraged.

"Lottie is under my protection. Give her back untouched, and I won't rip out your throat," Frendall said through gritted teeth. Klara had never seen his rage like this before.

The blood from Matthias's wound coated his cheek, neck, and the general's hands, holding him in place. The room waited for his response, but the alpha said nothing, did nothing.

A bemused Lucifer clapped slowly before breaking them apart.

"Now, now, what is all this about?" he said, his voice laced with charm.

"Lottie, the rightful alpha, has been taken by this false leader. This act breaks any such treaty," Frendall barked.

Klara gasped. He had snapped at the King of Hell in front of the courts.

"Take your hands from him, General. I will not ask twice," Lucifer said. He spoke calmly, but Klara noticed the veins bulging in his neck, then the smile on Matthias's face.

There was a moment's hesitation before Frendall released Matthias's collar. The four slashes travelled from the side of the lycaon's nose to the tip of his eyebrow, but his skin was already healing.

"How are we to settle this? One issue replaces another." Lucifer tutted.

Before anyone could speak, a dangerously soft voice rose above the rest.

"A challenge, since Frendall has already drawn first blood. It seems only fair." Aemella was probably hoping a challenge between the two lycaons would end one if not both of them, but Klara saw her opportunity and took it.

"I accept," she said boldly, taking the attention away from the lycaons. "Matthias is your ally. Lottie is my charge. If I win, Matthias returns my ward without a scratch and *alive*." She directed her words towards her mother. This was between them and no one else, and Klara knew she had to be specific in her demands. A hostage could return without a scratch, but also without life.

"I don't see how I'm involved," Aemella said, feigning ignorance.

"Did you know Matthias held Lottie?" Klara knew it was hard for a fae to answer yes or no questions; that way they couldn't weave a web of mistruth.

Aemella smiled, placing her glass of venom on a tray, and Klara watched her guard take a step closer to their queen.

"Yes or no?" Klara pressed, and the room waited in silence for the answer.

"Yes," Aemella admitted, as if it caused her physical pain.

"Well, since we are their rulers, then we are responsible for these events."

"And if you lose?" Aemella smiled sweetly.

"I will not challenge the factory any longer," Klara offered.

Matthias went to speak, his eyes flashing amber, but Aemella's hand silenced him.

"When?" the fae queen asked, clearly thinking she had already won.

"Tomorrow eve, when the red moon is at its highest. That should give you both time to prepare and rest. My doomed have already prepared rooms for you and your fae," Lucifer said to Aemella, ever the gracious host.

Frendall glared at Klara, but she ignored him.

"Most kind of you. I accept the terms," Aemella agreed, and offered Klara her hand.

Klara shook, and the challenge was set. Frendall left

the room while Matthias took a drink from the doomed's tray, perhaps to dull whatever pain he felt from Frendall's attack.

That didn't go according to plan, Klara thought as she watched the room return to previous conversations. *Hours to complete what should take days. Time moves slower in Hell than it does on Kalos; the delay will play to my advantage. I need to get a note to Mila, let her know the plan has been altered.*

Since Mila had revealed her acquaintance with Lokey, Klara knew he would be able to get to her in the tunnels. With the fae now staying in the manor, she couldn't risk being seen scheming. Klara hoped he wasn't interested in an early night—especially since Lucifer had returned Damien when the fae arrived. She despised the idea of putting his family in the middle of her troubles, but Lokey was a high warlock as much as he was a demon, and his wife belonged in Malum; so did their child.

If anyone cared, it would be her.

39

Klara snuck into Lokey's room, just down the corridor from her own in the manor, once the fae had settled for the night. She was almost insulted that his chambers were nearly twice the size of her own.

"What are you doing here?" Lokey asked from his desk, a candle lighting the parchment on which he wrote.

Klara looked to the bed to see a fan of red hair on the pillow and tiptoed into his quarters, only opening the door a crack to prevent the light from streaming in and disturbing Glaudine or Damien in the crib.

"I need to ask you for a favour," she whispered.

"Glaudine only just returned. Does it have to be right at this moment?" Lokey rubbed his face. Gone was his light-hearted and mischievous nature; when it came to his family, he became someone else entirely.

"Yes. You can sleep when I'm dead." She was being

dramatic, but then again, you never knew when you'd take your last breath in Hell.

"Keep going the way you have been, and I will get more beauty sleep than I require," Lokey said, folding the parchment and she wondered what he was trying to hide.

"What's going on, darling?" Glaudine asked. "You're going to wake Damien." She lit the lamp beside the bed. Lokey motioned towards Klara, and Glaudine jumped to see her queen lurking by his desk.

"I'm sorry to disturb you, but it concerns the Forest," Klara said quietly.

Glaudine's eyes sharpened as she glanced at her son and then to Lokey. "Your Majesty, I did not see you," she said politely. "You can't do it without his assistance?"

"I'm afraid not." Klara felt Glaudine's worry, and glanced at the scars Lokey bore from the last time he had taken her side. "I wouldn't come to you unless it was important," she added.

"Help the poor girl. I want there to be a Forest for our son to grow up in," Glaudine said firmly.

Lokey sighed and kissed his wife's cheek. "You're lucky she likes you. What is it you need?" he asked Klara.

"I need you to get this message to Mila." She handed him her own piece of folded parchment.

"Mila? So, you finally decided to listen to someone other than that general of yours." Lokey smirked.

"Don't act surprised—I know you've been plotting something with her. The duel will take place when the red moon is at its highest," Klara said. "The note will tell her what happened."

"Why can't you give it to her?" Lokey said. They both knew a note was evidence of plotting, and any fragment of that was a dangerous thing.

"I don't have time to get to the tunnels, and the fae are sleeping within these very walls. I can't be seen wandering about. If I'm to make it back before I'm missed, I need for you to portal me to Kalos about five minutes ago."

"I've only brought you to and from Kalos in a mere amount of days. Do you think I'm a bottomless well of magic?" he said, feigning a yawn.

"Yes." She grinned, soothing his ego.

"You would be right." He half-smiled and rubbed his eyes again, then looked at the door. "You're not taking your lover? He won't be pleased about being left behind."

"I don't think he's all too pleased with me regardless. He disagrees with my alliance with Mila, and I can't say I blame him, but I can't stomach my mother's shackles for another moon," Klara said.

Before Lokey could respond, he was silenced by a hush from his wife.

"As fascinating as this is, let's not disturb the child," Glaudine whispered, and Klara tipped her head in apology. Lokey zipped his lips with a wink.

Klara looked at the infant's crib, seeing how much it looked like the one in Kalos. She wondered if Lokey's child would one day deceive his parents as she was about to.

"It was nice to see you again, and thank you for your assistance with the witches," she said politely.

Glaudine offered her a weak smile, but Klara could feel the concern emanating from her. Klara had already forced their family into hiding once, and from the look in Glaudine's eyes, she suspected it was about to happen all over again.

"I think it should be I who thanks you for the guards you sent. But witches? Why are you thanking me?" Glaudine asked.

Klara moved closer in case she disturbed Damien. "For sending the witch to me?" she said to the leprechaun, surprised to see the look of confusion on her tired face.

"I'm sorry, Klara, but I never sent any witch to your door. I would never impose like that," Glaudine told her, clearly confused.

If she didn't send the witch… then who did?

"My mistake. Has Lokey had recent dealings with the witches?" Klara asked, knowing he was the next plausible choice. It was that very witch who had set everything in motion.

"No, not that I can recall. We've been too busy dealing with the dark fae lingering around Tapped and harvesting the next batch of syrup from the toadstools. I'm sorry, I can't offer you more."

"There's nothing to apologise for. I must have misunderstood," Klara said, watching Damien stir in his crib. "I'll leave you before he wakes."

Glaudine appeared grateful, but the question played in Klara's mind. *Who else could have sent the witch my way? And why would she have lied about who sent her?*

A swipe of Lokey's hand against an oval portrait of himself, in his signature waistcoat and top hat, opened a secret room of his chamber.

"Take this. It should help you return in case you can't call for me," he said, taking a silver coin marked with a pentacle from a pot on the small wooden desk. "Throw it against a wall or door and it will open a portal—but be sure to think about where you want to end up. It's the best I can do. It'll be easier to conceal than a potion, and if you're captured, you'll be able to get out," he explained.

"Thank you." Klara placed the coin in her pocket. "What if the cell is lined with iron and it blocks the magic?"

"It should be strong enough; I use them for getting between realms when I'm doing *business,* but just in case—" He tossed another at her, and she caught it mid-air. "If you end up in Aemella's cell, try to get out before you toss it, but if that's not an option, two should force the portal open. Not for long, though, so I wouldn't linger or try to save anyone." There was no humour in his tone.

She was grateful for even this much; she felt a small amount of relief in knowing that someone wanted her to stay alive. She wasn't sure if Frendall did at this current moment in time.

"I don't understand why you don't portal in yourself. You're strong enough," Lokey said.

She was, but it used a great amount of magic that she didn't want to spare. "Aemella would sense it. My magic can't get through hers without using extreme force. I barely made it through her and Abadan's glamour concealing the factory, and my wings have yet to recover," she explained, still feeling the sting in her concealed wings.

"Very well. I'm weak from bringing Glaudine to the manor, but I'll do my best." He took a piece of chalk from his desk and drew a pentagram on the wooden floor. He snapped his fingers, and a lit candle appeared at each point. He guided Klara to the centre. "See your destination in your mind's eye, and don't look away from it."

Pentacle portals were extremely temperamental, commonly used by witches. Knowing that they loved to send their passengers to any realm they wished, Klara struggled to focus her mind on the factory.

Before she could catch her breath, she felt the floor open beneath her.

40

Klara sighed in relief as she landed on her feet—she didn't think her ribs could take another bashing. She noted this fae room was similar to the one she had visited before, but this was larger, with a plush bed instead of a cot and expensive wallpaper covering the factory brick. A room for someone of importance.

Suspicion crawled up the back of her neck, and her relief was short-lived when she heard the click of the door. *Damn pentacle portal.* The only exit to the room was behind her.

"I have to admit, you're the last person I expected to find in my chambers," Jasper said. She tried to turn, but he was already at her back. "I suggest you don't move, unless you want my spear through your neck."

Klara felt the weight of her axe disappear from her back as he took it.

"For a queen, you're awfully good at following orders," he said, his voice so close to her ear she felt his breath against her neck. She wanted to grab him and fling him over her shoulder, show him exactly what her axe could do, but she needed to bide her time.

"A spear wouldn't kill me," she laughed.

Jasper walked around her, and she noticed he held no weapon other than her axe. "Good thing I don't have one, then."

She clenched her fists and glanced over her shoulder to see his spear resting against the wall.

"I thought you'd be happier in your cabin than within the factory," she said, trying to distract him.

"Since your last visit, I figured it would be best to remain close."

She sensed no fear in him. He was perfectly at ease, and she was anything but.

"I assume you're here because of the vote," he added. "I had a feeling you wouldn't be able to leave it alone, and with Frendall's fabulous display of anger I thought I had better return—just in case." Jasper leaned against the carved end of the bed, her axe in his hand.

"I wanted to inspect the place myself," Klara said.

He lunged forwards, bringing her axe to her throat.

"This will go a lot easier for you if you don't lie to me. I knew the vote would never carry in your favour, and that's precisely why you're here." His face inches from hers, she noticed his bright eyes and perfect skin. There wasn't a mark on him.

"What if I said I was here for you?" she lied. *He wants me to bind myself to him. Let him believe that's what I'm here for—to make a deal.*

He looked surprised.

"I highly doubt that. You could have found me in

the manor, but instead you came all the way here?" He smirked, brushing her hair behind her shoulder. The blade was still barely an inch from her throat, but she stepped closer.

"There isn't much privacy in the manor. I knew you would follow me; as you said before, we are much alike." She stared at his lips, raising her eyes slowly over his features to notice his pupils dilating. *So this is what you truly want: me.*

He smiled faintly. "Walk with me." He waited for her to turn and head out the door before following.

The fear in the walls of the factory smacked into her as they walked from the room. Jasper was careful to keep her axe in the hand furthest from her, with his other casually brushing hers with every stride.

"You come from a great line of the fae. I'm sure you imagined better things for yourself than this; maintaining the factory is beneath you," Klara commented, playing to his ego.

"The queen needed someone reliable, considering that recent events left a fae missing a hand. I think she was right to have someone more senior look after the place."

"A hand? How terrible," Klara said sarcastically, and Jasper snorted. "I thought you would have relished in the factory being destroyed. You'd be free to run your house, gather the silver for the angels without any delay or interference, instead of babysitting the draining of creatures in this grim place." A group of bound creatures passed them, and she couldn't take her eyes from their drawn faces and defeated posture.

"Shows how little you know about Aemella. Once she sets her mind on something, there's no stopping her.

I fear that trait has been passed on to her offspring," Jasper said, admiring her openly.

"I can't say we aren't determined—which is why you should take my side. I'll have Hell at my back one day, and I don't think you want to give up such an ally. I can feel your ambition, and this place is far from what you want." Aemella had mentioned his ambition, and she could hardly imagine that the factory was what he had his sights set on. Jasper seemed all too refined for such distasteful tactics.

"I hate to be the bearer of bad news, but you'll lose. Aemella has a new strength that's growing every day. Something is changing her, and I don't plan on making her my enemy." Jasper stopped suddenly and brought his face so close to Klara's that their noses brushed. "Even if you are very tempting." His eyes were on her lips.

She moved as slowly as possible to take back her axe, but he pulled away too quickly and continued ahead. She sensed no fear or worry in him; she didn't know whether he was incredibly stupid or incredibly brave. *All the more reason to have him as an ally. A new strength? Aemella won't have much power once I take this place down.*

The heat and smell of faeces only amplified as Jasper brought her through to the room of cauldrons, the factory floor. She knew he had done it to provoke a reaction. She studied his face, and there wasn't even a hint of remorse or pity from him. How he managed to keep his light dumbfounded her.

She took in the terror in the creatures' eyes. Some were able to muster enough energy to sit up; some glared, while others stretched their arms through the bars for help. There were twice as many fae guards along the walkway as before, and no sign of Abadan.

"You enjoy it here? Enjoy watching them suffer?"

Klara asked, feeling sick to her stomach. Her outburst gained her a smile, and she heard a broken potion bottle crushed under their boots.

"It serves a purpose, and I serve the queen—though there is no love lost between myself and the creatures." He grimaced, and she wanted to know what could have possibly happened to him to cause so much hate for those in the room. The bitterness she felt when she brushed her hand against his threatened to choke her, but he was blocking her from seeing any more.

"I admit they have their faults, but this is a fate worse than death."

"Yes. It is." His tone and expression were flat.

He paused outside the door to Abadan's cell. Klara saw that they had been quick to replace the door that had been destroyed last time.

"If you think I'm going to walk into a cell without a fight, you're dumber than you look," she stated.

He took a deep breath and dismissed the guards at the door. "I merely wish to show you something," he said, extending a hand. He closed his fist when she refused to take it. This time she waited for him to go first.

Before she could ask where the fallen high queen was, she heard a deep groan, like an animal that had got caught in a snatch. Klara looked further into the silver cell, and there was Abadan, embedded into the wall.

Her hair covered her face, and all Klara could hear was the quiet groan. Abadan was bound to the cell by silver branches woven through the brick, as if the factory was a monster trying to swallow her whole. Klara could barely make out the outline of her wasting body—only fragments of inflamed skin from the contact with the silver. Her eyes went to Abadan's hands, hanging through the heavy vines and branches. She was so encompassed that there was no need for shackles. Klara moved closer instinctively and saw the single vine wrapped around her neck, burning her while also keeping her upright. The once-ruler of Malum was as much a part of the factory as the bricks and cement. This was Aemella's way of making sure the factory remained.

"If you destroy this factory, then you destroy your ally," Jasper said at Klara's back.

Klara might not have cared about Abadan, but she had proved useful, and Klara owed her a debt for helping her escape not once but twice. She had promised to bring an army—and yet here she stood with one of Aemella's allies.

"You thought showing me this would stop me from destroying this place?" she whispered.

"You won't kill her. She's too valuable to you; she helped you escape, and I don't think you'll leave that debt unpaid, even if she was once your sworn enemy." Jasper stared at Abadan triumphantly. He rested a hand on Klara's shoulder. "If you're serious about binding yourself to me, then I'll help you free her and bring down the factories."

"*Factories?*" Klara said, snapping around to face him.

His laughter reached the high ceiling. "You didn't think Aemella could raise such an army and provoke such fear with only one tiny factory?"

"Son of a bitch," she rasped.

That wiped the smile from his face. "I'd prefer if we didn't bring our parentage into this," he snapped.

"You barely know me. Why would you want to bind yourself to me in this life and the next?" An alliance was one thing, but being bound was a ritual that lasted for an eternity.

"Alliances can be bought and made—think of how your parents created you. Peace comes at a high price; you just have to be willing to pay it. Together, we could rule Malum and Kalos, and with Hell combined no faction of creature or fae could rise against us. You might not feel anything for me now, but we're young. A hundred years from now you might never want to be without me."

Klara dreaded the thought, but she let him continue, letting her believe she was considering it.

"What if I killed that general of yours—would you come to me then? I can sense that you feel something when I'm close, that my skin craves you. The fae in you calls to me. You just don't want to listen."

His hand lightly travelled down her arm and in the pit of her stomach, she knew he was right. There was a tiny hum, a spark she couldn't ignore.

"You're right," she said, and his eyes widened. She placed her hand on his. "I do feel something. I have from the moment I met you, from the moment you held me during that first dance," she continued, and he pulled her close to him.

See what you're trying to save, he projected as his lips found hers. There was no emotion in it, only his mind connecting with hers as they stepped into his memory.

Klara stood in the faint Kalion breeze, amongst the green grass and flowers, and watched a young boy cry great tears that rushed down his round cheeks. He was staring in horror at the blue flames flickering before her eyes. Witches and dark fae held torches against layers of autumn vines that surrounded an enormous white house, and Klara heard the cries of at least a dozen fae.

When I was only a boy, the witches tempted a few dark fae to raid our lands and sacrificed my family in the process. Now we're expected to let them in here in the dozens? Jasper passed the thought to her.

Klara broke free of him as she tasted the smoke in her mouth. "A few witches and dark fae, nearly two decades ago, raided your lands—so every creature who now enters Kalos has to suffer? How many have to die before it satisfies your need for revenge?"

His face was ugly with rage as they stared at each other. She took advantage of their proximity and his emotional distress and gripped his wrist at her waist, twisting until she heard his bones crunch. A strangled groan escaped him, and her axe fell to the ground. Jasper fell to his knees, but before she could deliver a silencing blow, he shook his head with a demented smile.

"You have no idea what you are starting," he wheezed.

"Yes, I do." She delivered another blow and he collapsed, a cloud of dust lifting from the cell floor. A small trickle of blood traced down his forehead; he wouldn't wake any time soon. Klara pitied the boy who had watched his family burn, but the past didn't excuse anyone's actions. *Tragedy should breed compassion, not more tragedy.*

"How do I get you out of this?" she asked, rushing to a dazed Abadan. The fallen high queen whined as Klara lifted her head gently and brushed the hair from her lined face so they could talk face to face.

Klara flung her axe at one of the branches, but a protection spell reacted to the force of the blow and tossed her across the room, landing her hard beside Jasper. She cracked her neck back into place and rose on shaking legs. *Holy shit. Aemella spared no magical expense.*

"I was going to warn you, but you're still determined to act before you think." Abadan's voice was barely audible. Klara wondered how she could smile while bricks and branches pierced every part of her worn-out body. Her old glamour barely held, revealing Abadan's true nature and age.

At any other time, Klara would have been delighted to see her enemy in such a state, but 'the enemy of my enemy is my friend'. She lifted her axe to try again, but Abadan shook her head.

"Leave me here," Abadan whispered. "I have enough strength to topple this place, but I had to wait to see if you would return. To tell you there's no way to reverse Aemella's protection. She's using another source of magic that I can't penetrate. You can't undo her magic. There's no way to separate me from this place."

Klara had never thought she would hear the Mother of Demons resigned to defeat.

"What about him?" she asked, wishing she could take Jasper's head.

"He'll probably survive the destruction; his blood comes from strong ancient lines of fae, I can smell it. He holds too high a position to kill—it would bring the fae down on you. If he's merely injured in the rubble, I'll be blamed and she'll have no cause for war," Abadan panted.

Klara knew she was right. As much as she wanted to kill him, to weaken Aemella, she couldn't risk it.

"He wants something from me—feels something, even if it's twisted by revenge, so there's a chance he'll keep my involvement to himself. But I need you to tell me if what he said was true. Do more factories exist?" Jasper couldn't lie, but she needed it confirmed by someone, anyone else.

"I don't know how many. I have no control over them. She has another source—one I think I was only here to mask. I've grown too weak since I destroyed the ceiling for you. Tell Frendall I'm sorry." The room suddenly smelt like death. "I loved his father more than any gold I could have possessed."

Klara wasn't sure how much of that she believed, but she owed Abadan for helping her escape.

"I'll tell him," she said, but she had to ask. "Is that why you're doing this? To make amends?"

Abadan bowed her head. "I wish that were—true. And maybe—it is, but what I—really want is for—Aemella to rot for... for what she's done to me." Her breathing was laboured. The ground began to shake.

"It couldn't be more apt that in your dying moments all you want is revenge." Klara almost smiled, placing her hand on Abadan's for a brief moment.

"I've been this way for centuries, and staring death in the face won't change that. Now go," Abadan rasped. "Get out. Once I start I won't be able to stop." Black veins of pure dark magic threaded through her aged and cracked skin, infecting the branches encasing her.

Klara backed away as the bricks in the cell began to fall. She hesitated beside Jasper, a voice telling her to take him with her, but another large brick fell, almost hitting her, and she ran. She stopped only to drive her axe through the bolts on the cells, freeing as many creatures as she could. If they wanted to survive, they would have to make their own way out. They would be able to escape the glamour, and in such volumes, they would be hard to track. Her actions weren't entirely selfless; their escape would also distract the factory's fae from hunting her.

The bolt had been hacked from the last cell when two fae appeared at the stairs, trying to stop the creatures. They were quickly overwhelmed. A beam fell from the ceiling and nearly crushed Klara as she reached the factory floor. The cages there had opened as Abadan's strength was diverted to the factory's destruction.

A group of fae ran down from the walkway above, and Klara threw herself against the side of a steaming cauldron, the contact melting the fabric of her shirt to her skin. She grunted as it toppled, feeling some of her skin peel away with her shirt. She jumped up and hung from the walkway as the fae's screams echoed, the raw magic washing over and swallowing them. Klara peeled her eyes away from the melting flesh and basked in the silence that followed. The thick liquid dissipated once the fae had been consumed.

Light streamed in from the missing bricks, and wooden beams that held up the ceiling began to fall. The walkway collapsed, and she fell with it. The metal structure blocked her path, so she was forced to turn back for the cells. She passed a fallen fae crushed by bricks and had to step over them to make it down the steps. *Poor bastard,* she thought, descending to the cells, hoping a wall had opened up to ensure her exit. She didn't want to take another fae life if she didn't have to.

Suddenly a sharp whistle caught her attention. A spear was heading in her direction. She threw herself to the ground before it could pierce her side, and it cut through her thigh with a mind-curdling crunch as it hit the bone.

"I should have snapped your neck," she muttered, looking up to see Jasper flying towards her. She pushed herself back along the stone floor.

"Planning on going far?" Jasper drawled. "Don't look so hurt; it won't kill you."

He landed a few feet from her, clearly enjoying watching her pain. Klara shoved herself back into the closest cell in hopes of protecting herself just long enough to escape. She pulled the coins from her pocket, gritting her teeth through the pain, and kicked the iron door shut with her good leg, leaving Jasper on the other side.

"You know you can't keep this door closed forever. This is solid iron," he teased, his voice delighted.

God, how I look forward to mounting his head on a spike one day, she thought, knowing her own magic would be useless soon. *Please work,* she begged, tossing the coin as hard as she could against the door. She blocked out Jasper's mocking voice and pictured Hell's infirmary in as much detail as she could in her current state. She was relieved she had picked that specific location for the switch with Mila—she was losing a lot of blood.

The first coin opened a crack in the realm, but not wide enough for her to pass through. Klara stared at the silver spear, not wanting to bring it with her as evidence, but when she gripped one end and pulled, the pain was almost too much to bear. She tossed the second coin when Jasper started throwing himself at the door, trying to fight his way in.

I hope Mila looks as shitty as I do for our exchange to work, she thought as the coin hit the iron.

A portal engulfed her just as Jasper opened the door to the cell. She hoped she would never forget the shocked look on his face.

41

Klara coughed as the overwhelming smell of burning sage worked its way into her nostrils, but it was something to distract from the throbbing pain in her leg. She pulled herself onto the splintered and cracked wooden table in the centre of the infirmary, which looked more like a witch's apothecary, with shelves of herbs and potions and an open furnace in the corner rather than the sterile infirmary in her own castle.

She leant back on the table and tried to catch her breath, but the spear prevented her from feeling any comfort. She lifted her eyes to see a warlock standing in the corner, frozen in shock as they stared at her. She noticed the chain that wove around their ankle and connected to the wall.

"Sorry for the intrusion," she grunted.

"Your Highness?" they stammered, coming out from behind a cauldron. From the number of herbs and extracts laid out on the small table by the fire, they were working on something, probably for the king.

"The one and the same," she gasped, looking at her hands, coated in blood. They offered her a small handkerchief. "How kind of you," she rasped, taking it. It wouldn't do much, but it was something.

"Kindness wins trust," the warlock said, and she noticed a glint in their eye that unsettled her. Warlocks didn't end up in Hell's infirmary due to unprecedented kindness, but then again, Klara didn't care what their sin had been in her current predicament. Luckily, the small infirmary was free from anyone else. *Figures that it's empty here, yet the torture tunnels are highly occupied.*

"So does silence," she responded.

The warlock put a finger to their lips and nodded.

"I need you to get this out," she told them, holding the spear steady so it didn't do more damage. She ripped the side of her trousers with the other hand, exposing more of the wound. Her body was trying to heal, but it wouldn't work with the spear in the way; the head had gone clean through. She wouldn't be able to pull it out without causing more damage.

Why do I always end up with a hole in me? At least it wasn't in my chest this time—this is much less painful. She would have smiled at the thought if it hadn't taken so much energy.

"I think I should inform the king of your injury. He will be concerned," the warlock said, peering over their wire-rimmed glasses. They were right to call for the king; if they didn't, they were more than likely to suffer.

"Get it out, or you won't see tomorrow," she threatened, lifting her axe in their direction. The warlock ducked under the beam, their height competing with the low ceiling, and observed the wound.

"I will have to pull it through, causing you much pain," they said.

"Just get it over with," she said, and gripped the sides of the table. Their hands grasped the spear, the increased weight causing the pain to twist deeper. "Wait," she panted. "Have you got something to bite down on?"

The warlock paused and scratched their head before going through the vast array of jars in the cupboards. They came back to the table laden with herbs, seeming pleased by what they had found.

"Chew on this—it's the best I can offer," the warlock said, offering her dried and fermented white willow bark.

It won't do much, but it should help with the sting. Klara chewed the softened bark as quickly as she could. Breathing was hard, but chewing proved nearly impossible this close to passing out. The fermenting process had made it almost gummy in texture.

The bitterness coated her tongue when she had managed it, and it didn't take long for her body to absorb the numbing properties. The warlock's fingers wrapped around the spear and pulled it through, and she took some deep breaths, trying to stop herself from fainting.

"I think the tip of the spear has broken off inside," they said, looking at the jagged head of the weapon.

Before Klara could say anything, the warlock dug their long fingers deep beneath her skin, and spots appeared in her vision. There was a violent jerk, and the corner of the spearhead was pulled free. Klara resisted the urge to cry in relief as she felt her healing magic rush to the area.

"I will dispose of this immediately. Sit still a moment. Your artery was pierced, but it should heal quickly without the fae spear embedded in you," the warlock said, obviously knowing what it meant to have such an object in Hell. They hobbled over to the furnace in the corner and tossed in the bloody rags they had used to stop the bleeding. Hell's flames were so hot they could burn through bone and metal in seconds without leaving any trace, and Klara was overwhelmingly relieved as she watched the warlock toss in the spear and its fragment. The silver would be melted down and forgotten in minutes.

She felt her muscles repairing with each passing second, and no more blood escaped. She examined the wound, noting no angry veins or traces of poison. *At least Jasper granted me that mercy.* She would be sure to thank him in kind—although she had to admit, she *had* left him to die in Abadan's crumbling cell.

"That will need to be wrapped," the warlock said, clearly afraid to touch her skin.

"I don't care about your secrets," she said, watching her skin attempt to heal itself. She didn't have time to wait for it to seal completely. The warlock placed a bandage beside her. "So, what sent you here?" she asked, curious. Since she had to wait for Mila to appear, she figured she had time.

"I'm a warlock sentenced to this sorry excuse of an infirmary. Not that Hell has much use for one. What do you think?"

"Experimenting?" she asked, and they nodded. "With what? Souls?" Messing with the king's souls was forbidden. The look of horror on their face told her she had guessed incorrectly. "I might be dead soon, so you might as well tell me," she reasoned. *If Mila doesn't turn up soon, safe to say we'll both end up dead.*

"Necromancy," they admitted. "The high warlocks frown upon it. I was stripped of my rank and cast aside. I tried to cross to Kalos, but Kharon sent me into the Styx for trying to bring souls back to life."

"With your knowledge of anatomy..." she realised.

"It was here or the tunnels, and honestly," they said, leaning in closely, "who can stand the smell down there?"

"Thanks for this," Klara said as they wrapped her leg tightly, offering her some support as she healed. She laid her hand on theirs in thanks, but when she made contact, she slipped into their mind.

Lucifer stood in the dim light of the infirmary, directing the warlock to wait for Klara's arrival.

"You were expecting me?" she asked the paling warlock.

If Lucifer knew this was her and Mila's meeting place, her half-sister would not be showing up. She had either betrayed Klara, or their plan had been discovered. She looked at the table of herbs the warlock had been preparing when she arrived.

"Those were for me?" she asked, and the warlock nodded.

"I'm sorry, Your Highness. The king told me to prepare a few things in case you were injured upon your arrival," they said, bowing their head.

"I take it you are to tell me where they're expecting me?" she asked, resigned to what was coming next. *At least Father allowed him to bandage me up before summoning me.*

"The k-king is expecting you in the throne room," the warlock stammered.

Klara reached into her pocket and found a silver coin. "Thanks for patching me up," she said, tossing it to them.

The warlock was looking concerned as she slung her axe over her shoulder. "They know about your plan," they blurted out. "Mila was discovered. I had to make her a tea to stop her from bleeding out, but it was laced with alder to bring out the truth."

Klara was hardly listening. She would learn the truth soon enough.

42

No doomed were present at the doors to the throne room. Instead, two demons with yellow eyes watched the doors. Klara passed them without a word, though she could feel their beady eyes on her.

Once she crossed the threshold into the scorching throne room, the heavy doors sealed her inside. She could almost taste the anticipation in the air. The throne room was darker than it had been when the courts were in attendance, and it seemed all too big without them. Everything seemed to slow down; she noticed that the fires were slowly dying, and she suspected it wouldn't be long before the doomed had to come in and refuel them with enchanted logs that burnt for days and not hours.

Matthias and Frendall sat at the long table in the centre of the room. Matthias looked positively cheerful, while Frendall looked anything but. The top buttons of his shirt were undone, and strands of hair fell into his face. Aemella stood staring into the fireplace, tapping her heel ever so gently against the black marble floor.

"There she is!" Lucifer clapped, snapping Klara out of her daze.

She felt the animosity of the room deep in her gut, even if her father greeted her with a forced smile. Something else radiated from him as she looked into his soulless eyes. *Disappointment.*

"We didn't expect to be kept waiting so long, though we figured it would be best for the courts to leave before your arrival," the king said.

"Did you have a pleasant trip?" Aemella asked, moving from the flames to stand beside Lucifer at the head table.

Klara moved further into the room and smelt blood. Her hand instinctively went to her leg. "I've had better."

It wasn't until she reached the other side of the table that she saw Mila on the floor, her head resting against the table. Klara noted the bleeding wound on the side of Mila's forehead, matting her vibrant purple hair to her skin. A broken cup sat in her lap. *The warlock told the truth about the tea.* She was relieved, though. Mila could have been tortured just as easily, but it seemed that her father had chosen tea over knives. Klara wondered how much her half-sister had confessed to. It couldn't have been long since the fight; blood still dripped down her tired face. The crystal was gone from Mila's neck, and instead sat in front of her father.

"I'm happy to see that you two have managed to reconcile your differences. However, I'm disappointed that you have chosen to deceive us both," he said, passing the necklace to Aemella.

"Did you believe such a trinket would protect your

secret?" Aemella said, holding up the crystal, only to crush it in her palm. Klara watched the shimmering dust fall onto the table. "I expected more from you. Did you *really* think such a simple trick would fool me? You dishonoured me in front of the courts," she continued, her voice disturbingly calm. Klara wondered if the three queens had been disappointed in the lack of time she put into her plots, or if that was solely a fae queen thing. Perhaps the white willow bark was numbing more than her leg…

"The crystal was the best I could do in a short time," she offered. *It's the truth.* "I have to wonder, though—how did you manage to see through it? Simple or not, you cannot see your own kin's glamour without permission." *Someone told her about it—betrayed me.*

Aemella lifted her eyes as if to identify the person who had exposed her secret, but stopped. Instead, she clasped her hands under her chin. Klara glanced at Mila, wondering if she was the traitor, but Mila stared right back, offering a light shake of the head that confirmed she was not.

"If only you had been able to leave well enough alone," Aemella said, standing beside her fae guard. "It only took a moment to rip the damn thing from this one's neck. Too much time in the tunnels—she's out of practice fighting others who can fight back."

Klara looked to a fading Mila once more, sensing the brutal beating she had taken.

"I used a proxy to fight you. It's not uncommon," Klara said half-heartedly, but her father's fist threatened to break the table in two.

"Enough of your cryptic words, both of you!" Lucifer hated the strained truth of the fae; he would rather rip out tongues than be deceived. "I suggest you drop the act so we can have a civilised conversation about this matter, *without* your axe in hand."

Klara opened her mouth, but Frendall came to her, placing his hand on hers over the axe. *The king is trying to protect you. Try and keep your head—if not for Malum's sake, for Lottie's.* His eyes pleaded with hers.

The factory is gone. Your mother destroyed her soul and took it with her.

There was a flash of sorrow across his features. Klara didn't want to delay and make their exchange obvious, so she handed her axe over to him.

"A treaty was signed and agreed upon, and yet you took it upon yourself to break it," Lucifer began.

Klara laughed. "Treaty law was broken long before I intervened. What was it you said—it takes ink to create a treaty and only a drop of blood to break it? I think Malum's sacrificed creatures and my own blood amounts to more than a drop. Can't say it wasn't worth it. What I did in Kalos amounts to nothing more than a sting; isn't that right, Mother?"

"What's in the past is done. However, your vote for the factory to close has already been called, and you lost. You signed in blood and then invaded my land only hours later," Aemella said, raising her perfectly manicured eyebrows in apparent bemusement.

"The factory… yes. *One* factory was called into question during the vote." Klara leant forward, elbows on the table. "There are more factories for you to feed from, not only containing Malum's creatures but also dark fae. Now that's just cold-hearted." *That's why Glaudine was having a hard time with dark fae at Tapped. They were terrified and acting out once they were under the effects of the fungus,* she thought, putting the pieces together.

"Multiple factories?" Lucifer demanded, his head snapping towards Aemella.

"She's only being dramatic to make her point. She takes after you." Aemella rolled her eyes, though she didn't deny the taking of the dark fae.

Klara paused when she noticed Frendall looking at Mila with concern.

"Come on now, you're free to admit it," Klara exclaimed. "Abadan destroyed the factory, and though I managed to free some in captivity, you'll have it back up and running by the morning sun."

"Then why do it? Why invade my land if your cause was hopeless? If these multiple factories exist, where is your proof?" Aemella asked.

Klara looked to her father, who remained expressionless, reminding her that this was between the Queen of Malum and the Fae Queen of Kalos.

"Proof? I'm the proof—and because as long as I breathe air, and even if all the elders stand behind your self-righteous back, I won't let you take from *my* Forest. I'm the Queen of Malum. You made sure of that. This is what you get." Klara was willing to die for the Forest, even if it was only to see Lottie safe. She couldn't help but think of her elders, how they had been frightened into submission by the mere sight of an army.

The room went silent.

"Give up these foolish attempts at besting me. You. Will. Lose. And you'll only tear down the realm you have worked so hard to build up," Aemella threatened.

I'm sorry I failed. She was too strong, Mila projected. *You aren't to blame. I should have come up with a better plan.*

"Bow in apology, and I will allow you to see Lottie," Matthias said, clearly only wishing to humiliate Klara. She refused to move, determined not to bow to anyone.

She caught the look of disgust in Aemella's eyes as he spoke. They might be allies for now, but Klara was sure that once Aemella had reclaimed Malum, the lycaons would be the first to be wrapped in silver chains. They would be a threat to her power, just as they had been a threat to Abadan.

"How dare you ask your queen to bow to another?" Lucifer said, rising from his chair.

Klara was surprised by his reaction. He was meant to be a neutral party, though she was glad for his interference.

"She needs to learn respect." Matthias glared.

"*You* need to learn respect!" Lucifer countered harshly.

"Someone needs their chew toy," Klara mocked, and Matthias bared his teeth at her. "Using a child to threaten me!" She smirked. "Your cowardice knows no bounds. It's a disgrace to call you an alpha."

"It's frightening to me to see how you think you've done no wrong. You've brought war to our doorstep and show no remorse," Matthias snapped.

Klara bit her tongue so hard she drew blood. "*I've* brought war? How blind can you be?"

"Apologise for breaking the treaty and threatening the very lives of the creatures you seem to want to protect so much, and I'll show you that I mean no harm to Lottie."

"No harm? You left a gutted hound in my home. This is your way of ensuring peace? We both know that you'll take her head as soon as she matures. Save your lies for your pack."

"She has broken the Laws," Aemella put in. "Have you seen such factories? Have you seen proof, or only heard rumours and hearsay?"

Lucifer held up his hand to stop the quarrelling.

"This is not a situation to take lightly. For two lands to run side by side, there must be law. An agreement was made amongst all—that one would not step foot on the other's land—and that trust cannot be broken. We are not senseless humans; we do not bring discord to our own. Regardless of this agreement and the reason for your little adventure, you have broken this trust, daughter," he said, resting his knuckles on the table.

Klara was taken aback by her father's position. He wasn't siding with her, but he wasn't siding against her. His restraint worried her. *Does Aemella have something on him? Appeasement is not in his nature, neutral or not.*

"I did what I did to protect the creatures," she protested, and Lucifer didn't dare meet her eye.

"Nevertheless, there must be consequences to your actions. A caging of some time should be sufficient until the lycaon has reached maturity. Six years—that should be ample time to reflect."

Klara stilled, afraid her heart might stop if she uttered a word. *He's going to cage me—the very thing he fears most for himself. If I'm caged, I can't get out, but no one can get to me. How will the creatures survive without a ruler for six years?* Even with the gatherings and listenings, it was a constant battle to keep the peace amongst the creatures. Aemella would thrive on the chaos and use it as a reason to invade. Six years was only a moment in their long lives, but in Malum it only took six minutes for the balance of power to shift.

What the hell is your game? she wondered, staring at her father. *Even if I am caged in the castle in Malum I won't be alone. They don't know about Lilith.* The idea provided some small relief.

Aemella pouted. "That seems fair, provided that I'm compensated for the damage to my land."

"Gold, it always comes back to gold," Klara muttered

in frustration, but she saw an opportunity. Had the king set the time on purpose? "I will go, provided one thing."

"You cannot have a companion, if that's what you're thinking." Aemella sneered at Frendall, but Klara couldn't even bring herself to look at him, let alone think of what the next six years would mean.

"I need to know that Lottie is safe—see her in the flesh. And since I'm to be released on her reaching maturity, if anything happens to her while I'm confined, I'm to be released immediately—or so help you God and his angels won't be able to save you." She said it with a smile, and for the first time, she saw her mother pale.

"Fine. We're in agreement?" Lucifer said, looking to Aemella.

"You can see the child, but you are to be supervised," she corrected, trying to prevent Klara's escape.

I already have one. There was no way Matthias would allow Lottie to reach maturity, whether Klara was caged or not.

"Frendall can accompany you," Lucifer said, and she knew it was his way of protecting her and his own interests. She was still the heir to Hell.

"And Matthias will show them the way," Aemella concluded. Klara noticed her father's jaw flex. *Lottie is at the caves after all.*

"If you cause even an ounce of trouble, you will force my hand," Lucifer warned as iron cuffs were placed on Klara's wrists. "No queen is free from punishment," he added, but she watched his eyes flick to Aemella and back to her.

What are you trying to tell me? she projected to Lucifer, but he only winked.

"I'm counting on it," she said aloud, looking back at her mother. "I hope Jasper recovers quickly. I wouldn't want to have marked his pretty face permanently." Bitter joy bubbled inside her as she watched her mother's nostrils flare.

You really are your father's daughter, Aemella projected with a sneer.

I did have one Hell of an upbringing, Klara teased, and Aemella rolled her eyes.

Klara forced herself to keep smiling, to remain strong. She couldn't show how much the idea being separated from those she cared for frightened her. She might survive the six years, but would they? What if they needed her? What if Lottie needed her and she couldn't get to her? The thought was too much for her to consider in present company.

"Get a move on," Matthias ordered, shoving Klara forward. Frendall got between them.

"You forget your place, brother," he growled.

"There is to be no bloodshed on this trip," Lucifer said, and Frendall took a step back from the alpha. "Aemella and I will meet you at the castle for the caging ceremony upon your immediate return from the lycaons."

As Lucifer finished speaking, a portal opened in the fireplace, and the chill of the Forest emanated into Hell.

43

Gates and high, barbed fences penned in the lycaon territory long before they reached the caves; gone were the trees that had once marked their borders. Matthias had done all that he could to secure their area. Klara regretted expanding their territory as it reached far in the distance. Many of the trees on the outskirts were still scorched from Abadan's flames, but right now the only person she wanted to set alight was Matthias.

He led the group up a gravel path, and Klara eyed the newly planted crops on either side of them. Plants and vegetables grew wildly—she suspected some magical influence. A stupid grin spread to his amber eyes.

"We have made some improvements," he commented.

Klara caught the look of disgust in Frendall's eyes.

"You really think Aemella won't take you out as soon as she's done with you?" she asked flatly.

Matthias stroked his beard. "She can't get rid of an alpha if she plans to take over Malum; the lycaons are too strong."

"*Were* strong—but you being alpha drains them, and she has another. Lottie. Who's easier to control, a child in need of a mentor or a false alpha who does nothing but stroke his own ego?" Klara countered, watching his eye twitch.

He made no response, but she could see his mind buzzing with her words. It was the truth and he knew it. It was an excellent strategy on Aemella's part, and Klara couldn't help but admire her dedication. She dreaded to think what the fae queen would do with the rest of the lycaons once she made her final move on Malum. With no ruler, the realm was ripe for the plunder.

Elder Yadira of the elves might stake a claim to rule Malum in her absence; she had an army of elves at her back, and her attending of Aemella's gathering meant the fae queen wouldn't expect such a move. But whoever tried to take her place didn't matter. All Klara cared about was Lottie's survival. She couldn't let her become caught in the crosshairs of the queens' war. If Aemella got her hands on the young lycaon, it would grant her a new generation of lycaons to control.

They reached the entrance to the caves, where dozens of cabins had been built. Lycaons stared as they passed, many covered in sweat and mud; they obviously worked hard at logging all day, selling timber to the port so the elves could make ships. Abadan used to take their profits; Klara was glad to see the lycaons looked well fed now. Their clothes weren't riddled with patches, and their shoes looked new and strong for the work they did.

It was hard to get a read on whether the pack despised her or whether their stares were just surprise; who knew what tales Matthias had spun about her. The last time she had visited the caves had been to help with the rebuild, just after her ascension. That had been before her duties had overwhelmed her and pulled her away.

"We have her with the other young ones," Matthias said, and Klara saw Ceylon and another lycaon waiting outside a large cabin with a cherry tree in full bloom beside it.

"We didn't think it would be fair to separate her," Ceylon said.

"After all, it's not her fault that those meant to protect her couldn't." Matthias grinned as he opened the cabin door.

The smell of wood chips from the fire at the end of the cabin wafted around her. There were rows of small beds for the children, who were crowded around a small table, and a few of the youngest were on the rugged floor, playing with small hand-carved toys. Oblivious.

"Many of them lost their parents to the flames. Some even changed young. We find housing them together keeps them calm," Ceylon assured Klara, not bothering to look at her alpha for permission to speak.

"Has she changed since she's been here?" Klara wondered if fear had got the best of Lottie. "She doesn't mean to lash out. Her memories of the burning come back, and she can forget who's around her sometimes."

"No, she hasn't hurt anyone. She asks for you every night, and refuses to run with the others."

Klara wondered why that was. Lottie had run every day in the castle; she must be fighting the urge with a strength Klara was glad to know she had. She would need it while Klara was locked up. It killed her to know that she wouldn't be there to watch her ward mature.

"Klara!" Lottie said, looking up from her cross-legged position on the floor. The other children stopped playing in shock. "I knew you'd come! They didn't believe that I lived with the queen." Lottie stuck her tongue out at the other young lycaons in the cabin. The little beast ran to her mentor and squeezed her so tight that Klara didn't ever want to let her go.

"Are we going home now? I want to see Henny." Lottie's eyes drifted coldly to Matthias. "And they don't teach potions here," she whispered.

Klara took her aside and crouched down to her. She slipped into Lottie's mind and saw the lycaons burst through the castle doors.

"We have not laid a hand on her," Ceylon said, understanding what Klara was doing.

"Excuse me if I don't take you on your word." Klara watched Lottie hide in the wardrobe in her sky room while two lycaons smelt her out. Klara didn't recognise them—she was glad to confirm there had been no side-switchers in her guard. The lycaon gripped the back of Lottie's neck as she tried to change, to get away. There was pressure, but not enough to hurt.

"They're my friends," Lottie said aloud, breaking the connection between them. They were the words Klara had feared. *If she lets her guard down, even I won't be able to save her in time.* "Why would they hurt me?" Lottie frowned.

Her naïveté constricted Klara's chest. *Speak silently,* she urged.

I know the alpha isn't my friend—he hurts the others! Forces them to change early, but I help them, Lottie projected proudly. *He's trying to make them stronger, but I won't run with him, so he won't see how strong I am.*

Klara had to stop herself from sighing in relief. She took Lottie's hands. *You're smarter than you look. I'll come for you as soon as I can, but until then, trust no one. If you hear anything about Matthias and the fae, I want you to run—go back to the cabin where the toadstools live.* Matthias didn't know about Tapped and the concealed cabin; it would be the safest place for Lottie, especially since Glaudine had returned to oversee it.

Lottie seemed to take it all in. *Hug me if you understand,* Klara added, trying to conceal the fear in her voice.

Lottie's eyes reddened with tears as she wrapped her arms around Klara's neck.

"Did I do something bad and you don't want me any more?" she asked, her eyes welling with tears. It broke Klara's heart. "I want to go home. I'll be good! I won't be loud or ask to go anywhere, I swear!"

Klara hugged her tightly, feeling Lottie's small heartbeat thud against her chest.

"You did nothing wrong. Nothing. I'll come for you soon, okay? This is also your home, remember? Make lots of friends." Klara wiped the tears away and remembered the last time she had left Lottie crying. Frendall had been dead on the Neutral Lands, and she had been about to meet the mother she had never known existed.

"Are *you* in trouble?" Lottie asked, looking at Matthias in the corner, his false alpha eyes trained on them.

"No. Nothing I can't handle," Klara said softly, and she heard Matthias scoff. "I have some things to attend to, and once they're all cleared up, I'll come and get you."

"Promise you'll come back?" Lottie pleaded, but that was a promise Klara couldn't make.

"Soon," she repeated.

"I wouldn't wait up," Matthias muttered loudly. His ego made her skin crawl. She looked forward to the day when Aemella turned her back on him. He was no alpha, and his actions only confirmed it—he did what was best for him, not the pack. Certainly not for Malum.

Klara kissed the top of Lottie's head and watched her hug Frendall goodbye. He whispered something in her ear that made her smile. Klara lifted her eyebrows to ask, What? But Frendall shook his head, telling her it was nothing important.

She had expected a bigger goodbye, but Lottie simply wandered back to her new friends, and that pained her more than anything.

"You've seen her. Now let's go." Matthias tried to grip her arm, and Klara shrugged him off.

"I'm still a queen, and I have the power to skin you alive without breaking a sweat." She got up in his face, her power burning in her limbs as she sensed his hatred of her.

"But you won't," Matthias shot back. "Not unless you want me to turn your little beast into a rug for my cabin."

Frendall shoved Matthias away in spite of his bared teeth. "The King of Hell is waiting. Let's not waste his time with idle threats."

Klara glanced over her shoulder when they left the cabin to see Lottie watching her go from the barred windows. There was a smile on her lips, but Klara could sense the fear and sadness in her young heart. Ceylon sealed the door after them, and Klara wanted to rip the door off its hinges and take Lottie home where she belonged.

As Matthias was distracted by a few lycaons who questioned her presence, Ceylon drew near to her.

"I won't let anything happen to her," she murmured.

"How can I trust you? I can sense your loyalty to Matthias."

Matthias has my brother, Percy. He went missing after he discovered Matthias is forcing our young to shift early. I can't sense him anywhere in the territory. I'll help you bring Lottie to power in time. Matthias can't remain alpha or the pack will destroy itself, Ceylon projected.

Klara sensed no deceit in her words, and was taken aback by the risk Ceylon was taking in confiding in her. She remembered Percy from the first meeting; he had been Matthias's ally. Admitting he had lost the faith of an important pack member would be too devastating to Matthias's ego. They both knew he would kill to keep that doubt from spreading.

"I'm loyal to the true alpha, and if the day comes when Lottie defeats him, I'll be loyal to her. Matthias doesn't doubt me; he's too proud to see his enemies within the pack. The loyalty in our blood is hard to resist, but she does have friends here that won't let him harm her," Ceylon whispered.

"If he harms *anyone*, I won't hesitate in killing those who helped him." Klara hoped Ceylon would understand that she would help her find her brother when the time came, though she doubted he was still alive.

"I don't doubt it, but please don't forget that you have allies here, even if the vote made it seem otherwise. Fear can be a powerful thing," Ceylon replied as Matthias made their way back to them. Klara sensed no malicious intent in her—there was ambition, but not enough to be alpha. There was an internal struggle in the beta, and Klara just hoped it would be enough to stop Matthias.

44

The moonlight broke through the clouds, guiding them up the mountain pass. By the time the group reached the top of the Queen's Mountain, Aemella and Lucifer were already at the closed doors of the castle with some of Lucifer's demon guard and Aemella's fae. They waited in silence, unable to gain access without Klara's permission.

She looked out at the Forest below, savouring the fresh air, aware of the castle that was about to become her prison.

"Isn't it a beautiful evening?" Aemella said, standing beside her, both looking out over Malum.

"It has its moments. I can see why you want to re-claim it," Klara taunted, and her mother rolled her eyes.

"When I divided Malum and Kalos, there was a rea-son for it. I thought I could spare myself and those who sought good from the darkness, but it always has a way of creeping back in," she admitted.

"Is that why you want to reclaim Malum—because you know you can't rid the realm of darkness?" Klara asked.

Aemella leant in close.

"No. It's because ridding the realm of darkness will be much easier once my soldiers march through this land," she whispered in Klara's ear.

Klara pulled contemplatively at her shackles, the iron digging into her flesh and slowing down her healing, keeping her from any escape attempt.

"The creatures will fight for themselves whether they have a queen or not," she said, knowing the strength of her own Forest. "The Forest has made them cunning and unforgiving. An army of untainted fae would do well not to underestimate them."

"Open the doors, daughter," Lucifer ordered, cutting off Aemella's reply.

Klara limped away from her mother and passed Frendall to place her hand on the castle door. They all watched as the tall doors opened. The castle was colder than usual, and Klara sensed no one inside. *Bromwich and Larkin were meant to be here with my guard... Lucifer must have called them back to Hell,* she thought as the chandelier and torches lit upon her entry.

"Find the vault," Aemella immediately ordered two of her guards, who were in full armour. Lucifer turned to Klara.

"I never thought I would have to cage my own child," he said sadly.

"I never thought I would be disappointed to call you my father," she retorted. "You know what she's doing and yet you turn a blind eye. I don't know why you suddenly care for treaties and law—you're the King of Hell, for Judas' sake—but I *will* find out what she has on you."

Lucifer clenched his fist. Klara was sure he would strike her for insulting him in front of his demons, but the blow never came.

"This is for your own good," he told her. "Everything I have ever done has been to protect you. You'll come to see that in time."

"Whatever you need to tell yourself to sleep at night," she muttered, noting that he hadn't actually responded to anything she had said. She walked into the castle with her head held high.

"I've called your guard back to Hell. Even the lycaons decided to join my ranks," Lucifer informed her when there were no demons to support her within, and only lycaons she didn't know from the caves stood waiting. She was relieved that her guard was safe in Hell. Her sending Bromwich and Larkin to the castle had most likely influenced their decision to join her father. "They'll be returned once your sentence is complete; for now they will join Frendall's legion to maintain their training."

"My lycaons, however, will watch over the perimeter of the castle during your sentence. There will be no further need for their presence within, given that there will be no way in or out. The lack of company will give you plenty of time to reflect," Matthias said, and Klara didn't need to see his face to know he was smiling.

"Surely demons should be the ones to guard the heir to Hell?" she asked her father, silently begging him to let her in on whatever plan he was hatching. She knew there had to be one—he was too calm, too collected.

"My demons are needed in Hell. This is a time to show penance for your actions against another ruler.

460

Invading another's land is treason, and this is your punishment. When enough time passes, you will be free to rule once again."

"Once you learn not to overstep," Aemella seethed. Klara got the impression that the fae queen wished for her head after seeing the new and improved Malum for herself. "You played a dangerous game with both our lands. I hope this will be an invaluable lesson. I knew she wasn't ready for Hell, and this is the proof—don't you agree?" Aemella added, addressing Lucifer.

"She still has some to learn. There are plenty of books in the library to teach her," Lucifer said with a discreet glance at the second floor.

The library?

"I wonder how the angels would feel if they saw their ally so comfortable in the presence of the King of Hell," Klara said meaningfully. "I doubt they would feel at ease granting you and your people light if they knew about the factories."

Aemella was suddenly only an inch from her. "The angels have what they need when they need it. Unlike you, they don't ask questions they don't want the answers to," she hissed. "You insist on provoking me when the game is lost!"

Klara shrugged. "I don't mean to provoke you—only to remind you of the truths you seem so desperate to escape."

"Come," Aemella barked. "We shall leave before she provokes me further."

Klara wondered who she was talking to, when Henrietta came out from the shadows and joined Aemella and Matthias. Aemella dropped gold coins into her scarred hands.

Klara's blood ran cold.

"Henny… why would you do this?" Bile rose in her throat.

"I—I couldn't help it. You freed me from Hell, and the queen promised I could go to Kalos. Start a new life," Henrietta stammered, not meeting her gaze. Klara could see the struggle in her friend's eyes, but her love of gold and the promise of freedom had deafened her sense of loyalty. She didn't know why she was surprised; Henrietta's soul had been doomed because she lusted for material gains. She had murdered many innocents during her days as a thief.

Before Klara could speak, two fae guards came through the corridor carrying sacks full of gold.

"I see you found the vault all right," Klara scoffed. *It always comes down to gold and power.*

"It was once my vault, after all—and don't I deserve reparations for what you've done to my lands?" Aemella brushed back a strand of hair that had fallen in front of Klara's face. "I hope we can move past this; I don't want us to part on bad terms. We are both rulers, after all—even God can't expect us to agree all the time."

Klara went rigid as her mother embraced her, desperate to shake off Aemella's arms. The demonstration of affection gave the fae queen the perfect opportunity to mock her.

"With your darling doomed's help, it was a breeze getting past your guard. How did you think Matthias was able to get Lottie out without a scratch?" she whispered.

Klara's fist connected with her mother's jaw.

Matthias shoved her away before she could do any more damage. Klara almost lost her balance, the pain from the wound in her leg radiating up into her hip.

Aemella ordered Matthias back to her. "Don't. She can consider it a small victory after such a defeat."

462

Klara smirked, watching a trickle of blood stream from the fae queen's lip. She could have used magic to wound her, but she had wanted to feel Aemella's skin split under her fist. *So you do bleed,* she projected.

Aemella wiped her lip. *I'll give you that one. I'll be sure to make your creatures pay for it.*

"Enough of this! Are you happy with the reparations?" Lucifer said emotionlessly.

"I'm satisfied," Aemella said, after she'd opened the bags and checked the collection of crystals and jewels. *Great armies cost a lot to feed.* She winked, and Klara resisted the urge to respond.

"Say your goodbyes—this place is freezing. I don't know how you can stand it," Lucifer said as his demons removed the shackles from Klara's wrists.

"I swear on Lucifer's life I will get Lottie back," she whispered in Frendall's ear as he wrapped his arms around her, not caring who saw. It was a relief to know she had one true ally on the outside.

"I'm sorry," he said against her hair, and as her hands rested on the back of his neck, the air slipped from her lungs.

A memory danced before her eyes: Frendall telling Aemella about the crystal necklace, about Mila's glamoured appearance. Klara felt his shame, but he was glad he had done it. She felt like the spear was back in her leg, metal twisting against bone, as she watched him betray her.

"*You* told the queen about Mila?" she breathed, releasing her grip on him. She had watched the betrayal with her own eyes—he didn't have to admit it—but she needed him to say it aloud.

"It prevented a war," he said coldly.

She pushed him away.

I knew you could do better, Aemella projected into her mind, and Klara could almost taste the fae queen's delight in his betrayal.

"I don't want to overstay my welcome. I'm glad that we were able to resolve this matter without any blood spilt," Aemella said aloud, oozing enthusiasm. *Thank you for improving Malum—it will make the creatures all the more potent for my factories.*

Frendall had to stop Klara from lunging at her mother again.

"What could I have said to enrage you so?" Aemella feigned concern.

"If you touch one hair on any creature's head, I will burn that shiny palace of yours to the ground," Klara threatened, and it was Lucifer's turn to hold her back.

I look forward to it. Now, enjoy the prison of your own making. Who would have thought having a daughter would be so much fun?

Aemella disappeared with her guard. Klara was glad to be rid of her, but she couldn't help but be saddened to watch Henrietta fall in line. She might have freed her from Hell, but Henrietta had no idea what new hell she was walking into.

She was afraid that if Aemella had stayed a moment longer, she would have shown her exactly whose daughter she was. Klara would have paid any price to see the fae queen's face once she saw what was left of her factory—though the thought of others still functioning dealt a blow to her small victory.

Fun. That's all this was to her. A bit of excitement to brighten her life of absolute purity. Klara had never considered that being good could drive someone so mad.

"Calm down. Your rage will not help you," Lucifer warned, still holding her.

"Let me go," she ordered, backing away from her father, who looked more hurt than anything. She couldn't bring herself to look at Frendall.

"I will leave you to your goodbyes. And for your sake, daughter, I beg you to reflect on all that has transpired. Once those castle doors close, the cage will be set." Lucifer placed a light hand on her shoulder.

She waited for some thought, some explanation to come, but he simply disappeared from sight. Klara looked over her shoulder to the lycaons posted outside the open castle doors. She ran her hands over her face as she tried to gather her thoughts, then turned on Frendall.

"How could you side with her?" she yelled, fighting back tears. "She'll see that I never leave this place, and if I do there'll be nothing left to rule!"

She was met with a blank expression. "I follow the king's orders, as I always have, and I warned you I always would. He wants you confined. Maybe while you're here, you can figure out a better plan." Frendall sounded less like her lover and more like the cold-hearted general who served at the right hand of her father.

"You heartless bastard. There is no right plan. She wants war so she can take back Malum."

"It's for all the right reasons. Trust me, your father has good cause," Frendall said as the doors to the castle started to close.

"Trust you? Don't you leave me here like this without any explanation!" Klara gripped his shirt, only for him to remove her hands and step away. "I know you're keeping something from me. What does she have on him? Or does she have something on you?" she asked frantically.

He said nothing. She could sense his quickening pulse; she knew her words were hurting him, but he refused to let his mask drop.

"I'm not some princess you can lock in a tower!" Her outburst shook the very foundations of Malum as he turned away. "Give me a reason! You're the one who wanted to be bound to me, and instead you're leaving me bound to this place?"

Frendall turned back sharply, grabbing her face in his hands as he kissed her. No tenderness or love, but as if he didn't he would break as she was breaking.

"I can't lose both you and Lottie. Please," she begged.

"The library," was all he offered, his forehead resting against hers, and as much as she hated him in that moment, she didn't want to see him go. "I tried to warn you of what would happen if you kept pushing ahead. There are secrets I can't share," he admitted.

He released her as though her touch caused him pain, and walked away without a second glance.

Klara gritted her teeth so hard she thought they would crack. The doors clunked and clashed as they sealed on her, separating them for good.

She watched the cage, a red, water-like film, flow over the walls as the cage was set in place. The castle was now her prison. Klara went straight for the door, but instead of opening, the watery magic that now enveloped every exit and entrance of the castle burnt through layers of her skin, eating its way up her arm until she dropped her hand.

She panted, holding her burnt arm in her hand as she sank to the floor, utterly defeated. Her sobs died into silence as she stared at the magic her father feared the most and yet had used against his own blood. The chandelier dimmed as she cried. Just as she thought she would pass out, a hand fell on Klara's shoulder. She looked up to see Lilith standing over her.

"You have really damned yourself this time."

466

"They never found you?" Klara asked dazedly.

"No. They didn't know to look, and your side-switching doomed never thought to reveal my presence." Lilith smiled.

"Then you're as caged as I am," Klara said dully, looking back at the door.

Lilith's smile widened, and a spark flared in her eyes. "Not quite."

ACKNOWLEDGMENTS

I will never be able to put into words how much I love my readers. I'm grateful for all of you each and every day. A special thank you to all of you that have shared, liked and helped spread the word about my books, I wouldn't be able to do this without you. To my family, thank you for your unwavering faith in me and my dreams. To Emma and her sassy editing comments, writing wouldn't be as fun without you. Again, thank you, Eve, for the wonderful map of Malum and Kalos. Thank you to Sara for the beautifully designed cover—I couldn't have imagined it any other way. I'm so grateful to Enchanted Ink Publishing for their wonderful formatting, there wouldn't be a book without you. Last but not least, thank you to my proofreaders for being the extra cherry on top. I can't wait to share the rest of this series and many more books with you.

ABOUT THE AUTHOR

Kate Callaghan is an Irish writer from Dublin, Ireland. When she is not writing, she loves reading, yoga and watching movies. Some of her favourite genres include fantasy, horror, thrillers and romance. If you ever need a pen, she will surely have one at the ready.

Don't be afraid to reach out on:

Instagram & Twitter | @callaghanwriter

Email | callaghanwriter@gmail.com

Website | www.callaghanwriter.com